A M
VALLE

DUSTY RICHARDS

AMBUSH VALLEY

PINNACLE BOOKS
Kensington Publishing Corp.
www.kensingtonbooks.com

PINNACLE BOOKS are published by

Kensington Publishing Corp.
119 West 40th Street
New York, NY 10018

All Kensington titles, imprints, and distributed lines are available at special quantity discounts for bulk purchases for sales promotions, premiums, fund-raising, educational, or institutional use. Special book excerpts or customized printings can also be created to fit specific needs. For details, write or phone the office of the Kensington special sales manager: Kensington Publishing Corp., 119 West 40th Street, New York, NY 10018, attn: Special Sales Department; phone 1-800-221-2647.

PINNACLE BOOKS and the Pinnacle logo are Reg. U.S. Pat. & TM Off.

ISBN-13: 978-0-7860-3197-9
ISBN-10: 0-7860-3197-2

First printing: March 2014

10 9 8 7 6 5 4 3 2 1

Printed in the United States of America

First electronic edition: March 2014

ISBN-13: 978-0-7860-3198-6
ISBN-10: 0-7860-3198-0

PROLOGUE

An auctioneer's chant carried to where Chet Byrnes stood looking at the ranch yard crowded with people. Folks buying things he couldn't or didn't want to move. Excited children were exploring everything. Chickens squawked in homemade crates. The Byrnes were leaving the home site that his grandfather and father had chosen years before after coming down there from the Arkansas hills. The place his father and his mother's father built and kept from falling into the hands of the bloodthirsty Comanche, except for the three of his siblings who were swept away in Comanche kidnappings.

It was the ranch his father came back to after his military service with Sam Houston's ragtag army who finally whipped Santa Anna to raise the Lone Star Flag over the republic of Texas. Later on his father was brought back there by some Texas rangers, a broken-down near-delirious man, after searching too long and hard for three of his stolen children. Hardly dry behind the ears, Chet took over managing the ranch.

Then a bitter blood feud with the Reynolds took its toll on the family. A woman of interest to him, Marla Price, was murdered by some of the feudists who were hung for their vicious deed. His brother Dale was shot down in Kansas by some of the Reynolds while driving a large herd to the Kansas markets. Chet's nephew Heck had been murdered by some worthless road agents when the two were coming back to Texas. Another woman who stole his heart in his childhood, Kathren Hines, came back into his life, and he was sad on that sale day; because of her family loyalties she could not leave Texas, but had to stay behind to care for her older parents.

The man who never had his chance to go ride over the hill, do some wild things in his youth, was the steady hand who raised the –C into a profitable working ranch in the Texas hill country. The ongoing feud forced him to buy a new ranch in the Arizona Territory, and he was moving everyone out there except his nephew Reg and his bride Juanita. Those two stayed to care for an elderly childless couple, Henry and Millie Price, and some day they would inherit their ranch operation.

His sister Susie, in her early twenties, who was his mainstay, didn't complete her attachment with Sheriff Trent due to her need to run the ranch house's operation. His forty-two-year-old Aunt Louise was brought to his side when he saved her from being ravaged by some hired thugs. His brother's widow May with her own baby daughter

Donna and her two stepchildren, Ray, nine, and Ty, seven, were a part of his extended family. The boys' younger sister Rachel had died of complications, and like Chet's parents, were buried in the Yellow Hammer Creek cemetery.

In Arizona, a rich widow Marge Stephenson waited for his return, hoping for him to marry her. A large newly purchased ranch, the Quarter Circle Z, which straddled the Verde River, needed to be rebuilt. He finally sold the –C ranch and wound up his business in the Lone Star State to go west.

They and their farm wagons, horses, and goods were hauled by rail to Fort Worth and then to West Texas on the new Fort Worth–Denver Railroad with tracks already built near the town of Tascosa in the panhandle, and from there they planned to go overland by wagons on the surveyed Marcy Road to Arizona.

CHAPTER 1

The too-bright West Texas sun shone off everything including the ground with a mirror's blinding rays. Chet held on to the rope halter on his palomino stallion Barbarossa, leading him down the fresh-cut lumber chute. Barbarossa was his pride and joy. Once on the dirt, the frisky stud circled him on his lead and Chet laughed.

The tiring three-day-long train ride with some layovers ran from San Antonio to Fort Worth; then they switched lines to the new Fort Worth–Denver Railroad line and took it to the end of its tracks. They'd have to drive their wagons the next six hundred or more miles across the thirsty earth to get to their new home in the Arizona Territory.

Barb, as he called him, was being securely hitched to the stout hitching racks set up for tethering animals. He made loud challenges as Chet pulled the tie down tight. He clapped him on the neck. "Go easy big man. We're half of the way there."

The others were unloading the farm wagons with a team of Belgium mares to back up and ease the wagons down the steep ramps. Tents were going up and the Mexican boys hired by the railroad agent were helping them to get set up. Susie with her skirt in her hands was running about directing the unloading, in charge of that business. His sister-in-law May kept the young boys back from the wild operations while holding her upset baby daughter Donna in her arms.

The draft horses and then the saddle horses came out of the stock cars until they all were hitched at a long rack. His eighteen-year-old nephew JD had charge of that operation and with the drivers was busy harnessing the teams to hitch to wagons so they could unload the furniture and commodities out of the boxcars and not have to reload them later.

"How is it going?" Chet asked Susie, who looked distressed.

"It will work out somehow."

He caught her shoulder and stopped her. "I have plenty of help hired here. Slow down. Tell me what's wrong. I can get it under control."

She swept the curls back from her face and her shoulders sagged. "I just want it to be right."

"It will be."

"Do we have to go on tomorrow?" She looked hard at him for an answer.

"Not necessarily. But it would be better if we did.

From the standpoint that every day we waste, we don't make twenty miles."

"I understand, but the train ride has been very tiring on May and the children. I thought we needed to let our lives catch up. Your aunt is very tired and she hasn't done a thing."

He chuckled. He knew how good Louise was at that.

"*No. No,*" Susie spoke in Spanish to a boy with a wooden crate he carried around. "That goes in wagon *numero* three."

"Oh, *sí, señorita.*"

"He don't know three from four."

She laughed. "I guess you're right."

"It will be a deal to get going. So I'll tell the boys what we're doing. Staying a day won't kill us. You settle down. I'll get a cowboy to run this Mexican help. You go sit down."

She nodded.

He pointed to the number 3 on the box and directed the youth to find the *carita* marked 3. The youth agreed and acted surprised that a number and a wagon were the same thing.

The sun went down and the flat cars, stock cars, and boxcars of the railroad were at last unloaded. He shook the agent's hand and wrote him a check for the amount of a thousand dollars. The man made him out a receipt in the campfire light and thanked him. JD told him the horses were all watered and fed. The crew and family formed a line where beef stew was being served with Dutch oven biscuits. Apple dumplings half filled another large Dutch oven for dessert.

Two young Texas rangers came by and visited with him. They were on duty, not only watching the track building, making sure no union problems occurred in the progress, but also doing peacekeeping as well.

Crane, a young ranger who hailed from close to where they lived, could hardly fathom why Chet had sold out. He said, "I'd've shot every one of them bastards."

"You can't kill everyone, they've got too large a family. Besides they shot my brother clear up in Kansas. No, it was time we found a new place to throw down our bedrolls."

The other one's name was Hamby and he agreed that a feud was hard to stop. "That sheriff should have asked for rangers."

"He tried hard. Come eat, boys. My sister has plenty of food."

They stood up and brushed the seat of their pants with their hats and thanked him. They all washed up at the start of the line and JD joined them.

"You get many law breakers over here?" he asked them.

"Quite a few," Hamby said. "They've run out here 'cause there was so little law and we get several wanted ones and some new cases too."

"Is it exciting?" JD asked.

"Naw, once in a while we have to buck up to

arrest some guy. But most throw down their guns when we ride up."

"You fellars must have a big rep," JD said.

"Naw, we's just rangers is all."

Susie handed the first one a tin plate. "Don't you men skimp none at eating. I'm glad you all are here. We have plenty."

"Yes, ma'am." Crane about swallowed his whole Adam's apple at her words.

Chet was glad his outfit was going to stay over to check everything the next day. Maybe they'd all get a rest because by the next month they would be a long ways west of this spot.

He and JD rode over to look over Tascosa the next day. A town the rangers said was tough. When they got there, some men were having a shooting contest and the boy that won it was William Bonney. He hardly looked out of his teens. He dressed sloppy and had a Mexican *puta* that hung around his neck all the time. Someone told them he was an enforcer for John Chisum, the big rancher, and probably had some stolen horses he'd brought up there to sell.

Chet and JD both drank a beer and started back to camp, still unimpressed with what was labeled "the greatest town west of Fort Worth." They also learned the railroad wanted ten thousand dollars to lay tracks to their city and no one there had that kind of money.

Bonney stopped them in the street. "I hear you're moving to a big ranch over into Arizona." His weathered felt hat off his head, he beat it with his left hand on his leg. He had to sweep back his uncut hair because of the wind. "Need a good hand or two?"

"Not today, we've got enough help thanks."

Bonney nodded like he was thinking about it, then when they started again, he said, "Hold up, I know that road real good."

"I imagine you do," Chet said. "But we have our own help. Thanks."

"Yeah, watch out for them damn Navajos, they'll rob you blind."

"Thanks."

"Sure. You guys ever want to have a shoot off, come see me. I'm the best in the West."

"I believe you are," Chet said and they rode off.

When they were far enough away, JD looked back then asked, "Was he wanting to have a gunfight?"

"I think so. I didn't buy his bait."

"Just so I didn't miss the point." JD shook his head warily. "He sure was a cocky bastard."

"I have heard his name before."

"Have you?" They were trotting their horses across the West Texas sagebrush and bunch grass.

"Yeah, they call him Billy the Kid."

"Yeah, I've heard of him."

Things went uneventfully in camp, except three rangers this time came for supper that evening, and to meet his sister. Chet believed if any one of those lawmen stole her, he'd beat them up and drag her back.

That second morning, May had the baby in a

cradle and looked rested when he came by the tables. The chubby widow of his brother came from a rich family who had shunned her when she married Dale. Chet always thought his brother married her to take care of his three sons and baby daughter. But she was sweet, worked hard, and never complained. The teenage older son of Dale, Heck, had been murdered by road agents. The boy and his stepmother had a struggle getting along. Which is why he took Heck to Arizona looking for a new ranch. He'd grown up so much on their trip—damn, he could hardly even imagine that boy was dead.

Their things were all loaded before the sun came up. Susie and May had a wagon to drive. He knew mules would have been better than the Belgium mares, but he felt even if they had to haul some forage and water for them, in the end he'd raise some great draft mule colts from them.

A Mexican boy named Rio herded the loose horse stock, the other brood mares, and saddle stock. His brother Juan led Barb, the stallion, from his horse, a tough, well-broke gelding. JD was the scout and Chet the trail boss.

Seven veteran ranch hands drove the other teams. They were all experienced cowboys that he knew and trusted. His Aunt Louise drove one of the wagons and Chet knew she would be his biggest pain in the rear of the entire outfit. May's two younger stepsons had small horses to ride, but he made them ride in a wagon the first few days.

They did lots of awing about that but he didn't want them lost or separated.

They took four days to get to the New Mexico Territory line. A New Mexico rancher there with plenty of water welcomed them. Chet offered to pay him but he scoffed away his offer. "My wife will be proud for the company."

A man in his thirties, Roy Arny said he'd fought for Texas in the war and was glad to hear someone who talked with a drawl. Chet's outfit impressed him and Arny sent word for his wife to come meet the white women.

"So you've got a place in Arizona?" Arny asked.

"Yes. On the Verde River."

"When I went out there in '65 that was all Apache country. That was right at the end of the war. Indians around here weren't mad, so I came back closer to Texas."

His windmill was working hard pumping water and creaking in the strong wind. The drivers were watering their stock and had set up a tent for the ladies.

"Nice teams. The trip will be hard on them. I'd have used mules."

"I can afford to baby them. I plan to raise mules with them when we get out there. They'll have good mule colts."

"They damn sure will. Might really bring some top money, too. You sell your place back there?"

"I did. An investor wanted it for his son-in-law. We sold him the cattle, mules, and lots more. Oh, and two colts out of my stallion. They paid for the railroad bill to get us up here."

He and Chet leaned with their backs to the tall corral. Arny rolled a cigarette, lit it and puffed on it. He offered the makings to Chet. "You want a smoke?"

Chet shook his head.

"I seen that claybank hoss. Where did he come from?"

"Mexico. The Barbarousa Hacienda. I bought him as a colt. They seldom sell their stallions."

"He looks like a helluva horse."

"He really is."

"You must have had a big outfit down there in Texas."

"We did, but a family feud developed and I lost my brother. We were shot at and lots of bad things happened. Made up my mind I needed to find some new ground. I was lucky this ranch we have now was run down. The owner lived back East and I think he was afraid of the manager he had hired. I bought it—I think it's worth the money."

"You know that Arizona ain't the Texas hill country?"

Chet nodded. "But you can't live in a land where your life and your family is threatened every day."

"No, I guess not. Which one of these ladies is your wife?" Arny asked as his own wife, carrying a child and followed by two more, came up the sandy driveway.

"My sis is the gal over there. Her name is Susie Byrnes. I don't have a wife."

"Would you introduce my wife Neddy to her?"

"Sure."

After the women were introduced, Susie took her and the kids inside the tent. He and Arny talked more about ranching.

JD rode in and dismounted. Chet introduced his nephew to Arny. Then he asked JD how the next day looked.

"Fine. There's some water about twenty miles west in a small dry wash."

"Dead Man's Creek," Arny said. "The next water is thirty miles from there. Then it's thirty more to a trading post."

"We've got a water wagon to get us by."

"Fill it up every chance you get."

"We will," Chet said. "The women must have coffee on by now. Join us."

"Sure sounds good. We run out a couple weeks ago. Roasted barley won't replace it. I need to go get some."

"JD, go get his wife some Arbuckle coffee from the supply wagon."

Arny frowned at him. "I never said that to get charity."

"Ease off. We're watering stock, filling our water

wagon. A couple of pounds of coffee ain't a high price to pay for all that."

"Whatever you say. That coffee will damn sure make Neddy smile." The two men walked to the tent.

They'd covered a hundred miles and had at least five hundred more to go.

The next few days some mountain would stick up way off, and it would take several days to reach its base. They found grass for their stock and water. Some of the water had so much alkali in it was hard to swallow. They tried to keep good water in the drinking barrels on the wagons but each mile the wheels turned, that task grew harder.

San Juan Mission had several small deep lakes of fresh water. The people were Hispanic and acted glad to see them. They took a day off, washed clothes, and bathed. Everyone needed a rest. A rancher sold them more hay. They had not used a lot of it, but Chet wanted to be certain so they added to the supply.

One of his drivers, Billy Cotton, has a bad boil rise on his butt that needed lancing. Blond-headed and hardly out of his teens, the lanky boy was operated on by a white doctor and told to lie flat down on his belly for the next few days while it healed. Chet drove his mares and Billy was on a bed in Susie's wagon, red-faced most of the time as a boy could be about his condition, surrounded by the women.

Chet wasn't sure who was the most glad when he healed enough to sit on a pillow and could drive his own wagon again. Flocks of sheep herded by mere boys roamed the country. They had several "guests" stop by at night and stagecoaches passed them in the daytime coming and going.

A few of the drop-ins were rough men who from behind their beards looked like cutthroat killers, but they acted polite and Susie shared her food with them like they were neighbors. Chet imagined that they were so damn glad to have a woman-cooked-meal, they'd act nice at any cost.

Most of their kind ate cross-legged on the ground outside the tent and were armed to the teeth with pistols and large knives, and wore buckskin clothes. Their horses, jaded mustangs, were ridden hard and put away wet. But they acted polite like their mothers had backhanded them often for any infractions to her code.

May complained that some of them made her shudder with how they gazed at her. Chet told her that outside of Indian women most white women were a treat for those men to simply look at.

She frowned at him. "If one of them ever asks you for me, tell them no."

He'd hugged her shoulders and said, "Why they may be rich."

"I don't need them. If they can't take a bath and shave once in a while, I want no part of them, rich or not."

The closer they drew to the Rio Grande, which he considered a third or so of the way, they moved into more mountains and junipers. Even a few pine trees and cooler nights. So far they'd only lost one Belgium mare to colic and she had to be destroyed.

He had a brief talk with Susie how on the Rio Grande at Bernallio Crossing they would take some time to catch up and repair everything that needed their attention.

"Two days we will be there, but I understand that mountain road goes out off into there is real steep. We may have to double-team the wagons and use a log brake on the hind wheels going down there. We could've gone to Santa Fe, but I figure that would take almost a week longer."

She bobbed her head in agreement. "We didn't need any longer. I am just glad we had the money to take that train ride to Tascosa and the end of the tracks. But we made half that trip in three hard days. Here we've been over half a month just getting to the Rio Grande."

"It's a long ways out there. I only hope the barrier between us and the Reynolds is great enough."

She agreed. "You look tired. Are you getting any sleep?"

"Enough. We'll rest and wash up at the river."

"Good. Step by step we're getting there." She reached over and squeezed his hands on the table. "No one said this would be easy. But I agree life back there was impossible."

"Maybe I should have found a place closer?"

"No, when I heard you first describe the ranch

you had bought, I knew it would be a grand place for all of us."

He nodded and closed his eyes. "It will be. I promise."

Bernallio Crossing on the Rio Grande River consisted of a mission, a small town on the banks of the river, a ferry, and several farmers on irrigated farms up and down the valley. He bought frijoles and shucked corn, some of which he had ground at the water mill into meal for the women to use. They loaded some good hay and the town had a fiesta for them. Chet knew the Hispanic people and they needed little reason to host such a firecracker-popping event with wine, dancing, and a good time to be had by all.

He danced half the night away with a dark-eyed woman in her twenties named Consuela. Her husband had been killed in a flood trying to save some of their stock. She spoke some English and he savvied enough Spanish so they had a great evening. They laughed and she talked about her village, her life, and him about moving.

Late in the night the music went on, and she invited him to her *casa*. He told her he must first check on his people and his camp. That he only had one horse with him.

"Oh, *mi amigo*, I can ride double if he don't buck me off."

"He won't buck."

"Good. Let's go then."

He mounted the stout bay, bent over, gave her his arm and she swung up like a feather behind him in a pile of slips and petticoats. She clung to him. The horse acted stiff legged the first block of dark street but then set into a running walk. At the camp, two of his rifle-armed cowboys came out and told him all was well.

He thanked them and from there she guided him to her *casa*. Leaning forward, she pointed out the way through the mesquite trees, barking dogs, and dark houses. Her arms around his waist, she squeezed him from time to time and laughed

"Will we wake anyone?" he asked.

"No, my children are at my *mamacita*'s."

At her front door, he drew his spur-clad boot over the saddle horn and dropped to the ground. He caught her in his arms and kissed her. Then he carried her through the door.

She laughed easily. "Oh, *hombre,* you will be fun for me to entertain you."

With a big smile, he agreed with her.

CHAPTER 2

The mountain range in the west rose tall and hosted a long hard nine mile grade. Halfway up he looked back at the green farmland that lined the river. *Good-bye, Consuela.* On the grade he found one wagon stalled, so he tied his lariat on to the tongue of JD's heavy wagon and made a dally on the horn. The bay horse helped the team dig in, going uphill over the worst grade of all. At last on flat ground, he went back to help the others. They were all soon on top. Near noon they all rested atop the flat country dotted with small farms. Parked beside the road they waved at a dust-stirring stage that passed them eastbound.

Chet's wagon train drew its way westward. They found water and then used the tank wagon in dry stretches, refilling it at missions and small villages. He was so grateful his horses were shod and had everyone take great care crossing the volcanic fields with their sharp-edged glasslike rocks, which worried him for close to a day. On the western end they pulled off and made certain all the stock was safe.

"No problem," JD reported.

"We all better offer a prayer," Chet said, grateful for the safe passage. The ones close by gathered and he offered a short thank you to God for their delivery.

In another few days they reached Gallup and then the final fort in New Mexico. They took a day to rest and gather their wits. By his calculation they were within two weeks of their destination in Camp Verde. With no serious safety mistakes, besides being weary, they lounged around in camp and got some catch-up on their sleep.

His Aunt Louise complained she was no muleskinner and when would they reach this next hell he had picked out for them. Chet wanted to tell her he had offered her a place in town and a stipend to stay in Texas. An offer she scoffed away telling him she could drive any team he had. But he kept his tongue—there was no way to reach her at times when she was in her cranky stages.

Susie made a survey of her supplies and told him they would have plenty of everything. JD and the men told him things were going much smoother than they thought it would. He thanked them all for trying so hard. He was so pleased they had not driven their cattle as well. From his previous experience driving herds to Kansas, he'd found such treks to be bitter journeys.

The wagon train moved on the next day. There

were fewer settlements in the region ahead and his written guide of the Captain Marcy Road that he and JD used indicated that water sources would be harder to find.

West of Gallup, an Indian woman wrapped in a trade blanket stood beside a small wagon with a dead horse in the shafts lying in the road. Chet rode up, dismounted, and removed his hat.

"How did he die?" he asked, motioning to the dead horse.

"He was fine until he stumbled and fell face-down," she said with a shrug.

Amazed that she spoke English so well, he nodded. "How far are you from your home?"

"Two days."

She looked to be in her late teens. A handsome young woman and very straight-backed.

"Is there anyone can take you home?"

"I have no idea. I hoped some of my people would be coming along."

JD rode in and stepped off his horse. "What happened, Chet?"

"Her horse fell down dead."

"What do we need to do?"

"She says she lives two days from here and hopes some of her people will come by."

"What can we do?"

Chet turned to her. "Is your place west of here?"

She nodded.

"We can hook your wagon to one of ours and haul you in that direction. My name is Chet Byrnes. This is JD my scout."

"Nice to meet both of you. My name is Judy Bell."

He looked at the food and supplies that she must have brought in her wagon.

"Mrs. Bell, I think your supplies will ride in the wagon if we don't go too fast when we pull it behind one of ours."

She reached out and touched his arm. "My name is Judy. I have no husband."

"Oh. All right. I am sorry."

"No problem. I would appreciate that very much."

"Good." He stepped out and waved Frank, one of his drivers, over from the file, and JD began to unhook the harness. They stripped the dead animal out of his harness and the three men and she pushed the wagon back. The shafts were soon hooked and tied to Frank's wagon. Her harness was removed and loaded. Next the dead horse was dragged off the road. Chet took her up the line to Susie's parked wagon. Meanwhile JD and Frank made sure the wagon would follow.

"Susie, this is Judy Bell. That was her horse that died unexpected. She will be riding with us. She speaks good English."

"Oh, so nice to meet you," his sister said.

"No, I am so grateful to all of you for stopping for a poor Indian woman."

"Come get in our wagon. I am certain we can move on."

Chet nodded and he helped them both into the wagon. With a salute, he mounted up again, gave a shout, and the wagon train was on its way again across great sweeping grassland. The belly-tall grass fascinated him. These regions had never had buffalo like the central plains, so the grass was waving to any stockman who crossed it.

The day was uneventful, and that evening Chet spoke more to the Indian woman.

"Do you live with your family?"

"No, I live with an older woman, her name is Grandmother. We have sheep and goats. We weave rugs and blankets for sale."

"Navajos don't live in tepees?" he asked.

"No, we have hogans. Six-sided log cabins. The sun shines in our front door every day."

"I have seen some that are abandoned."

"If a person dies in one, we simply move out of it. No one will ever live in it again."

"Where did you learn English?" He was looking at his hands so he did not make her too uncomfortable to talk to him.

"We had a mission school in my village."

"Did you go to the prison camp?"

She nodded about the incarceration of her people down in New Mexico where they died in great numbers before finally the Navajos promised to fight no more. Then the government turned them loose and many more died on the walk back to their land from way down south in New Mexico.

"You have no husband?"

"No. Maybe I speak too much."

He laughed.

She drew her spine up. "My people lost many

leaders in our confinement down there. We need strong people to keep our nation strong. I must scare men away when I shout, 'Stand up!' They say be quiet Judy Bell, the white man may send us back to hell."

She amused him with her strong ways. He was reminded of the woman Mary, who led the Yavapais and who he helped so her people survived. This woman had the same strength.

That evening he told her about a horse they would give her from their saddle stock. "JD and the other drivers think we have a horse that will pull your wagon home. He will be our gift. He's a saddle horse and very gentle. You can drive him tomorrow and see so when you have to leave us that he will work for you."

"That is very generous of you and your family. I don't know how I will ever repay you."

"He's a gift."

"I know a gift. But I am also proud."

"Unless you can magic-like make a horse, you'll have to accept our horse." He shook his head. "I am not being mean or bossy."

He thought she would cry.

She dropped her chin. "I am grateful for all you and your family have done for me."

"No need to be sad."

She tried to smile. "You wondered why I have no man. I wonder why you have no wife. Your sister may be the reason. She is a great leader for you. She does much work."

"Susie is a good person. But she's pushed me at

a woman in the past—it did not work out. The woman had to stay there and care for her folks in Texas."

"Oh, I am sorry. We all must do things that are not our cause. I will drive your horse with pride and return him some day."

"He is a gift for you to keep."

"I may want to see your land."

"You will be welcome."

"Oh, I am sure of that."

"I better go check on things." He excused himself.

The next afternoon she drove away, headed north on some wagon tracks. He watched her disappear in the brown windswept grass and sagebrush. A strange woman he'd liked to have known more about—but he had a ranch to worry about. Better keep moving.

"You liked her," Susie said quietly as he walked her to her wagon.

"I like women. Strong ones. You will meet another in Arizona."

"I am looking forward to that."

He chuckled. "Susie you are the light in my life. Thanks for all your help. In a few days we will be there. I want you to find a strong man."

His sister gave him a we-will-see reply.

They left the Marcy Road on a cutoff that would shorten their miles. In two days they camped at a small natural lake. The place was a wonderful spot in the pines and produced fat cutthroat trout the younger boys hauled in on bent willow poles. They were within days of reaching the new ranch.

Chet spoke to JD and the drivers before he left. "This is still Apache country. The army is chasing them, but be on guard and take no chances on them. They could slip in and kill some of us. So be wary all the time."

With care, he went over the details of the map with JD and then he set out for the ranch. He rode a big stout bay horse they called Holdem and made Camp Verde the first night. He had a short beer in one of the saloons in the block of businesses that the town consisted of, then went on to the ranch after sundown.

Someone shouted, "The boss is back!"

And he was swarmed.

Hoot came running out beating on a large kettle. "Well ain't you a picture for sore eyes. Get in this house, you rascal. We've been talking bad about you and you must've heard us."

"Where's your outfit?" Wiley Combs, the shortest man in the outfit asked, hitching up his pants.

"They're two or so days east of here."

"They need any help?" his foreman Tom Flowers asked, pushing forward through the men to shake his hand.

"We can send a few men if you can spare them to relieve some of the drivers and my aunt."

"How far off are they?' Tom asked.

"Maybe thirty miles or so. They're coming across from the east. Ten wagons of them. We cut off the Marcy Road."

"We can damn sure find them," Hampt said, bear hugging him.

"We're all still here," Sarge said. "'Cept Busby Stone."

"What happened to him?"

"Oh, he's working his own place. You recall Mrs. Kelly O'Bryan?"

"A round redhead?"

"That's his bride."

"Good for him. Tom, how is your wife and kids?"

"Fine, sir. They're here."

"Mr. Byrnes, I ain't shook your hand yet." It was the kid Corey who helped Hoot.

Chet leaned back to look at the improved-looking youth. "My gosh, you look like a cowboy to me."

"Well I'm trying."

They shook hands.

"I sold the Bar C mostly lock stock and barrel, boys. Got a good price and didn't have to trail them cattle out here. We came a third of the way by freight train."

"Aw, boss, come inside. We've got coffee made and some apple raisin pie left," Hoot said. "You can tell us all about it."

And he did.

CHAPTER 3

His foreman Tom's new house for him and his family was nearly done, Chet learned that evening. That was good, he decided the next morning, walking around the fine log structure. There was lots of craftsmanship in the fashioning together on the two-story log house. The wide porch welcomed them. Mill-made glass windows in the front looked at the Verde River. Millie, Tom's wife, showed him where the living room, dining room, and kitchen would be. The aroma of the fresh-cut sweet pine lumber stayed in his nose. Rock fireplaces were on both sides of the living room and half completed. Stairs went up to a fenced landing. The kitchen would have a pump in the sink and a new large wood-burning range to cook on.

"I hope you like it," Millie said.

"Hey, this is your house. Do you like it?"

She nodded her head and chewed on her lower lip. "It's a mansion."

He hugged her before she cried. "Good. You'll like my sister Susie. You two will get on fine."

"I'm looking forward to meeting her."

"I better go find Tom. I'm certain that there are things we need to fix."

"Chet Byrnes."

"Yes."

"Thanks for hiring Tom. We love this ranch and with the house it will be even better."

"Good." He went and looked for his foreman.

They met and discussed things. Tom planned to go look at some cows for sale. He had a good plan to ship some of their older cows and replace them with better ones.

After lunch, Chet saddled a big stout horse and rode off to Preskit. He planned to get a haircut along with all else, but forgot it. He made good time completing his other business and in late afternoon, he reined up at Marge's ranch gate. Drew a deep breath and turned *Brother*, his renamed horse, down the lane.

He didn't see anyone exercising horses, so he stopped at the house, hitched his horse, and went through the yard gate with the Scotch Collies barking excitedly at him.

"Oh my God—" Knuckles on her mouth, she looked pale enough to faint. Marge stopped halfway out of the open door. "You've come back from Texas."

"Like an old tomcat. It's me. Are you all right?"

"No. I about fainted. I don't usually do that. Oh, Chet it is so good to see you." She fell in his arms and they kissed. And kissed. "I'm sorry, but it shocked me so much to see you on my porch, I wondered if I was dreaming it all."

"It's me all right. I knew I needed to stop. I sure never aimed to shock you half to death."

"Oh, come in and sit on the couch and tell me all about Texas."

He put his hat on the rack and settled next to her on the sofa. "Texas is still there. I don't own a shred of it. My family is about a day or so east of Camp Verde. I sent some of the boys to go meet them tomorrow."

"How—how did you come?"

"First six hundred miles we made in train cars. Took three days . . ." He had to take a moment to kiss her again and then he went on with his tale. When he finished, she jumped up.

"My new housekeeper must have supper about ready."

"New one?"

"Yes. My long-term friend had to go to Tucson and take care of her mother down there."

A Mexican woman came in the room. "*Señora*, is your friend here going to eat with us?"

"Yes," she said, then turned to him. "Dad's over in California on business. All my men are out chasing some horses that were turned out by someone."

"Trouble?" he asked.

"I hope not. With my father gone—why I hope the gate simply came open and someone did not steal them."

"If they did let me know. We can find them."

She smiled. "We better go eat. Monica, this is my good friend Chet Byrnes. He sold his holdings in Texas and has bought the Quarter Circle Z ranch at Camp Verde."

"So nice to meet you, *señor*."

"Yes ma'am."

"His entire family has been on the road moving here."

"Oh, how far is that?"

"Close to twelve hundred miles by my guess."

"Oh, did anyone die on such a long trip?"

"No, we only lost one horse."

He seated Marge and she made him sit in the head chair. When Monica left the room he kissed her again. They both laughed. Neither of them could take their eyes off each other. But somehow they managed to eat and after Monica cleared the table, they were still looking at each other.

Marge made certain they were alone before she said, "You must certainly stay the night."

A horse came in on the run down the lane in the bloody sundown.

She rose. "I wonder what's wrong?"

A short man under a sombrero came on the run. "*Señora*, the rustlers shot Logan and Buck. I came for help. What should I do?"

"They what?"

"Can you take me back there?" Chet asked him, taking charge.

"*Sí*, but it is many miles, *señor*."

"Marge, go find the sheriff or Roamer. Tell

them I will leave markers so they can find me. What is his name?"

"Raphael—"

"Raphael, go get yourself a fresh horse. Marge, get me a rifle and some cartridges. I may need them."

"Take my father's good horse," she said to her man and ran for the glass gun case. Looking at the half empty case, she turned to Chet. "The men must have taken the good ones. Is a .44/40 all right?"

"Fine."

She handed him the new-looking rifle and then two boxes of shells. "I will go get Sheriff Sims or Roamer. Maybe Raphael can tell me where the rustlers were at."

"Good idea."

"Oh, I hate to see you going after horse thieves."

"Hey, we need to stop them."

She agreed. "I'll get some jerky, a blanket, and something."

"What is wrong, *señora*?" her housekeeper asked.

"Raphael just rode in. He's taking Chet back. Both Logan and Buck have been shot. Get some dry cheese, crackers, and jerky for them. I'll get him a blanket."

"Who will tell the sheriff?"

"We're going to drive to town and do that when they get gone."

Monica said, "I can hitch the horses."

"We both can. Get the food for them."

He kissed her good-bye with his arms full. Her

Mexican cowboy was back with a big fresh horse out front. When he came in the house Marge filled his hands with food. Then the two women ran by him to go hitch the team.

With a blanket over his arm, a box of ammo and rifle in his hands, Chet headed for his fresh horse. Marge's cowboy loaded both his and Chet's saddlebags with the food. He jammed the rifle in the scabbard and tied the blanket on behind the cantle. When they were both in the saddle, they whirled their horses around and headed up the long driveway. They turned hard at the main road and headed east. By Chet's calculation they had less than a half hour of light and then it would be dark. He hoped that Marge and her housekeeper would be all right going into Preskit. By this time, several of his Arizona cowboys had already met his wagon train. They should be good. They raced through the small mining town of Mayer and off the east mountain toward the Verde well downstream from the ranch. Forced to cut down the speed of their mounts to a hard trot, going off the mountain, he decided to quiz her man.

"Could you tell how many rustlers had the horses?" he asked.

"Three or four. One of them, maybe a boy. They had taken twelve of our good ranch horses. When we got close to them, one of them dropped back and began firing at us with a rifle. Buck was hit in the leg and he told me to go for help. I think Logan was already dead. Nothing I could do but what Buck said. I told him I would and the bullets whizzed by me like hornets but I was soon out of range. I was plenty scared and never looked back. They may have killed both of them."

"You did real well, amigo. Where were they headed do you think?"

"Buck said before the shooting that they were going to Bloody Basin."

Chet shook his head. "I don't know this country and I have never been there."

"Me either *señor*. But it is south of us according to him."

"We'll just follow them after we check on those two men that were shot."

"I hope that Buck is alive. He is a good *segundo* and I sure like to work for him." Raphael crossed himself and looked up at his sombrero for celestial help as well.

Chet marked where they took the trail off the road for the posse to see where to turn. A note said they were on the trail ahead of them.

Both horses were still breathing hard as the twilight set in, and recovering from the hard race they made to get there. The country was mostly head-high juniper and open spaces. They spooked range cows and calves and a British breed bull or two. Couple of them were Herefords and some were red and roan shorthorn males. They reminded Chet about his own planned upgrading breeding program. He'd have to buy more of those kinds of bulls. The mountains ahead looked tougher and he knew the quarter moon wouldn't rise until later.

Pretty brazen rustlers to take ranch horses out of a pasture, then halter and lead that many away. It was a big decision because folks would sure notice that many passing by. He bet several folks saw them when they came through Mayer.

"How much farther to the ranchmen?"

"*Señor*, it is over another mountain from where we are. Those banditos were really moving on when we discovered there were men leading them. I saw them from one mountain to the next. I guess they saw us coming too. Buck was mad as hell."

"I can't stand a thief either. Back in Texas, three men once stole my whole remuda and I hung them when I caught them about two hundred miles away from our ranch. Over eighty horses,"

"Oh, how did they do it?"

"Just rode in and took them. One of the mothers of the hung rustlers later said, 'Oh, they would have brought them back.' Dumb woman. We caught them near the Red River—that's the line that goes into the Indian Territory. Their execution caused a feud with that family that made me move out here."

The starlight grew brighter, but the trail grew much steeper and slowed their pace even more. A coyote howled and another answered. An owl hooted for its mate. Chet settled in for a long night. The trail was obvious enough that he figured the law could trace their tracks in the daylight. They'd bring a posse. But this was tough terrain they went down then up again, and their horses had to cat-hop up. It would sure sift out the weak ones in a big hurry. He wished he had his roan horse that had been shot out from under him. The one he rode was tough, but that pony was made for this steep, hard country.

They chewed on jerky about the time the quarter moon rose. And the new light really outlined the steep mountains they were in. Way past midnight they approached the ambush site that Raphael had pointed out to him from across the dark canyon.

"They may have come back and caught their horses and took them too."

He agreed with Chet. "I bet they did."

That in consideration, they rode in silence off the mountain, then up the even steeper trail. Raphael held up his hand in the lead. "This is where they started shooting at us from up there."

Even in the starlight he couldn't see any bodies. There was little more than some pear cactus beds. Raphael was off his horse and looking. He struck a wooden match. "There's blood here."

Chet dismounted. "What in the hell did they do with their bodies?"

Raphael pushed his sombrero back on his shoulders. "I don't know. This is where Buck told for me to go get help."

"I don't doubt you. They must've taken the corpses with them. Let's go up on the mountain and wait until dawn so we can track them."

The blood was real. Why take the bodies except to hide them? Corpses would make a loud call for the arrest of the killers. Horse thefts were just things that happened every day, though ranchers were upset any time they happened. But dead men raised big rewards for the capture of the killers.

"I hope not, but I think they're dead and the thieves want to hide the bodies."

"I savvy. But when I find them I may strangle them myself with my bare hands."

"I understand," Chet's stomach roiled over the thoughts of the men's demise. Not a good picture to consider.

They emerged on a large mesa of grass and pear cactus beds. With matches for light, Raphael studied the tracks. His words sounded sad. "They must have taken them with them."

Chet dropped heavy from the saddle. "I have a blanket. It'll be cool up here by sunup."

"I have a blanket-lined jacket here on my saddle, *señor*. You use that blanket. I don't know if I can sleep anyway."

"I understand. It will be past noon or later before the posse shows up here. I will leave them a note about what we found."

"Good idea."

Chet used the side of his boot sole to clear a place of any debris and rocks from his resting place.

With a stub of a pencil he found he would write it in a small tally book he kept notes in. By the light of Raphael's matches he wrote a short note. He planned to tie it on yucca stem in the path for them. On the hard ground, he grabbed some shut-eye, waking every hour or so until he sat up and wondered if they could see anything yet.

The short man came over and squatted on his boot heels. "I never sleep much."

"Neither did I. But can we see yet?"

"No. But my anger fires me." He pounded his chest with his fist.

"Me too. Let's give it a little more light. They have to sleep too." Raphael agreed.

Chet's eyes felt like they had been sanded by a dust storm. He hoped they soon would become wet from his lashes fluttering over them. If those outlaws dumped the bodies they might be hard to find. They could not afford spending much time on the search and let them get away. As much as it sickened him, they needed to hound these men's trail or they'd evaporate. That was something he didn't want to happen no matter how far they had to go to get them. He left the posse a note they could hardly miss, mentioning they thought the rustlers had taken the two bodies. He added, If we find any evidence of the bodies we will leave a note for you where they are. *Personally he intended to keep after the thieves, no matter the outcome.*

The first light showed the trail went to the east and off the mesa. This jumble of mountains was a real wilderness. Raphael told him the Apaches had used this country to hide in as well.

"I can see why. Are there any ranchers in here?"

"I think so. But I have never been here before either."

Mid-morning, they spotted smoke and could smell it on the wind. It proved to be a ranch. Not much of one, but they must have water and their horses needed some. The adobe jacal and the corrals did not look prosperous, but several tanks held water, no doubt from a spring. Some goats greeted them and a few burros stood hipshot around the house.

The shock came to Chet when they rounded the house and faced a woman in a wash-worn dress armed with a .22 rifle. Her hair was dark and un-kempt. Thin faced, she looked like she was badly upset.

"Stop right there. I can shoot this damn gun and it'll kill you."

"Whoa, ma'am. Our horses need water. We are after some men that stole our horses and killed two men. Have you seen them?"

"Get your horse watered and get the hell out of here. I can shoot you both and I will."

"Did you see these men?" He knew they had been there. The shod hoofprints and fresh horse apples showed they might have been there for a while.

She shook her head. The rifle butt was against her shoulder. Her dark eyes looked hawklike.

"Lady." He led his horse toward the trough. "I can read signs. Those men were here. If you gave them any comfort, the posse of lawmen behind us may arrest you as an accessory to murder and horse theft."

"Shut up and water those horses and get the hell out of here."

"Do you know the men who killed our ranch-men?"

"Shut up!" She stepped over so she could aim the rifle, threateningly, at him.

"You know these men?"

She never answered and he felt she was so upset she might really shoot him. The situation was close to exploding. Concern written on his face, Raphael had mounted his horse and looked like he wanted Chet to do the same.

Chet had one more question. "Did those men rape you last night?"

She looked ready to squeeze the trigger. Then she dropped the barrel and shook her head. "Did they say they did?" she asked.

"Ma'am, I'm sorry. Raphael and I are not going to rape you. Those men killed his boss, a man he really liked and a fellow worker. They stole those horses from the ranch he works for. A lady I like owns that ranch and I am here to get those men. Do you know their names?"

She staggered backwards against the wall of the house and cried. "I know one was Robert some-one. I heard them call him that. They all—"

He took the .22 rifle from her. She moved away, so he didn't touch her and she shook in her resolve not to even have a hand on her.

"Who else?"

"A breed called Wolf. Another man was Jeff, he has bought some cows from my man."

"There was a boy with them?"

"He was no boy. His name was Bud, he said. He was bad as the rest."

"Where is your man?"

"Working at a mine."

Raphael tossed his head toward the west, meaning the direction of the mine. He looked more concerned about her as she huddled against the wall in her own arms away from Chet.

"Who besides this Jeff had been here before?"

"I never saw the others before." Her thin shoulder shook. "I never offered them a thing. They tore my clothes off me and then—"

"My name is Chet Byrnes. Did they have two bodies on the horses?"

She nodded and then she took his kerchief that he gave her to wipe her wet face.

"Do you have any supplies to eat here?"

"Not much."

"If we come back we will bring you a deer."

She nodded. "I could use it."

"Do you know where this Jeff lives?"

"No. My husband sold him three steers that had his brand on them. They were mavericks. He never stole them."

"I never said that. Will you be all right now?"

"I have to be."

She handed him back the kerchief.

"There will be a posse behind us today. Tell them what they did and who they were. They won't hurt you."

She nodded, but never looked at him.

He leaned her rifle against the wall, stepped up on the bay and followed Raphael who acted anxious to be away from her. When they were going down some wagon tracks away from the ranch, Raphael looked back and then turned forward. Still upset over their confrontation with her, he said, "I thought she would kill you."

"No, she was very upset and I hated for us to have to leave her but we can't afford to lose their trail."

"How far will they take those bodies do you think?" he asked.

"No telling. We should watch for buzzards I guess."

"These horse turds in the trail look fresh."

"They are. If they all four raped her, they spent some time there. From the fresh horse shit around the yard I'd say they were there for several hours. They would need to sleep and we may run into them before this day is over."

Raphael still sounded concerned about the matter of the woman. "I thought she would shoot you."

"She was upset all right. But she also was not a real killer like a man would have been. I agree it was very dangerous but now we have names for some of them."

"Anyway I think you are a *mucho* brave *hombre*."

Chet nodded. He'd merely found out from her what they needed to know. They'd bring her a deer to eat when they rode back. Several mule deer had broken out of the brush at their approach. They owed her one. No telling what she had to eat. He doubted she had much of anything. Those four killers needed to be stopped before this was over.

Midday, they found a wet spring and some cattails that offered water to their mounts. The tracks were fresh and the dim road easy to travel. They pushed their horses hard.

Chet reined up at the sight of another ranch. He wished for his telescope or field glasses. They rode off into the junipers to be less visible in case they had a lookout.

"Did you see any horses?" Chet asked him.

"I thought there were some down there. What should we do?"

"We need to circle and see if they are there."

Raphael nodded his sombrero in agreement. "They will watch their back trails."

"We better hobble our horse and tie them. I'd hate to walk back empty-handed."

"*Sí.*" He bailed off and they soon had their horses tethered good. Chet took his rifle and the ammo. Going low, they used the bushy evergreens for cover and moved fast to come in from the north side of the house and corrals. This way would be time-consuming getting there, and the killers might be gone when they got into place. Still, to ride in with only two men would be deadly, considering they knew the killers could be there.

They soon were in the corrals. Then Chet realized a low flying buzzard came gliding in close over his head.

Raphael tugged on his sleeve. "Those bodies are still on the horses."

"Good, if we get between them and their horses, we'll be in charge."

"Hold it." Raphael caught his sleeve and pointed to a man on the roof with a rifle.

Chet set the rifle on the corral rail to take aim. "Shoot to kill when it starts," he whispered.

The rifle roared in Chet's hands and the lookout was struck hard, and pitched head first off the roof. He swung the lever out and reloaded the chamber and aimed at the edge of the house. A man armed with a pistol came running around the house and began blasting it at them. He met a .44/40 slug in the chest and crumbled to the ground. The long gun reloaded, Chet looked for any more. No more appeared. Chet and Raphael moved closer to their horses using the cover of the corral. Those men had to have their mounts to ever escape in this wilderness. Chet felt confident he and Raphael had them under their control. Then there was some commotion in the yard but they could not see what it was from their position.

Soon two horses were racing away on the far side of the house and Chet shot at both riders fleeing the ranch. But the gap they passed through between two buildings was too small to be sure he hit anything. That must be the horses that were left. They moved carefully toward the house, making sure no one remaining in the house shot at them.

Then a woman screamed, "I am coming out with my kids!"

"Watch her. It may be a trick."

A woman herded her three small kids from the house. "We have no guns."

"Get over to the side." Chet waved her to get

more toward the sheds in case the outlaws began to shoot at them.

She took the children back into a shed and crouched down. He crossed there and kept his gaze on the house.

"Who rode away?" Chet asked her quietly.

"I don't know these men. They beat up my husband. I fear he might die unless he has care."

"I'm sorry we didn't get here sooner. Are they still in the house?"

"No. The other two rode away."

"Raphael, she says those two are gone. The one on the roof and the other man we shot makes four. Her man is badly beaten in there."

Raphael holstered his gun and they hurried for the house. Chet took the lead. The man who had charged them was dead or unconscious. He told Raphael to see about the one shot off the roof. With a nod, he headed to check the west side.

He set the rifle down at the wall before entering the house. A man sat up on a bed with his head in bandages. "Who the hell are you?"

"A man who came to save you and your family. Who got away?"

He laid back down, obviously in extreme pain. "I only knowed Jeff. He'd bought some cattle from me. They came in here and slapped my wife around and beat the hell out of me."

"You're lucky. They shot two men and raped a woman up the road."

"Did they rape Annie Smart?" He looked upset.

"If she lives north of here, yes."

"Oh, that is bad. Are my wife and kids safe?"

"They'll be in here shortly." Chet looked up when Raphael came in the door.

"The one that was on the roof is dead."

"We need to lay out the bodies for the posse. Those two killers that got away don't have any horses except this man's I'd guess." He turned to the beat-up rancher on the bed. "Were they saddled?"

"I had a fresh one saddled, and I'd rode the bay horse all day. That other outlaw rode off bareback on him, I guess."

Chet closed his eyes. "Raphael, you stay here and meet the posse. Get these bodies ready to take back. If a few tough ones or if Roamer comes they'll want to follow me. I'll leave notes until I catch them or they kill me."

The man looked sad. "I can handle this. You be careful *mi amigo.*"

"Try to shoot Mrs. Smart a deer on the way back."

"I'll get that done. What will I tell *Señora* Stephenson?"

"Tell Marge I have to settle this deal if I can. She knows my ways."

"*Sí, mi amigo.* I was proud to ride here with you."

"Any time I can help you, call on me."

"*Gracias.*"

He went out and walked uphill to where their horses were hitched. Holdem was ready when he swung up, holding the rifle in his right hand, and rode out to the east past the ranch house. When

Raphael waved at him, he shouted to him. "I'll get them."

Raphael nodded like he expected him to do that

The last two killers were on the run. He needed to track them down and quickly.

The rifle back in the scabbard, he wondered where they'd light next. Holdem's rocking gait was carrying him steadily after them.

He could lean over and read the tracks in the dry dirt. In an hour or two, he knew they were going downhill to the river—it must be the Verde. When he reached the shallow river it smelled fishy. They had crossed it and came out the other side. The ground was still wet where they'd charged out and their horses had scrambled up the bank.

When had he eaten last? He let Holdem get a drink and bellied down himself to get his fill. The water tasted fishy too. If they discovered he was tracking them, they might set a trap and kill him. From here on, being this close to the pair, he had to watch himself.

They'd lost the horses they'd stolen. Two of their buddies were dead and if they found someone was on their trail—his hours would be numbered and no one would ever know what happened to him. Eerie business to be in a strange wilderness like this and not have a destination. No wonder they couldn't ever catch the Apaches in this land. Too much wild country. Steep-sided mountains. Lots of junipers, like the hill country had cedars.

He chewed on hard spicy jerky and rode on the

trail with only two sets of horse prints; the rest were cloven hooves of cows and deer. He'd seen several more deer and hoped that Raphael was able to shoot one for the lady back there. A bear had left tracks down on a shoal and also a big mountain lion had watered there. Man, his paw tracks were nearly as big as his hat size.

He rode up the deep canyon and stopped to listen several times for any sound of horses or man. Many times he looked back. Big cats stalked people sometimes. He'd only known one man who'd been attacked by a panther. But he had scars all over his body from that attack. Said he finally killed it with a big hunting knife, after he lost his pistol. It all made a helluva spooky tale.

Birds were down by the water. Big crows—they called them ravens out there. Lots of little wrenlike birds in the junipers and a quail with an Indian headdress scurried about, but they hardy ever flushed like bobwhites did at home. They made a sharp *whit-whew* sound. And several kinds of doves that cooed. Folks in Texas called them rain crows. Hell, out here they could coo themselves sick and not get any moisture.

Then he heard some voices chousing their horses to go up a mountainside. They were causing some rocks to fall down.

". . . can't make it come back." They sounded close.

Lots of their cursing. "All right, but it's a lot farther to Rye that way."

". . . one I'm riding is weak."

Chet got off and made sure Holdem didn't nicker to the outlaws' horses. The other one was coming back down. For sure he couldn't dare leave his gelding and go spy on them. His heart was beating hard under his chest and his breath was short. Not yet. *Not now.*

They talked more, but he couldn't understand them. Then they were on the move again and he breathed easier.

Where was Rye? He'd never heard of it. Might be a town? Good, they'd have their guard down if no pursuit had showed up. He was too damn close to them, he'd have to be more careful and listen closer. Later in the afternoon he stood in his saddle and saw the man riding the saddle and the boy riding bareback. He watched them until they disappeared down a wide sandy creekbed and turned east. This must be the long way to Rye.

He built no fire at dark. Holdem was hobbled. Wrapped in the blanket, Chet slept in short stretches. Coyotes howled and a bobcat screamed. Wasn't a big enough yowl to be a mountain lion. Come daylight he checked his revolver and his rifle. They were loaded. His muscles were stiff and even his vision seemed foggy. At last he got in the saddle. He saw some houses and shacks off in the mesquite and juniper mix. Dogs barked but stayed at their homes. This must be a settlement. The wide dry wash was silt and sand, and some old gnarled cottonwoods grew on the banks. A few trees had been dislodged by past floods and they had huge dead roots showing where the raging water left them.

The fugitives had ridden up this easy way. There was an unpainted church steeple with a cross sticking up above the junipers and next he saw some store buildings. But what caught his eye were two jaded horses, one saddled and the other had a salty spot on his back where someone had ridden him bareback. They were hipshot at the rack, sleeping standing up. The sign said BAR in faded black letters. No one was in sight except a friendly yellow and white collie dog. He could hear some kids playing and by the sun he judged the time was about seven in the morning.

He eased up to the front of the building and, ready for any reception with them, he strode in the open door. The pair was pouring whiskey into glasses when his eyes adjusted to the darker room.

"Who the h—" But they froze facing his cocked Colt.

"Bartender, I am a lawman from Preskit. Don't either of you move. These two men killed two ranchers, stole several horses, raped a rancher's wife, and beat up another man over in Bloody Basin."

He stepped in, disarmed them and busted the older man hard on the forehead with his pistol when he made a move.

"Don't ever try a thing with me." Blood began to spill. He forced them to put their hands on the bar and took knives from them and tossed them aside.

"Barkeep—you got a pencil. Write down their

names and their next of kin's name and the town
they hail from.

"Tell the man your name kid." He jabbed the
kid in he kidneys with the gun barrel when he
didn't answer right away."

"Joseph Marie Lane."

"Give him your folks' name and address."

"Tom Lane. Wildcat Crick, Texas."

"Now you."

"Thellman Catlin. I ain't got no kin."

"What town did you live in?"

"Fort Worth."

"You got any rope to tie them up with?" he
asked the barkeep.

The near-bald man in his fifties nodded. "He
needs a towel for his bleeding?"

"No. Get me some rope. I can pay you."

"I won't charge for the rope. You work for what
sheriff?"

"Sheriff Sims. Yavapai County."

"This is Gila County." The barman's hands were
shaking while handing him a rope good enough to
tie their hands. Chet did the kid's first, ignoring
the man's words. Then made the kid get facedown
and tied one boot up to his hands. Then he did
the bloody-faced Thellman the same way.

"Now go buy me a hundred fifty feet of good
hemp rope over at the store."

He put a ten dollar bill on the bar. "I'll watch
the bar. No one will bother a thing."

"You—you're going to hang them."

"Just get the rope, please, or you can hold that

sawed off shotgun under the bar on them while I go get it."

"No. No. I'll do it." He took the money and ran out the open door.

A freckle-faced boy less than ten was on his hands and knees peering inside from under the batwing doors that had swung shut.

"Go home and stay there, right now!" Chet shouted at him. The kid flew backwards and he could hear him running down the boardwalk.

When the man came back, he spilled the change and folding money on the bar. After swallowing his Adam's apple twice, his face bleached white, he managed to say, "That's lots of rope."

"It will be enough if it is all there."

"Phillip measured it."

"Fine. You two get up on your feet." He bent over and cut the rope on their boots. "If you try anything, I'll gut shoot you and let you die in agony."

"Mister I never," the kid protested.

"Bad company hangs with bad company. Shut your mouth or I'll bust you with my pistol."

Outside of the bar, he told them to start walking and he led the horses. When they reached the sandy creek bed, he said for them to go right on until they came up the dry creek. A good distance from the saloon, he made them sit down in the creek bed and began to fashion two nooses. The first one done, he put it on the kid and cinched it. Then he took it off and methodically made another. He had drawn a crowd of men and women onlookers hanging back on both sides of the wash at a distance to watch him. They talked in such quiet voices that it was hard for him to distinguish the words.

He mounted Holdem and stood on the saddle seat talking to him the whole time while he tied the nooses on the biggest, lowest thick limb he could find. That completed, he slipped down in the saddle, got off and put both men on their horses. He led their horses over one at a time. Then on his knees on his own saddle, he slipped the loop around Thellman's neck.

"You son of a bitch. I'll see you in hell," he spit out.

"You better not 'cause I'll cave your sorry ass in."

He did the same on the sobbing kid's neck.

All set, the crowd in the distance gave a loud moan and he led Holdem back and made him ground tie. Then on foot, he rushed their horses, screaming at them, and they ran away. The on-lookers' chorus went, "Oh, no!"

Both men must have had their necks broken in the fall. They never kicked. But he was certain the kid's bowels had flushed. He climbed in the saddle and caught the two horses. He never looked back. Headed west, he reached the Verde by sundown and was at the beat-up man's ranch by the sunup with only a few hours sleep.

Bandage-headed, John Yeager and his wife, Shelia, came out to greet him. They introduced themselves and were grateful for the return of their horses and his saddle.

"I never expected to see them again. But Raphael told me he knew you'd get them back."

Chet nodded and said nothing.

"The sheriff didn't come and that man you spoke about, Roamer, he wasn't with the posse, who were all worn out. I worried about you going alone, but again your man said, you would get them. Obviously you must have."

"All I want to say, is they won't ever beat up anyone else."

"Stop, Mr. Byrnes, and eat something. You look so worn out and drawn. Please let me feed you," Shelia asked.

"I'll be fine. Two days I'll be home."

"God bless you, sir."

"Thanks, I'll probably need it." He swung his horse around and rode on. A couple miles from their place, three deer broke cover. His hand went for the Winchester in the scabbard and with a quick shot he downed a yearling on the hillside. Wading through the pungent sage brush, he cut its throat and then he dragged it out by the leg to his horse. He threw the carcass over the saddle, climbed up, and held the limp body on his lap.

The sunset was red as fire off in the west when he reined up at the woman's doorway.

"Who's there?" she asked trying to see in the glare.

"Another deer killer, Mrs. Smart. I have a fat deer for you."

"Oh, you are the man the Mexican said went after those bastards."

"Yes, Chet Byrnes. They won't ever bother you again."

"Wait, we can hang it out back and I can gut it. Lands, I'll have enough jerky meat for a year." She halfway led his horse around to her cross bar and handed him some rope to hang the deer by the legs.

Hands up to shade her eyes, she looked at him. "You look tired as all get out. Climb down. Is that dried blood yours?"

He dropped off his horse. "Not mine. We need the hide off it and the guts out or the meat will taste like stinking deerskin."

"I'll get a light. We can do this in ten minutes."

With the lantern, they skinned and gutted the carcass in no time. She carried water in buckets to wash it out.

"You go wash up. I mean wash up. I got a night-shirt of his you can wear. I'll do your clothes while you sleep. When have you slept?"

"Oh, here and there."

"I'll fry up the fresh liver, I ain't got any onions, but it will be good for you." She waved him on. "You just get undressed and pull on that rope. It will give you a shower. I won't look. Just get your-self clean. There's soap and towel up there. By then I'll have you his nightshirt."

"I don't want—"

"Go on. You will feel ten times better."

The shower was sun warmed and he did feel better after his bath. The garment was almost big on him, but he put it on. And he had a hard time staying awake eating his hot peppers and liver.

"I aired out them blankets, so they don't smell like them killers. Get over and catch you some sleep."

"My horse?"

She pushed him down. "I'll care for it. You get some sleep."

He lay down on the palate and it felt soft to his tight back. His eyes closed like a trap door and he slept. He awoke in the night and realized she was in the bed with him. He got up, emptied his bladder, and went back to sleep with her. They both awoke about dawn.

She sat up and wet her lower lip. "I hope I didn't bother you last night. I just needed someone to be near." She shook her hair. "That sounds like some dove talking I know—"

He put his finger on her lips. "I enjoyed your closeness. It's lonely trying to sleep wrapped up in a blanket by yourself, I know."

"How I'll ever repay you I don't know. But some day I damn sure will."

"Don't worry about that. I better get back home. My folks will think I left them for good."

"You going to marry Raphael's boss?"

"I don't know. I just got back from Texas."

She laughed and jumped up, took her everyday dress in her hand and ran outside to change out of the nightshirt she'd worn. She came back swishing the dress around for it to be straight. "I'm making you some pancakes and all I have is some prickly pear jelly to spread on them."

"You must eat like queens here."

She frowned and shook her head. "No, no, but one day we'll have cattle enough to make a living here."

They laughed and he agreed. After breakfast he rode on.

He was coming off a steep mountainside. From way across the canyon he heard a voice. "My lands, there he is and he's still riding hard."

Hey, Hampt, who's with you?" he shouted.

"JD. And we've been worried half sick about you. Get on over here."

Half laughing, he guided Holdem around the cactus and down the steep path. They met in the bottom of the canyon, shaking hands and looking each other over.

"You get 'em?" Hampt asked.

"My uncle hates horse thieves worse than any-thing," JD said. "He'd not be coming back today if he hadn't."

Chet nodded. "They won't steal any more horses."

"How far did you have to go?" Hampt asked.

"You ever been to Rye?"

"No, why it's way over in Gila County."

"A fur piece. Everything fine at home?"

"Now you're all right it will be" JD said, twisting in the saddle to look around. "I love this country."

"Good, I have to go apologize to a lady who I ran out on."

"She's the one who sent us. Her man told us all about your getting them," JD laughed. "Hampt, my uncle can find some wonderful women. Let me tell you about them some time," JD said as they mounted up.

"Mrs. Stephenson sure isn't bad looking," Hampt said. "No. No."

Chet smiled. He'd known some nice womenfolk in his life, but his luck to hold on to them wasn't that great. Lord it would be good to get back to the ranch—sometime.

He might rest for a week.

Later in the day at the road fork to Preskit, he parted with the two men and told them he'd be on home in twenty-four hours. They both laughed and teased him. He was still laughing when he reached Marge's place.

When he dropped wearily off his horse, she burst out the door with "Thank God you're all right."

He swept off his hat and shook his head. "I'm fine, Marge."

Nearly in tears, she hugged him. He must have forgotten, she was damn near as tall as he was. Her hair smelled like flowers and her wet eyes looked so sad, he kissed her. Whether it all was real or put on, it sure sounded and looked sincere to him. He tried not to compare her with others, but Marge was dramatic. His ex, Kathren, was as straightforward as a man. Both had hearts of gold, but they damn sure were worlds apart.

"Come in. Come in. Have you had any food? Are you all right? I mean did they wound you?"

At the front door he held up his hands. "Whoa, I'm fine. A little saddle weary but fine."

"We have food. If you can eat?"

"Of course I can eat." He put his arm on her shoulders so they'd be close. He could see she liked that—good.

"Monica, he's back nearly unscathed and hungry."

The sweet Hispanic woman stuck her head out. "For what?"

"Why food of course—" Then Marge blushed and buried her face on his shoulder. "That sounds so bad."

"No, it was funny." Then he turned to the other woman. "Food for now."

They shared a quick smile and managed to part long enough to sit side by side at the table.

"Do you want a drink?"

He shook his head and tossed the hat he'd carried in the corner.

"Oh, I'll get it."

"No, sit down. It won't rot over there. Do you want to talk about it?"

"They brought back four bodies. The funeral for my men is tomorrow. They put those other two in the pauper's graveyard night before last. Sheriff Sims has applied for wanted rewards on them for you. I have forgotten their names."

"*Señora?*" Raphael came to the front door and called to her. "He is here. No?"

"Put his horse up please. No, come in please, Raphael."

Chet stood up and nodded to him.

"Those other *hombres*—"

He shook his head. "They won't steal any more horses or kill anyone else."

The short Mexican nodded. "*Gracias, amigo,* I am glad you are all right."

"Is it all right that he puts your horse up?" Her reserve was up like she'd overstepped the boundary and wanted back in.

He nodded to her and thanked him. He'd damn sure cut off his own possible retreat from her by doing that. Maybe he was too tired, maybe lots of things, but he felt comfortable in her company—a new situation. Maybe his guard was down. Nevermind. Whatever came of their evening he felt sure something was going to happen—for the good.

After the food, she wound up the bright sounding music box and they waltzed in the dining room to the music. It wasn't as good as fiddles playing it, but he liked it and holding her in his arms was like watching soft waves on the shore of a lake. They kept rolling in.

Monica had done the dishes and told them good night. But the dance went on and on and on. The big clock rang the midnight bell and they were kissy face in the dim candlelight.

The chimes made them stop.

"We are both grown people." She paused. "I have been married twice, unfortunately, so I am not some teenage girl." Another pause. "We are grown-ups and I won't tell anyone if we—"

"I won't either."

"Good, then let's go to bed."

"Fine." He kissed her and then they blew out

the candles. He hoped she wasn't disappointed when she closed the bedroom door behind them.

He woke about dawn. Carefully he came apart from her, slipped out of the bed and began to dress.

"I know you must run away. But I am pleased we had such a wonderful evening, Chet." In the dim light she held the sheet up to cover herself. "I hope I did not scare you off with my boldness."

He put his knees on the bed, leaned over and sipped on her lips. "You are an angel. I even hate to leave, but I must get back to business."

"You will be at the dance Saturday night?"

"Right now I plan to be there."

She smiled. "Save the last dance for me?"

"Yes, ma'am."

He tiptoed downstairs and was headed for the back door, when he discovered there was still light in the kitchen.

"*Señor*, stop, I have coffee, pancakes, and oatmeal made for you special."

"Well," he drawled. "I guess secrets ain't secrets anymore."

"I won't tell if you don't." Armed with a coffee-pot she poured two cups.

Then she looked toward the upstairs. "I know you made her happy, now you will make me happy eating my food."

He set his hat on an empty chair and took a place at her table.

"Tell me about Monica." He picked up a spoon for his oatmeal and looked over at the woman's pretty brown eyes.

"I was born in Sonora and my family came up the Santa Cruz River to farm for a man at the Tubac Mission when I was a little girl. I learned how to read and write at the church school.

"When I was fifteen I married a man twice my age who was a vaquero. His name was Paco Realas. We had some children, two, but they died in an epidemic. He left me after that, sick in his sadness. I wandered around and finally came to Preskit. I met the *señora* one day and she asked me what I did. I told her I cleaned people's houses. She said, 'I will try you, because my best friend who did that has left me.' So I am here."

He nodded. "Thanks for the breakfast." He stood astraddle the chair ready to leave.

"Do me one favor."

"What is that?" he asked after finishing his last sip of coffee.

"Help Raphael get the foreman's job. You know him, he is a good man. I can help him if numbers get too large or if he needs to write letters. I know he is a Mexican, but he works hard."

"If they ask me, I will tell them what a good man I think he is."

She smiled relieved. "Today is the funeral."

"I know but I must get back to my own people. They just got to the ranch and I was gone."

"*Vaya con Dios*," she said.

Raphael led his saddle horse over to the back-yard gate.

"You spoil me."

"I wish I could've pulled the rope on those bastards. How is the woman I gave the deer to?"

"I took her another. She is doing fine. They won't ever come back and haunt you."

The man saluted him. He mounted and returned the salute before he rode off for home. Sounded strange to say the ranch was home. It would never be the same as the –C on Yellow Hammer Creek, but it was his new place to sleep. He glanced upstairs on her house. She wore a fluffy housedress and waved from inside the window. He returned it. Their escapade of the night before was damn sure no secret and he wanted to laugh—on how hard they'd tried to make it one.

First person he saw when he rode up to his ranch headquarters was his sister Susie. He hitched the horse and she grabbed his arm. "It's about time you got back here. The boys said you were all right, but I am glad to have you here."

"What's broken down?" He clapped her hand on his arm as they went in the house. Tom's wife, Millie, smiled at him with a broom in her hand. Then his Aunt Louise, at the head of the stairs with her hair wrapped in a towel, said, "This Arizona dust is not one bit better than Texas."

May had joined them and he said softly, "Louise's

forgot there was any dirt in Louisiana where she came from." Millie and May really laughed.

"Don't make fun of my home state. It is a grand place to live."

"I don't see any alligators hanging around here," he said and followed Susie in the kitchen for a cup of coffee.

"Well we've only heard half the story," Louise said from the doorway.

"I trailed the other two to a place called Rye over in Gila County. Then I took the man's horses back and came home."

"They in jail over there?"

"I guess they call them pine boxes."

She closed her eyes. "I'm sorry. I wasn't picking on you, Chet. I recall my own redemption on the Pedernales River. You damn sure are a brave man not to change the subject, but when do we get to approve or disapprove of this Marge woman we've been hearing about?"

"Saturday night at the Camp Verde dance."

"Good enough. You know we have to pass on her before you throw her in this barrel of fish of a big house."

"Yes ma'am."

Louise left their company shaking her head.

May quietly spoke to Millie. "She's on her best behavior."

The four of them laughed.

"What is the country like over there?" Susie asked.

"Very much wilderness. Junipers, cactus, and wild

critters. I saw a real black bear and big mountain lion tracks. Some pine trees in the real high country. There aren't many folks over there."

"Where did those men come from?" Susie asked. "Did you learn?"

"One said someplace in Texas. Another Fort Worth. One of the gang had bought cattle off the small ranchers in that country. They had no permanent base over there. They were strangers in the small town of Rye."

"Where is it?" May asked.

"Across the wild mountains east of here." Millie said. "The country that the Apaches used to hide in from General Crook a few years ago."

"Did you see any Apaches?"

He shook his head. "No. And that gang is gone. The shame is the good men they killed and bad things they did in their wake." He sipped some more of the good coffee. "Is there anything bad here?"

"No. We need Millie's house completed. The mechanics are doing all they can. The men will need a bunkhouse before fall. They're living in tents."

He nodded. "I'll go see who I can hire in Preskit. There must be some men need that kinda work."

"We understand that a timber crew quit up on the rim." Millie said. "They all went to Tombstone. The mines paid more money for timbering than we do."

"Are we out of loggers, too?"

Millie shook her head. "I just heard that rumor. But we sure aren't getting the lumber we need."

He scowled at the situation. "When Tom gets back I'll go talk to them. We surely need to push this building deal some more."

"Millie says we need to buy apples in the next month and dry them for winter. There are some grapes down in Hayden's Mill and we need to dry some grapes for raisins."

"We can send JD in a wagon. Find out when and where we need to go."

"And blackberries are ripe up on the rim country. Can we go pick them?"

He laughed. "You and the bears?"

"I can run them off," Susie said.

"Talk to someone who's done picking at the dance. I can spare a hand or two to go along with you. That's a vast country up there, too. I brought those criminals back from up there last year. You'd sure need a guide."

"Good. We will make a plan," Susie said.

He closed his eyes and shook his head. "All I need is three more wives. I feel like the Mormon head man."

"Brigham Young?"

"Yes. I appreciate all of you. We will make this a great ranch here in Yavapai County."

"And Mrs. Stephenson?" Susie asked.

"After the dance Saturday night, I imagine she'll have you invited for supper. Is that all I need to worry about?" He looked around for his answer.

Susie hugged his head to hers. "You are excused, little boy."

"Good. Millie, don't join them. They are mean to me."

He rose and went to check on things. In the kitchen he confronted his cook and helper. "How you two making it, Hoot?"

Hoot's helper was pealing potatoes. "Fine, sir."

"Those women want my job?" Hoot looked mad.

Chet shook his head. "They want us to have supplies is all. They need to do things too."

"Me and this boy can clear out if you say so."

"Things ain't going fast enough is all. You're the cook. Get off your high horse. Women are a part of us."

He noticed Tom had ridden in and went to see him at the tack building.

"Good to see you alive."

"It was a good option. The females are upset about our construction progress. And I guess I'll have to decide who will run the kitchen. What about the timber deal?"

"Several of the lumberjacks went to Tombstone. They pay more money."

"What can we do?"

"Find more timber men." Tom took his saddle off his horse and carried it in the shed.

"Arizona isn't an easy place to get folks to come work for you without trains to get them here."

"I guess we could take some of our men up there and have the guys show them how. But they can drive horses. We have some of those stout teams you drove out here. That might be a big part of it."

"Tonight get an opinion who would go up there and work for a while. We can get the trees to the mill with our horses."

Tom nodded. "I guess if we can get some lumber down here we can find some more carpenters."

"We may need to switch help from job to job. I saw maybe enough framing lumber to start the bunkhouse stacked out there. Then we can go back to work on your house when we get supplies to do it."

Tom agreed. "We have some more troubles on the west end of the ranch. I think we have rustlers. You know Ryan sold calves instead of keeping them till they were grown, so we don't have a back-log of two- and three-year-old steers that pay for a ranch. I think someone is pulling the ones we do have out and driving them somewhere."

"Where could they sell them?"

"If I knew that I'd have caught them."

Chet laughed. "Maybe we need a spy out there."

"I think it would be a good plan." Tom took off his hat and wiped his sweaty face on his sleeve.

"Let's get a few heads together and talk serious about that."

His foreman agreed. "We can do that. These bulls need to be scattered more. Those Herefords aren't as aggressive as those longhorn ones. We may need one bull to fifteen cows. I found two or three bulls at a waterhole, that means they aren't spread out where the cows are at."

"You're on the right plan there."

"You told me to look for more cows to buy when you went back to Texas. I've not seen any numbers of them I'd want. They all had lots of broken-mouthed cows in every bunch when I got them up. We have too many of those kind ourselves."

Chet agreed. "Running a ranch is never easy."

"I got word several Utah ranchers want to sell some cows."

"How will we get them over the Grand Canyon? Swim them across at Lee's Ferry?"

"Yes, when the river is low. But we could buy cattle in Colorado or Kansas easier than that."

Chet nodded. Something he'd have to figure out. "I'm going to try to go back to Preskit and do some business tomorrow. I need to see Jenny at the café too. The sheriff. You seen Roamer? I expected him to lead the posse. He wasn't there."

Tom shook his head. "That surprised me too when I heard he wasn't the man. I heard that none of them went on to help you either"

"I expected Roamer to come." Chet had looked for him right up until he took the prisoners.

"Those rustlers all drifters?"

"One of the guys named Jeff had bought cattle from the small ranchers in the Basin. The rest no one knew."

Tom made a grim face. "I guess they won't bother any of us anymore."

"Not unless they can throw six feet of rocks and dirt aside."

Tom nodded.

The men were coming in and shaking Chet's hand.

Before dawn he rode to Preskit. He didn't dare stop at Marge's house and went on into town first. He hitched the horse at the rack at Jenny's café and pushed his hat back. When he came through the door she shouted, "The great state of Texas has returned, ladies and gentlemen."

The crowd jamming the place applauded. She ran over and kissed him like an old-time lover of his. He held her out and laughed. "You are one great friend, girl."

"Keep talking. You hear him call me girl? Ain't that nice. You aren't home two days and you're off running down outlaws."

"Someone had to do it." He waved his hands for reprieve. "Are there any carpenters in here out of work?"

Two men stood up.

"Get out to the Quarter Circle Z on the Verde. We can use you."

They smiled. It drew a good shout.

"The guy who ordered this has got time, so here's you a big breakfast, cowboy." Jenny put a loaded plate down in an opening on the counter and waved him in. Followed with a mug of steaming coffee she faced him off eye to eye. "It's damn good to have you back, mister."

"Good to be back. I missed your warm receptions."

"Oh, I could track after you barefooted, Chet Byrnes."

"Too many cactus needles." He began to cut up his ham.

She kissed his forehead and left him to go back to eating.

He resettled his hat on his head and watched her exit into the kitchen. That would be Susie's choice for him. She had big blond braids piled on her head—a big woman to keep him warm in winter like the German girls she suggested that were in their nearby communities in Texas.

After Jenny, he saw the banker named Tanner, who welcomed him back. They had cordial words. He made plans to transfer more of his money out there.

Sheriff Sims came next. When Chet came into the outer portion of the sheriff's office he waved him inside. The man got up and closed the door.

"How have you been, Mr. Byrnes?"

"Fine."

Sims reached in a drawer and put the *Globe Arizona* newspaper on his desk. "Maybe you've read this story?"

Chet shook his head.

"This story came from a resident in Rye. He gave no name."

Two men showed up in Rye one day last week on jaded horses, they headed for Clyde's Bar, and paid for a bottle of whiskey. The man's last name was Catlin and he hailed, he said, from Fort Worth. His partner was a boy in his late teens also come from Texas, perhaps not directly, because according to others they rode in out of Verde River country.

A tall man came in an hour later and he said he was the law and came for two horse thieves. He got the drop on the two from Texas and asked Clyde for some rope. He tied them up and put them on the floor. He paid for the rope and their whiskey. Then he gave Clyde the money to go and buy two ropes seventy-five feet long. Clyde went to Barnes Store, procured the rope, and brought it back. The man politely thanked Clyde. I never asked but I do not believe this man had partaken of any of the whiskey.

Clyde said the boy was crying. The other man stiff lipped. He drove them on foot a quarter mile down the Rye Wash. There he sat the two prisoners down in the sand. Their hands were tied behind their backs and like an experienced executioner he made two hangmen's nooses.

The witnesses said he stood on his horse and tied the ropes on a stout overhead limb of a large cottonwood tree. Then he tossed each man on the horse that they rode in on and he got them seated. From there he rode in and he placed the knots beside the left ear of each man.

No one among the onlookers heard what the two doomed men said to him. He reined the big bay horse back and dismounted. Then he took his lariat in his right hand, and a hat in the other. With a hoop and holler, he choused the two horses away.

Witnesses said both of their necks snapped in the drop. They never suffered. This stranger gathered the other horses, took them, and rode away. None of us knew his name.

Let all the horse thieves in Gila County know this story and sleep in fear. The Phantom of Justice will find you.
(from a concerned citizen of Gila County)

Chet looked up. "Interesting story." He put the paper back on his desk.

"I thought so. I guess you're back from Texas. I guess I should thank you. I don't condone rope justice."

"I understand. Those men shot two good local men. All of them raped a rancher's wife up there and stole two more horses from another rancher they beat up." Chet had his back up. "And if this phantom of justice had not followed them I suppose they'd have gone on to do more bad things."

"That was the story?"

"Yes, sir. I won't try to tell you your business. Where was Roamer?"

"I did not send him."

"I know that."

"I'm the sheriff of this county and I'll assign who I decide is the best man for the job."

"You knew those storekeepers would peter out getting up there. And you sent a man of like qualities. Didn't you?"

"I'm the sheriff—"

"Today you are. Did you know any of those men?"

"Are you accusing me of something?"

"You wear that badge 'cause people want you to. They can vote you out of office fast as you got in."

"Is that a threat?"

"No, it's the truth. I've heard lots of folks say you're an office lawman."

"Get out. And Byrnes, if you lynch anyone in my county, you will pay the price."

"Good to know whose side you're on." He went out the door firing mad. Crossed the street to the Palace bar and ordered a beer. Someone elbowed him and he about swung at them—then he recognized Jane, the short barmaid.

"Where's Bo?" he asked about the real estate agent.

"I don't know."

"Why not?"

"Him and I broke up."

"He's dumb then," he said in disgust.

"Word is you already ran down some horse thieves?"

"Don't spread it around. The sheriff ate my butt out over a like deal. What's he got against Roamer?"

She frowned. "I don't know but I'll damn sure find out."

He slapped a silver dollar on the bar for her. "Thanks. I'll kick Bo's backside when I find him for quitting you."

She put the coin down between her small breasts and nodded. "Thanks."

Once the beer was downed, he paid the bartender and left the Palace. He walked to the hitch rail on the other side of the courthouse square, untied his horse, and headed east. Still mad about Sims's attitude toward him, his plans were to stop and see Marge. A brief visit with her might settle him down. From the top of the hill, he looked back at the gray stone courthouse—something was going on down there. Maybe he'd learn what it was about. It wasn't all over the lynching, there was another issue. One that evaded him at the moment.

No matter, he'd find out in time. He was in Arizona for the long haul.

An hour later at Marge's yard gate, he dismounted and heard the door open. When he looked up she came off the stairs and flew in his arms. "Oh, I wondered if you were ever going to come see me again."

He shook his head, swept his hat off and with her in his face, he whispered, "I was here all night."

"That's an eternity," she said. Again he had forgotten how tall she was. They kissed and he dropped his hat to really hug and kiss her again.

Her forehead pressed against his, she shook her head. "I have never had a man in my life that I wanted more than you."

"Marge, I'm a man loaded down. Everything is going fine, except I hired two carpenters. Not three. JD is taking a few men and some teams up on the rim next week and get us some logs out if we can get the sawmills to run up there. We have to finish my foreman's house as well as a bunkhouse before fall."

She took his arm and snuggled to him. "What else is wrong?"

He looked around to be certain they were alone. "I made the sheriff mad somehow. He had the *Globe Arizona* newspaper with an unsigned letter to the editor about the whole deal that he showed me. Then I asked him why he didn't send Roamer over there, instead of some deskman and a damn town posse over to help Raphael. I expected Deputy Roamer to come on where I went, but he never sent him, and I asked if those two killers were some buddies he wanted protected."

"Oh. What date is that *Globe* paper? Dad gets that." She put her knuckle to her lips. "I never read it."

"Don't read it. You may get shocked and hate me."

She shook her head at his reply. "Now you know I will have to read every word of it."

He closed his eyes. "Marge, should I bring my sister and the others or will you invite them?"

"Oh, I'll invite them."

"There is my sister Susie, my sister-in-law May, and my Aunt Louise. May probably won't come; she has a baby daughter about a year and half. Oh, and Millie, my foreman's wife."

"Come inside. Wait there a minute, I think Raphael is coming to check on your horse."

She stepped out to the edge of the porch. "Yes, put his horse up, he's staying for supper."

"He don't need to be unsaddled, partner."

"Yes he does," she said. "Never mind him."

The man waved and led the horse away. Chet shook his head. "Will he be your next foreman?"

She frowned at him. "That is my father's decision."

"Come on Marge. Will he make him foreman?"

"Are you on his side too?"

"He's a good guy. He'd get the job done."

"I guess if anyone else is hired, I'll lose you and Monica both." Then she laughed and drove him inside.

Once in the living room, she put him on the couch and then went over to a fresh stack of newspapers beside a Morris chair and soon came back with a paper. "I had them stacked for him to read when he gets back from California."

"Get ready for a shock then. He showed that to me when I got to his office."

"The one about the Phantom?" she asked, and reading away, she dropped on the couch holding the paper in her hands.

"That's the one."

"Oh my gosh, Chet. You never told me this."

"I've never told you anything but the truth. I know that is grim but we live in a grim time. Those four men ambushed two of your people. They raped a poor rancher's wife. A dear person who lived all alone, her husband works away at a mine. They obviously took turns on her."

"Raphael told me about the woman he thought would have shot you." She went on reading. "He never mentioned what they did to her."

"No one wanted to talk about it. She probably only told me and him. Then they beat up the next rancher with two of his small children watching them and his wife too."

"My two men were already dead, weren't they?"

"Yes. Those two would have escaped on that rancher's horses if I hadn't tracked them down. I expected Roamer to show up. All the way over to Rye. The sheriff never sent him. He sent some desk men and anyone knows those kind of posses are good for less than two days. They went back."

She put down the paper to look at him. "This is why Raphael was so upset when he got back. He said, the deputy would not let him ride to help you. I never understood why? He didn't either, and about cried over it when he got back. Said he knew you needed him."

"We may never know."

"No. The deputy told him that you were a fool and were no doubt dead too by that time."

She folded the paper and replaced it. "Oh, Chet, I am so sorry. You had no one to help you?"

"There are some things that simply fall in your lap and they must be handled. I could not personally let those two killers and rapists ride on for what they'd do again."

She sat on the sofa and held his head. Her wet eyes made him sad. But she knew what he had to do. Knew what her foreman felt when the deputy told him, "That man's dead."

"Did you meet the writer?"

"No, I don't think so. There were many people at a distance on the bank of that dry wash. I wanted to scream for them to go away. I would have had to shoot at them to get them to leave. So I ignored them. None came over or even offered a hand. It was a grueling time for me."

"What did you think?"

"I can't recall I thought of anything but getting it over. That kid was eighteen. He knew better. No telling the rest of his crimes. She said they all four had raped her and took turns after that. She was all alone out there—helpless. Then they pistol whipped that rancher—"

He leaned his head back on the leather couch and closed his eyes.

"This man who wrote this saw you doing it and he thought they deserved it."

"It might have been a woman."

"You're right. We will never know."

"Just as well."

She leaned over and kissed him softly on the lips. "Poor Raphael, I was mad he couldn't ride on to help you, but he obeyed the law. Didn't he?"

"Yes, he also did what I asked him to do. Shot Mrs. Smart a deer. He did and so did I when I came back so she had some more food."

"I will listen close to see if I can learn anything else about that matter. You had a right to be mad."

"I guess Sims was upset, maybe about something else. I'd like to know that too. My infringing on his business, perhaps." He noticed Monica coming in the room and sat up.

"I am sorry to bother you two," Monica said. "I have some smoked ham, yams, and fresh green beans. Would that suit you two for supper?"

Marge waited for his answer.

"That would be fine—but I need to—"

Marge pushed him back into the couch with the flat of her hands.

"I'll stay for supper," he said in defeat.

"Thank you," Monica said melodically and went back in the kitchen.

Marge looked at the ceiling tile for help. "You can stay here instead of falling off Mingus Mountain in the dark."

"I have a ranch to run."

"You won't do anything tonight relevant to your operation that can't wait until the morning when you get there."

"I smell like a horse."

"I personally like horses."

"Not sleeping with them."

"We can go down and run you under a sheep-herder shower after dark. How does that sound?"

"You sound delighted that I'll freeze to death."

She glanced over her shoulder. "Then I can bring you back to life. Won't that be charming?" They both laughed.

"How do all your ranch women like the Arizona Territory?"

"You can ask them when you meet them." He held his hands up. "I won't touch that with a ten-foot pole."

They twisted around and kissed facing each other. He pushed the curls back a little from her face. He'd never realized her height before he went back to Texas. Why not? He'd tried to keep her distanced back then—he'd owed Kathren that much even if it didn't work out and she couldn't come because of her parents' failing health. He'd danced with Marge the year before, but if they'd asked him how tall she was he'd have said five-eight. She was six foot tall. What else did he know? She had a heart of gold. Well educated and after she read that letter to the editor, she accepted it as him. He'd worried about that and was ready to defend it. Didn't have to. She was grown-up enough to know what he'd done and why. She sounded like she knew someone had to do that to protect others. That was important to him.

* * *

Over supper, they talked about the weather. How his bunch came too late to do much gardening. She offered to share her ample supply. He told her to work that out with the girls. Then he thought about Hoot as the cook. He'd have to have a mess for his men and let the women work out of the house part. They'd held off telling him about what they thought of it. He chuckled, refilling his plate with the fresh-picked green beans.

"What is so funny?"

"Hoot is the cook down there. At home the women fed the family and crew. I am going to have to separate them before they kill one another."

"Did they complain?"

"No, but Hoot threatened to quit. I talked him out of it."

"You work on that operation of yours all the time, don't you?"

"Yes ma'am."

She sipped on a glass of wine, he drank coffee after the meal. They went back in the living room so Monica could do the dishes after Marge couldn't talk her out of doing them till morning. In the living room, she moved the cowhide rugs aside and wound up the music box. They danced until after Monica told them good night.

Then they both went down to the sheepherder showers in the starlight and she brought along a pair of her father's felt slippers and a longtail nightshirt for him to wear going back to the house. He got under the shower in the moonlight, lathered all up, and then rinsed. The water was warm until he shut it off. Then the dry air began to evaporate it off his skin and he hurried to get dry. In the nightshirt and boots he felt like he must look strange if anyone saw him.

Hand in hand, hauling his clothes and gun belt slung over her shoulder, they went back to the house and blew out the lights. Nothing was on his mind but that the two of them were going to be together.

CHAPTER 4

In the predawn he found his horse saddled and ready after he ate Monica's hot oatmeal and pancakes. He checked the cinch and swung aboard. It was all such a clever plot by Marge, Monica, and even Raphael, he felt certain like he was being led into the web of a black widow, and that when she was with child, she would kill him. No. No, that was too grim. But the two of them had talked the night before about it and *if*—with either husband she had never been with child. Doctors could not tell her a thing that was wrong. She warned him to know with her for a mate he might never have any heirs. Good enough she'd been frank with him.

He descended into the Verde Valley on the narrow road that snaked down the mountain as the rosy dawn broke its existence. The ranch hands had already left for various duties. Tom was sipping coffee when he rode up and dismounted.

"Find some loggers?" Tom asked.

He shook his head, "Got some men coming that will drive nails."

He continued with his ideas to Tom. "You, I, and JD need to go up there tomorrow and talk to the mill owners. We need some understanding about this deal. We have paid them for the lumber we have received?"

"Yes, I made sure we paid them monthly."

"Then why haven't they sent us the lumber we need?"

"The guy that delivered the last load said they were short-handed. Like I said, everyone up there quit and went to Tombstone to work down there 'cause they paid more."

"A trip up there might settle this."

"I'll get ready to go."

"Good. I'll catch JD tonight. Maybe we can iron out the situation. Who do you do business with up there?"

"Ted McKnight."

"We better take our bedrolls. The trip will take a day anyway to get up there."

Tom agreed. "May be gone three or four days."

"I need to be back here by Saturday night."

Tom smiled and then shook his head. "That will be fast."

"Or I may be in duck soup." Amused, Chet shook his head while unsaddling his horse. He better go settle the cook business. He dreaded that too. His life was going to be one of going up and down the line setting sailing boats upright that had turned over on their side.

"Hoot," he called out, entering the back door into the house.

"What do you need?" his cook asked, coming in in his apron.

"Where is the roundup chuck wagon?"

"What for?"

"I want it and a tent set up. You will feed the crews up there. These women can cook for who they want to who aren't crew members."

Susie came down the stairs, two at a time. "What is this?"

"We are splitting the duties. You will have the kitchen. Hoot is going to use the chuck wagon and a tent to feed the ranch hands."

"Why?"

"Things are different here. In Texas, we were family and a few hands. Here we have lots of employees."

"Why didn't you ask us?"

"I'm sorry. I needed to make a decision. Hoot feeds the crew. We will build a mess for him before winter. Tom, JD, and I are going up on the rim tomorrow and try to resolve this lumber business."

"Fine, you can eat out there too." She stomped back upstairs. Mad as he could ever believe she had gotten at him in her life. What would be the result? The women could do what they wanted and probably would. But the fighting would stop— Hoot had his kingdom and they had the house. He better get lots of lumber coming off the mountain and get the construction over with.

It would be a damn sight easier to herd cattle than run a place with this many problems.

The next day, Tom and JD rode with him over the military road to the top of the rim. He took a long look of the vast valley and the red mesas to the west, then they started across the pine country. On top, they could see the San Francisco Peaks in the north. They hurried along to the loggers' camp and steam mill.

The whining circular saw told him they were sawmilling. They dismounted and hitched their horses at a log building with a sign that read McKnight Lumber Company. A big man came out onto the porch wearing a suit and a gold watch chain.

"What brings you clear up here, Tom?" he asked.

"Ted, this is my boss, Chet Byrnes, and JD Byrnes. We need to talk about these short orders of lumber."

"Come in, gentlemen." He swung the door open and let them in. They found seats and he ordered coffee for the men from an underling.

"Was it a good ride up here?"

"It's pretty country up here," JD said. "My first trip."

McKnight nodded. "You know I've lost lots of help. These miners down in Tombstone stole my help with their high wages. I am working short-handed."

"What're you short on?" Chet asked, leaning forward.

"Lumberjacks. Log haulers. You name it."

"I don't have lumberjacks, but I do have draft horses that can haul logs."

"How many?"

"Eight teams of good Belgium horses and men that can drive them. I saw lots of cut logs along the road that need hauled in here."

McKnight nodded. "That would help for a while."

"Can you find more lumberjacks?"

"I sent a man to California to get them. I think he'll bring a crew back."

"Would those teams help you?"

"Yes. There is lots of cut timber out there we could make into lumber. I'd pay for that haul."

"I don't want to lose money," Chet said.

"How much will they cost?"

"Five dollars a day."

"I can afford that. Will they bring a load of hay up when they come up here?"

"Probably cost us ten dollars a ton, Tom?" Chet asked.

His foreman agreed. "We should be able to get that."

"I'll pay for that. Will these men work?"

JD nodded. "They will haul logs when they learn how."

McKnight acted satisfied and went on. "I have decent quarters and a good mess for them."

"Now about the lumber we need," Chet said.

McKnight leaned forward with a look of relief. "You three are going to save my business. What you need we'll cut as quick as we can. Will you quit me when you get that wood?" he asked.

"I will support you for six months and if we can make money or break even, we will look at it. We made you a cut-rate offer that I might not be able to afford forever."

"Mr. Byrnes—"

"Chet," he corrected him.

"Chet, how soon can they come?"

JD took the lead. "Five days to a week. We will be here to haul logs."

"McKnight, these men are tough cowboys. They may not like this work. But we will try to keep the ranks full."

"That is all you can do." McKnight stood up. "How about a drink of good whiskey to toast our business."

"Gentlemen, I need to get back to the ranch," Chet said, and stood up. "Excuse me. You two have a drink. I am going back." He shook the man's hand.

"Tell her hi from us," JD said and they laughed at his expense.

His nephew wouldn't want to stay in a logging camp for long. But he could establish their presence and then replace him with someone who liked the work. His plans were to find another ranch up on the rim for his nephew to run anyway. Maybe near Hackberry where he'd arrested those shooters the year before.

On his stout horse, Chet made a great distance and dropped off into the Verde Valley off the rim as the sun set in the west. He'd be at the dance all right the next evening, and he was excited about seeing Marge again. She'd sure become a lot more important in his life. With his sorry luck at matching up and making it work with a woman he hoped that things went better in Arizona than they had in Texas.

His discovery of Marla's bloody body still reminded him how she wouldn't face a divorce from her cheating husband, and marry him despite his urging. If she had she'd probably be alive and be his wife. Then came Kathren and they made plans. He thought that was a heavenly arrangement, but his bloody feud with the Reynolds forced him to move his family out of Texas. And her parents' health forced her to stay and care for them. Nothing he could do about that. Then the tall lady paid all his bills in an effort to be certain he survived in Arizona. He chuckled to himself riding downhill on the steep military road off the rim under the stars. She had been serious and endeared herself to him after he got over being mad.

He reached the ranch after midnight and unsaddled his weary horse. It had been a helluva trip. The rig dumped on the horn in the tack shed, he put the pony in the corral. The cow pony, he noted, was tired enough he didn't lay down and roll.

He wondered if his bed in the office was empty. He looked at the dark stairs. The coolness of the night wind crossed his face.

"Getting in late aren't you?"

"It's a long ride from up there on the rim."

Susie was sitting up under a blanket in a stuffed chair in the dark.

"You against sleeping?" He stretched his arms over his head and yawned.

"No. But I wish I'd stayed in Texas."

His sore eyelids hurt him. They could talk about it in the morning, but that was not going to work.

"You're mad about my decision to give Hoot the mess for the cowboys."

"Yes."

"We have close to two dozen employees."

"I have always fed the ranch help."

"Difference. Family and employees. In those days we had little help. We need a separation of us here."

"I may go back to Texas."

"Susie, what for? Your family is here. I count on you."

"No, you don't—" She jumped up crying. "All you think about is your damn business."

"It's your ranch too,"

"No, it is not. Your new lady was here. She was concerned about you getting back. I guess she doesn't have to worry now."

He closed his eyes. "Did she invite you—"

"I am not going anywhere."

"Did she insult you?"

"No. She is very proper and polite."

He nodded.

"Do you think you will fit in her world?"

"I kinda hope so." He felt trapped between the two women by her challenge.

By then she was crying on his chest and he hugged her. "We can work it out. I need you, Susie. Understand, we aren't in Texas on a family ranch. JD is going to take a crew up there and haul logs to the mill. He won't really like that and I need to find him a ranch in the future."

"You're tired, I know. Go to bed and I will try to understand what you expect from me."

"Thanks." He went upstairs and fell to sleep on the cot until the noises of the children downstairs and ranch activity woke him up. He combed his fingers through his too long hair and tried to clear his head. The timber deal might work. Ranch operations came next. Tom could buy the hay they'd need and acquaint JD to the people who sold it.

Rustlers in the West. Tom had his concerns about them. He needed to look at that. Where did Sims have Roamer? He really respected the lawman for all his aid getting the ranch deal settled and taking it away from the crooked foreman Ryan. He went downstairs and May fussed about, making breakfast and coffee for him. He stopped and waited for her to get it completed and they talked about her stepsons.

"They catch fish every day. They won't drown down there on the river, will they?"

"The river is shallow but they need to respect it. There's current and they could be swept away. I'll check on them."

"They have become great fishermen."

He laughed. They were healthy boys and full of spunk. Before they'd left Texas they rode their small horses all over. They would here as well.

After his large breakfast, he thanked May and went out to check on things. Hampt was shoeing a horse in front of the shop and looked up, surprised. "I thought you were up on the rim?"

"I came back last night."

"Are we going to get lumber?"

"Yes. Our men will haul his logs in for him to keep the mill running."

The big man looked up and frowned. "I hope I don't have to go do that."

Chet smiled. "I won't ask you to do that."

"Good." He sounded relieved and was back to tacking the shoe on.

"Tom is concerned about some rustlers working our cattle in the West."

Hampt nodded, dropped the hoof, and then blew his nose in a red kerchief before he said, "He and I talked about it. I don't have any notion. But I suspect we have had some rustling out there."

"There aren't many small ranchers out there, are there?"

He shook his head, standing up to his full height—well over six feet.

"Think you could go out there and visit our lady friend casually and find out what she knows?"

Hampt checked around to be certain they were alone. "I can sure go out there and check on things."

"We need to resolve that rustling. Take some

supplies. Edna Pryor's absentee husband doesn't overstock her with supplies."

"I'll keep it all under my hat. I may be be gone for a week or two."

"Don't take them on. We can mount a force and do it. I don't want you hurt. Promise me?"

"I won't—I promise." Hampt looked around some more. "Next time you run down horse thieves take me with you." He paused. "I read that article in the *Globe* paper. I'm sorry as all get out that you didn't have more help."

"My actions made some people mad. I don't give a damn, but it did."

"I don't doubt anything. You tell Tom where I went and I'll keep mum. And just be making a round out there checking on our strays."

"I knew you'd enjoy yourself."

"Good, don't worry any more. I'll find out if there were or if there is some rustling going on."

"I count on it. I'll tell Tom." He left Hampt to finish his shoeing.

Maybe Susie would cut his hair. She was the barber. His hair was sure shaggy. He'd forgotten the last time in town to see the barber. The ranch cooking operation was making smoke at the chuck wagon. Hoot and his man were busy getting the night meal ready. They looked settled.

He found his sister in the kitchen. "You have any shears?"

"Is it sheep shearing time?" She smiled. "I am going to eat. Do you want some food?"

"No, May cooked me a large breakfast."

"You have time for me to eat?"

"Sure." He took a seat at the long table. "I'd like you to reconsider going to Camp Verde tonight. No need in you and Marge being separated."

"I thought her name was Margaret?"

"I shortened it."

"She's been married before, hasn't she?"

"Her first husband died in the war. Number two was killed in a horse wreck."

Susie laughed. "Well, she couldn't have poisoned them."

He shook his head and laughed too.

She poured him coffee and then began on her sandwich. "Do they dress up?"

"Do they ever. They dress just like country dances at home."

"I bet she does."

"I never noticed."

"Sounds to me like you've been really noticing her." He never answered her. Half of her sandwich eaten, she went for the shears and a sheet.

Chet sat in the sun on a kitchen chair out on the porch, under the sheet tent, she clipped away. "Tell me about her."

"I told you about her paying every bill I owed. We had a discussion over that and I paid her for everything including the Chinaman with the bathhouse and the barber. I was having hell out here with that foreman Ryan and I am sure she had my interests at heart. And I told her I had Kathren in Texas. Well that flew away. And I'm back."

"She must've went to finishing school?"

"I suppose she did, but she's not a prude. She found that story about the horse thieves that I told you about. She was really upset that they told her man he could not follow my tracks and help me."

"Who did that?"

"Some desk deputy who Sims sent over there. I thought he'd send a man named Roamer who helped me before. I got in an argument with him over that and he told me he was the damn sheriff."

"Have you been picking fights with everyone these days?"

"No. But Raphael came back and told her he hoped I was all right. He knew I was looking for Roamer to back me and the deputy he sent wouldn't even let Raphael go help me. Marge said, he told her the deputy said that I was probably already dead."

She looked down the right side and then the left side of his head to be certain the cut was the same. "Would you have brought them back for trial if he'd been there?"

"Maybe if Roamer had insisted."

"It's a tough country. Did the deputy who went over there know all they had done?"

"He should have. But he's a deskman like his boss. Two days in the saddle would kill them both. If I wanted a posse I'd call in ranchers, not store clerks."

"You going to run for sheriff?"

"I don't plan to."

"You'd have to be a lot more pleasant to get

elected. There. Your hair is shorter. I will go to the dance."

"And have a good time?"

"I'll try."

He kissed her on the forehead.

"We will talk about the arrangement again." Then she stalked off into the house with the sheet and barber things.

He took some clean clothes, towel, and soap down to the sheepherder shower. Bathed under the sun-warmed water, he dried and put on his clean clothing. Then he took a lariat off the gatepost, stepped in the corral, and roped a big gray ranch horse.

"Uncle Chet, you know what we catched today?"

He looked at his well-tanned two nephews on the top rail.

"No, boys, what did you get?"

"Thirteen big fish. And we got a big carp. I mean a big one. May said he had too many bones. Why does one big fish have too many bones?"

"Yeah, how come?" his younger brother asked.

"Oh, carp are just boney fish."

"She made us feed him to the house cats."

"Did they like him?"

"If he don't kill them cats."

"How is that?" The gray horse acted sort of snorty and he wasn't too sure about his choice.

"I mean Maw said we could die getting fish bones in our throat or in our belly. Will eating him kill the cats?"

"Whoa," he said sharply at the head-tossing

gelding. He slipped a noose over his nose. "Aw, cats won't die eating fish bones."

"Good. 'Cause they ate most all of him and fought over the last parts. If one would die Aunt Susie would whip us."

"Yeah, she'd plaster us hard."

"Now you boys don't let a big fish pull you in the river. He might drown both of you."

The two looked at one another like they faced another busting.

Oh, hell, they'd been in the river to catch that big fish—he knew it by looking at their faces. "Ain't no fish worth going in the river after."

"We won't the next time. We promise. They ain't worth it. Them cats can catch their own carp."

"Good. Now get back. Spook here's kinda feisty." He slapped him with the tail of the lariat and shouted, "Whoa."

"Horse you better listen," the oldest one, Ray, said. "Or he'll really whup you."

"Kin we get back on the fence and watch him buck you off?" Ty asked.

"Sure," he said, hitching the gray to the rail. Then he went in to get his saddle and blankets. By then he could hardly keep a straight face.

"What do they call him?" he asked, knowing the boys probably knew the names for all of them. They'd been down there every morning watching the hands saddle up and ride out. Every once in a while they'd have a bucking contest.

"Zero."

He turned and frowned at them. "Why's that?"

"Wiley said it was because no one has ever rode him."

Chet closed his eyes. He couldn't put him back. Those young boys would tease him for years. No, he'd have to ride him, or at least try.

He noticed more folks were taking places to watch his business. Hoot and his helper Cory were up there by the wagon with their arms folded. Sarge was sitting like a ramrod on a horse he'd just rode in on.

Chet went to ignoring all of them. When Zero here got through with him, he might not be able to dance. He cinched him tight. When he dropped the stirrup down he saw the house crew was on the front porch. All the women were out there too. Well, it was do or die time for him.

The bridle headstall held hard against his left leg, he swung up. Zero spun around in a circle as Chet found the right stirrup with his toe and reined him in. Even on a short leash, the big horse reared on his hind feet and then dove out ahead.

One of those younger boys on the fence said in a shocked voice, "Wow, that son of a bitch can really buck."

He closed his eyes, gritted his teeth for what was ahead and hoped their stepmother hadn't heard them. From there to the open front gate that horse had a real series of fits. And he'd sworn he was up in the air more than on the ground. But he was only crow hopping going down the road toward Camp Verde. He lashed him from side to side with the reins. If he wanted to run he'd show him how far he could run. His name was not Zero anymore. He'd call him Ono.

The gray was really handling well when he reached the campground around the school and searched for Marge's outfit. The big horse was handy as a cat and he really enjoyed him with his fit finally over—for the day, anyhow. Then he saw the men putting up the tent and rode over that direction. Reined up, he saw the smiling Raphael come out from under the canvas side.

"Ha, my *amigo, Señor* Byrnes."

He swung down and tied the horse with a lariat to a hitch rack, not trusting him not to break his set of reins.

"Oh, he must be a little broncy," the Mexican said and shook his hand.

"A little and its his first trip to town." He hugged the shorter man. "Marge said they wouldn't let you go and help me."

"That won't happen again. I told her I did not want to make that man mad. She told me no one was my boss in a case like that."

"She told you right. Did she come?"

"Of course I came." She rushed around the structure. "My foreman tell you everything?"

"No, but congratulations, *hombre*." He realized she'd promoted him.

"*Gracias*." He showed his snowy teeth. "Now I am the boss."

"What do you know?" he asked her quietly.

He kissed her on the forehead and damn near had to stand on his toes to do it. "Good to see you.

They said that you met my ranch women this week."

"Oh, yes. You do any good up there with the loggers?"

"I think so. We're sending them some horses, men, and wagons so they can get the timber out. The old bunch got bought off to go to Tombstone and work in the mines down there."

"You sure moved around a lot in a week."

"Trying to hold a ranch together."

"I know. Is your sister coming?"

"I expect her. How have you been?"

"Sad."

He took off his hat and beat his leg. "Why?"

"I didn't have you to hold my hand." She took his arm as they walked toward the tent. "These men don't need either of us. Let's go talk to some others and see what else is happening."

"Sorry, Raphael," he said over his shoulder. "I'd help you but she needs me."

His friend laughed.

"I'm glad you made him foreman."

"How could I do anything else? Monica and you were both hounding me."

He nodded. "You find out what had the sheriff up a pole."

"I spoke to him when I was in town. He sounded awfully interested in my business."

"Was it because of us?"

"He has a wife. I never have been anything but on the up and up with him."

"Sometimes men attach themselves to other women. Even married ones."

She frowned at him. "Oh, I can't believe he did that."

"Good." He still felt there was something the man was stirred up about.

They stopped and looked over the camp from the highpoint in the grounds. "I love your sister."

"She said she met you. She's coming."

She lowered her voice and toyed with the side of his wool vest. "Would you ever think about simply getting on a good horse and riding off with me?"

"When can we go?"

"I've thought of it many times, since you came back."

"Running away from me."

She frowned and then laughed. "No, silly, *with* you."

He laughed. "Your daddy sent you to finishing school and all that so you could run off with a poor Texas cowboy."

She winked. "I would."

"Oh, we both have responsibilities. Let me get my boot soles on the ground better. I need to do several things."

"Chet Byrnes, you will always have lots more things later. I know how you think." She pulled him behind a thick cottonwood tree and kissed him. "They won't ever—ever all get done."

His palms cradled her face and he looked deep in her eyes. "The rangers brought my dad home plumb delirious when I was teenager. They'd found him unconscious somewhere out in West Texas, brought him back. I was about eighteen. We'd lost a boy younger than me when he was ten. No one ever saw him again. Then there were the twins, and Comanches got them—a boy and a girl. He was out there looking for them. He'd stayed out there too long and never was right after that. I took over the Bar C and my boyhood was gone. I never rode over the hill and found a woman of my own. Never went on any wild goose chases. I spent my time building a ranch. And I built one. I looked around and I was twenty-five, still no time for myself. I wanted to let go, but there was no way. The feud only made it worse. The woman I loved wouldn't leave her husband who treated her like dirt. And when she decided to, my enemies murdered her, and her husband never read the letter she wrote him that she was leaving him. I tore it up and burned it."

"I'm listening," she whispered, sounding very somber.

"The feud got worse. They shot my brother in Kansas. Took me weeks to gather the cattle herd and take them on. We got the rustlers and killers. What I am trying to say is, I have this ranch to run and all these people count on me making it work. This is a long ways from being what fed us in Texas. I'll need to do lots to make it a real big one that I need. . . ."

"All right, I can wait. I know I simply want to

separate you off to myself. I've had such lousy luck with men."

"Welcome to my world." His arm around her neck, he kissed her. "We can take a break and go see the moon once I get all this tied down."

"I will hold you to that. What did it look like up there?" she asked.

"A wonderful country."

"I've never been up there."

"Never? One day, if your reputation can stand it, we'll make a trip up there."

She gave him a push. "My reputation is no worry to me. If I can go with you, I'd ride to hell and back."

He nodded that he'd heard her.

The dance started on time, right after they had slow barbequed beef, beans, and fry bread, plus cherry cobbler at Marge's tent. Susie, his aunt, Tom's wife Millie, and a big share of the ranch crew all had greasy lips and were ready to stomp. It was Saturday night in Camp Verde and the fiddles were tuned.

Kay, Floyd Kent's wife, came by and gossiped with everyone. The short blond woman whose husband ignored her spoke to him. "Where's JD tonight? Did he not come?"

"He's up on the rim running our crew, who are hauling logs to the sawmill. All his teamsters and loggers left him for better pay in Tombstone. We weren't getting any lumber we needed from up there."

"He's a wonderful dancer. I'll miss him. Tell him I said hi."

"I will, Kay. He likes to dance."

When she went off, he wondered about his nephew who was close to eighteen or had turned that, and the thirty-year-old rancher's wife. Well he'd have to see. She was a cute, nice lady, and a good friend of Marge's. He couldn't even imagine her husband ignoring her.

"That's our waltz," Marge said, and took him out on the floor. They whirled around the room and he was grateful he had her in his arms.

"Kay ask you about your nephew?"

He nodded and guided them past a slower couple. "They must have struck up a friendship?"

"I think so. He really can dance."

"Should I be concerned?"

She shook her head. "They simply danced. They did it very well and he danced with others. Why?"

"She's unhappy in her current life, I know that. Any time you aren't wanted, change is an option."

"Oh, he's how old?"

"Eighteen. But a grown-up eighteen. He's seen enough hell in his life."

"Has he ever had a serious girlfriend?"

"You know I don't know. His older brother Reg married a girl named Juanita who worked for my sister and lived on the ranch. I never knew about them either until they announced their plans. His mother had a fit because Juanita was Catholic and

Mexican, but she calmed down. I really miss having Reg to help me. He was a tough young man."

"Aren't all mothers upset when their son leaves them for another."

"I guess so."

He danced once with the schoolmarm Miss Costello. A lovely thin girl about nineteen who was a big hit with the cowboys. She came from Nebraska and signed a contract not to marry anyone until the end of the school year. Schoolteachers were hard to keep single in a land short on women like Arizona was, and for some reason only unmarried women were allowed to teach. He never asked why. But he knew she wouldn't have any problem finding dance partners that evening.

They set out a square dance. Marge went to get them some iced lemonade, and Allen Gates who owned the CXT came by to sit next to him on the wall bench. He was in his forties and had a much younger wife Madrid who was square dancing with someone.

"I wanted to talk to you some one of these days about the Hartley brothers. They've moved several head of cattle in here and act like they're bringing in more."

"I never met them," Chet said.

"That's the T Bone outfit from east of Mayer. Brand their stock with a big T B."

Gates crossed his legs and acted like he had something big to tell him. "They act like they own everything. I guess where you are, you ain't met them yet. But you will." The rancher looked around to see if anyone was close. "That Carl is a cocky little bastard."

"No. I haven't met them so far."

"This is a dry country compared to back in the East. You can eat all this grass down and not have any if we ain't careful. They don't seem to give a damn."

Marge was back and offered Gates her mug of lemonade. He politely thanked her and excused himself.

When she sat down, Chet asked her if she knew the Hartley brothers.

She gave him a cold frown. "Which one, Carl or Willis?"

"I'm sorry I asked." He chuckled at her sour look that he brought on by his question.

"It isn't funny. I think that Carl is a smart mouth and no gentleman." She squared her shoulders and straightened up.

"Oh?" He made note of her rigid posture.

The tone of her voice was cold as ice. "He has no manners—"

"Sorry I asked. Gates is concerned about them overstocking the ranges up here."

"They came here about two years before you did. Carl came over and told my dad that folks better take notice that he and his brother were fixing to take over the cattle ranching business around here. Before he left that day he took me aside and propositioned me like I was some lady of the night. I went to the house for a damn gun."

Chet drew back from her, amazed at her anger. "Did you shoot at him?"

Her eyebrows were like a hawk's wings ready to pounce on something. "No, but if I had, there would have been only one brother left to ranch over there."

He hugged her shoulder, but he could tell she wasn't over thinking bad about this guy. That really took some nerve for the smart mouth to have done that. Hartley better not ever say anything to him about her, or he'd wish better of it when he got through with him.

Susie came by with the tall rancher Tom Hanager, and she spoke to them. Tom was in his thirties and usually had his teenage daughter Caylin with him. She was nowhere around him now, and Susie and he looked comfortable together. He'd noticed the two of them dancing. They still looked at arm's length, but maybe something would grow— he'd hate to lose her, but he knew she needed her own life.

"Those young cowboys of ours are dancing the soles off his daughter's feet," Susie said and both of them smiled over it.

Hanager agreed. "Caylin loves to dance. I'm glad your sister came with you. Susie is a nice partner for me to get to step on her toes."

They both laughed. Hanager was a good dancer and Susie was an easy person to dance with.

A fight must have broken out. Several men ran

to the front door. Chet held up his hand for Marge to stay there, and hurried through them to see what was going on out in the schoolyard.

From the porch, he could see two men about equal in size, exchanging fists like a pair of boxers. They made some furious moves to make contact, and then danced back, defending themselves. He joined Sarge and asked his cowboy what the fight was about.

"That redheaded guy claims the other one has been trying to steal his wife. The other guy is a cowboy works for a ranch over east of here. I don't know him. The redheaded guy does freighting."

The men charged each other, exchanged a few more fists, then danced away again. There was lots of cheering by the drunks in the crowd.

Sarge asked Chet if they should stop it.

Chet gave him a nod. "There's too many kids here."

Marge joined him and held his arm. "What's happening?"

"Two men are fighting over the redhead's wife. We're going to stop it. Too many children here."

Sarge stepped in and held his hands up for them to quit. "Hold it right there. This is a family doings. This does not set a good example for those children."

The redhead swept the hair back and threatened Sarge. Two of Chet's ranch hands pulled him back by his arms and gave him a threat Chet couldn't hear. But it drew the fight out of him. The two fighters exchanged some verbal threats and the crowd began to fade.

"The Quarter Circle Z crew settle the matter," she said, looking at him pleased.

"This isn't the place for a fight. My men know that."

"Obviously. Who was your mentor out there?"

"Sarge, he rode with General Crook in the big Apache roundup. Said he ate too many beans. He's a good man to have on your side."

"Thanks," someone said, who realized it was his men that backed Sarge's breaking it up.

"No need in showing the kids here how to solve their problems."

"I'm Clark Evans. Own the X Two ranch south of Preskit."

"Chet Byrnes."

"I know you. That was nice of your men to stop that. I agree, too many children are here. Next month, we're having a meeting of area cattlemen in Preskit. I'd like to invite you."

"What's happening?"

"There are people forcing others off the range that really belongs to all of us."

"Let me know. Me or my foreman Tom Miller will be there to listen."

"Thanks. You get mail at Camp Verde?"

"Yes, we do."

Chet went back inside with Marge and they danced. He mentioned the man's deal to her. "Clark and some others are hosting a meeting about the range overloading."

"Hartley brothers?"

"I suspect them."

"My father is upset about them too."

"I'll be sure that he knows about it."

"Good." She searched around to be certain no one was close enough to hear her. "When can we slip off and be by ourselves?"

"You have a private tent?"

"Yes."

"Let's go."

"That's not too wanton of me to ask, is it?"

He shook his head. "No. And who can we hurt?"

She squeezed his hand. "Thanks."

Ready to go, they told some ranch folks who had been around them for the evening that they were turning in. After the farewells, they hiked to her camp. The night was pleasant under the quarter moon and stars. Raphael met them short of her camp.

"Was the fight down there tonight serious?"

Chet shook his head. "No, but it was unnecessary. That is a family event."

"Yes," she agreed.

They told her man good night and went on.

"He watches things closely," she said. "I feel very safe with him around."

"We told you that you needed him."

She poked him in the ribs. "Both of you."

He looked back over the campground. Things were quiet enough. Maybe too quiet. Unrest from the Apaches in this land wasn't over, they simply were not settled into reservation life. But they weren't going to storm Camp Verde, however they could, on the run, hurt some isolated families in their way or for their needs. And the Hartley brothers—he needed to look at them more seriously.

Grateful for her hospitality, he smiled at her in the candlelight and toed off his boots. Shortly in her nightgown, she blew out the candle. It would all work out.

CHAPTER 5

The next week went by quickly and a trip up on the rim to check on JD and the men used up three days. He found that everything was going fine up at the sawmill and JD was going to bring lumber down on Saturday and stay for the dance. Chet knew Marge would be upset about their being apart so long, but on Thursday he stopped off there for one night, coming back from talking to a man who ranched down by Congress, south of Preskit, about buying some more Hereford bulls.

Saturday night after the potluck supper, Marge's friend Kay, the short blond rancher's wife, danced with him. Kay told him she was so glad he had come back to Arizona and was with her best friend.

"I want to thank you. Those polite cowboys that work for you have asked me to dance, too."

"Good bunch. I know you've met my nephew JD."

"Oh, yes." Her reply sounded like a swoon. "He's a real mature young man for his age."

"He's been working up on the rim. He planned

to be here tonight. I am surprised he didn't make it. Must have had some trouble getting back."

"Well, maybe he'll still come tonight."

"Yeah, he's a great young man. His brother stayed in Texas to run a nice ranch for some older people and earn the ranch since they have no heirs."

"That sounds like a very good thing."

"Oh, Reg is good man. His wife Juanita worked for my sister for a year."

"This other lady Louise is your aunt?"

"Yes, her husband, my uncle, was killed in the last days of the war."

"I understood she was a widow."

"Louise is definitely something."

Kay laughed. "You're so sweet."

"No, I'm just myself."

"Thank you for the dance."

He bowed his head. "Thank you, too."

Then he and Marge left her in the small group and waltzed away.

"What did she tell you?"

"Oh, how you hated that I ever came back—"

Marge leaned back as they danced and frowned at his words. "She never did that."

He swung her around and then said, "No, she said she was grateful I came back for your sanity."

"That's the truth."

He squeezed her. "I like her. I guess nothing is changed. He doesn't dance."

She whispered, "Or even sleep with her."

"She's a delightfully bright woman."

"I worry about her safety living with him."

"Some women will stay no matter."

She agreed. "Your friend that was murdered did, didn't she?"

He nodded. If Marla had divorced her husband she'd be there with him at this dance. They walked outside to get some air.

By the blazing bonfire, a fistfight broke out. Chet told her to stay there and rushed down to stop them. The two men were throwing fists at each other. Neither looked familiar as he ripped the first man backward and then slammed his flat hand in the other man's chest.

"Stop this. This is no way to act with children and women here."

Both looked numb.

"Who the hell are you?" The second man wiped the blood from his nose on the back of his hand.

The other man looked bleary-eyed and shaken. "That son of a bitch started it."

"I don't care who started it. If you can't act decent, go home. This is a family deal, not a saloon."

"Where do you come off from?" Bloody Nose asked.

"I ranch and live here. My name's Byrnes and if I don't stop you someone else will."

"I ain't through—"

Chet whirled around and gave him a fist under

the jaw that came from his knees. The man fell on his back and didn't move for a minute

Hands on his hips, Chet waited for him to recover. "Had enough?"

Shaken, the flattened man nodded.

"Now everyone get back to minding their own business."

Ranchmen came through the crowd. Busby in his cracked voice said, "He won't forget that for a while. We got here too late to stop it."

"It's over." Chet rubbed his sore hand in the other. Marge was at his side looking concerned.

"Your hand hurt?" she asked.

He shook his head and spoke to some of the men who thanked him.

She didn't press him any more.

"Thanks, Chet," CXT ranch owner Allen Gates said. Chet shook his sore hand with him and they went on.

Thomas Hanager did too. His fifteen-year-old daughter Caylin at his side smiled. She said, "Whew, don't get mad at me!"

"I won't," he said, and started to leave with Marge at his side.

"You want to soak it?" Marge asked under her breath as they went back toward the schoolhouse.

"No. I'll be fine."

"Let's go to the tent and sit down."

"All right," he agreed.

Susie came by. "What happened?"

"Your brother simply settled a fight."

She nodded flatly at Marge. "He's good at that."

"Just stupidity," he said. "You having fun?"

"I am. Glad you made me come."

"Well, I'm fine. Go back to dancing."

"Keep him out of trouble," she said to Marge.

"I'll try."

When Susie started back, she was escorted by Sarge to the schoolhouse. If you were part of his outfit you were in good hands, he decided. He and Marge ambled over to the tent out under the stars. The interior was lighted and they pulled two folding canvas chairs together. She examined his knuckles again.

"They're swelling," she said.

"It will be sore. I'll live."

She leaned in and kissed him. "I won't tell you not to be yourself. But I can worry about it."

"That's your business. I have some strong feelings and fighting has no place at a family affair."

"I know, and lots of folks told me you and your men were enforcing it. That's good." She moved over to sit on his lap and in the exchange the chair fell over and spilled them out on the ground. Laughing, they untangled and kissed each other seated on their butts.

"That did not work."

He laughed. "Stay here."

"All right."

Her humor pleased him. With his finger on her lip, he stopped her apology with his finger. "I thought it was funny."

"What project is on the top of your list for next week?"

"Tom and I are going to check the range and cattle."

"So I won't see you all week?"

"No, I'll be there one day if you are going to be home."

"I'll be home all week if you are coming one of them."

"I'll brush you off. We better get back."

"I'd sit here the rest of the night with you and talk."

He pulled on her arm. When she stood, he went to brushing the dry grass off the back of her dress. They went back to the dance laughing and danced together for several songs. They parted after midnight, him promising to visit her later in the next week.

JD had arrived late. They'd had a wagon breakdown coming off the mountain, but he and the other drivers were fine, which relieved him a lot. He noticed him dancing with Kay. And Susie danced several more times with Tom Hanager. They made a nice couple.

Afterward, Chet rode back with the crew, taking a lot of teasing about his gray horse choice. The spirited horse pleased him and he took their words as funny.

Wiley drove Susie home in the buckboard, busting with pride. Dismounted at the ranch, one of the hands took his gray to put up and the two walked to the house.

"Those cowboys are nice guys," Susie said. "Tell me about Tom Hanager?"

He shook his head. "I don't know much. Marge knows him. She introduced him to me. He has a daughter Caylin. I think he owns a ranch down the river. Why?"

"I don't know. He was very polite. How old is he?"

"Old as I am? Are you interested in him?"

She nodded. "We will see what we will see."

"Did you invite them out to eat with us some night?"

She frowned before going in the house. "No. I barely know him."

"I'm sorry." He held his hands up and she shook her head. "Do you want me to invite them over?"

"I'll let you know."

May was up waiting like he figured. He kissed her on the forehead and then left them to talk like sisters. He wished he'd gone home with Marge— but that wouldn't work every time. Undressed, he climbed in bed and fell asleep fast.

CHAPTER 6

Morning came too early. He wished the sunup had held off for a few more hours. Up and dressed, he went downstairs, recalling how his sister had given him a haircut. Susie was up and she asked him what he wanted for breakfast.

"The two boys had their oatmeal and have already gone fishing."

"They're serious. We talked about that trophy carp. I think they were disappointed about the cats eating their huge catch."

Susie shook her head. "They're a mess."

"Oatmeal is fine."

"Coffee is hot. Help yourself."

"Fine." He walked to the back porch and watched the activity at the chuck wagon. Hoot didn't look busy. Most of them probably had slept in. It was Sunday, a day off unless things on the ranch were under stress. He wondered what Hampt had learned about rustler activity up in the Sycamore Creek area. The polygamist's wife, Edna

Pryor, who lived alone on a small ranch in that country knew lots about what went on in that area. She at least had a good man out there to look over the activities going on west of the ranch.

He was busy working on his books for ranch expenses when Susie came up and told him a man was there to see him.

"Who is he?"

"He didn't say."

"I'll be right down." He wondered who was there and came downstairs to see.

The familiar face of Roamer stood there holding his hat. He nodded in approval at the sight of Chet.

"Did you meet my sister?" he asked the deputy sheriff and turned to her standing by.

"No. Ma'am. But I sure am glad you came here with him." He gave her a smile.

"I'm glad at last to meet you, too. Come in the dining room. You two can talk privately in there."

"Fine," Chet said. "What brings you up here?"

Roamer looked around. "I know I'm late to come up here about this, but I had no time off the past few weeks. He's short-handed for deputies. I'm sorry about the horse rustling. But Sims has had me working down in Horse Thief Basin. I figure he thinks I got too much publicity out of helping you get ahold of this ranch and might shake his chances of holding the sheriff job."

"Hey, I got the cold shoulder over the letter to the editor about a lynching."

"That's why I rode up over here today. When I

read it I knew you had expected me to join you in pursuit of them when you went on. But I wasn't available, and knew nothing about it for a week."

"Whoever he sent wouldn't let Marge's man Raphael even go and help me."

Roamer dropped his head. "I couldn't do a thing where I was at, and when I found out the details I really was upset."

"Listen," Chet said. "He gets too tough on you, you can come work for me."

"Thanks, I'll consider it. I just came over today to apologize."

"I appreciate it. But I knew it wasn't your fault. How is your wife and all the kids?"

"Great. We'll have a new one in the fall."

Chet shook his hand.

"I'm glad I found you here."

"Hey, do you need anything?" Chet asked.

Roamer put down his cup. "No, I'm fine,"

When he started to leave, Chet at least had a much better idea about what concerned Sims.

"He's a cute guy, freckles and all," Susie said, standing behind him when Roamer rode off.

"Him and his wife have plans for twenty kids."

She closed her eyes and shook her head. "I'm glad she has him."

"He answered a question or two about the sheriff and why he handled things like he did."

"What was that?"

"He was concerned we had out-shined him in the operation of taking this ranch away from Ryan."

"Oh."

"He must be quite unsure of himself."

She agreed.

"Are you still thinking about a certain rancher?"

She about blushed. "I wonder is all."

"It's a secret with me."

"Good. You want more coffee?" she asked.

"No. I may go see Marge. I can be there in a couple of hours."

"Go. You might get your gray horse completely broke to ride."

Mid Sunday morning Chet short loped the big gray gelding to town. The big horse was fleet and full of energy. He never let him buck, but they argued all the way to the front gate before he gave up the notion to duck his head and settled in to moving out.

Before he left, Susie said she needed some baking powder. He decided to stop at the small grocery store in Camp Verde and put it in his saddlebags so he didn't forget it.

Two men wearing canvas dusters in the heat of the morning had dismounted at the store before he came down the dusty street. From a block away he knew he'd never seen them before. But he didn't know very many people of the population as a rancher, and the area was so vast. He reined up short on a hunch, like he had other business. The notion grabbed him with suspicion, Why in the heat of the morning were they so dressed? The azure sky was cloudless. Both men looked around warily at everything before they entered the store.

In the deserted street no one stirred. It was mid Sunday morning and most folks were in church. He imagined that Marge was sitting in a pew in Preskit. A shot rang out from inside the business. No surprise, and one of the men appeared with a smoking pistol in his hand.

A bartender ran out of a saloon's batwing doors from across the road with a shotgun, and distracted the armed man. That gave Chet time to draw the rifle out of the scabbard and to lever in a cartridge. The bartender fired one barrel. The men's horses must have been struck by some of the pellets and they tore lose from the hitch rail. The pistol-armed lawbreaker shot at the saloon man and then Chet shot him with his Winchester.

Next a screaming woman with the other bad guy's cocked pistol held to her head showed up in the doorway. He said, "Drop them guns or she dies."

The bartender, holding his wounded arm, backed through the batwing doors into the saloon.

"Now, you there, cowboy—put that rifle down."

"Go easy," Chet said, concerned about the safety of the redheaded young woman he was holding the gun to, and he had hold of a fistful of her hair.

"Someone go get me a buckboard for me and her to get out of here."

"Everyone's in church," Chet said.

"If you want this woman to live, cowboy, go get me a damn buckboard."

"I don't live here," Chet said.

"You better get smart then if you want her to live. If I die, so does she. Find me one."

"All right, don't hurt her."

"Cowboy! Drop that gun on your hip, too. I ain't blind."

Chet used two fingers to pull it out and let it fall in the dust. If there was a buggy or buckboard it would have to be at the church. The steeple of one was somewhere behind this block of businesses.

"I'll go try to find one."

"You better hurry or this sister is dead."

Setting out in a run, when he rounded the corner, he saw four men dressed in suits coming on the run with their guns drawn. He waved them back. They halted and he quickly told them he needed a buckboard because the store robber had a young woman as his hostage.

"Don't go out there. The live one who robbed the store is desperate. The only chance we have is to answer his demands and then separate him from the young woman he's got for a hostage. A bartender is shot, but it may not be life threatening. Get me a buckboard and team."

One younger man nodded and started on the run back for the church.

"How is Crosby?"

"I don't know him." Chet shook his head.

"He owns the store."

"I have never met him. I'm new in Arizona.

There was a shot inside the store earlier. I don't know anything but a madman has this woman and she needs help."

"Crosby's a good man," an older man said, holstering his gun. "I hope they haven't hurt him."

"The woman he has as a hostage is redheaded," Chet told them.

"That's Bob Barkley's daughter, Renia."

Head nods confirmed the fact.

The young man reined up a team beside him. He handed Chet the reins and jumped down. "Be careful."

"Don't any of you expose yourselves, but be ready to follow his escape."

The men agreed and headed back for the church. A crowd was coming out.

"Make them stay out of sight." He pointed at the churchgoers. Then he clucked to the horses and they broke into a run. He slid them around the corner in a cloud of dust.

The outlaw dragged the screaming woman into the street with one arm and waved the pistol in his other hand. Chet stopped and the robber said, "You're going to drive us out of here. No tricks."

The woman screaming at the top of her lungs and fighting his hold on her hair distracted the outlaw enough that he tried to stop her from escaping. Chet feared he would bust her over the head with his gun. He dove off the buckboard and took him down in a tackle. His right hand had a hold of the wrist with the gun hand. His pistol went off and the shot made Chet scared that, in

the cloud of gun smoke, he may have shot her. But
she was still using her lungs and kicking the squirm-
ing man underneath him. Chet finally struck a
blow to the man's midsection that drove the wind
out of him, and then Chet wrenched the gun away.

"Don't move." Three of the churchgoers had
their guns pointed at him.

Chet struggled to his feet. "You all right, ma'am?"

Tears streamed down her dust-floured freckled
face as she tried to straighten her dress. "Yes,
thanks to you, mister."

"Has someone checked on the bartender?"
Chet asked.

"Yes, they've stopped the bleeding," one of the
older men from the church said.

"Crosby's all right," another of them said,
coming outside the store.

"Good," Chet said. He felt more concerned
about the woman, who was obviously upset and sitting on the boardwalk, crying, with her shoulders
shaking.

"What's your name?" a tough older man asked
the bandit.

"Tim Malone."

"You wanted?"

The outlaw shrugged.

"Hold it," Chet said, and put his hands out. "Tie
him up and I want three serious men to take him
to jail in Preskit."

"I say hang the sumbitch."

Chet shook his head. "No. We will see what the
law does. He is such a worthless piece of shit. We

need law. I'd say hang him too, but let's try the court way."

"Mister, you did so damn much to solve this without any more losses, most of us will go along with your judgment."

"I need three men and a buckboard to deliver him and his partner to Sheriff Sims. Who will do it and swear that they will get them there?"

There was some grumbling among the men about lynching them. The four men he'd already met stepped forward. Chet thanked them. "Is the other outlaw dead?"

"Close to it."

"Do what we can for him. Get a buckboard. Load both men up. Two of you ride guard on horseback, another one can drive. Or two can be on the seat, I don't care, so long as they get there."

Things began to take shape. He went over to where a burley-built man comforted the woman on the boardwalk.

"My name's Chuck Denton." The big man shoved his big hand out to shake Chet's. "I owe you for saving her. Renia is my intended wife. She's waiting for a divorce from her husband."

"Nice to meet you. Renia are you all right?"

She nodded and indicated. "Now that he's here."

"Take good care of her. She's had a very frightening experience. I imagine the prosecutor will want testimony from you," he said to warn her.

"You think law is the way to do this?" Denton asked, hugging her to his side.

"Yes. We need to show Arizona has sense enough to become a state."

"Rob Tagget is a good leader. He's the one in charge of taking them to Preskit."

"Good. Take good care of her, she's a brave woman to have fought him like she did or I'd never had a chance to jump him."

"I will, and thanks again."

Someone brought Chet his own six-gun and rifle. Another led the gray over to him. He thanked them and after dusting off the rifle, he slipped it in the scabbard. Then he used his kerchief to clean his pistol. Checked it over and then he holstered it. His hat came next, and he thanked the bearer.

The bright-eyed older storekeeper in his white apron stuck out his hand. "My name is Crosby. Thanks."

Chet shook it. "How is the bartender?" he asked the bystander, and looked in that direction.

"They say he was only nicked. They've got him fixed up."

"Good. He was the first one to come out and shoot at those robbers."

The church-dressed men had taken charge of the prisoner operation. Malone was loaded and tied down, the unconscious man beside him in the blankets. Two men sat on the buckboard's spring seat in their Sunday suits and one carried a long gun. The other two riders were armed and ready. They left the crowd and Chet mounted on Ono with the can of baking soda in his saddlebags and he rode with them.

There was little conversation. Everyone acted very serious about their task and they wound their way up Mingus Mountain and reached the flat in mid-afternoon. He parted with them at Marge's ranch gate in Preskit Valley and rode up to the house.

Her buggy was parked in front so obviously she was back from church. A boy came on a barefoot run to collect the team and buckboard. He stopped to let Chet go by and hitch his horse.

"You doing all right today?" he asked the youth.

"Yes, sir." Then he very carefully turned the team around and took them around back.

"Have you had lunch?" Monica asked him from the doorway.

"No, ma'am. Where is the boss lady?"

"Upstairs changing."

"So you're the greeting committee?"

She laughed. "I am all you get. We will have a late lunch shortly."

"Don't fuss over me."

"Oh, yes, you are very important to us."

"I'll read the newspaper," he said. "Don't worry about me."

"That is not my orders," she said, leading him inside the house by the arm. They both laughed.

"I'm coming," Marge said, brushing her hair, standing at the top of the stairs.

"Rest easy. I'm fine." He undid his gun belt and hung his hat over it on the wall pegs.

Over the meal he told them about the attempted robbery at Camp Verde. Marge shook her head at him. "You need to stay out of those things, you'll get yourself hurt."

"Aw, Marge, you can't stand by and not do the right thing."

Laughing at his response, she passed him a bowl of mashed potatoes. "I know you have this little man in your brain who kicks you every time to get involved."

"Maybe I should fire him."

She winked and shook her head. "You won't listen to me anyway. How is the ranch operation going?"

"Slow but we are hurrying." He made sure they were alone and turned back to his food. "Tell me about Tom Hanager."

"Is something wrong?"

"No, I just wondered what happened to his wife?"

Marge stopped eating. "His wife left him."

"Oh, I thought he was a widower."

"He is a very nice man and he has tried hard to be a good parent. But his wife ran off with another man. It's been five or so years ago."

"I can see that. Him and his daughter are close."

"She's his life."

"Were they divorced?"

"I don't think so. She ran off with some man I did not know and no one knows where she went, or at least that is what I understand. Why do you ask?"

"I wondered if he had any interest in anyone?"

"No. But he's a straight shooter in my opinion. He was very shaken when his wife left him."

"He ranches?"

"Yes. I would say he's successful. His neighbors like him."

"Thanks."

"Any time. Monica has some pie for dessert. Do you want some?"

"Sure."

"You will excuse me for not eating some of it?"

"Oh, yes."

"Marge, he wants some pie."

"Coming."

The large slice of apple raisin with a heavy scent of cinnamon drew the salvia in his mouth. "Thanks. That looks great."

Marge beamed, gathering their dishes.

He savored the pie, bite by bite. Then they went in the living room and visited some more, seated together on the couch. Her father was coming home. His business in California was about over, he'd said in a letter.

That would complicate things about their arrangement. But they'd work out something, he felt certain.

CHAPTER 7

Monday began the next week when Ono about threw him. He loved that gray bucking horse, but he knew the judges, his two young nephews on the corral fence, enjoyed the show the gelding gave them. Settled down on the road to town, Chet let him use up some of his energy in a short lope.

When he saw three men on horseback coming from Camp Verde on the road that went west, he reined him up to stop and talk to them. They had two packhorses loaded down, obviously going somewhere.

"Morning," he said, sitting on the gray who was still upset enough to bob his head, clunk the bit on his teeth, and shift around some under him.

"Morning," the hard-eyed man who looked in charge of things said.

"My name's Byrnes, Chet—I own the Quarter Circle Z ranch."

"Loftin's mine, that's Bart and Kyle. We work for the Hartley brothers over in Mayer. We're going to set up a cow camp up on the Verde. We've got two thousand head of cattle coming."

"Hold up just a minute. I own the Perkins ranch. It's deeded land. So keep on riding to Sycamore Canyon."

"I guess we'll set up where we want to."

"No, you won't. That land west of here is deeded land to where Sycamore Canyon flows into the Verde. If you want those cattle in there you can drive them up on the rim and come off that way into that back country."

Loftin frowned. "Them ain't my orders."

"Well, you're going to change them. I'm not standing for you to drive that herd through my ranch. You better ride back to Mayer and tell your bosses that they need a new plan."

"I guess you haven't met my bosses yet." Loftin forced a smile. "You may not know them but they're going to drive their cattle into that country I can assure you."

"Turn your butts around. I'm saying you can't go in there on my land even to get to it."

"You threatening us."

"No, I'm telling you. Don't ride across my land or even try. Now that's clear enough, isn't it?"

"Mister I can tell that you're new here. No one tells the Hartley outfit where they can ride and can't."

Chet's eyes narrowed a notch. "Then it's time they found someone who stands up to them. Turn your butts around and go back to Mayer. Just because it isn't fenced doesn't mean it's free range."

"Mister, do you like living?"

"Yes, I do, but let me tell you something. I've whipped tougher men than you've got here over less than this trespassing. Tell them brothers I said they ain't coming through here with that many range cattle. The forage won't handle them and I won't stand for it."

"Come on, boys. When Carl gets through with this rebel son of a bitch, he'll be begging for us to come though here."

"Loftin!" Chet shouted at him. "The next time you call me a son of a bitch, you better have your pistol cocked, 'cause I'm sending you straight to hell. Consider yourself lucky to be alive. Next time you won't get it all out of your mouth before I blow the daylights out of you."

The man hunched up and spurred his horse into a run to get away. The other boy looked fear-filled and the one leading the packhorses about jerked off his horse's head because they balked. Chet charged Ono at the two and the packhorses left ahead of the boy leading them. Pots and pans clanging, the two packhorses passed the two young riders.

Chet wheeled his gelding around and rode for the ranch headquarters. He needed to find Tom and warn the crew that the Hartleys had thrown down the glove. There would be less sleep on the Quarter Circle Z. If those brothers thought they were tough they had not met the Byrnes family. They knew how to fight—what was left of them.

"What's wrong?" Susie asked when he slid the gray to a stop on his heels at the hitch rack.

"You heard me mention the Hartley bunch?" He dismounted and wrapped his reins on the worn rail. "Well. I just sent their advance party packing. They wanted to drive two thousand damn head of cattle up on the Sycamore Creek. That's west of the Perkins ranch we bought as part of this property. There isn't enough feed up there for that many cattle—they'd eat the country into the ground in a year. I told them it would be over my dead body before they drove those cattle in over our land."

"Who was it?" Susie asked when his aunt and May came out on the porch to hear his story. Tom's wife Millie joined them.

"Some foreman named Loftin."

"He's shot a few men," Millie said and shook her head. "Those Hartleys are not nice either. Did he threaten you?"

"He called me a son of a bitch and I told him to have his hand full of a gun butt next time, 'cause I was killing him."

"Well, get down and come inside. You're all wrought up, I can see that," Susie said.

"Is Tom coming in today for lunch?" he asked, loosening the girth on the gray.

"He's supposed to," Millie said.

"It can wait till evening. I may ride in and talk to Marge's father. He's supposed to be back this week. And I guess before it becomes full blown I better go talk to Sims."

"Just be careful," Susie said.

"When Tom comes in tell him to warn the crew. We need to go loaded for bear about this deal." He jerked up the girth, untied the horse and swung in the saddle. "I guess, ladies, we can't avoid controversy anywhere."

"We can hold the fort," Susie said, and they waved good-bye.

In three hours he was at Marge's house. He found her busy using her jumping horse to complete the range of fences to fly over. When she realized he was there she rode over to the fence. "What's wrong?"

"One of the Hartleys' foremen came riding up the road to my place, telling me they were going to set up camp on the Perkins place to receive two thousand cattle they were driving in."

"That's deeded land?"

"Yes."

She slipped off the English saddle on her horse and strode over to the wooden fence. "He can't do that."

"Loftin says they plan to do that, like it or not."

"Did he threaten you?"

"He called me a son of a bitch and I told him next time he called me that he better have a gun in hand and cocked, 'cause I planned to shoot him."

She gave the reins to the Mexican boy and he took him. In her English boots she climbed over the fence and he helped her down. "You looked good jumping him. He's came a long ways, since last year."

"Glad you noticed." She kissed him—he couldn't hardly get used to her height. She was right there in his face—and a neat lady as well. "What will you do?"

"Go talk to Sheriff Sims. If they try to cross my property there will be bad blood spilled and some lives lost."

"Let me change. I won't be long and I can go with you."

"Aw, you have things to do."

"No, nothing any more important than you are to me."

"Fine. I'll hook up the team."

"No, let Jesus do it. He can and will do a good job. I want him to be a smart boy who can do anything. He's learning how to shoe horses now too. He has brains; all he needs is an education in these things. I will have a great horse trainer in him some day."

"I'll ask Jesus to do it then."

She looked up at the house from the foot of the stairs. They kissed again and she ran up them to go change, and he started off to find her horseman.

"Until later," she said after him, and went inside.

Sims's office always was neat. He had posters and papers in neat piles. There was nothing out of place. The westerly afternoon sun shone in the room on that side of the courthouse and from there he could look down on Whiskey Row. The

Palace Saloon and all the others were strung out for a block in close proximity to the county jail so that drunks could quickly be handled.

Sheriff Sims was in his forties and looked more like a banker than a lawman. He wore a flat brim western hat and a short evenly trimmed mustache. He was a thin built man and looked comfortable in the wheelback desk chair that was so well oiled it never creaked. He was a man who left nothing to chance. In the saddle he looked too stiff to Chet and it was not the man's place. He belonged in this neat room on the southwest side of the Yavapai courthouse.

Sims glanced up and rose to greet Marge when she came in the office first.

"How are you, Margaret? Hi Chet Byrnes, you two have a seat. What can I do for you?"

"I came to explain about a serious situation that has arisen, if you have the time?"

"First I want to thank you for your help at the scene of the store robbery at Camp Verde Sunday. That second outlaw is going to live. Those men from out there in the valley said it was your level head that saved the young woman's life he held for a hostage. I've been so busy I planned to thank you sooner for your handling of this mess. I've been working on so many cases, getting jurors to sit on the trials, I hadn't had time to send you word about how much I appreciated your efforts."

"No problem. This morning I stopped a man called Loftin who works for the Hartley brothers over in Mayer. He told me that he was setting up a cow camp on my deeded property and moving two thousand head of cattle in that country. I told him he would have to drive them up on the rim and then off down into that Sycamore Creek country beyond the deeded land. There is no way, except with several line riders, could I keep that many cattle off my deeded land; and they'd eat us out of house and home in six months."

Sims sat back in the well-oiled chair and tented his fingers. "I am certain the Hartley brothers have no wish to disturb your private land rights. The man may simply be talking about something much less than he described to you."

"Maybe you better advise them. I won't stand for trespassing on my ranch to send cattle up there to eat out the grass, then push their way down on my land. I will meet them with force if they even try."

"Oh, Chet, why can't all of us sit down and discuss this matter?"

"The talking is over for my part. It got over when Loftin told me he'd show me and called me a son of a bitch. I told him that he ever did that again, I'd shoot his head off. Now do I need a lawyer to get an injunction against them or can you talk them out of it?"

"Oh, there is no need in all that. I'll go over and talk with Carl and Willis. They're practical businessmen and should see you can't simply drive cattle over a man's place—not that many anyway."

"I believe they'll try it. I'm going over after this

meeting to talk to Margaret's family lawyer about preparing a case for court."

Sims shook his head. "No need in paying a lawyer. I will go see them and straighten the matter out."

"Thank you. But I'll file the case anyway. I intend to enforce my rights. They will not cross Quarter Circle Z land to get their cattle up there. They can take them up on the rim and go in up there and I can't stop them."

"That's nearly two hundred miles around. But you know how far it is."

"I do but that's their problem."

"Oh, yes, I agree. Rest easy a few days and let me work this out."

"I can tell you now they won't drive their stock across an acre of my land."

"I'll try to handle it."

"Good." He rose and shook the man's hand. "I appreciate your consideration."

Sims nodded. "I will go see them this week."

"Very good."

Once outside in the courthouse yard, she asked him, "Do you think he can talk them out of it?"

"No. Where is this lawyer Sam Eagan?"

"Across the street on the east side of the square."

"Let's talk to the man."

Sam Eagan was a short man in a nice tailored suit. His walnut desk was broad and smooth. He smiled at Marge and shook Chet's hand, offering them seats. A man in his fifties, he had a clear, loud voice that they must have taught him years earlier in law school.

Egan sounded articulate in discussing the territorial law. He could ask the court for a holding writ that the brothers could not trespass or drive their livestock over his property. Then he explained more about the law, and Chet agreed.

"They're big bluffers and I understand that they have run over many people. I will enforce the no-trespassing writ with my men if necessary," Chet said.

"If we get this order from the court and they do trespass they will be subject to arrest for violation of the court's orders. Serious business, especially in this jurisdiction."

Chet thanked the man and told him to proceed. They left Eagan and started back to Marge's ranch in her rig.

"Been a long day for you," she said, taking off her straw hat and letting the afternoon wind cool her face and her hair.

"It's been a nice day for me to have you along. You were the brightest point in my day. I hate trouble but by damn, I do get mad when people challenge things like this. And I take them personally."

"You know what I think about the Hartleys. I am with you all the way. Other ranchers will be too."

"Good. We can go to hell together."

She pecked him on the cheek and laughed. "If I have to do that to have you, turn the heat up."

They both chuckled. At her house, he bowed out of staying overnight with her. Though he wanted to badly, he worried he needed to prepare his crew. Law or lawyer, he was going to be ready for them should both fail. He still could see that man with the dark eyes, black hair, and mustache calling him an SOB. He'd see who that was before this matter was over.

CHAPTER 8

Tom Miller met Chet when he rode in and prepared to unsaddle the gray. "Let the boys do that," Tom said. "I want to hear about this confrontation out on the road that you had this morning."

"Sure, let's go to the house,"

After he told Tom the details, his foreman shook his head. "I guess I've heard a lot about those brothers. They've ran over lots of folks in the past and I thought Sims turned his back on some who had legitimate complaints about what happened. You need to keep a sharp eye on everything. They're bullies and have some men on their patrol I would call out-and-out killers. I could have gone to work for them when Ryan fired me. Willis came over to the house and offered me a job. But I never trusted either of them. I won't work for anyone like that. Costed me some wages, 'cause all I could find was day jobs. But—" He shook his head. "I just don't think they're real truthful or even honest."

"What we need to do is mind our borders. I

expect Hampt to be back in a week or so and he might know about this western situation we talked about and have some good ideas how to watch that part of our country. We need any warning we can get, because driving in that many cattle like they talk about will ruin that range."

"I agree. Mind me you be careful," Tom said. "I don't think they're above back shooting anyone who gets in their way. I noticed we have more T B cattle on the range than ever before. I guess they are drifting in here. We may have to drift them out."

Chet nodded he agreed. "Have those cowboys go in pairs."

"I'll do that. Good idea."

"And I'll give you some spending money, so two at a time, the cowboys can go drink a beer or two in Mayer and Preskit. We will need any rumor they can learn."

"That will work. We all get so busy out here we haven't time to know what goes on around us."

"You knew Roamer came last Sunday and apologized about the Rye deal and him not being available to help me?"

"Yes, Millie said he'd come over."

"He thought Sims was concerned he and I made him look bad, running Ryan off this ranch last year. And so he sent him to that Crown King mining camp to get him out of sight."

"Protecting his butt, huh?"

"I'm still not sure about Sims and the Hartley brothers. He acted like he could handle it."

Tom shook his head. "It will damn sure bear watching."

"I'm going to be edgy about this deal until we're both satisfied we've stopped their efforts, and not just hear from Sims that he stopped it."

Tom agreed and they went their ways.

Things pretty well in hand, the next morning he saddled up a big sorrel horse and went to see Marge. She was exercising her jumping horses when he rode up. A smile big as Texas lit her face when she discovered he was there. It was near lunchtime and her boy Jesus took their horses. Then he went on riding her horse to exercise him. She took Chet with her to the house to change her clothing.

"To what do I owe this visit?" she asked, squeezing his hand.

"Oh, just momentarily caught up."

"I can't imagine you being that close to completed."

"They'll finish Tom's house next week. The crew has the bunkhouse corners done and will start framing it after that. And we are simply catching up. I want to go look for another ranch on the rim. Would you consider going along? We'd take a packhorse or two and camp."

"I'd love to."

"It might spoil your reputation for good."

"I really don't believe I care."

"What will your father think?"

"That we're testing the water."

He nodded. "Kind of bold for me to ask that of you. But I really enjoy your company and I need to find another place. There are railroads coming they say, and when they do they'll bring big money from the East, and owning a ranch out here won't be bad. I think I need to move on finding that place."

"Have you talked to Bo your agent about it?"

"No, Bo is avoiding me. He left the woman he was living with and must be gambling hard. Probably drinking too much. He has to grow up. He knows that I'm back."

She nodded and they went inside the house. He hung his gun belt and hat on the hook in the hallway. Monica came from the kitchen and greeted him. She announced the meal would be served shortly.

"You have never seen the Grand Canyon country, have you?" Marge asked.

"No, ma'am."

"I haven't either. Maybe we can go by there?"

"I don't know why we can't. I'd like to see it."

"When can we leave?"

"Should we wait until your father is back?"

"That sounds fine. I expect him any day. What about the cattleman's meeting?"

"Tom can go to that. We talked this morning about what we need to do to prepare to meet them with force if they try anything."

They were seated on the couch, stealing kisses. She checked to be certain they were alone. "You've turned me into a love struck girl whenever you come around," She reached down and squeezed both of his hands. "Oh, Chet, I enjoy your company so much."

"A week or so of camping out might change your mind."

"I really doubt it."

"Good. Do you have a sound, easy riding horse?"

"Of course. He's a real mountain horse too."

"Be sure he's fresh shod. I'll find some pack-horses and pick me one out."

"That big gray?"

"No. He's good but not for that kind of a ride. He's too headstrong. Can you make me a list of things we'll need for food and things?"

"Sure."

"There won't be a camp cook but we can share those chores."

"You name the day."

"Fine. After we eat, we can drive into Preskit. I want to see an old friend."

"Who is that?"

"My friend Jenny who owns the dinner. I want you to meet her, if you don't already know her. Through her I found Hoot and the others last year. She's no competition to you, but she's a friend, and I also need to talk to the liveryman, Luther Frye. He promised me a couple of real mountain horses like the one I had before that Ryan shot mine out from under me."

"Food is served." Monica announced and they laughed, getting up to go in the dining room.

"I know Luther" Marge said.

"He sure treated me nice for a horse trader." He scooted the chair under her.

"I don't mean to drag bad memories up. But do you still miss your nephew Heck?"

He nodded and, seated, put the napkin in his lap. "At eleven or twelve, not much older, Heck rode a couple horses into the ground getting back home to me and giving me the word about his father's death in Kansas. I almost lost my mind when those stage robbers kidnapped him as a hostage, and I'll never forget you coming down there in my worst hours and saving me from going crazy after they killed him."

"I knew you needed me then. If there was any way for you to become untangled back there, I came to help you."

"And you waited for me. I wasn't very nice to you. You had quite a while to wait when I was busy closing out the ranch."

"You mailed me three letters."

He nodded, recalling how hard they'd been to write. "Short notes were all."

"I cherished them." She squeezed his hand close to her.

Monica served them thin sliced beef in brown gravy to go over the steamed rice. Then she brought out some hot sliced bread and butter. And refilled coffee cups. "Anything else?" she asked.

"How is the pie business going?" he teased.

"Wonderful. I will bring some for dessert."

"Ah, some man is going to run off with you," he said.

Marge frowned. "He better be buckshot proof 'cause I'll shoot him for trying."

All three laughed.

After lunch they drove to town and he found Frye in his office standing over a woman in her thirties, going over his books.

"Why, Chet Byrnes, I heard you were back a few weeks ago. This is my wife, Gloria. She does the book work for me."

"Can I hire her to do mine?"

His words drew a smile from her and she went back to work.

"No, pure and simple, I have to have her. What can I do for you today?"

"When I lost my horse last year, you said you'd find me another, or even two."

"I know who has them. Gloria, who is that man from Star Valley has those two roans?"

She looked up and squinted her blue eyes for a minute. "Jason Humbolt."

"See, I don't have any mind left. She can recall more than I can dig up. Thanks dear."

With a shake of her head she went back to work again.

"I can have them up here to look at by Friday," Frye said, and seeing Marge outside in the buggy, he said, "Good to see you, Miss Stephenson."

She waved. And said the same thing to him.

"Is that good enough, Chet?"

"I'll be here then. How much will they cost?"

"Eighty bucks a head, but—"

"If they're as good as the last one, fine."

"You know they're special. There is talk you have a special claybank stud horse you brought up here from Texas?"

"He's from the Barbarousa Hacienda."

"I have a long barrel mare."

"Is she open?"

Frye looked hesitant. "How much is the stud fee?"

"A hundred dollars, but to you, nothing."

"You don't need to do that."

"I know who I owe and don't owe. I can take her back or send a boy after her."

"Hey, I'll send her up there if you'll breed her."

"Whenever, just tell my man what I said. The deal will be all right."

Back in the buggy, he clucked to the horses.

She nodded. "He just got married a few months ago to that woman, Gloria. Did you meet her?"

"Yes, she's working on his books. A nice lady, she appears to be."

"I think she's educated, and I am not merely telling you for gossip's sake, but she was a widow with three young children. Her husband was killed in a horse wreck that broke his neck. He owed money on the place and she couldn't meet the payments and lost it. She brought the children to town and lived in a dirt floor shack. She worked nights in Mrs. Kane's house of ill repute to survive and support those kids. Frye found out and took her out of there and married her."

"She's one of the very lucky ones."

"Yes, and he's quite a man for taking on a woman with three children."

He drove the rig over to Jenny's and parked, then helped her down.

Time was mid-afternoon by then and the place was about deserted. Jenny came out of the kitchen, reaching in her apron pocket for a pad and pencil. "Well it's about time you brought her by, you rascal. I'm the last one to meet her."

"Jenny, meet Marge."

"Sit on a stool, you two. Lands, I have seen you at a distance, but up close I see why he likes you. You are a lovely lady." Then she stuck out her hand. "He's mighty well thought of in here. And he's right back righting wrongs in this country like the last time. We love him."

"So do I," Marge said, about to blush. "Thanks for keeping him here, so he came back."

"No problem, 'cause if you hadn't roped him, I'd've branded him for myself."

They both laughed and Jenny served them all some fresh coffee. It was a pleasant conversation and he recalled all of Jenny's help finding him Hoot and Tom along with the rest.

They drove back to Marge's place after she picked up some things Monica needed at the store.

"Guess I'm lucky to have you," she said, leaning on him, going down the road. "I think she would have taken you."

"Oh, she simply helped me and in turn I hired her customers who were out of work. But I always have to laugh at my sister Susie who wanted me to marry one of those German farm girls back in Texas. She promised me they'd produce me a large family, a big garden, and put up with me."

They both laughed.

"She had some good advice, didn't she?"

That evening Gates came by her house and stopped to talk to him. He'd heard he was with her in town and wanted to catch him. The three talked about the Hartley brothers' threat in her living room, and Monica served them supper.

Over supper, Chet asked him, "Do they really have two thousand cows somewhere to drive up here?"

"I'm not sure. But if they do they have a financier someplace. They are borrowed pretty close to the bankers' limit around here."

"That's interesting," Chet said.

"I have checked, and from what I can learn, they are really stretched financially. Bankers don't like to admit that because it could cause a panic if depositors knew something like that. But they owe sizeable sums of money backed by their cattle on hand and ranch property. That you can learn at the courthouse records."

"That might force them to take bigger chances, like ram a big herd down my throat?"

"Exactly. That was a lovely meal, Margaret. I have to get home tonight."

Chet walked him to his horse and the man mounted in the light of the bloodred setting sun. "I hope this squeeze doesn't come on you. I'll check around and see if there are any big herd movements coming."

"Thanks." Chet watched the man ride off. Marge joined him and hugged his arm.

"He will find out if this is a real threat, don't you think?"

"I'm hoping so."

"Will we need to postpone our camping trip?"

"I don't think so. Cattle move at ten or so miles a day. We're far enough into summertime, most of the easy water will be dried up. I don't think they can move them until fall."

"Good."

He kissed her and they went to sit on the porch swing.

He had lots to think about as the cricket chorus began in the twilight. Comfortable in her company, he wondered where they'd live if they did marry. On the ranch or at her place? No matter, he felt they'd be happy wherever they settled down. He needed to settle down and make some better plans for him and her. Then the Hartley brothers left lots of questions on what they really planned to do next.

CHAPTER 9

Livery owner Frye sent two three-year-old roan geldings and a light dun mare to the ranch. A boy about fifteen delivered them. Chet was taking a siesta when Susie woke him.

"You have horses here. Luther Frye sent them. He said you knew about them."

Moving his legs off the edge of the bed, he took a boot from her to pull on. "Must be the horses I ordered."

"He's a nice polite young man."

"I don't think he has a son that old."

"The boy didn't say."

He pulled on the last one and then stood up. "Tell him to come up and I'll write him a check for the pair of horses. I need Rio to breed that dun mare to the Barbarousa horse for him."

"I can do that. What horses did you buy?"

"I had a great mountain pony and that damn Ryan shot him. Frye's been looking for me some. I sure loved that other one, and Tom rode him up over the mountain to Preskit one night when we were surrounded here."

She returned with the young man and introduced him as Roy.

"Did Frye say how much I owed him for the horses?"

"No sir, he said you'd pay him when you came to town. They are sure good horses. I rode one of them up here and led the other three. One's for me to ride back on."

"Stay for supper and spend the night. It's a long ways back in the dark. You can tell him I made you stay."

"You have your choice," Susie said. "You can eat here at the house or up at Hoot's chuck wagon with the crew."

"Reckon I belong at the crew. You sure have a pretty place up here. I've never been to this place before. Those young boys yours that are fishing?"

"That's our nephews, Ray and Ty. Did they have a mess of fish today?"

"Oh, yes and they told me that a man was going to take all their carp. Bones and all, he liked them."

"Good," Susie said. "They would hardly speak to me over them. I made them feed a big one to the cats. They have so many bones in them."

"Yes ma'am. They are boney. You and Mr. Byrnes ever fish?"

"Oh, no. I am his sister not his wife."

"Oh, I see."

"Those boys have a stepmother. Their mother died and their father was shot."

"Gosh, that's bad. They're polite enough. I'll go speak to the camp cook. Thanks for letting me stay over. I was dreading the trip back."

"Thank you," Chet said, and rose from the desk.

When he left, Susie turned to him. "Tom Hanager was by today"

"I guess he came by to see you."

"He started off telling me he thought you might be home. He had the excuse of wanting to talk to you about the Hartley brothers. Then he drank some coffee and we visited. I asked him to bring his daughter and come join us for supper next Sunday."

"That's good," he said, pleased that Tom had noticed his sister who she had shown some interest in.

"Now just hold everything." She spread her hands out in front of her. "I like him but I am not at this time really thinking about a man for myself."

"Did I say one thing?"

"No, but you thought it. I can tell by the look on your face."

"Which reminds me. Would you think Marge would want a big wedding or something simple?"

"If it was me, I'd take a simple one, but I didn't go to finishing school either."

"She's not a snob."

"No, but if it weren't for wanting you so bad, she could become one."

"Do you really believe that?"

"She's wanted you since you came here, hasn't she?"

"I guess, but I didn't consider her a snob."

"She is just Margaret and she has that finishing school . . . air about her."

"When her father gets back from California, we're going on a look-see trip. I want a ranch for JD up on the rim."

"Are you going to get married or are you simply going to drag her around and have everyone talking about it?"

"It's not easy to decide. Lots of things to consider. Where should we live? Decisions I don't know the answer to."

"I would think you'd do the respectable thing. Get married. But you've had some good affairs with some nice ladies."

"I am spoiled, aren't I?"

"Yes, you have been. But if I wasn't your sister, I'd want you. You kept Marla Price a big secret for a long time. I sure didn't know you were seeing her and I'm not digging up things. And Kathren, I hoped you two'd make it. Then all that fell through. Do what you need to do, but yes, you asked me. I'd marry her."

"Thanks."

"You know after all that has happened, we don't act or feel like a family anymore, do we."

"What do I need to do to restore that?"

She shook her head. "I fear it is like water under the bridge, gone downstream."

"You want to feed them all is what you're saying?"

"No, you knew it wouldn't be family like before and now I see it. Reg is even gone. Our brother, plus Heck, Mom and Dad. I hate to even consider leaving May here. I thought she'd find someone. But she's not looking."

"Is she my responsibility?" he asked.

"No, I don't think that. She would marry you in a minute, but she's not at your speed. Margaret is."

He nodded in agreement.

"Do you think I'd make a good stepmother to Caylin?"

"If she wanted one. Does that worry you?"

"I know about family ties. She hasn't had to share her father growing up."

"I bet you'd win her." Susie must be thinking serious. He excused himself and went to saddle a horse. He was about to go see Marge. No need vexing about it all week.

"I won't be here for supper," he said to her, leaving the house.

"Tell her hi from me," Susie said from the doorway.

He waved that he heard her and went down to the chuck wagon and spoke to Hoot.

"Everything is fine. Best damn outfit I ever worked at. Every man here works hard to do a day's work and we all want this ranch to work for you."

"Good. I need to go check on some things."

"Them Hartley brothers ain't done nothing else have they?"

"No, not yet."

"Good." He went off to check on his cooking. "Ride easy, boss man."

It was past dark when he arrived at her place. Her boy came to take care of his horse and Marge came out on the porch.

"Put him up, Jesus. He'll stay, I am certain."

She came on down and hugged him. "I won't ask why, but I am so pleased you came."

"We need to talk, I guess."

"Good, let's sit on the swing. It's not too hot now."

"I've been thinking I was very brazen to ask you to go on this trip. I realize that it will smudge your reputation and it was selfish of me to ask you."

She kissed him and laughed. "I was not afraid of that."

"Do you want to have a big wedding?"

"I don't have to have one."

"Be truthful."

"I am. I don't care."

He chewed on his lower lip for a second or two. "Will you marry me?"

"Oh, yes, Chet Byrnes. Anywhere, anytime that

you want me to." She sucked in her breath like it had caught.

"Will your father be back by Saturday night?"

"I am certain he will be back by then."

"Let's get married at the Camp Verde dance."

She threw her arms around his neck and smothered him with kisses. "Oh, Chet you have made my day."

"Now wait. We have lots to settle. Where will we live?"

"Wherever you want to live."

That let him down a little and he about slumped in the swing. "No, we need to settle lots of things."

She shook her head. "I will be your wife, not some law judge. I'd go live in a tent or tepee—wherever you want to live."

He squeezed his forehead and shook his head. "You aren't any help."

"Excuse me," Monica said coming out on the porch. "Supper is ready to serve."

"Come." She pulled him up. "Monica, we are going to celebrate my engagement to this lovely cowboy."

"Oh, *Señora*, congratulations! I have some wine," her cook said.

"Good, break it out," he said. "I am going to need something."

She pulled him to her and kissed him. "I don't want one thing from you, Chet Byrnes, except you to keep loving me. I'll help work, do whatever I need to as your mate—" She closed her eyes. "I simply want your love, big man."

"I'll be there for you, Marge."

"Good. Will you find a preacher or should I?"

"You know who you want. I know it ain't a church wedding but I won't treat it any way but the best I can do to please you."

"And we will go on this camping honeymoon?"

"That's why, and the fact that I want to share my life with you, we're getting married."

She threw her arms around him and kissed him hard. Then out of breath between huffs, she said, "I am the happiest woman in the world."

"Good. Some day don't tell me we needed to have straightened all that out years ago."

"I won't. What dress should I wear?" she asked as he seated her at the table.

"Heavens, you look good in anything." Then he leaned over. "And without anything too."

She blushed and shook her head. "I can see now I am in for it."

He hugged and kissed her, sitting side by side.

"I'll send word for JD to be sure to come down." Then he looked at her fingers. "What size are they?"

"I don't know. Do I get a ring?"

"It's not the biggest or prettiest, but my mother wore it."

Her eyes flew open in shock. "Do you have it with you?"

"I do, but it better not be bad luck to show it to you."

"Silly, that's not bad luck." Then she sucked in her breath at the sight of it. "That's gorgeous."

"That stone's real. First trip we made to Kansas with cattle my father brought that back for her after we sold a thousand steers. She fussed about him spending the money. She didn't know he had over seventy thousand dollars on him."

"That was sweet of him."

"For an old Arkansas hillbilly years ago, he was a neat man."

"He must have been."

"Them Comanches killed him. He wouldn't quit chasing them looking for those kids they'd kidnapped. Never found them. He and my mother both slipped out of their minds looking for them and pining for them. Bad deal."

They ate their engagement celebration meal and then danced to the music box waltz. He didn't figure you could have got any more excitement out of a woman than he got from her. Her cook and housekeeper left them after the dishes were done with a soft "good night" from the door.

"I don't know how to tell you how happy you've made me," she whispered in his ear.

"I hope you stay that way for the rest of our lives."

"Oh, Chet, I will."

"Good, 'cause our life will have some crooks and turns along the way." There he stood face to face with a woman tall as he was and as easy to kiss as to move four inches. But he did believe her. She was as thrilled as he was about the deal. Then no one could complain about their living together before they were married. He hoped that worked for her sake. He'd better go home and tell Susie. Marge wasn't her choice, but he didn't think he'd ever be happy with a chubby, German-accented bride. He kissed her again thinking about it. No, Marge was more to his liking.

CHAPTER 10

JD came down from the log camp for the wedding and so did his crew. The ranch was crowded with folks. Hampt came back and had a conference meeting with Tom and Chet. Hampt had learned that a few rustlers, who had been out there earlier, probably stole some of the ranch cattle and drove them to a butcher over on the Williams River in a mining camp, and had later pulled stakes from there. So there was no one else operating in the western country at the time. Chet felt he had the best information they could get from out there.

Millie and Susie sewed him a new white shirt to wear for the wedding wingding. They made a good team, and things were settled down. The cowboys' cook shack food was going up, and the bunkhouse as well. Things were taking shape. Tom was going, the next week, to look at some shorthorn bulls for sale down at Hayden's Mill. There weren't enough

Hereford bulls around there that were old enough to breed cows for sale.

Chet had four packhorses and his two new mountain horses for him and her to ride. Marge said she'd even ride a mule as long as she got to go along. He'd ridden both new horses and was pleased with them. Packhorses were selected, the gear was all laid out. The Mexican boy Victor, about sixteen, who served as the horse wrangler, was the choice for handling the packhorses and the others. Rio said he was a hard worker and a loyal guy.

They sent him up on top on Saturday morning to make camp near the sawmill. Chet and his new missus were to join him Sunday evening up there. They'd spend the first night in a borrowed cabin near Camp Verde. Sunday, they'd ride up on the rim to Victor's camp setup.

The crowd at the dance was double the usual numbers. Susie had fussed at him all morning about what he needed to do before, at, and after the wedding. Like she was his mother, and it amused him.

Finally she said, "Margaret really wanted you mighty bad to put up with this honeymoon on a pack train. Mercy, she went to finishing school. Aren't you worried she will quit you and go home in the midst of it all?"

"We have talked about it a lot. She's serious."

"I can't imagine how."

May laughed at the two of them fussing about it.

"Why I'd go with him if he was going to be my husband."

"See there, May would go," he said and shared a wink with May.

Susie shook her head. "I sure hope it works."

"It will. I'm going to town and I'll check to be sure she ain't run off. She'll be worried that I'm off on another wild goose chase."

Susie agreed. "I'd be concerned too."

He left on the gray horse. The ranch hands were bringing the roan ones with them. Their "honeymoon horses," he called them, and the men laughed. They were all shined up for the event and he knew he'd get lots of kidding when he got back. But he really looked forward to what lay ahead. His tall bride and he were going to enjoy their lives together. After so many false starts in his life, he counted on them having a good union.

He found her at noon with a large tent set up and her cook along as well. Her father still wasn't back and that niggled him. He hoped it didn't upset her too much. She rushed out and kissed him. They stood under the fluttering leaved cottonwoods and savored each other's mouths for a while. Her foreman took his gray horse and they walked down by the river.

"All's going all right for you?"

"I am as edgy as sixteen-year-old. I feel so giddy inside and even on my skin. I guess this is number three and I really want it to be so much better than my others. But let me tell you, I am so proud I know you so well. I have truly enjoyed our, well— *cheating* being together. You are a generous, patient man with me, and I so appreciate that. Some day I'll tell you more about things like that. But you know me well enough for now."

They kissed. He saw some boys wearing cutoff britches splashing in the river as they strolled on the higher ground. His nephews would have enjoyed that. Then she led him behind a tree and they kissed again.

She rested her backside against the bark and her eyes sparkled in the sunlight filtering down. "It is hard for me not to say, We're married already, let's go be by ourselves."

"Oh, today will teach us to be patient."

"Whatever you say, big man. I will be good."

He hugged her tall form and savored her body against his own. "You are always good."

"I have you fooled completely."

They both laughed.

"Has JD said anything about Kay to you?" she asked.

"No. Should he have?"

"I'm not certain. But I think she is going to take the children and leave her husband."

"How does my nephew fit in that deal?"

"Maybe I have said too much."

"I'll take you back and go find him. I better know what he plans if she's made some plans."

"I hate that. But I agree. You may need to know."

"I'll be back before suppertime." They kissed and parted not fifty feet from her camp.

He caught Susie. "You seen JD?"

"Not since this morning. What's wrong?"

He looked around to be certain they were alone enough to tell her. "Marge is afraid Kay and him are going to elope, with her kids as well."

Susie frowned. "Really? Oh, his mother will have a fit."

"Not much she can do about it. Kay's husband is not a happy man anyway, and I don't know how he'll take it either. She still is his wife."

"I'll go look for him and tell the boys to do the same," Susie said.

"That will be good. He may be head-over-heels in love with her, but I worry more about her husband's reaction."

"Here you go worrying about the outfit on your own wedding day. We can handle it."

"Wedding or not some things need to be settled."

Susie agreed and hurried off. He went and spoke to some ranchers he knew. About then a buckboard arrived and a crop of little kids lined the sides. A red-haired woman who held a baby in her arms sat on the spring seat. His buddy Roamer had just arrived. He went to shake his hand and meet the small woman with the baby who wanted to populate the territory.

"Word was out you were getting married. We didn't want to miss the occasion. So I got some time off to come over. How have you been?"

"Good. Take your wife up to our camp and they'll help watch the kids."

"Darling, this is Chet Byrnes, the Texan I told you about."

She smiled big and Roamer starting unloading his crew. "Nice to meet you, Mr. Byrnes. He's spoken a lot about you."

"Good to meet you too, ma'am. He's got a right to be proud of these young'uns. They sure look neat to me."

"Thank you, sir."

Roamer headed them up to the ranch camp. Meanwhile, Chet found Tom and Hampt. He drew them aside. "Marge told me that Kay Kent is planning on leaving her husband at this dance and she thinks JD is also involved. Don't let anything happen to either her or him. I fear her husband might be mad about it and I don't want either one of them hurt."

"Get married, boss man," Hampt said. "Us boys can manage the rest."

Tom agreed with a grim nod. "Her husband don't treat that woman right, anyway."

"I just hate to leave you all with my problems."

"Naw, we're all proud to be working for a man who cares."

"Look who's arrived," Tom said. "Henry McClure."

His father-in-law-to-be drew up his team and smiled big at the three men. "I hear my daughter is marrying some Texan today. Any of you know him?"

"No," Hampt said. "But if he's any one of them

Texans I know I'm sure feeling sorry for you."
Then he laughed.

"Well, Chet, I've been coming all the time. Figured she wouldn't miss me if I didn't make it here
today, but you might never forgive me."

Chet shook his hand.

McClure clapped him on the shoulder. "Good
to have you coming into the family. I know it
pleased her. I am grateful to have you in the family
circle. I owe you for recovering my horses, too."

Chet shook his head. "We're glad to have you
back. She's up at your tent."

Roamer joined them and he shook McClure's
hand. Hampt went to see about JD and the rest
went up to Marge's tent, talking about everything
from the government to outlaws.

In a little while, Hampt located JD and brought
him to Chet. The two spoke outside of the McClure
camp.

"I'm sorry, Chet, that you had to hear about this
from others. I told Kay some time ago that if she
needed to leave him, she could come to our ranch
and Susie would be the one to keep her straight if
she wished to file for a divorce."

"Have you told Susie that story?"

"Yes sir, a little late there, too."

"What did she say?"

"Told me to bring her on, we never turned
strays away at our place."

"I reckon you're serious about her?"

"I am, but I don't want her reputation turned
into some dirty deal."

"What about your mother?"

He shook his head. "Who knows about her?"

"She'll have a lot of screaming to do. So you better tell her, too."

"I can do that. Kay Kent is a nice lady. I think when she gets shed of him she can do what she wants to do."

"Good. Simply avoid any gunplay with him."

"I will. And Chet, thanks for looking out for all of us."

Six p.m. Chet was in place, standing where the preacher had set up his stand with JD, who had the ring. They played the wedding march and here came Marge on the arm of her smiling father. The blue dress she wore was gorgeous and flattered her trim figure. Excitement danced in her eyes and she looked perfect standing there with him at the preacher's position.

He didn't recall much about the whirlwind ceremony, except, "I do." Then he kissed the bride and they were swept off to the food table in a dream flight to cut their cake. He wasn't sure he could eat anything on his butterfly stomach, but she helped fill his plate and they went off to eat some and to be congratulated.

One of the first to come by was Kay to hug both of them. She bent him over to do that and whispered, "Thanks so much."

Before he remembered what for she was gone in the crowd. Why did she feel the need? There was no asking Marge. In the uproar around them, they were covered with well-wishers. Later, the bride went back to their camp and changed out of her wedding dress and came back in a riding skirt, blouse, and jacket, plus a hat; and the two roan horses stood saddled and ready for when they showed up.

He boosted his bride in the saddle and swung up with one hand on the horn on his own. They waved and galloped away in the bloody sundown. The borrowed cabin was only a short distance from the school grounds and she held the horses' leads while he unsaddled them, then put them in the pen with water and hay for the night. At the rough wooden door, he swept her up in his arms, carried her through the opening, and set her down inside. Both were laughing at his efforts.

In the middle of the room was a bed made for them with a Texas Star quilt on top. He stood admiring it.

"It's a wedding present from my lady friends. They made it and it was a surprise."

He kissed her and then they began to undress. For a long moment they stood there holding each other skin to skin. She was finally his wife and his heart pounded with the news.

"This is too damn much to be real," he whispered in her ear.

"Damn it, Chet Byrnes, this is as right as it will ever get. Things are going uphill from here."

He still wished he knew why Kay had said thanks for everything. But by then he and Marge were on the bed in each other's arms. Everything else could wait for another day.

CHAPTER 11

He woke with his arms and body coiled tight around her. There would be no disengaging himself without waking her up. All he could recall about the night before was that he couldn't get enough of her, and she was the same about him. Then she stirred and opened her eyes. No woman in his life had ever been closer than that. Awake, she raised up and shook her head, then went to laughing.

"Sneaking away, huh?" she accused.

"I tried."

"I knew it. I knew it. You're tired of me already." Then they kissed and snuggled flesh to flesh.

"Oh, yes. How long have we been married?"

"Years." She threw her arms back. Then she quickly returned to savor their closeness.

"How many anniversaries have I missed?"

"Not many, thank God."

"If I don't get out of the bed we both may get wet."

"Oh, serious, huh." Reluctantly she gave him up.

The second part of making this adventure so neat was her genuine laughing. Nothing forced. Free laughter came from her that eased the whole situation from being somewhat awkward to settling between a man and wife. She could find humor in everything they did. Not silliness, but sincere laughter that made him happier by the moment with his choice.

They finally got up and she made coffee. There were some Danishes for breakfast. Monica was going to gather the bed covers and what they left. The rest was on the packhorses waiting for them in camp up on the rim. The ride up was pleasant and en route they watched a large herd of elk, cow, and calves. Mid-afternoon they reached Victor and the camp. Everything was in order.

Victor met them when they rode in, took their horses, and he told them he had supper cooking for them, and to get some rest. Chet smiled. There would be no rest in the tent and cots set up inside, but they did enjoy each other.

The next morning at the sawmill, he spoke to McKnight, who said that it was all going good and he had plenty of logs at the mill thanks to JD and his crew. Chet hated that his nephew hadn't come on that Sunday. JD could have told him about Kay's separation from her husband as well as if it had occurred before they left the mill. They rode across the Marcy Road used by east–west bound stagecoaches and went around the high San Francisco Peaks to head for the Grand Canyon.

They spent a few days exploring along the south

rim. Chet was impressed with the colors and majesty of the large chasm, and felt very small in the presence of the mighty cut into the earth. Some people had warned him that the Hualapai Indians who lived west of there could be cranky. But most folks thought they were tame enough not to bother them. The tribe lived down in the canyon itself, so they stayed clear and finally reached the community of Hackberry, which consisted of a few bars, blacksmith, saddle repair shop, and two stores, and had not changed much since he was there a year before.

He met both storekeepers in the village. A stoic man named Herman owned one, and an Irishman named O'Malley who did a jig for Marge and laughed when he shook Chet's hand owned the other one.

"Welcome to me land. And where do you two lovely folks hail from?"

"Camp Verde."

"Ah, indeed I've been there a time or two."

"Next time look us up. We are west of the town. Quarter Circle Z ranch."

"I'll do that very thing. What brings you to Hackberry?"

"I'm looking for another ranch for my nephew to run up here."

"Ah, and there is a big one north of here for sale."

"How big?"

"Six sections deeded land."

"That sounds interesting." Marge nodded to his words in her approval.

O'Malley asked, "Do you know how the United States government issues sections of such land to the railroad to raise money for their tracks?"

Chet shook his head. "I don't, perhaps Marge does. But tell us."

"They give them as apposing sections of land. One section would be on the right of the line, the next one would be on the left of that line. Well, this man bought them from some line headed west and exchanged them with the government for land up here, 'cause he said the land they had given him on those other tracks had no water. They showed him a plat up here and said this land isn't far to the Colorado River." The storekeeper slapped his legs laughing. "And he took it sight unseen. So it sure is for sale."

"Who is this guy and where do I find him?"

"His name is Boxley Austin and he lives in Saint Louis. Maddest man I ever met when he came back from looking it over. He stomped around here for days, finally went down and used the telegraph in Preskit. But the government said it was too late, they had already made one trade with him. He had to keep it."

"What about the land? Where exactly is it?"

"Starts about five mile north and runs over this rangeland east to west for six miles. He spent a fortune having it surveyed before he came out here."

"Is there a guide who knows it and can show me that land?"

"It's a girl, one of the Wright sisters. She'd do it for two bucks a day. I can send word and they'd be here in no time—say in the morning. They're tough ranch hands, any one of them girls."

"Let's do that. That may be interesting." He looked at Marge and saw she was interested too. "Yes, we will meet her here about sunup."

"That'll work fine."

All the way back to camp he and Marge talked about the possibility of having perhaps found a bird's nest on the ground. A man who bought a ranch he can't use sounded too good to be true.

"Why we might buy this one cheaper than the valley ranch," he said to her as they rode back to camp across the rolling plains of juniper, pear cactus, and lots of grass.

"It also could be lots of work, too. Building headquarters, developing stock water, finding land suitable for haymaking," she pointed out to him.

"It is lots of land and this country has grass and water in places." He laughed. "But I'm not counting on the Colorado to supply much."

She broke up over his comment. "No, it would not be likely to supply much."

"Tomorrow we can see the terrain with our guide." He watched three shy mule deer slip off into the junipers after a curious sighting by them.

"This cowgirl guide may be interesting," Marge said. "She sounds like a real one."

When they drew closer to their camp, they could hear Victor chopping wood with an ax. Chet knew him from the trip out from Texas, but he had decided from the first day on this trip, this youth was a hard worker. Keeping camp and things going for two honeymooners was no small job. And he took it serious like he'd been doing it all his life.

"What do you think now about our adventure?" he asked, helping her dismount.

"I absolutely love it. I first thought taking a honeymoon on a camping trip might be boring." She removed her hat and shook loose her hair. "Anything with you is a great adventure and fun. Tomorrow we go look at the man's ranch on the river and I'm excited. It sounds interesting."

Then with her familiar laugh she hugged him tight. "I simply wish we had been teen lovers and had spent our entire life together. It would have been so neat."

He hugged her. "The best part is we found each other. I lived in Texas, you were out here, and we might never have known each other except for the problems that drove me out here. Fate was kind to both of us."

"You know I lived in total fear you'd not come back after your nephew's death."

"All of it was tough business. But I had a family to protect. And I'm glad I came back here. One less thing for me to dread in my life. Besides, I have you."

After supper, they helped Victor clean up and did the dishes, while Victor played the guitar. Marge knew the words in Spanish and those two sang the ballad about a wild *cabayo*. His music went on as they sat by the campfire under a blanket while the night's coolness came in on a soft wind.

"We better get some sleep," Chet finally said. "Tomorrow we are going to look at another ranch."

"Will you sell the ranch back at Verde?" Victor asked.

"No, no, this is another ranch," he said to the youth.

His brown face looked relieved. "Oh, good, I like that place."

After telling him good night, they went arm in arm to their tent. She pulled off his boots and teased him. "Aren't you glad you have a wife now?"

"Oh, yes, I used to sleep with them boots on and they always got tangled in the sheets."

Laughing, she tackled him on the bed and the force of their collision turned over the cot, spilling them both on the ground. He reached over in the tangle of blankets and kissed her between laughs. "Since we're here, guess we can sleep here as well."

She was laughing too hard to protest.

CHAPTER 12

Their guide the next day, Lacinda Wright, was perhaps eighteen, maybe older. She wore a dress over her jeans and reminded him of that "girl that Susie spoke about." The chunky-built young lady wore boots with spurs and a once-white hat with a floppy brim over her short-cut blond hair.

"They call me Lacy." She shook his hand with the callused palm of a man. Then did the same with Marge. "O'Malley said you want to look over the railroad survey up north. We can see some of it in a day. Except for the nearby Colorado River that that old man screamed about when we showed him that down in the canyon."

"We heard about that."

She smiled. "The Canyon River is over twenty miles north of this land."

"Lacy, we don't expect any water from it."

"Good thing, Mr. Byrnes, 'cause I ain't got a rope that long to dip a bucket in it."

They were laughing going out the store door

after he thanked O'Malley for finding her. She stopped on the porch and looked at their horses. "Wow, you sure got some real ponies. I've got Jud and he's got lots of bottom, but he ain't half that good looking."

Marge chuckled. "You're going to keep me in stitches all day. I hope you don't mind my laughing."

"No, ma'am, go right ahead. I'm just a scatter-brain cowgirl and say too much sometimes."

"Not for us," Marge said. "We really want to see this ranch and appreciate you taking time to show us."

"Lordy me, do you know what I'd had to do today at the ranch if I hadn't got this job?"

"I have no idea."

"Why, shoe a couple of horses. My dad's back is stove up and he can't do it."

"Whew, you shoe horses. I won't give you any lip."

As they rode, Lacy went to shaking her finger at her. "Why I know now who you are. I've seen you at Preskit on the Fourth of July in a nice dress driving a buggy. I know you're his wife, but what are you doing up here?"

"This is my honeymoon. I mean our honeymoon."

Lacy's blue eyes narrowed in wonderment. "I thought, well, ladies like you went to, like, Paris for those sort of things. Camping out?"

"Hey, I'm as content as anyone out here with him looking for another ranch than I would be over there—even more so."

"You don't sound like you'd be happy over there."

"I wouldn't be. Fancy people trying to impress other fancy people. I'm ten times happier being out here with you doing this."

"You'll have to meet my sisters. They'd love you."

"I will meet them. Do they have a dance up here?"

"Don't they have one of them everywhere in the West?"

"Come to think of it, they do. Do they have them in Texas, Chet?"

"Heavens, yes. Let's trot, we've got lots to see."

"We better get back to business, Lacy. He's busting to see this place."

They all three laughed.

The country ranged from wide open to clustered in canyons. Some even had pines. Many he found showed some water that needed to be developed. His family had done lots of that originally in Texas. Built cypress boxes they buried in the creek sand, and they soon filled with water.

There was a lot to see and they found a good spring and a steep set of hills to protect a headquarters from all the north wind. It was well inside the second section that the man owned.

"I like this spot," he said, dismounted and passing out some jerky he'd brought to feed them.

Marge had taken a large drink from the powerful spring chocked with watercress and was getting off her knees. "That is wonderful water."

"It's ice cold all year round too," Lacy promised them. "There's some other sites we can look at, but this is the one that would be my choice for a ranch headquarters."

"Girls, we better get back. Tomorrow we'll move our things over here and camp since I want to see all of it. Do you have the time to show it to us, Lacy?"

"It's Friday today. I'll come get you tomorrow right after lunchtime here and take you two to the dance and supper, if you want to come with me."

"We'd love that. Lacy, Chet can dance our boots off."

"Good. I'd be real proud to have you two go with us."

"What can we bring?" Marge asked.

"Yourselves. They will all want to meet you."

"Good, we'll ride east from here to our camp and get back here to reset up in the morning."

"Shucks, my sisters and I'll be here to help you do that tomorrow."

"They don't have to."

"We can help. I think you will be our new neighbors from the way you have looked at this land."

"At least part of us. We have about fifteen men, not counting ranch hands, now at work on the ranch down there. They can move up here next if I can buy it."

Lacy half laughed and kicked a small pinecone off for a distance. "Why that old man went crazy when he saw this country, but the ride to the river was the funniest part. He kept going back and forth to get peeks at it way down there and cussing like a sailor."

"O'Malley said he was mad. Good, we'll try to buy it if it looks like a ranch to me. Thanks for your invite, we will be privileged to be your guest tomorrow night."

"That will be mine." In a large swing off the saddle horn, she was back on her horse and in the saddle.

When she was gone, Marge laughed. "I really can't see either of us in Paris."

He agreed and hugged her. "No, we don't fit the part. My sister had a fit. 'You can't take her on a honeymoon on a camping trip!'"

"She was wrong. I wanted you, not some fancy man. This is getting somewhere. I can see this as a great ranch. The water's cold, but I'd take a bath downstream in it."

"Get naked. There ain't nothing to peek at us but camp birds."

"Wonderful." And she began to undress and waded out in the water. He went after soap, towel, and a blanket from his horse. In minutes they were both in the cold water and with a shiver sharing his bar of soap and lathering up. Then they used handfuls of water tossed on each other to rinse off. Then they sat in the bright sun and dried the rest of the way.

And like honeymooners, they made love next on the blanket.

Riding back to camp, they discussed their day.

"It has lots of grass."

"Developing water will be a big need, but we can do that. I've done that in Texas, though it will be a bigger challenge up here. Looks to me like it will be something we have to stay after."

"Where will we live?"

"Oh, I think at the Verde ranch. You will some day have your father's holdings and the ranch over there will grow. It's been so mismanaged by the last guy. We will be years making it as smooth a ranch as the one in Texas."

"I never dared asked you before but did it hurt you to sell it?"

"Sure, but I was so committed by then, I knew it was the only way for my family to survive."

"I could feel every inch of you even at a distance."

"I thought you might find someone more dependable than me."

"No. My mind and heart was set for you. When I went to get you and his body, I knew if there was any way I could have you I wanted you for myself. I thought I didn't have much appeal when you never took me to bed in those long days. I wasn't some innocent girl. But then I realized you were still obligated to her like you said, and that had to be settled. When you came back I was trembling— that first day at the house I knew it was too good to be true."

"Oh, you were hard to resist, but you sure stood by me. I'll never forget that day either. Let's get back. I want to be up here tomorrow." They put their horses in a lope for camp.

In the morning, the three were loaded by sunup and headed for the new place. They came at a long trot and reached the site. At his first sight Victor nodded his approval. "Oh this is a great place for a big ranch. Who are they?"

"The Wright sisters," Chet said, looking at three cowgirls in dresses with jeans on under them, talking to Marge who had already joined them.

He soon met them. Lacy introduced her middle sister, Fern, who was the tallest and a much better dresser than Lacy, but still a cowgirl; and the dark-eyed younger girl, about fifteen, Hannah.

"This is my *segundo,* Victor," he said, and his intro about made the boy blush. They shook his hand like men and welcomed him.

"Good day, *señoritas,*" he managed to say.

They each took a packhorse. Then tie-down ropes and canvas flew off the panniers. Chet knew it sure unloaded a lot faster than it went on. Marge made them coffee, and they took a break to sip it. The girls sat cross-legged on the ground so she never set up her canvas chairs. Chet and Victor joined them.

"Sis said you were real serious about building a ranch up here," Fern said.

"We'd like to. We have one down at Camp Verde. But my nephew needs one."

"I see. This place could be a good one."

"Thanks. Marge and I have only seen a small

part of it. That's why we moved over here. Sure was a lot faster with you girls helping us than us doing it."

"Hey, we can use some good neighbors."

"Do you have some bad ones?" he asked.

"We got some ain't worth the powder to blow them up."

They all laughed.

"Were you the man," Fern asked, "who about a year ago arrested those men in the saloon that you'd trailed all over, and took them in chains back home?"

"Yes, that was me."

"My, my, I never thought I'd get to meet you. Why when that man and his boy got back from hauling them, folks had him tell that story a hundred times."

"Where are those two?" He'd wondered about them.

"They went on to California. Kinda hard to make a living here. I bet several folks will recognize you at the dance tonight."

"No big deal."

"Marge, does he say that all the time?" Lacy asked between sips of her hot coffee.

"A lot. He came to see me after he got back on his first visit, and he took off before I could hardly kiss him, and went after some men who had rustled some of the ranch horses. They killed my foreman and another good worker and he ran them down. For days I didn't know if he was alive or not."

They began to laugh at how she told them the story.

"We see why you took a honeymoon with him," Lacy said.

"Only way I could keep up with him." Marge exchanged a wink with him.

After the camp was set up, the girls shed their jeans for the dance. They washed up and brushed their hair. Chet and Victor got a kick out of them getting ready.

"You want to go with us?" he asked his helper.

"No, I can watch the camp."

"Grab that guitar, Victor," Lacy said. "Won't no one bother your outfit up here. They can always use a musician."

"Oh, yes," the youngest one said. "They can sure use some help."

"Saddle a horse," Lacy told him. "They pay in good food for your help."

"If I don't have to cook it, I'd like it much better."

At the schoolhouse, the girls had strung a thick rope up for a picket line. Their father, a big man, had brought their pies in a buckboard. After telling Chet and Marge his name was Jake, the girls ran off to check on the pies he'd already set on the table. Chet figured by then that they ran everywhere they went.

"Good to meetcha," Jake said, shaking Chet's hand. Then he did Victor the same. He nodded to Marge. "Lacy said you liked the Railroad ranch."

"I think it could be a good one."

He nodded. "I was here in town the day you got those guys. That sure took lots of nerve."

"You do what you have to."

"Glad I never had to do anything like that. Ma'am?" He removed his hat for her. "Them girls are talking up there, just go on up there and join them."

"Thanks," she said, and nodded to Chet.

"I'll be along," he said after her.

"Grab that music box, Vic," Jake said, like he knew the boy all his life. "I'm going to introduce you to them players."

Chet nodded for him to go with the man. "I'll go check on the women. Good to meet you, Jake."

"Me too." And Jake went on with his conversation with the boy.

Marge joined him and the three girls who were talking to several ranch wives. Marge had a piece of fruit bread for him that one of them had given to her. The cake on his first bite flooded his mouth with saliva at the flavors of cinnamon, raisins, and sugar.

Later, after a wonderful meal, he danced the night away, meeting wives and husbands, and he was a dance partner with the Wright sisters and Marge.

Victor told him on the break they really were nice to him and wanted him to stay.

At last together on the bench along the wall, Chet and his bride sat out a dance and talked about things.

"They really think you're a hero. Of course I knew that, but they all remembered you."

His arm around her back, he hugged her, then he whispered in her ear, "Not much ever happens up here in Hackberry."

They both chuckled.

"You're probably right."

"I am. We'll take a few more days to look at the ranch and then head home."

"Good. I'm in no rush. It has been very entertaining. And I am so glad you found the place."

"I think so too."

He wondered about JD and what he might be into. He was a big boy. He'd have to figure out this deal with Kay by himself. Especially with him at this distance from the main ranch, Susie and Tom together could probably work most things out. He simply hoped he had not left them in a big mess. That situation could have escalated.

When he heard about it, Victor was excited to be going home. He had found him a place with the musicians and he told them all about it.

"Why, Victor, as good as you play, anyone would have you in their band," Marge said.

"I thought I would never find a place to play."

"Did you ever go to the dance in Camp Verde?"

"No, *señora*."

"We'll take you there next time we go."

"Oh, *gracias*."

Chet wondered about the Hartley brothers that night. Had they tried anything else? He might need to station someone at the western end of the ranch in a line shack to turn back cattle and keep his own in check. He'd speak to Tom about that when he got home.

They headed home at the middle of the next week. They checked at the sawmill for JD, but his man, Robert Brown, who JD'd left in charge with the horses, said he was still down at the ranch. They were doing fine and didn't need a thing.

"What did you learn?" Marge asked when she joined them.

"JD is still at the ranch."

"Isn't that strange?"

He mounted up and agreed. "I think we ought to push for the ranch and let Victor bring the packhorses along slower."

"Fine with me. You better tell Victor."

He twisted in the saddle. "Victor?"

"*Sí, señor?*"

"You take your time going home. Marge and I are going to hurry home today."

"Will you need me there?"

"No, we can handle it. Take care of the horses and camp somewhere tonight before you go down off on the military road to the Verde."

"Be careful. I enjoyed going along with you two very much. *Señor*, I never laughed so much in all my life. She is a good woman for you."

He nodded and agreed with him. They set out in a long trot through the pines.

The sun was setting in the west when they came off the rim. He slowed their descent down so they didn't end up off the steep sides. It was close to midnight by his clock when they reached the ranch. Dogs barking caused some lights to come on. A youth came and took the horses.

"Is Victor all right?" the young man asked.

"Yes, he will be here in the morning. He's fine," he told the horse handler.

"Is that the honeymooners?" Susie asked from the porch.

"Yes, don't shoot."

Susie was already hugging her sister-in-law on the steps.

"Is JD here?" he asked.

"He's fine."

"Is she here?"

"No." Susie led them inside the house. "Let's go in the kitchen and I can explain it all."

She stoked up the stove to reheat some coffee. "It all happened fast after you left and I had no way to send you word. Kay and the children came here. Of course I knew they might come and we unloaded them. JD had gone to the rim and I sent word for him to come back. Tom and the crew were ready to meet her husband if he came for her.

"There was no sign of him, and last Tuesday, JD was going to drive her into Preskit to see a lawyer. I told Tom to send two ranch hands with them. Her husband has a bad reputation for getting mad and I felt they needed to be careful. Hampt and Billy Joe went along. They were men could handle guns if it came to a fight."

Chet agreed and shared a nod with Marge sitting beside him.

"They said they met Floyd Kent on the road in Preskit Valley. Somewhere near Marge's ranch. He'd been drinking and tried to draw his rifle out, cussing all of them. Hampt rode in and jerked it out of his hands and then slapped him over the head with his pistol barrel to shut up his cussing. Kent fell off his horse and the three men carried him off the road. He was unconscious but alive. To be certain he didn't try anything again, Hampt kept the rifle.

"When they got to town they went to the sheriff's office and gave him Kent's rifle and the details. Sims sent a man out there to see about him and they took possession of Kent's rifle. JD and her went to see the lawyer to get the divorce proceedings started. About an hour or so later, the deputy returned and he had found her husband had shot himself when he came to. So she was a free woman."

"JD is helping her at her place?"

"Yes, and Tom went up and checked on the mill crew. They're fine. He made one of them foreman to take JD's place up there for now."

"Good. I talked to Robert yesterday."

He told his sister about the ranch project and she agreed they still might need it.

"Let's go to bed, Marge. We can go see them tomorrow. I need to find Bo, my land agent, also."

"Thanks for getting us up to date," Marge said. "We had a very special, wonderful honeymoon."

Susie shook her head in dismay. "You two are so crazy in love anything would be nice."

Started up the stairs, he shook his head. "We'll see what you do some day."

"Only maybe. Good night."

Marge had ahold of his arm and squeezed it with a smile. They went on upstairs to his room.

Come daylight, he was at Hoot's cowboy chuck, taking his share of ribbing. Eating flapjacks, fried side meat, and some raisin pudding, he knew his men weren't mistreated.

Tom soon joined him and slid in on the bench with a coffee cup in his hand. "You see much country?"

"We did. I think I found a ranch northeast of Hackberry as well. I'm going to check it out further. Has some good water and a great place to set up. Lots of grass as well."

"How big is it?"

"Oh, six sections laid out railroad style from east to west. No improvements even started."

"I've seen that country before. It gets cold up there."

"We'll need hay up there too. I've seen some ground to raise it on."

"You heard about JD and Kay?"

"Susie told me her husband shot himself."

"Sad deal, but he never was a happy man."

Chet agreed. "What about the Hartley bunch?"

"Gates held a meeting last week and they say there is no thousand head of cattle between here and Tombstone. Folks have checked. Those cattle about had to come out of Texas. There is some beef coming from there for the markets in Tombstone and the Indian reservations. So it might all be a bluff. Lots of word that they may be in trouble with their bankers." Tom turned his palms up. "I sent some of the guys to town and to Mayer. Their hands complain, they only pay them in long intervals like three months apart. Not a one knew anything about a thousand head coming. They did say Loftin is holding a grudge against you for turning him back."

"He can hold it long as he wants. I'm not afraid of him."

Tom smiled. "I didn't figure you'd lose any sleep over it. I about have a complete count of our mother cows. We need a contract to sell about a hundred and fifty old ones. The Indian agents will buy them. Ryan never culled any of them, but we need to get something out of them instead of letting them die of old age out on the range. Besides they eat our grass and most won't have another calf or else they'd do a poor job of raising it."

"He never saved many heifers either."

"Not if he could find a buyer." Tom swallowed some of his coffee.

Chet shook his head over the man's foolishness. "We also need to move the outside cattle off our ranges."

"I planned to start in September doing that if that suits you?"

"Fine, we will need to assemble a larger remuda to be ready."

"Yes, it will take forty or fifty more horses. Do you like that high country?"

"Oh, yes. Plenty of grass up there and we can develop water in enough places to make it a sweet ranch. I like it a lot. Have you heard of any more cows to replace those we need to cull?"

"No."

"I may need to go over in New Mexico and see what I can find."

Tom agreed.

There was still lots to do. But he had a good man in place to straighten out the Verde ranch.

He took his bride to her house and agreed he could move up there easier than she could move to the Verde ranch. After leaving her at the house, he drove into Preskit and went looking for Bo Evans, his agent. He wasn't hard to find. The morning Palace bartender sent him to a shack up in a canyon east of town.

At the front door of the about fallen-in raw shack, he reined up the team. He tied the reins off and some woman in a wash-worn dress too tight for her soggy figure and an unkempt mop of brown hair appeared looking blank.

"Tell Bo to get up. I've got a job for him."

"Who? Who are you?" she asked as he swept past her and went inside the dim light of the ransacked looking room. He saw his man in his gray underwear sitting on the edge of the exposed mattress holding his face in his hands.

"Time to sober up. I need you. You've been lolling around here long enough. Get some clothes on. You're going to town, take a bath, a shave, and a haircut, then get your ass to work. Come on, get dressed."

"What the hell do you want, Chet Byrnes?"

"If I have to tie you to a post, I'm sobering you up. Now move."

"Aw. Leave me alone." He waved at Chet like he was a pesky fly.

"I can take you in your underwear. Get dressed."

"Oh, God, Byrnes, leave me here."

"No way, get dressed."

The woman, if he could call her that, was backed up to a dry sink drinking cheap wine out of an open bottle. "You leaving me, Bo?"

"Ask him," he said, pulling on his pants. "You're crazy, Chet Byrnes, you know that."

"If you don't have sense enough to get sober and back to doing business where you belong I'm going to treat you like a dumb kid. Get your boots on."

"Aw, Bo, don't go. You belong with me, baby."

"Lady, he's got more to do than you." Chet slapped a hat from the wall onto Bo's head and shoved him toward the door. This might take more than a simple chewing out, but he wasn't accepting letting Bo destroy himself.

With Bo on the spring seat beside him and the sour stench of his body odors in his nose, Chet turned the buckboard around and headed back for town. He caught him twice by the collar before he pitched off the seat.

"Sober up, damnit."

After a bath, shave, and haircut, Chet came back from shopping with some new fresh clothing. He took Bo in his new suit to Jenny's and in mid-afternoon the café was near empty.

"I want to hire two men tough enough to keep him sober and keep his nose to working for me."

Jenny blinked at him then looked critically at Bo. "That's a tall order."

"I'll rent two rooms in a boardinghouse. Provide room and board to those two men and pay them two dollars a day to keep him sober and at work."

Jenny's lips creased in a smile. "I have two unemployed customers need that work. When do they start?"

"In an hour. I have a ranch to run."

She waved a youth over who was sweeping the

café floor. "Homer, go find Davis Green and Bud Carter, tell them I have them a real job. For them to get over here at once."

"Where are they?"

"Probably at the grain mill—they've been stacking ground sacks of grain. This is a real job." She sent him off.

"Take a seat, we'll eat lunch," he said to Bo.

"Thank God. I need—need a drink."

Chet could see he was shaking all over like a leaf. "You have something like a shot of whiskey?" he asked her.

She rushed off to the kitchen and came back with some brown liquor in a glass. Bo downed it with both quaking hands. He gave her back the glass and quietly thanked her.

After they ate a plate, the boy and two burley men arrived covered in cornmeal dust and anxious to hear about the new job. Jenny herded them over to the table where Bo and Chet sat.

"Sit down. That's Chet Byrnes and his problem Bo Evans beside him. Tell them the details," she said with her arms folded over her ample chest.

"This man is a drunk. I don't want him to drink a thing. I want him to work on the job I have for him to buy me a ranch. I want him to operate an office every day to sell real estate. He is not to drink or party with any ladies of the night. He is to have severe curfew hours and I expect one of you to go everywhere he goes. You two can share a boarding room, next to him. Tie him up if necessary.

"I'll get him an account at Marconi's store if he needs more clothing. But I am paying you two so one of you is with him around the clock."

"Ah, Chet—"

"You heard me. These guys will tie you up if necessary. You are going to dry out and I mean it."

"For how long?" Bo moaned.

"I am going to pay them for three months and if you aren't dry by then it goes on."

He handed him a piece of paper with "Boxley Austin, St. Louis, Missouri" on it. "Find him, and it's the six sections of land he owns near Hackberry, Arizona Territory."

"If I get that bought for you is my sentence over?"

"No. You will be a sober land agent when we get through with you."

Bo slapped his forehead with his palm. "I'll die doing this."

"Get busy. It will be over before you know it."

He shook both men's hands. They were big callused-hand galoots. They'd sober him up. "Need more help, holler. Jenny can get me word."

The bigger man, Green, shook his head. "No worries, Mr. Byrnes, we can handle this situation— and thanks for the job."

"Wait, wait," Bo said in a worried tone. "I'll do all you say. Don't leave me here with these gorillas. Chet . . ."

He shook his head. "You do as they say and you will be out of their care in no time."

Then he waved to everyone and kissed Jenny good-bye on the cheek.

He arrived back at Marge's house. Chet stepped off the buckboard by the saddle shed. Jesus made him stop taking the harness off the horses. "That is my job, *señor.*"

Chet looked hard at the youth. "You telling me that you want me to hitch my horse at the rack, too?"

"I will hurry and unsaddle him. If you wish to ride on, hitch him out front and I will ask for your wishes, *señor.*"

He paused holding his elbow and squeezed his chin. Then he nodded, "I've got it now. Thanks, Jesus."

"Same to you, *señor.*"

He was already on the run to ambush his wife and peddled backwards to tell the youth, "Thanks, you do good work."

"Well?" She flew in his arms. "What did you learn today?"

"I have two men hired to keep Bo sober. We will be learning about this man in Saint Louis shortly."

Wrapped tight in his arms, she closed one eye and used the right one to examine his face. "You did what?"

"Bo was living with some drunken slut in a shack. I removed him and hired two tough men to sober him up and keep him that way so we can make the land deal."

She laughed and shook her head, still in disbelief. He kissed her, still amazed how tall she was and how easy it was to kiss her.

"He's too damn good a man to hide in a bottle. It will work, trust me."

"Chet Byrnes, I always trust you to do the right thing. But sober a man up for him to do business for you is another side to you I can hardly imagine."

"All I can say is he's worth it, darling."

"My father is gone to Hayden's Mill. Some deal he is looking at—so supper is the two of us."

"I don't mind. I'm going to the ranch tomorrow. Then the next day we can drive out and see if my nephew JD needs anything."

"Good. I'll visit with Kay while you two talk."

They went to the house as arm-locked lovers. Monica greeted him. "Good to have you back. She walks the floor when you're gone."

"Maybe you could show her how to crochet."

Marge looked at the ceiling for help. "I don't need that. But I may go to the ranch tomorrow with you. I suppose you want to get up at four a.m.?"

"It's a good ride down there and I'd like to be there before the men ride out."

"Yes, slave master."

"Hey—"

She pressed a finger to his mouth. "I was teasing. I know how spread out you are these days."

"Does this place need me to do something?"

"No, it's fine."

He seated her at the supper table. There were things about their camping out he'd really liked—maybe the sitting around the campfire with her so casual. You had to trade some things to have a wife as great as her. In the morning, they'd go in the dark to the ranch. Be good to have her company.

Monica served a tasty beef roast with mashed potatoes, fresh green beans, homemade fresh bread, and cow butter. Her coffee was just right, along with delicious blackberry cobbler under whipped cream. He'd damn sure get fat eating at her table. Maybe he could work it off. Wonderful food. He bragged on her and she smiled.

"Breakfast at four a.m.?"

"He says so."

"I will have the oatmeal cooked." Then she laughed and left the dining room.

The next morning in the cool air, the two arrived at the ranch while the men were saddling up to ride out. Marge went to the house to see Susie and May. He headed to get a cup of Hoot's coffee. The place smelled of fresh cut pine and the frameworks of the bunkhouse and the cook shack were in the sky.

"Wow, you musta got up at midnight to get here." The gray whiskered older man poured him a steaming cup. "Did yah see the Grand Canyon on your honeymoon?"

Chet nodded. "Hell of a big hole, ain't it."

"They got another over on the Rio Salado in the 'pache country. I was packing mules for Crook once and saw it. What a damn hole it is. How's married life?"

He blew on his steaming coffee and nodded. "I'm doing fine, Hoot. How is the ranch?"

"Tom's got her running good. He's been driving in lots of those shelly cows he told you about. Looks like it'll rain somewhere today. I figure the monsoons are about to start."

"I saw a few clouds. We can damn sure use it." The coffee was cool enough to sip and not burn his tongue.

Tom joined him. "I got a price of ten cents on the cows we need to sell at this agency and Fort McDowell."

"Sounds good. Better than them dying out on the range eventually."

"Some won't make the drive to McDowell."

"Give them to these Indians here for free. May make us some friends. Those people were starving last year and I got the military to intercede for them in Washington."

"I recall us doing all that. This new agent is a preacher. He's more concerned about those people. They don't complain either so they must be getting better supplied."

"Any word on the Hartley brothers?"

"No. But we're listening. I don't know where they'd buy that many cows let alone drive them in here."

"They didn't send that crew over here for no good reason."

"Maybe they were testing our strength?"

"They went to a helluva lot of trouble to do that. All they had to do was ask me."

"I think our new bulls are spreading out. I feel certain we have all the longhorn ones neutered. Next year's calves will be lots better."

"This ranch should be using second generation British cross cows. Ryan was an idiot. All he knew how to do was steal."

"Someone said there was large herd of pure Herefords coming from New Mexico this direction. Straight Hereford cattle. You remember ever meeting the mailman that came from Gallup in a buckboard that used your route?"

"Yes, only vaguely."

"He said they had lots of cattle coming slow."

"Are they the Hartleys'?"

"No, they're some ranch moving out here from all I can hear. He ain't hurrying them none. Must be graze up there."

"There is lots of grass, but we had to haul water to make it over here."

"No way to do that." Tom shook his head.

"I better ride up there and see what I can learn."

"Want me to send someone?" Tom asked.

"No, I'll go. I heard that a man named John Chisum over in New Mexico has cows for sale."

"You know him?"

Chet about chuckled. "JD and I met one of his

enforcers. Billy the Kid they called him in Texas. He wanted to work for me. Said he knew the way."

"I've heard of him."

"He's a buck-toothed kid, but I think he's deadly with a gun. Had some teenage *puta* hanging on him most of the time."

"I know the kind. What are you going to do today?"

"Probably make arrangements to go meet that herd. Can you spare Victor?"

"Sure, do you want the same outfit you two took to Hackberry?"

"Yes. Hook it up and send him to her place this afternoon. We can get supplies tomorrow in Preskit and be on our way the next day. Keep culling cows, we can find some more. Do you have most of the mavericks caught up?"

"Yes. We all knew Ryan wasn't doing much ranch work. But we found over a hundred cows and calves not branded in the past year."

"We knew it would be work. Thanks, Tom. I'll go check on the girls and tell Victor to bring his guitar."

The two shook hands.

He found Marge, Susie, May, and Millie all talking a hundred miles an hour at the table. "Well, do you all have the world in shape?"

"Not yet, Marge told us about you sobering up your land agent."

"I have that in hand. Susie, do you recall a mail

carrier who brought the mail from Gallup to Preskit? In a buckboard, I guess."

"Yes, he was a big hunk of a guy. We talked to him several times when he stopped at our camp."

"His name is Guy Nelson. You ever heard his story?" Marge asked.

"No, fill us in."

"This Nelson came along one year when the mail was getting waylaid time after time by outlaws, and the letters opened to find money and then scattered by those bandits. He told them he wanted to try and get it through. It was getting up toward Christmastime. Folks were upset, too. He took over and there were no more robberies. Folks said he left them to lie and die by the road if they tried to hold him up. When that got around the holdups ceased. The Christmas mail came through and everyone heralded him as the hero of the holidays. The service still works perfect."

"We talked to him about taking the cutoff. I recall that," Susie said.

"He told someone here, there was a large herd of Hereford cows coming out of Kansas, slow like. The owners want to set up a ranch in Arizona according to what they say. I'd try to buy some good cows from them if they would sell."

"What are the plans?" Marge asked.

"Victor's coming to our house this evening. We can get supplies tomorrow and the next day we ride east if you want to go along."

"My dear husband, you couldn't tie me down and leave me," Marge said.

Everyone laughed.

"I'll go check on JD tomorrow then, and let you all know anything I can find out, if things have changed."

"Good," Susie said. "Guess you two will miss the dance this week then?"

"This week, but save us some dances."

His wife laughed. "You all have fun. We are going traipsing again. And I like it, too."

They rode back with her listing what they'd need for supplies.

"I've never been over there," she said. "I'd like to see the country."

"We will see it and probably lots more. I love camping with you, and Victor makes a great hand."

She took off her hat and shook loose her curls. "Chet Byrnes, I like going anywhere with you."

He rode in close and hugged her. "That makes two of us."

"Good. I knew I'd enjoy your whirlwind ways if I ever got on your boat."

"Well good. I know I do things quick, but I don't regret leaving Texas one minute." He gazed off in the south at the gathering thunderheads. "We better ride for the house. That rain's coming."

Thunder rolled in the distance and they ran for the driveway, then the house. They were wet before they made it. Finally they were standing kissing on the porch as the flood of water came off the eaves and the drum of each strike rolled across Preskit Valley. The dark wall was sweeping down on them. The monsoons had started like Hoot promised him earlier. Every afternoon there would be chance of a rain starting to fall. Some would not settle the dust. Others would flood the dry washes.

"Maybe we should go hide upstairs."

"Great idea," he said. "You think of the best things to do."

Shaking her head in amusement, she led him inside the house. He took a last deep breath of the rain—he loved it.

CHAPTER 13

In town the next morning he found his land agent, Bo, a little haggard, in his office with his guard Bud Carter reading the newspaper close by.

"I have sent off several telegrams to Saint Louis to locate this man Boxley. It will take several days to receive an answer, I am certain. Now can I go on living my own life?"

"Keep busy working." Then he turned to his man. "You are doing a great job. Thanks."

Carter gave him a sure nod.

He left the pleading Bo and went across to the Palace Saloon. In the darker interior, his eyes adjusted and he smiled as Jane came across the large room with a tray under her arm. "Bo is sobering up under guard. He is not drinking."

She smiled, smug like. "Good, I'll take him some straight lemonade one day."

"You might do that. How are things going? Any talk about a herd of cattle coming?"

"No. But I can get you word if I learn anything."

He handed her a ten dollar gold piece. "I appreciate any news I need."

"Certainly. You think this plan of yours will work on his hard head?"

"He's worth saving."

"Thank you, Chet."

He left her and met Marge at the mercantile three blocks over. She and a stout boy doing the hauling about had the buckboard loaded with their needed supplies. He helped her on the seat, tipped the boy a dime, and joined her. He swung the team around and they headed for Kay's place west of town.

JD was off checking on cattle and they found Kay cooking a large roast in her wood burning kitchen range.

"I can slice some off for us to eat," she said, hugging her friend Marge.

"We can eat," he told her.

The two women laughed at him.

"Where are your children?" Marge asked.

"My parents took them for a week. They knew I was under lots of strain after the funeral and all."

Kay soon had the roast out, cut some slabs off it, and returned it to the oven. She sliced some fresh white bread and made coffee for them. The meat was tasty and they decided they better head for home after lunch.

"If JD needs anything, send word. Tom is at the ranch and has men that can help him," Chet said.

"I'm certain we will be fine," she said. "But Marge said that you two won't be at the dance this weekend?"

Marge shook her head. "We're off on another camping trip—to buy cows this time."

Kay frowned.

"Don't worry about me. We have lots of fun and I enjoy them."

"You always were the horsey one of us girls." She wrinkled her nose.

"Thanks for lunch." Chet said.

They drove off and headed back for her place.

"What do you think?" he asked.

"I think she's happy. She should be, he no doubt is paying her some attention."

"If he does any at all, she's better off," he said.

"Oh, I can tell she's a lot more settled."

"Will she marry him?"

Marge nodded. "There is no long line of suitors is there."

"Pardon me. I thought you had one."

"If I did I ignored him when I met you on the stagecoach."

He clucked at the team to make them step out. "We did ride up here together. I'd almost forgotten that—I remember you best though in my darkest hours. You driving clear down there to save me with the boy's body."

She agreed and kissed his cheek.

* * *

They left her place in the morning. Victor acted so pleased to be along he played his guitar part of the way off Mingus Mountain. By evening they reached the small lake northeast of the Verde Valley. Chet took some catgut line and a hook with a fat earthworm and used a willow switch pole to fish. On the first cast he caught a fat cutthroat trout, and then as the sun set, caught his twin. Gutted, cleaned, and rolled in cornmeal, Marge fried them crisp and that was their supper in the dark night full of crickets and a blazing campfire.

They never set up a tent that night so they could take off quicker the next day. In the predawn they left northeast on the road across the rolling high plains grassland. The third day they stopped in the camp of Colonel John McKay. The colonel was a rather dignified man who wore a suit. His wife Pauline, at least twenty years his junior, reminded him of some socialites he'd met at a fancy party in San Antonio.

After introductions, the colonel showed them to some folding canvas chairs under a canvas shade that popped some in the strong wind.

"My main purpose for this visit, sir, was to see if you'd sell me some of your Hereford cows."

"You need to buy some cows?"

"I'd like to, sir. Have you considered selling any of them?"

"They may be way too high-priced for you to buy any."

"You let me worry about that," Chet said. "What will you sell me?"

"I'd cut three to four years old out for you at a hundred dollars a head."

Chet did some quick math. The culls Tom was selling would bring half of that. He nodded as if in deep thought. "I'd consider them at ninety dollars a head."

Marge never said a word. The Colonel's lady sat still. The wind popped the canvas overhead.

"I could do that, sir."

Chet stuck out his hand. "You've got a deal."

The Colonel shook it. "Where will we cut them out?"

"There's a lake about thirty miles southwest of here. I don't want it ruined by this many cattle but a stream flows out of it. We can water them in smaller bunches on that creek. I'll send Victor home in the morning to get my foreman and several hands to accept the cattle."

"We'll have to do it careful. There are several small calves among them. That's why we have been so slow coming across—to save as many as we could."

Chet nodded. "I have a water wagon I can have them bring if you'd like to use it to sort out the pairs."

"That might be an idea. I'll speak to my foreman about it. Would you care for a drink?"

He shook his head. "My wife might want a glass of wine."

Pauline rose and asked her what she might want.

Marge answered her and together they went for it.

"Bring me some scotch and water and my guest some water as well," he said after them and his wife nodded.

"Victor will leave before dawn and bring the men back but the tank wagon will come slower. If you want it."

"I'll use it. Thanks. Where is your operation?"

"West up the Verde River from Camp Verde."

"How long have you had it?"

"About a year ago. I moved my family a few months ago here from the hill country of Texas."

"Like this better than Texas?"

"I had to move. We were in the midst of a bad feud. They murdered my brother and it was too bloody to stay."

The colonel nodded. "Tough deals, no one wins in those situations. How did you find this ranch?"

"The man who owned it was afraid of his foreman, who was robbing him blind. I ran him down before I was through and he's in Yuma Prison with some of his help."

"We have a place down on the Mogollon Rim south of here."

Chet nodded. "I guess you have seen it."

"No, but it was examined by some friends of mine. So it will all be a surprise. I am shocked at the lack of water in this country. That is why I sold you those cows. To have enough water for my herd after this journey worries me. There is lots of grass, but you need water, too."

"You really do. Have you ever seen the desert in the south part of the territory?"

"No, but I have seen some drawings of it. Rather spiny place, huh?"

Seated in the chair, Chet studied the clouds building in the south. It was raining on someone down there. He'd closed a good deal that would build his ranch. Things were going well.

The next day the Colonel moved his camp to the lake and whipped out his fly rod. In no time he was completely shocked at the great fishing.

He told Chet that officers he knew told him that the fishing in Arizona was wonderful. He never had believed them. Marge told him it was because the Apaches didn't eat fish; they were practically untouched.

The Colonel laughed. "I bet you are right."

In two days, Tom arrived with a crew and some supplies. He and Chet rode quietly through the grazing Herefords.

"How many of these cows did you get?" Tom asked under his breath.

"A hundred. Young ones."

"They are gorgeous. What did they cost?"

"Ninety bucks apiece. High, but we got forty or so for the culls, didn't we?"

Tom quickly agreed. "Would he sell more?"

"I don't think so."

"You made a helluva deal."

"We'll need to cut them out and separate them

and then drive them home slow. Many have calves. The man's foreman—Jarvis is his name—has done a hell of a job nursemaiding them to get that many calves to here. At this rate in a few years we'll be all Hereford cows."

Tom nodded. "I won't miss those wild longhorns either."

"Memories is all we'll have." Chet squeezed his saddle horn. Things had been happening fast. It was going to rain again somewhere that afternoon. They'd better get back to camp.

CHAPTER 14

The cattle movement operation took some time. Hampt took charge and Tom hired him four local boys to go along with three ranch hands. They moved them slowly and Victor fed the men with his packhorse outfit.

Chet and Marge went home with everything in good hands. The next morning, cleaned up and shaved, he drove her into town. They stopped at Bo's office first. Bo rose from behind the desk looking fresh and rested. Bud Carter, in the chair, put down the *Miner* newspaper and nodded at him. "He ain't had a drink since we got him."

"Good. What news do you have?" he asked Bo.

"Mr. Boxley wants a million dollars for that place by his telegram." He handed Chet the two telegrams. He carefully read the first one. It was long and listed all his expenses including the five dollars an acre he paid the railroad for the original land. A survey cost of three thousand dollars and his various other costs like the government charged him a dollar per acre fee in the exchange.

The second telegram asked what they would offer for the property.

"Send him a telegram we'd pay twelve thousand dollars for a clear title and he has two weeks to respond."

"Why not offer him ten?" Bo asked. "He has no one else wants it. Saves you to pay me for all this business."

"Try it."

"I already have. I knew you'd say that."

Chet said to Carter, "See how good a businessman he is sober?"

"Yeah, he's real good at this business."

Bo reached in the drawer. "Here is his reply to my request."

Chet held the yellow paper up to the light coming in the front window. SOLD. "Send the necessary details to my office."

"Have you sent them?"

"Why, of course."

"Good. Now I want you to find me some land around this railroad's headquarters up there on the rim at the junction of the military road and the stage line one. That will be prime land someday."

He went out the door and waved to Marge seated on the spring seat. Her eyes flew open and as she came to the edge of the buckboard he caught her and kissed her. "Bo bought the land for a song. We've got another ranch, Mrs. Byrnes."

In his arms, they kissed like mad and he whirled

her around pressed hard to him. Folks on the street turned to see what was so wonderful. Chet had bought ranch number two on the rim. They had lots to celebrate about.

"Am I a free man now?" Bo asked, hanging out of his door.

"Not yet. But you're doing better. Get busy on the next deal."

He hustled her onto the seat. "Marge, we better get home. Tonight's the dance and we have lots to cheer over." On the seat, he pointed at the disappointed looking Bo in the doorway. "Make some more deals work. I'm not the only buyer in this territory."

"Can I have one drink?"

"No. You'd fall in that bucket and drown." He turned the buckboard around in the street and drove off with Bo waving and shouting after him.

That evening at the dance, he had lots of questions to answer. How did he get the Colonel to sell him the white face cattle? Had he heard any more about the Hartleys?

Was his nephew going to marry Kay? But from the small crowd shooting him questions he saw Susie in the rancher's arms dancing and he never saw her more serious with a man in his life. Good for her.

JD and Kay danced by real serious looking, too. He felt some concern about those two as well. He could not imagine his Aunt Louise not having a fit about it already. But he felt spared she hadn't given him an ultimatum about that business. Later,

Marge pointed out Louise and Harold Parker, a rancher from south of Preskit.

"Is that serious?" he asked.

"You haven't been watching them?"

"No, but he's nice looking and looks successful."

"Widower. He lost his wife a few years ago."

"Good. Maybe she's so busy with him, she ain't worried about JD?"

"She's busy." Marge smiled.

They spent the night at the Verde ranch house. At breakfast the next morning, Jesus brought Chet a telegram.

"It came for you last night, *señor*. Monica said it might be important."

"Thanks." He sat down and opened the envelope. It was from Reg. His stomach turned over as he read the contents—*more of the Reynolds war. God he hoped not.*

> *Juanita was killed in a buckboard wreck yesterday. The team ran away on her. Her funeral is today. I cannot stay here. I am coming west this week.*
>
> *Your nephew Reg.*

"What does it say?" Susie asked.

He nodded and spoke slowly. "Juanita was killed when her team ran off. Her funeral was yesterday back there. Reg can't stay there and is coming to join us."

"Oh, my God," Louise said. "That boy loved her

so much—" Holding a napkin to her face, she ran upstairs.

Wet eyes around the table, Chet nodded to his wife. "Louise told the truth. That boy really loved his wife. I am certain he is crushed about losing her. He can mend his heart with us."

"We've got plenty for him to do if he wants to be busy," Susie said, wiping her wet lashes.

May left the table crying. She was always the tenderhearted one and had taken all of the ranch family losses the hardest.

He and Marge went home in silence, most of the way. Pulling the hard grade, she said, "Will he work the new ranch, do you think?"

"Hard to say. But he might. Depends how broken up he is. That boy loved her and we knew her too. She helped Susie for over a year so we all knew her, and she was a kind, grateful person. She was a gorgeous woman."

"Susie showed me their wedding picture. She looked like royalty."

"Yes, she did."

She clapped a hand on his leg. "Hey, this is still our honeymoon isn't it?"

"I'm glad you reminded me. We get to the house we can celebrate."

At his words, she gazed up at her hat brim looking for help. Finally she shook her head at him then he twisted around to kiss her.

Pleased, he turned about halfway back around and looked back over the entire valley to the far high rim. Reg was coming to join them—good.

CHAPTER 15

Half asleep in bed, he heard Monica talking to someone from the front porch underneath their open bedroom window. She said she'd get him up. He could see the line of posse members through the lacy curtains. Familiar ranchers and cowboys sat on horseback in the early morning in his front yard.

"I'm coming, Monica," he said from the window, and finished putting on his pants. "What's wrong?"

One of the men responded. "Someone murdered John Artman and his wife Cindy and robbed them last night. His brother found them early this morning and we've been gathering help ever since."

"I'm dressing, boys, to join you." He buttoned his shirt while talking to them and hanging out the window.

"We're getting an Injun tracker to meet us at his place."

"It's down on the Verde over east of here," someone else added.

"I'll have Marge send a supply outfit behind us. We may be a few days since they got a head start."

The heads nodded and someone said, "We never thought of that."

"I can send Jesus," she said in a low voice. "He'll find you."

"Essentials only." He strapped on his gun belt. By this time the boy had heard part of the conversation and would have a horse saddled for him. Chet hurried downstairs and picked out a Winchester from the gun rack and a box of ammo. She caught up with him there in her fluffy housecoat. They kissed and she gave him a few sharp words. "You be careful."

"I will." He rushed out the front door and Jesus had the big gray saddled and ready. The big horse walked on his toes and pranced around him. He slid the rifle in the scabbard and thanked Jesus, taking the reins, then flew in the saddle hoping to catch Ono up enough to control him. But the horse lived up to his reputation, bucked through the parted posse and got lots of shouts.

Once the horse was under control, Chet rode back to Monica who had a big sandwich made for him. He told the other men to go on, he'd catch up. The gray really worried when the others left.

"You and Monica pack some supplies and then you follow us," he told Jesus. "Thanks love," he said to the cook, and then charged off to catch the others.

When he caught up with them all in a trot, he asked Gates, "Any suspects?"

Gates shook his head. "Artman was a loner but I suspect he had some cash."

"Sheriff Sims know about this posse?"

"I think folks ain't too satisfied with his efforts of late. There was a ranch wife raped in her own bed. He never did anything. Said she didn't give him enough description for him to find her attacker. It's kind of a sore point. Two men robbed an old man north of town. He said they likely were drifters and already out of the country."

"I got my ass chewed out that time before over those horse rustlers."

"Yeah, we all know the truth about that."

"Is someone going tell him?"

"Oh yeah, and he'll send someone out today."

Chet nodded. He knew the answer to the rest of the deal.

He looked back. It would take Jesus a few hours to catch up. But by nightfall if they hadn't found the killers they'd at least have something to fill their empty guts with.

At the Artman ranch, he met the man's brother, Nathan, a thin, hard-faced man at least in his fifties who looked like he had some Cherokee blood in his veins.

He raised the blanket from his brother. The man's throat had been cut open from ear to ear. Dried black blood was around the void and Chet had seen enough. His shorter wife had some stab wounds on her dried-up breasts and was equally dead. No one in the house said much, and they moved quickly to get outside in the fresh air.

Chet stopped the brother. "Did he have much money to steal?"

"He had three thousand dollars."

That was lots more than most such small ranchers ever saw in a lifetime, but he had no reason to doubt the man. They waited on the Indian tracker. After checking around, Chet could see by the tracks that when they left, one of the three riders was riding a mule.

"Leave a couple men here to bring them on after us. I can read these tracks. Let's ride."

"Good thing you came along," Gates said as they set out going downhill to the river far below. The river might be the place where they tried to hide their direction, but most criminal minds were simply set on escaping. No telling who they were dealing with in this double murder-robbery.

They reached the river and he bailed the gray off in the swift water to swim some crossing and he soon found the marks where they had come out. No backtracking or taking to the water.

He stood in the stirrups and directed them. "Come across at that lower ford. Looks easier down there." He waved the seven men with him to go to an easier place. Off his mount, he let his horse catch a drink from the stream.

"Tracks over here?" Gate asked, riding up and dismounting.

"Clear as daylight. Anyone know three men and the third one rides a mule?"

"I don't think they do. But it could be anyone. Maybe drifters coming through."

"No, I think it is someone who knew them," Chet said. "No one would have simply guessed they had that much money, living like they did. That place up there was a shack. They hadn't bought any new clothes in years. Those people lived like poor ones. Someone pointed them out or they learned something about them to find that money his brother said that they had."

"You ever been a lawman?" Gates asked.

"No, but I am learning."

"I'd say you'd make a good one."

"Tell me where I'm going to next, in that direction."

"That's pretty wild country beyond here. They either know their way around or they're off on a lark."

"Are there any ranches up in there?"

"I don't know anyone ranches up in those hills." Gates turned and asked the others. "Anyone know much about that country where they are headed?"

They shook their heads. One guy said, "There's a road up there somewhere that goes to Fort Apache."

"That's a long way over east," a young man offered.

"Good enough, there aren't many tracks in here. But the killers went this way. Anyone figured out who they are by the fact the third man rides a mule?"

"Several folks ride a mule," a young man said. "My dad rides one a lot in the rough country."

Chet nodded. "Let's go on."

They mounted up and started through some rough mountain country. This was no well-used track, and even the killers had to double back and try another game trail. He had expected the tracker to catch them by late afternoon and he wondered about Jesus and their supplies.

At last they reached the pines and the shelf they were on spread out in the timber. Chet had the tracks to follow, but wondered if he had outrun his supply train. It would be dark in an hour. He halted the men.

"We have an hour left of daylight. Our supply train is behind us. I doubt that tracker ever came. Let's set down and stop here. They're still making tracks."

The men agreed and gathered bonfire material.

"Are we close to them?" one of the men asked.

"I'm not enough bloodhound to know. They came this way headed somewhere. I don't know if those last horse apples we went by were steaming hot. They were fresh."

Everyone laughed. In thirty minutes, one of the men keeping an eye on the trail told him some horses were coming. He went over there on the edge and behind the lead man he saw Jesus's straw hat. Good. His supplies were coming.

"Food may not be great, but we'll eat, men."

"Good thing you went on, Byrnes. They said you were a bloodhound."

"We have tracks to here. I'd say they were going someplace. We should catch them tomorrow."

"Good. Anyone of us need to track them more tonight?"

"I don't want to spook them. We'll build small fires tonight and then push hard to catch them tomorrow."

"My name's Leif Times. My dad and I run the Rafter Eight ranch."

"Times, I hope we can get them tomorrow. The farther they go the harder the job will be. We have no witness to those murders. All we have is this set of tracks."

"You're saying they might get arrested and then get off?"

"I'm saying, those tracks are our only lead to the ones responsible for the deaths of those people."

Times nodded.

"You figure that out at Rye when you got there?"

Chet shook his head.

"They raped a poor woman without any regrets. They beat up a man before his children and they stole those horses. Why bother with messing with them? They had no regrets."

"They say Sims threatened you about that."

Chet shook his head. "I was near as mad over the way he sent a deskman leading that posse who stopped Marge Stephenson's foreman from coming to help me. I had expected him to send a real deputy. He has a man named Roamer who would have come on after them. Sims didn't like I ran down that crooked foreman and his henchmen that stole from the Quarter Circle Z or how I treated the stage robbers who murdered my nephew either."

"I had no idea."

"Keep it to yourself, but however this ends it will make him mad. He thinks he's the only law and he can't handle it all."

Times nodded. "Thanks."

Chet drank some coffee, had some beef jerky, and thanked Jesus for coming.

"*Señor*, your wife almost came with me to help."

"Good that she didn't. This is damn tough country."

"She is a powerful woman."

"I agree. Sleep tight. We'll have a long day to-morrow." All he needed was to have to worry about her safety being along with them. But she'd been on his mind ever since he rode off again on her. She might—no, she was realist and knew he had to answer such calls. But being separated from her had affected him more that he'd admit. He shifted his gun belt out of habit. Then he went to find a place to sleep. Dawn wasn't far off.

The posse moved out in the first pink of dawn. His eyes dry, he knew they needed to find some water for their mounts. Not a man in the half dozen men riding with him knew of any water source in this region. They were soon on an east–west road. The tracks went east.

Times rode up and told him, "This road eventually goes to Fort Apache."

"Are there any towns or settlements on this road?"

"I've never been very far on it. We elk hunted on it a few years back."

"You get this far east on it?"

"If I see anything familiar I'll tell you."

Chet smiled and thanked him.

They rounded a bend and he saw some horses beside the road and some campfire smoke. He sent every one backward and told them to be quiet.

"You see anyone?" one of the men asked him.

He shook his head. "I want three men on foot with their rifles to go up in the timber and circle them. If they flush, stop them. We will wait here to give you a chance to head them off. Be quiet and stay wide of them."

"We were lucky you saw them," Gates told him.

"I felt we'd find them sometime this morning," he said under his breath.

Three of the posse members with rifles took off into the timber and he waved them on. The whole lot were a good willing bunch ready to get the job done. If they'd been storekeepers they'd have already wanted to go back. These men with him lived in their saddles.

He hoped the three men hurried. No telling if

the ones camped ahead would be ready to pull out any minute.

The men were all dismounted. He listened and could hear men talking and banging pans. They were close, perhaps, to arresting the murderers. It could be innocent people. But he doubted it.

He selected Gates and two more to go south through the timber and circle in. "If things break loose don't shoot one of our own men. Bullets flying in a crossfire could get one of us killed." The three agreed and took off with rifles.

"Jesus and someone need to tend these horses. Shooting might spook them. A gray-haired older man volunteered. He picked the youngest rider to help them.

"I know you'd like to be there, but we need these horses to get home." He clapped the youth on his shoulder. "You're an important part of this posse."

"Thank you, sir."

"What's your name?"

"Potter Brown, sir."

"Nice to meetcha."

"Mr. Byrnes?"

"Yes?"

"You need another hand on one of your ranches?"

"Talk to me later. I can always use a real man needs work."

The youth nodded as if shaken by Chet's words.

"We'll talk later." Chet hurried back to spy on

the situation. A man with silver sideburns named Wheeling handed him the reins.

"About time. Mount up." He turned the gray and rode through the handful of men left. "Don't kill any of our men in the crossfire."

He drew his .44 and turned his horse for the charge. "Let's go."

He saw a bareheaded man ahead try to hold the reins on his spooked horse as they charged in on them. The reins were torn from his hands, he drew a pistol, and was cut down by rifle fire from the woods across the road. A bald-headed man had his hands in the air and his pants at his knees, obviously caught off guard. Someone was getting away. He saw the flash of a mule's butt going off into the timber. "Hold them, boys."

The rider was lashing the mule hard to make good his escape. All the timber proved a challenge, but the gray was cutting back and forth keeping his quarry in sight like he knew the mule was his goal. No low branches on these tall trees made the job easier, but the trick was too ride the big gelding through them and for him not to collide with one.

The mule rider had emptied his pistol with wild shots taken at Chet. No need to waste any ammo on him until he had a chance to stop him. He must have found a cliff down there. He wheeled the mule around and fled uphill off to the left of Chet.

He jerked out the rifle and when the mule came into a clear shot, he shot him. The mule went down in a pile, throwing his rider. Three more of the men on their horses rode to the scene.

Chet stepped down. "I didn't want to shoot that mule but I didn't want him to get away."

He caught the moaning man by his shirt collar and jerked him to his knees. "What's your name?"

"Who? Who are you? Why you trying to kill me? I ain't done nothing!"

"Just killed two old settlers and stole their money, huh?" He stuck the pistol muzzle to his cheek and cocked the hammer. "How is your memory now?"

"Not me. Not me. I believe I broke my arm."

"You boys take him up there. My trigger finger is too itchy."

Another of the men stripped the saddle and bridle off the mule and piled them on his own saddle to take them up to camp. Chet thanked him.

Gates was in charge. The shooter was dead. The bald man had his pants up. No doubt he was not constipated now. They had his hands tied behind his back.

"His name is Tremble," Gates said. He had it written in his logbook. "Garrison Tremble. That dead man is called John Smith. That's an alias."

The man who shoved the mule rider in the circle said, "He says his is Shaver. Nick Shaver lived in Tombstone last."

"He should have stayed there," Chet said. "Is there any water close?"

"There's a small stream over there." One of the men who had gone east pointed in that direction.

"Some of you men water the horses. Times, do you recall anything about this road?"

"It goes west to the Verde Valley eventually is all I can say."

They all laughed. "It will damn sure be easier than the way we came. Where is the money they stole?"

Chet looked around for any sign.

"Stole?" Shaver asked. He laughed. "We ain't got no money."

"There was several thousand dollars taken from those people in your robbery,"

"That shows you got the wrong guys, we ain't got a cent on us."

Chet stopped. He eyed the prisoner holding his broken arm. Had they stashed it on the trail? He couldn't recall many places that they stopped and could have ditched it.

"We ain't found any money in their things." One of the posse members turned up his hands. "It sure isn't here."

"That was why you killed them. Where is it?"

"I swear to God we never took any money from anyone."

Gates moved in close and whispered. "What if they didn't steal the money?"

"I'm not sure. But these three murdered that couple. The place did look torn up."

"I don't think they're lying."

"We'll let Sims figure it out. They did kill them.

There is dried blood all over Tremble's shirt and pants. He cut their throats, I can swear to that."

"Is the money on that back trail?"

"No. There is an answer to this and we'll figure it out. Wrap the dead man in a blanket. Those two can ride double. We're burning daylight."

The other men were coming back with the horses they'd watered. They cinched up and rode for Camp Verde. They reached the Quarter Circle Z close to midnight. The crew and women fell out to help. The ranch hands rubbed down their horses, gave them their beds to sleep in after a hasty meal was thrown together, and then guarded their prisoners.

After the shock was over, Susie and May gathered with Chet at the table in the house.

"These men murdered them to rob them?"

"They said he had three thousand dollars that is gone. I thought all the way that they'd have the money. But they didn't have a penny on them."

"Maybe they didn't kill them?"

"No, they killed them and we never found the money. Tremble had dried blood all over him and the dead man did too. That was Artman blood on those two."

"What will you do next?"

"Take them to jail and let Sims worry about them."

"And you're sure you got the killers?" Susie asked.

"Positive. The only screwy thing is they didn't get the money. Those three went to rob them and not leave any witness. I figure they tortured both of them and they never told them where it was at."

"Who knew then?"

"I've been asking myself that question for twenty-four hours."

"Sleep a few hours. You look worn out." Susie nodded to him.

"Thanks. Get me up in a few hours. I need to go see Marge. She's probably worried to death."

"No, she's simply lonesome without you. You fill some big holes in our lives too."

He shook his head. Wished he had time for a bath, but the hell with it, he needed some sleep. It could not have been any time till May shook him.

"I'm coming," he croaked, sat up, and pulled on his boots.

"Tell Gates to stop and get me at her place," he told Tom who was already up and at the chuck tent.

"I can do that."

One of the hands caught his roan he called Big Man. He brought him around for Chet, saddled. He finished his coffee and some of the raisin rice pudding that Hoot fed him.

"How are the Herefords?" he asked Tom.

"Good, I got a couple of the boys keeping them up at the Perkins place. There's lots of grass up there and it's easy for them to get fat. Not near as tough as some range country we use."

"Short as this country is on good bulls, don't cut

them. I think we can sell all those young bulls and make more money."

Tom agreed. "I've already been hit up for some."

"I knew we could make some money with them. Good, I think Bo has bought the ranch up there. I've got him on the sober train."

Tom laughed. "Ride easy. We don't want anything to happen to you."

Over two hours later, he reached Marge's front porch and dismounted. His face was so whiskered, he hated to even kiss her.

She must have been watching for him. Monica came out on the porch and, hands on her hips, tried to chew him out, laughing hard.

"Hold him down," Marge shouted from inside. "I've got the rope."

He caught her by the waist and kissed her when she rushed outside.

"I'm bristled like a boar hog."

"Don't worry. I love you. Did you?"

"We did capture the three men. Let's get inside. The posse will come by soon and I want to spend a few minutes with both of you before I go turn them in."

"Is there something wrong?" Marge asked, swinging on his arm.

"Yes. They did not have any of the stolen money."

"Did they hide it?"

"They had no time for that. We tracked them to where they were camped. We understood they took several thousand dollars from the Artmans."

"Where is it?"

"It still may be well hid for one thing. I really believe those three killed the couple and fled empty-handed."

"Are you going to look for it?"

He shrugged. "That's Sims's job. He will probably tell me to go mind my own business. I'll be shocked if he wants one more thing from me."

"One of them was shot dead when he returned fire at us. I know little about him. There is a big bald guy who I suspect cut their throats. He had dried blood all over him. Then the other one is a cocky mule rider who broke his arm when he tried to run off on his mule. They were some simple felons who heard about the Artmans having lots of money hid out."

"And you figured all that out riding them down?" Marge asked, and kissed him.

Her cook served him the breakfast she'd whipped up.

"Jesus is fine," he said to reassure her, ready to eat. "He did very well as a supplier and cook."

"You made the ranch last night?"

"Midnight. I had to sleep a few hours."

"You didn't have to come rushing back to me."

"Oh, yes I had to. I missed you."

She threw her arms around his neck. "That was sweet."

"No, simply what I needed." He finished his coffee and thanked Monica with a wink for her food. "I hear the posse coming. I'll be back in a few hours."

"We'll have something special for supper," Monica promised.

"Ah, I'm just glad to be back." He kissed his wife and headed for the front door.

At the courthouse, the posse dismounted. The two prisoners were in the back of a ranch buckboard, the dead man tied over a horse. Two deputies came out of the jail armed with shotguns. Chet had no idea why. Sims strolled out and frowned.

Gates looked at him and when he did not move, he pushed his horse in. "These are the men killed the Artmans."

Sims nodded. "What evidence do you have?"

Chet couldn't stand it any longer. He got off his horse. "Get down here, Sims. Get that Tremble over here."

He jerked the big man up in front of the sheriff. "See all this dried blood. That is Artman blood. Get that corpse off the horse—"

Sims held up his hands and turned to a deputy. "Get him inside and strip off his clothes. Take the others on along. What's wrong with his arm?"

"He broke it when he fell off his mule, trying to escape," Chet said in his face.

Sims ignored him. "Get all their clothes for evidence."

"You want to know what I think, Sims?"—hands on his hips, and breathing hard—"This posse should have hung these worthless pieces of humanity up there in the wilderness."

Still ignoring Chet, Sims asked, "Where is the loot?"

"They never found it."

"That's your case, Chet Byrnes."

"No, it is either hidden so well or someone knew where it was and stole it after the killers rode off."

"That's—"

Times rode in. "Hold up, sheriff. Chet Byrnes has this all figured out. We spent a day with those killers. They couldn't find it. That was the only true thing we believed."

"If I need your testimony, I'll serve you with a warrant."

"No," Gates said. "Yavapai County needs a new law enforcement officer, Sims."

The posse and many of the onlookers gathered shouted, "Yes!"

"Since the sheriff doesn't care we saved this county hundreds of dollars apprehending these felons who killed two old people, we do!"

Chet sat his Big Man. He was somewhat embarrassed since everyone was looking at him. And shouting, "Tell him, Chet." He pushed the horse in and held his hands up to get them quieted. "Sheriff Sims, if you need anybody to testify I am certain they will. I expect you will find that money, or who took it."

Sims stood on the steps, chest out. "I want all of you to disperse. I consider this gathering a breach of the peace in this city."

Chet closed his eyes in disbelief. Calling a citizen posse who brought in killers a breach of the peace may have signed the man's own resignation. He turned Big Man and went over to hitch him at the rack in front of the Palace. Word would travel fast. There would be a lot of whiskey and beer poured in glasses and mugs for the uproar only beginning to explode in this city.

A reporter from the *Miner* paper was in the bar-room quicker than a twitch of a cat's whiskers. He had a pad and pencil and scribbled down notes. Chet was seated at a table in the back and Jane brought him a cup of coffee.

"What has happened?" she asked, seeing the customers filing in.

"The sheriff threatened the posse who brought in those killers with disturbing the peace."

She looked in disbelief at him. "Really?"

"I couldn't believe he did that either."

"He must not want to be sheriff anymore. I've got to know, how is your sober party going?"

"I think he's bought me the ranch I wanted."

"When is this guard business over?"

"I can get you inside to see him."

"Not yet, I want him to come to me."

"I don't blame you."

She winked and left him.

Gates joined him, looking back to see who else was coming in the flow of customers moving inside.

"Should we go down there and find the damn money?"

Chet said, "I believe you can go turn it upside down. The money is gone."

"Who got it?"

"My number-one suspect would be the man's brother, Nathan."

"Why him?"

"I think after he found the bodies, he went and removed the money. I asked him how much it was. He knew it because he had the Artmans' money for himself. He knew they had exactly three thousand dollars."

"You figured that out?"

"Only thing made any sense. Those killers obviously left empty-handed. Someone told them the couple had a lot of money and they thought that would be an easy way to get some. So after torturing them and searching for it, their time ran out, and they finally killed them and went on."

Gates started to say something to a joiner at their table. Chet shook his head. "That's a secret."

"I understand. Well, did you hear our sheriff telling us off?" Gates asked the man.

"Yeah, who the hell does he think he is anyway?"

"Sheriff, I guess. Excuse me," Chet said. He wanted a bath, needed a shave, and missed Marge's company.

"We'll see you, Chet. Thanks again," Gates said after him.

He rode back to Preskit Valley and hitched the horse at the saddle shed. Jesus, already on the job, came on the run.

"You rested?" Chet asked him.

"No, but I had a wonderful time. It was exciting when you took them."

"Dangerous too. Remember that."

"I will, *señor*."

He caught Marge in his arms on the back porch, kissed her, and said, "I need a bath, a shave, and some overtime with you."

She laughed. "I love you, big man. How did it go?"

"Things went to hell. Sims threatened the posse to get them to leave."

"Oh, no."

"Oh, yes. I think he's hung himself. He acted like we had the wrong men as prisoners."

"He turned them down?"

"No, but he challenged us."

From the shelf in the back hall, he took a towel and soap bar, and left his boots to come back barefoot. She grabbed a sleeping shirt of her father's and smiled.

They headed for the sheepherder's shower. He hung his gun belt on the wall peg and his clothes with his hat. The shower was warm and he soaped down. She did his back, then stepped quickly aside to get out of the rinse.

"You can shave at the house where I have hot water."

"Good." He dried off and slipped on the sleep shirt, laughing. "I have not seen your foreman in a long time."

"Raphael works every day. I swear he knows where every horse, cow, and calf are at all the time. He's a good man."

"Damn right."

"Sit on a kitchen chair and I'll try not to cut your throat. I'm a good hand at shaving."

"I won't argue. I may sleep for twenty-four hours."

"I can tell you're tired." She lathered his face with the hog bristle brush and then took careful strips of his beard off. She was steady and her razor was sharp. He enjoyed the attention and just being close. Marriage was a nice place to be. All his years of being single never really produced a situation he enjoyed more than their union. Her ringing laughter sounded like special bells—and to think he almost ran her off. He thought she was some rich girl spoiled to death and would be harder than hell to please. Nothing like that—oh, well, he didn't lose her after all.

"Do you think the ranch deal will go through?"

"Yes, Bo is sober and working hard on it."

"Tell me about Reg? When will he get here?"

"Reg is a tall, square-shouldered guy about, oh, twenty-two. He can ride any horse, rope any bull, and throw his opponents over a wagon."

"He takes after his uncle, huh?"

"He's a hand."

She swished off the last of the soap from the razor. "It would be hard to lose your wife or husband like that."

"Damn hard. Those two were lovebirds. She was about the prettiest girl, too, in that country."

"What are you going to do with him when he gets here?"

"Put him on a saw and an axe and let him build the ranch house up there. He needs to be occupied. Building a ranch headquarters can eat up lots of sorrow. I built a lot of things on the old ranch to take up some spaces in my life. It's good therapy."

"Those boys are like your sons, aren't they?"

"And they're a lot better than their father. He was a dreamer. My dad was a hard worker and didn't know when to quit. That's what killed him, 'cause he came home the last time and knew nothing. Dad's brother Mark—well, I figured he'd show up some day. He was supposedly killed at the end of the war—but there were no records in those last days. I expected to look up one day and he'd ride in on a good horse. But he never did. He does now, they'll laugh at him."

"Will he come out here and find you?"

"I always thought he'd be back. Guess he won't never do that now. It's been over seven years."

"Does your aunt think he is alive?"

"My aunt is contrary. Spoiled. I sent her back to Louisiana once and she discovered that the white folks didn't live much better back there than their ex-slaves. Some hired killers grabbed her and thought she was Susie. I ran them down and brought them in for the law."

"What were they going to do to her?"

"Rape and then kill her. They thought she was Susie. Maybe sell her in the slave trade in Mexico."

"Oh, my God, Chet."

"It was grueling on her and I never wanted it to happen. But she don't chew my ass out anymore."

She rinsed off his face with a warm wet towel,

then dropped in his lap and kissed him. "I'm glad you're home in one piece and back with me."

Later, Roamer came by about dark. He didn't get off his horse. Chet stood on the head of the porch stairs with one hand hung on the ceiling trim over his head.

"What'cha need, Hoss?" Chet asked.

"I don't think I'm supposed to stop and talk to you. But what the hell, I figure you know the answers that I need. What happened to the Artmans' money?"

"One of two things."

"I appreciate any help I can get."

"Either no one found it or it's buried in coffee cans."

"What theory you hanging to the hardest?"

"His brother went over and found them dead. Knew where the three thousand dollars was at. He got it, then hid it before he went for help. I asked him how much money did they have and real quick he said three thousand dollars. I think he went and got some ranchers who he figured would lynch them as killers and the money never would be found. If you tell anyone that's my theory I'll shoot you."

"I won't tell anyone, but you damn sure changed my mind. Never would have thought of that, pard. I can handle it."

"How's the wife?"

He stopped, turning his horse around. "Feeling good. Getting closer."

"Tell her hi and she has my sympathy for putting up with you."

"Go get some rest, you look tired."

"I am," he said to himself and went back in to see his wife.

"Did you solve it for him?" she asked

"I'd bet so."

CHAPTER 16

Another busy week passed. Reg had not arrived, but Chet thought it was too soon. He had probably come on horseback to see the country. Bo was in the process of completing the Hackberry ranch deal via telegrams. Sober as a judge and bright-eyed, he even had sold a house to a new family coming to live in Preskit. Davis Green was his office companion that day. Both of the men were guarding him well. Chet decided they would also be very versed in the news from reading newspapers cover to cover. But his plan to wean Bo off booze was working very well.

The crew were building more corrals at the Verde ranch. He was anxious to move them north when the finishing touches were on the cook shack. Hoot was using it and bragged on the convenience of it all. In their spare time they greased the chuck wagon wheels and made some repairs to haul it up north when the time came.

The Fourth of July celebration was fixing to bust

loose out at the grounds. He donated two beeves to the event committee. He met one of the top hands at the events, a handsome man with black hair named Tom Horn. Horn worked for General Crook as the number two man over the Apache scouts, but he always came to compete at Preskit. There was gossip galore about him living with an Apache squaw and his efforts to get the bronco Apaches to come in and surrender.

Marge introduced them a few days before things started.

"I've heard about you," Horn said when they were alone and she was off to see about something.

"Not much to tell," Chet said.

"Oh, you tracked down some horse thieves to a place called—Rye. I've been there over by Four Peaks and they said you hung them."

"They say I did."

Horn laughed. That day he wore a brown suit coat and white shirt, no tie. "I've been in that wild country with General Crook and his forces. It's damn tough country even for the Dinea."

That was their word for Apaches—the people.

"I don't know. I went across it pretty quick."

"Word also got out about you heading a posse ran down three killers." Horn took off his hat and scratched his head. "I'd say you're a tough man, Chet Byrnes. There's one more about store robbers you drug in." Horn shook his head as if amazed. "Why do they pay old Sims to be sheriff?"

"I have no war with Sims. I have two ranches to run."

"No. These folks don't appreciate all you have done up here. I've done some of that work. It ain't easy."

"Someone has to do it."

"I agree. You came here from Texas, right?"

"I left Texas in the middle of a feud. Hey, you have a history book on me?"

"No, I just wanted to meet you. Your wife—" He tossed his head in the direction she'd gone. "My God, man, what a beautiful woman. Ranches, a darling wife, and you ride damn good horses—you can't beat that *mi amigo.*"

"They say you know Geronimo. Tell me about this man."

The two men squatted on their haunches, shifting their weight from time to time. Horn drew things in the dirt with a stick.

"He's a medicine man. You know three times that old fox told me something was going to happen and by damn it did. He once told me Lieutenant Gatewood would ride up on a white horse to meet us. The army didn't have a white horse. I thought he was crazy. But down in the Madres here Gates came—his own horse got colic and died, so he bought this one from the Mexicans."

"Tell me about your friend the Captain Crawford who got shot. I heard bits and pieces of that story."

"Maybe next time. That was the saddest day in

my life. Captain Crawford was a great soldier. Your wife's coming and I need to meet a man."

They stood up and shook hands. "Horn, some day you may need to write a book on your adventures."

"Take me a year to write it."

"Maybe longer."

"What will take longer?" Marge asked.

"Rubbing sticks together to make fire," Horn laughed and then hugged her lightly. "You've got a helluva great guy."

"I think so. Always good to see you, Tom. I'll tell dad I saw you too."

"Give him my regards."

They parted.

"What were you and Tom talking about?"

"Geronimo, mostly."

"He knows those Apaches and has lived with them. He's also a helluva a roper."

"I imagine so." He chuckled at her swearing; she must be taking up his bad habits.

"What is wrong?"

"I love you and we better get home or Monica will think we died."

In the morning he set out for the Verde ranch. Marge had things she wanted done at home and he rode his gray, starting out at dawn. He arrived and talked to Tom and the cowboys before they rode off for their day's work. Nothing sounded wrong and

Millie thanked him from the porch of her new house.

"I love it, Chet. Just love it."

"Good, you were supposed to."

When he arrived at Susie's kitchen, May's baby Donna was trying to walk around and explore things. His sister grabbed a pot and cup for him, avoiding the child.

"How is the romance going?"

"Which one?" his aunt asked, coming in the kitchen.

"Oh, am I behind on the news?"

"Days behind," she said, and Susie was busy frowning so Chet knew this gossip would be good.

"Mr. Hanager and his daughter Caylin were here for supper this week. And May got some hard candy from Worley—is that his name, dear?"

"His name is Waverly and it was just some hard candy. Nothing more."

"And I met a man named Parker."

"This house sounds empty already."

"Not so fast," Susie said. "None of us are leaving or planning on it."

"Good. I was hoping we'd hear from Reg by now. But I guess he's still coming."

His aunt gave a hard nod. "This place is not easy to find."

"We are closing the Hackberry ranch deal this week or next."

"Bo is still sober?" Susie asked with a smile.

"Yes. He even sold a house this week."

"Will we all be at the dance this Saturday night?" Susie asked.

"Marge and I will be there."

"Good. I'd like to have this family get together, we've all been so scattered. Now tell us all about the men who killed the Artman couple."

He told them his story, then he and Tom looked at the ranch books. There was lots of outgo and only the beef sales.

"I think we can gather a hundred and fifty big steers," Tom said.

"Where will we sell them and get a good price for them?" he asked his foreman.

"If they ever build a railroad we could ship them. Maybe we could sell them to the Navajo reservation?"

"That bunch down on the border and the Tucson ring has most of that beef contract business in southern Arizona for the reservations and the army tied up. Ike Clanton is the old man that rules that business."

Chet had heard lots about the Clantons' other deeds, plus their mining camp business. They were busy down there. Tombstone was the largest city between Saint Louis and San Francisco. There had to be a market somewhere for their beef. Navajos might be a good market.

"Marge and I may take a trip over there and see what we can learn."

Tom agreed. "If the railroad is coming, their work camps would make a good place to sell them."

"I think that one is still coming from Kansas, then across New Mexico. But we can check on them."

"Keep it in mind," Tom said.

"No sign of the Hartley Brothers' cow expansion, is there?"

Tom shook his head. "I think you bluffed them out of it."

"No, money is too tight for them. They haven't figured how to make any money out of all this range cow business. Too scattered to gather the increase and as far as they are from them, the more get eaten by folks who considered them lease money for eating their grass."

Tom laughed. "I agree."

"Don't scoff them away. They could get desperate and blow up."

"Maybe they thought they could use that west country of ours to gather them and keep them in that region."

"They will still need watching."

"Where are you headed today?" Tom asked.

"Back to Marge's house. Millie is excited about her house. She never expected such a place. It is nice. Keep your eye out for my nephew Reg who may show up any day."

"We'll give him a big welcome."

"I'm excited. Oh, let's look and see if we are making any money hauling logs up there. You're getting good at the books. Look at the costs."

"I am enjoying that. Susie is a big help and explains lots to me."

"We may lose her some day."

"I think he's serious too."

"Don't get me wrong, I want her to have a life of her own." Chet shook his head.

"Damned if you do, damned if you don't."

They shook hands and he went home. Caught in an afternoon shower, he hurried his big gray for the house. He still got soaked and laughed coming in the back door.

She had a towel and dry clothes on her arm.

"Great rain," he said, and hugged her.

When he looked up, Reg stood in the doorway behind her. He looked taller than he recalled.

"He asked in town where his uncle Chet lived and someone said, "Oh he lives with that woman out in Preskit Valley. 'Lived with'?" She was laughing and shaking her head.

"Maybe we should buy a big ad that we are married." He shook Reg's hand and then hugged him.

"You all right?"

"Long trip. I finally sold my horse and took the stage. I already saw you've got plenty of horses here. Yeah, your friend at the livery gave me a good one to use."

"Frye is a good man. He has a new wife too."

"Very nice lady. How is Susie?"

"Anxious to see you."

"JD?"

"That is a big story. Let me change and we can go in and—"

She put a finger on his lip. "We are going to eat

and talk. We just sat down when I heard you war whooping in the rain coming in."

Reg smiled like he did that all the time in Texas. "We brought back our remuda that some men had stolen. The three of us rushed for the house and he beat us."

They laughed. Marge took Reg in the kitchen and Chet changed.

Seated at the table after filling their plates, Chet told his nephew about his brother.

"I met Kay Kent last year at a dance and she was a good friend of Marge's. Everyone knew she had a problem; her husband wouldn't even dance with her. Marge knew more. Her husband wouldn't sleep with her anymore either. They had three nice kids and no one knew what his problem was. We think—" He paused and Marge nodded. "We thought she was at the end of her rope. JD came along and she convinced him to get her out of it. I don't blame her. So he took her and her children to the Verde ranch.

"When they started for town, we sent some hands with them. Her husband met them on the road out there and got into it with our men. He was drunk and a cowboy named Hampt took his rifle away and hit him over the head to shut him up. They said he was out cold when they took him off the road, and they kept his rifle. They sent a sheriff's deputy back to check on him and he had committed suicide with his pistol in the meantime.

"Marge and I went down there to check on them.

We got a cold reception and JD was off checking on her cattle. Was that all?"

"I think she is upset is all." Marge shook her head.

"I may need to go check on him." Reg looked over his coffee cup.

"After you see Susie down at the Verde ranch."

"Yeah, she'd beat me with a broom if I didn't." Reg laughed between eating.

"There is an area dance and potluck meal at the Camp Verde schoolhouse on Saturday night, which is north of here. We will all be there."

"She also has a serious suitor?"

Marge nodded like she knew all about it.

"Wow. How is May?"

"I don't know. Some cowboy gave her a sack of hard candy."

Reg snickered. "What else do I need to know?"

"I'm buying a raw ranch up on the rim. Interested?"

"Oh, sure. I need something hard and tough to dig my teeth in."

Chet agreed.

"You running for sheriff?" Reg asked.

Chet was taken aback. "Who told you that?"

"Marge had time to tell me all about your efforts to catch the criminals around here."

Chet shook his head. "We have a stick in the office sheriff, who doesn't like citizens to do anything."

Marge interrupted him. "He doesn't like anyone to solve crimes that he doesn't get the credit for doing."

"I wish I'd been there at—Rye? To help you. I read that story in the newspaper Marge showed me."

"Did your friend Roamer solve the lost money deal?" she asked.

"Sims will take that credit."

"You are as much in Arizona's welfare as you were at home in Texas." Reg smiled and shook his head.

The rain shower was over when Chet and his nephew rode for the ranch. On the top of Mingus Mountain, ready to go down into the Verde, Reg looked impressed at the vast valley.

He shook his head as if taken aback. "This is one helluva a big country."

Chet agreed and they went down to the ranch. When they rode up to the main house, the two women must have been looking for them. They ran out shouting.

Chet left him with them and took their horses to the corral. One woman on each arm, they headed Reg for the house.

"I guess your nephew arrived," Hoot said, standing on the rise wearing his apron.

"He made it."

"Damn, he's a lot taller than JD. He taller than you?"

Chet said, "Yes. How is it going for you?"

"It won't get no better. I can manage this job. The hands all will dig in and help me and the boy. Tom told that boy next year he'd make him a cowboy."

"Good. You will have to meet Reg. Those girls and his mother got him now."

"I'm looking forward to meeting him."

"Be good to have him up here." Chet left the cook shack. What would happen next? Things were holding fairly good on the ranch business.

CHAPTER 17

Saturday night, Chet wore a starched white shirt and a new tweed vest. He was introducing his nephew to all the folks he knew in his circle of acquaintances at the dance. Marge had bought Reg a new shirt as well. When JD arrived, he left Kay with the ranch women and joined them.

"How is the ranching going?" Chet asked him.

"Kent never did much for the ranch the last few years. She needs several old cows culled and some new bulls."

"Can she afford them?"

"He didn't have much money in the bank. His funeral and all."

"How many bulls do you need?"

"Six."

Chet nodded. "I can loan you the money. I'll try to find the bulls, too."

"I'll talk to her about it."

"Do that. Need anything else?"

"I hate to ask you. But I could use three or four ranch horses. The ones he had are all old horses."

"Reg can take them over next week. He said he wanted to help you some. The deal on the Hackberry ranch is going through. We may work all winter building some headquarters up there."

"Great. I get some time, I want to see those Herefords you bought as well."

"Any time. We're keeping them over at Perkins."

"Chet, thanks, I won't worry anymore."

"Hey, we're all family."

"I didn't know what you thought about me getting involved in her marriage."

"Hey, you thought it was right. That was what was important."

"Thanks." He smiled, looking relieved.

Back with Marge, she asked him what he and JD had settled.

"He needs some bulls and some saddle horses. I'll buy him the bulls and Reg can take him four horses next week. He said Floyd Kent had not done much with the ranch in a few years."

"Well, father." Marge grinned and swept him off on the dance floor. "I think you will have a brother-in-law—soon."

"Susie?"

"Yes."

"Good, I knew she'd never consider leaving the ranch if she fed those men. I made her mad but she also began to think about Susie. For a change."

"I think you are becoming the patriarch of this family."

"I have been ever since I was sixteen."

"I know you never got to be on your own. And now you have me to contend with. God, I wish we were on some camping trip. I'd have you all to myself right now."

"Let's go to Gallup and sell some beef."

She frowned, then let down. "Sure, why not?"

The next day he did some investigation at Sam Eagan's law office about where the Navajo Agency was located, and found there were several agencies at various locations.

"Each one no doubt handles their own purchases of beef," Eagan said.

"That's a big deal," Chet said aloud. "How would I handle it then?"

"There must be a lawyer in Gallup who handles those kinds of deals," Eagan said. "Let me find one for you and we'll write him and ask how we need to do it."

"Good enough. You checked the deeds and paper on this Hackberry ranch deed, and they're all okay?"

"Yes, we are going to register them in the courthouse tomorrow and release the man's money in Saint Louis via telegram. You know, don't you, these Indian agents expect some things from contractors."

"You mean money under the table?"

"You could call it that. Most folks consider it the cost of doing business. You understand, so don't explode when you are asked for something."

"I won't, but they do get paid for being agents. Like the one down at Camp Verde, that I got forced out over mistreating them last year."

"Yes." He smiled. "I simply wanted to let you know what to expect."

"Find out about them. Ranchers around here need a good market for their beef."

When he joined Marge later, they started home. She wanted to know all he'd learned about selling beef to Navajo agencies.

"Damn complicated. Eagan told me there are several agencies, not one. He's going to find me a lawyer up there in New Mexico and see how to do it."

"Then we won't get to go camping." She dropped her chin in disappointment.

"Hey, we can go anyway, to someplace."

"Good." She took his arm and clung to it. "Where are we going now?"

"Home for right now. I need to find JD six bulls. Tom bought some shorthorn bulls at Hayden's Mill from a man I may mail a letter to and see if he has any more."

"You will be in the bull business in a year, right?"

"Yes, we'll have white face bulls by then for sale—but he needs bulls now."

"So if you get the Navajo reservation contract, it could mean big herds of cattle to be driven up there?"

"Sounds big to me. But I think we've got the men and can get the livestock to handle it."

"Sounds like a mountain to me. Did Reg take him some horses to ride?"

"Yes, he took him six head when he went down there this morning. We decided he needed that many."

"I can't imagine her husband not doing better than that. Maybe he got so depressed was why he shot himself?"

"It's sad. I hope for both their sakes this deal works for them."

"I thought that you acted concerned about them. You are, aren't you?"

"I have a gut feeling it won't last. I've had for some reason since it began, and I want it to work and will do all I can to help them. But something ain't right."

"I'm glad you told me that. I simply expected it to work. Maybe I overlooked something."

"Can't help it."

"I have no problem, but you have lots of powers at seeing things for what they are. There is an article in the *Miner* about how Sheriff Sims solved the matter of the Artmans' lost money and how he arrested Nathan for the theft. I am certain you will be mad when you read it."

He clucked to the horses, still mulling over the Navajo deal. Selling them beef might be more work than he wanted as well. He'd try to keep an open mind. He knew the night he told Roamer his idea that Sims would get all the credit and he would never mention his deputy who solved it for him.

* * *

The next morning, he was ready to go check on things down on the Verde. Marge didn't go along. He threw his saddle, blankets, and bridle in the buckboard, and arrived mid-morning at the ranch. First he went to the house to see the girls, and then he went to checking on the hammer drivers. The roof was shingled on the bunkhouse and they were laying out the lath to put one on the cook shack next.

Hoot met him, drying his hands. "All these afternoon showers will sure grow some grass, but it's been hell, so they roofed both of them this week."

Chet agreed and drank a cup of coffee at the table with his cook. "All going right around here?"

"I'd say it was going damn good. What do you think?"

"Oh, I'm grateful to have a nice wife. So many hard workers and we're building a real ranch here."

"Been a helluva year and a half for you, ain't it?"

"You don't know, Hoot. If I lived it over I'd like Heck to be alive. He was making a real man."

"I know I couldn't believe anyone got that grown-up in such a short period of time. You going to sell some beef?"

"If we can find a market. We need that. Folks need beef but getting to them is a problem."

Hoot agreed, then turned his head northward. "How many years till they've got a railroad up there?"

"Oh, ten, maybe more."

"I heard the reason no one cattle ranched in this country before was they were too far from markets, so they ran sheep and sold the wool, which could be hauled down by wagon to Yuma and put on ships in the Gulf of California."

"I bet you're right. But we'll sell our cattle for a profit."

"I sure don't doubt that, boss man. You know they eat lots of beef down at Tombstone—of course old man Clanton has all that beef business."

"That market may be closed." Chet laughed thinking about it. He'd never seen Tombstone either. It was twenty miles south of Benson on the main stage line. Big place—lots of people were down there. There was also lots of talk about crooked businessmen who held all the government, military, and Indian contracts running things in Tucson.

"I need to check on a few things and get back home."

"Lots of folks been coming by looking at that Mexican horse you call Barb."

"He's been busy since we got here. Should be some grand colts next year."

"I am going to look for them."

"Where is Corey?"

"Ah, Tom lets him ride with the crew one day. It's making a real man out of him."

"Good." He left Hoot to his half-finished cook shack. Then he drove back to the Preskit Valley and his wife, who met him at the backyard gate. Jesus had taken the team to put up. He thanked him.

"Reg is here," she said, as he swept her up and kissed her.

"Good. What does he know?"

"I'll let him tell you. He's excited about the upper ranch."

"Good." He looked up at his nephew. "Hey, how is your brother doing?"

"All right."

"You know about ranching. Will they make it?"

Reg simply nodded.

"Let's go inside. You two can talk in there."

"Well, it didn't rain on me today. Guess my rain-maker power is getting weak," Chet said, herding them inside ahead of him.

"He mentioned or asked me for some bulls."

"He needs them. His bulls are culls."

Reg shook his head. "That probably is only half of his problems."

They took seats in the living room and Chet told Marge to join them. "She's family."

Reg agreed.

"What is going on?"

"Her husband hadn't done much in the past years. He had some alfalfa acreage watered by an artisan well. He must've stopped watering it. It's dead. That was horse hay, milk cow hay, and bummer calves feed. It also was their garden. Nothing."

"I can send her produce. We have plenty."

"I don't know, Marge. She's pretty touchy about folks helping her. Those two got in such an argument, I kinda felt out of place and told them I needed to check on some things. I hated it, but

I'm kinda upset anyway and I don't need that—I love him and like her but I sure am not going to sit in the middle of all that. I hope JD understands."

"He will in time. I don't think any of us can do much. They'll have to figure it out. I didn't want to admit it I guess, but you're right, the place has been neglected and run down. Any success they get is only going to come from getting things fixed."

Reg looked relieved. "You two tell me about this new ranch."

Marge beamed. "It's up on the high country. Tell him about how the man got it."

Chet explained how the government aided the railroad in building the tracks and how the sections alternated on sides of the track and how Boxley had traded his other land for some closer to a river out there. He'd not known the Colorado River was in a deep gorge about twenty miles north.

Reg shook his head. "How did you find this place? I mean know where it was located and all?"

"First we met an Irishman who owned a store at Hackberry."

"And he danced an Irish jig when he met us," Marge said, laughing. "He's a neat little man."

"He found us Lacy Wright, who is a real cowgirl, and her father Jacob, who owns a ranch up there. She showed us all over the place. There's a place up there has a big spring and would make a good ranch site. There's some sagebrush country that would make a great hay meadow close by. It is in real cattle country."

"Sounds great, how far away is it?"

Chet looked at her and she frowned.

"Oh, a hundred fifty miles. Maybe less," Marge said with a soft laugh. "We were on a honeymoon, Reg. Distance didn't bother us."

"I know what you mean. Would I need a map to go up there?"

Chet shook his head. "I can get you there, then you can find O'Malley and he can get hold of Lacy and she can show you the place."

"I think I want to see it. Sounds neat. You don't need me, I better go soon."

"I don't know her plans but you aunt may be making plans for a wedding."

"She talked all the way around it when I got here. That would be good for her. Yes. I don't figure in Texas she'd ever considered it," Reg said.

"We agree on that," Marge said.

Chet nodded. "Pick you out some horses up at the ranch. Victor can set you up with camping gear. Visit our boys at the sawmill. Robert runs that for us up there. Take whatever you need and when you get back we can go over the plans."

"Sounds great."

"It's wonderful to have you here with us. I'll figure out a way to help them two if I can."

"I think this trip to the new ranch will clear my head. I'm counting on it doing that. I hate to linger in the past, but I guess it's part of healing."

"You probably won't ever forget it, but you will get so you can live with it."

Marge squeezed Chet's arm. "You over it?"

"Most of the time. I don't think about it often. But it comes and reminds me that it happened."

She chewed on her lower lip before she spoke, "My first husband was killed in the war. I thought I'd never live again. But he faded, and number two rode out one morning and never came home. A horse threw him and broke his neck. Then your uncle came back from Texas at last to see me, and someone had stolen some of our horses. I had waited so long for him coming, and then he rode off to catch them. I thought oh, my God, I have lost him too."

Reg looked straight at her. "If they stole your horses, I know how he feels about that. I've been on those wild goose chases. But stealing horses really gets to him."

"But I had waited a year, maybe longer. His interest in Texas couldn't wait. I was so high and zoom he runs off to get them. I was white knuckled until he came back."

"He's been bad about that since I was a boy."

Marge kissed him. They all three laughed.

Chet was glad that Reg could talk about things. The new ranch might be just what Reg needed. What he could do for JD and Kay he had no idea. Time would work out things like that.

Late that night in bed, Chet and his bride talked about things.

"I don't want to pry, but I am concerned about your business," she began. "I mean I don't need to know everything, but how can you afford all this?"

"Kansas cattle drives. I made some big money driving the right cattle to Kansas. I planned to expand the Bar C for years, but never did it. I have a large war chest of money the family has saved. I don't trust all my money to banks. They fail from time to time. Both Susie and May know all about them. I have never told Louise."

"I understand." She smiled in the moonlight flooding the bedroom. "I won't bother you again about it."

"We've never spent it and we have plenty."

"Good. My father, as you can imagine, had investments all over but he's been trying to close them out. That was what he did in California. Sold some things he held over there. He asked me if you needed any money; that is why I asked."

"I borrowed money from him last year because I didn't have the money on me. But I paid him back."

"Oh, he said you did. He simply thought all this ranch building might be hurting you."

He kissed her. "No problem."

"Good, I won't mention it again."

"Hey, we're partners."

She sighed and then hugged him "I know and love it."

* * *

After breakfast, he saddled a horse and rode with Reg down to the Quarter Circle Z. They talked about his buying the Hereford cows and plans to improve the herd in the valley.

"Where would we get the cattle for the new place?"

"Maybe buy yearlings and stock it with them."

As they rode off Mingus Mountain, Reg nodded like he was considering such a change. "That would be different. But might be what we need and not winter them."

"I see it that way. But time will tell. I'm looking to provide beef to the Navajos."

"Is that a bribery deal?"

"I have no idea. Indian agents have a bad reputation. Our lawyer is trying to find another in Gallup to tell us the way to do it."

"You never run down, do you?" Reg asked.

"Hey, we have a big family and I want us all to have the best life we can have."

"This valley and that far rim is impressive," Reg said, admiring the vast scenery spread out before them.

"Wait till you see the Grand Canyon. I was impressed."

"I can't hardly wait."

"Good. This cattle selling, settling the purchase of the ranch and the rest, make me stay here."

"I know. I miss the ranch life we all had in Texas. But that part is gone. Aunt Susie missed it too."

"I know, but we all have our lives to lead. The Reynolds stopped that."

"I still liked it then."

"Maybe you'll like this new place as well."

"I hope so."

They found him two saddle horses and two packhorses that suited him. Reg said he wanted to explore the entire country. Chet felt that was encouraging. He wondered how the Wright sisters and he would get along. They obviously did not have many suitors up there, from what he and Marge observed when they went to the dance with them. Reg would have fun, perhaps.

Susie put together food and supplies that he'd need. Victor drew him maps and told him all about the things he'd find.

Chet's foreman Tom dropped by and told them about a rancher who lived downstream, Jack Greene, who had two beeves shot and the hindquarters taken from both with the rest left to buzzards. They called it slow-elking.

"He have any ideas?" Chet asked.

"No. He figured the first one was done by someone drifting through. But number two made him think about someone who lived around here. We have no evidence they have struck us."

"Reg is going up on the rim and check out the new ranch site."

"I understood that." Tom said. "He get what he wanted to ride?"

"Yes. Victor helped him and drew him maps."

"Is Victor going along?"

"No, I hadn't planned on that. I can ask him. Victor would make a good guide."

At lunch, Reg said, "I'd rather discover it myself. I need some room to simply think."

Chet accepted that as his answer. Susie fussed about her special guest and took some ribbing about her own situation.

"This Tom, what's his name?" Reg pointed his fork at her.

"Hanager."

"Do I get to approve of him?"

"You can stay and meet him." Susie acted busy with her food. "He'll be at the dance Saturday night."

"Oh, I want to ask him lots of questions."

"I have no idea what he'd say to that."

Reg laughed. "I wish for the best things to happen with him."

"Thanks," she said quietly.

After lunch, Chet asked Reg if he could use some money.

"I guess I could."

He gave him fifty dollars and Reg thanked him. With a few words to encourage him, Chet went back to Marge's and then drove her into Preskit. He stopped at Bo's office and the sober agent explained that the deed was coming and the ranch was his.

He thanked him and his bodyguard, then he left and crossed the street. Marge was shopping for something and he was going to check with Jane.

When she saw him she came over. "How is your man?"

"Still sober. What do you know?"

"Word is that your friend Roamer was shot last night and they're bringing him here from Crown King."

Chet felt cold chills on his cheeks. "You know who shot him?"

"I have no idea. They said he was alive."

"Where will they bring him to?"

"Doc Melton is the best surgeon. He has a practice two blocks north."

"I can find him. No story to go with his shooting?"

"It is all sketchy. There was some kind of holdup going on."

"That's enough. I'll go see if he's up there by now."

"Be careful."

"I will."

He took the buckboard in that direction and found the sign of Dr. Melton. He entered the office, which smelled of ether and disinfectants.

"May I help you?" a gray-headed lady asked.

"Is the deputy Roamer here?"

"Yes, but he cannot have any visitors."

"Who ordered that?"

"Sheriff Sims."

"I am a close friend of his. The sheriff can't keep me out of seeing him."

"He said—"

"I must see him."

"I can't—"

"I'll find him." He moved her aside.

"Doctor!" she shouted.

Taking off his glasses, a man came out in the room. "What is wrong?"

"I'm here to see Roamer."

"He was shot."

"That is why I'm here."

"He may be groggy."

"I trust your concern. But the man or men who did this are riding away."

"The sheriff said—"

"Doctor. I need to speak to him."

"I really think you're disrespectful."

"Is he dying?"

"I hope not."

"Then let me get what he knows about the shooter."

"Follow me, and lower your voice."

He opened the door and let Chet in the room. He went to the bedside and waited for Roamer to open his eyes. Then he dropped on his knees. "Who did this?"

"They tried to rob the store—I tried to stop them—Blake Ryder and some guy, name's . . . Bender—were the—ones—sorry I can't do more—"

"Get well. I'll find them."

Roamer nodded his blanched face at him.

Chet turned to the doctor and they left the room.

Outside, the doctor nodded. "You satisfied?"

"He's a good friend. I'll find who shot him."

"Sheriff Sims said the shooters would be apprehended."

"I hope he does. But if he don't, I will."

"Isn't it best to leave this to the law?"

"I have no argument with Sims. I disagree with his methods, let's say."

"Did you bring in those men that murdered the old couple?"

"I was with the men that brought them in."

Doc shook his head. "May you safely find them."

He wanted to tell the man safety was not an issue. Those men needed to be apprehended. That was the most important thing. They'd have a good head start by the time he got his feet planted down there.

When he reached the dress shop, Marge came out flush-faced. "Have you heard about Roamer?"

He loaded her on the seat, then got in behind her. "I spoke to him about it."

"Is he all right?"

He turned the team around and headed for her place. "Doc Melton said he should survive. Roamer looked tough to me."

"I expect you will go down there where he was shot."

"I need to get a horse, some supplies, and try to find out where they went."

She nodded. "I understood that. Will anyone go with you?"

"I have no idea. Those killers'll have a good head start by the time I get there."

She agreed. Holding his arm she asked, "Does this really require you?"

"If I thought Sims had this under control, I

wouldn't bother. But in both cases, those men would have escaped his grasp."

"Would you take Jesus along with you? I know Reg is gone."

"I could send Jesus to go to the ranch this afternoon and get Hampt Tate. He's a powerful man."

"I would like that. I don't doubt you'll be taking care of yourself, but a good man with you would make me feel better."

"I'll write Tom and him a note."

"I'll go get Jesus ready to deliver it."

"Wait." He reined up the team, seeing they were alone on the road. Then he turned her toward him and kissed her. "You are my life, Marge. But you know that."

She hugged him. "Oh, I have loved our lifestyle. I am not a housewife wife, and you're including me in so much has thrilled me."

"I won't quit until you are too tired to go."

"I love it. Thanks." She clapped his leg and shook her head.

They drove on.

Jesus rode off with his letter for Tom and Hampt. The trip would require four hours or more but he expected Hampt to be up there later that night. They were eating supper when Leif Times arrived, and Chet invited him in.

Out of breath when he arrived, he'd asked Chet if he had talked to Roamer. Chet said he had, and hustled him off to wash up. Monica brought a plate and he joined them.

"Are you going to Crown King?" he asked.

"In the morning."

"Excuse me ma'am," he said to Marge. "I would like to go along with your husband. And I know I am hogging this conversation, but I also want to know what Chet thinks."

She agreed. "I understand. We talked about it all the way home."

Chet nodded. "I spoke to Roamer. I never asked about his wounds. He said Blake Ryder and another called Bender were the ones robbing the store."

Times shook his head. "I never heard of them."

"I imagine they were miners."

"Sure, lots of them I don't know."

"They have a good head start on us."

"We'll get some descriptions down there tomorrow and then maybe we'll get a direction they went."

"You don't have any ideas?"

Chet shook his head. "But anyone that moves leaves tracks."

"Thank you," Times said to Marge for handing him bowl of gravy.

"No problem."

"One of my hands is coming to ride with us. I figure to leave about four a.m. We can meet you at the Black Canyon turn in the morning."

"Thanks. I'm proud to ride with you. I will be there."

"No, it's something we need to do."

"Has the sheriff sent someone?"

Chet shook his head. "I have no idea but he didn't send anyone, really, the last time, nor the time before."

"I know. So do many of the people in this county."

"I'll tell you something when we have these two criminals behind bars."

"What is that?"

Chet smiled. "I'll tell you that when they are in jail."

"Oh, yes, I understand. This was a wonderful meal. I'm headed home to load up and I will met you in the morning."

"Bring a bedroll, a slicker, and a rifle. Hampt and I will have the rest."

"Thanks again. I will be there."

Chet showed him to the front door and stood on the porch. "Ride easy, Leif."

"Thanks, Chet." He rode off.

Hampt arrived about ten that evening. Marge asked if he had supper and he told her, with a big smile, "I had it at the ranch before leaving. Thanks, ma'am. Is Roamer doing all right?"

"He was alive this afternoon."

"How far ahead are the men who shot him?"

"By the time we get to Crown King, they'll be gone two days."

"That's a big lead."

"I agree, but everyone leaves tracks."

"I'm with you. Jesus says I can sleep in the

bunkhouse. You may need to get me up but I'm with you."

"No problem. I'll get you up. Leif Times is going to meet you at the Black Canyon Road and ride along."

"I don't know him."

"Nice sincere young man."

"No problem. See you then."

After Hampt went to the bunkhouse, they went to bed. Four a.m. was going to be early and he wanted to be on the trail of these shooters. They whispered to each other and then laughed.

"Who in the hell will hear us?" he finally asked.

"I have no idea." They kissed then went to sleep.

When he and Hampt reached the Black Canyon Road, Times was waiting for them. Under the stars in the predawn coldness, he introduced the two men and they rode on. It was a long ride through the pine forests over the top of the Bradshaw Mountains to the mining camp. Past midday they were at the general store where Roamer had been shot.

Chet introduced himself to the store man. "My friend, Deputy Sheriff Roamer, was shot here two days ago. I came to hear the story of who did it."

"I told the sheriff."

"He didn't tell me. I want to hear your side of it."

"Two guys who'd been hanging around up here came in the store with masks. One was Blake Ryder and his pal John Bender. Ryder told me to open the safe and I did. I guess Roamer came in about then and caught them. They fired two shots at him and he returned fire, but he was shot by one of them and lying on the floor. Then Ryder snatched all the money he could and stuffed that in his shirt. They ran out and got on some horses and rode out."

"Tell me what Ryder looked like."

The store man looked at the other two. "You the law?"

"What did Ryder look like?"

"He's in his thirties, about six feet tall. Brown eyes, uncut brown hair. He weights about 190 pounds."

"Dress?"

"He wore a dirty shirt. It was stained. And some brown pants."

"How was it stained?"

"Tobacco."

"Beard or none?"

"He ain't shaved in a week."

"Hat?" Chet asked.

"Beat up."

"Kerchief?"

"It was red checkered."

"Suspenders?"

"Yeah."

"What color?"

"I don't recall."

"What kind of a gun did he have?"

"A bulldog-handled one. Not like yours. Round handle."

"Holster?"

"No, I saw it was in his waistband when he came in before."

"He ever say where he came from?"

"Yuma."

"Prison?"

"He said Yuma."

Chet turned to the others. "Anything else?"

"He have any scars?" Hampt asked.

"Some on his—ah—left cheek."

"Now describe the other guy."

"Small, five two or three and about thirty years old. Had whiskers like a rat. Brown eyes. He was the lookout. I only saw him once or twice before. They said his name was John Bender."

"How did he talk?"

"Squeaky with an accent."

"What kinda accent."

"Foreign, he was strange."

"Who shot Roamer?"

"I'm not sure, the place was full of gun smoke. My ears were ringing and I was afraid for my own life."

"How much money did they get?"

"Three hundred and twelve dollars."

"Which way did they go?"

"I'm not sure." The man shook his head. "They rode brown horses."

"Give me ten cents worth of hard peppermint candy." Chet hoped one of the three of them would recognize the pair when they met up with them.

"What did the sheriff tell you?" Times asked.

"He'd get the men responsible for this."

"No one went after them?" Chet asked.

"No. The only deputy we had was Roamer. He did a good job. But they ain't sent another one down here—yet."

"Thanks," Chet said, sucking on a piece of candy from the small sack. He offered it to the others and they each took one too. It was the only nice thing that happened all day since he'd kissed his wife good-bye. Outside on the porch, he studied the dusty street and cloister of log-slab buildings.

The two got on their horses and led Chet's. He'd told them he wanted to see the liveryman. A whiskered individual in some dirt-stained overalls asked him what he needed.

"The two men shot Roamer."

"They run off. Never paid me the bill they had for leaving their horses here."

"What kinda saddles did they ride?"

"They was dried out and curled on the edges." The old man shook his head like they weren't worth much.

"They have good horses?"

"Looked like half-starved Indian mustangs."

"Brown?"

"Yeah, they wasn't worth much."

"How far would they go."

"Not far."

"Thanks."

"You a lawman?"

"We're looking for them."

He nodded. "Catch 'em. They shot Roamer and he was a helluva good one."

"Thanks. I think so too. That's why we came."

"My name's Nabb. Any way I can help, call on me."

He shook the man's hand. "I'm Byrnes, that's Times and Tate. We'll find them."

Nabb waved at them. "Hang them somewhere and let them be a lesson for all of them would-be crooks to see."

Chet mounted his horse close to him and checked him. "Where did they go?"

"Hassayampa to catch the stage, I figure."

"Thanks." He booted the gray out on the road and they left Crown King. In late afternoon, halfway off the mountain, they found a dead horse beside the road. Chet was trying to piece it all together. It was still a long ways to the stage stop.

At dark, they rode up to a ranch house and woman in her twenties came out with a .22 rifle in both hands. The stock dogs barked. Chet rode up until she aimed the gun at his heart. Then he shut down the gray. "Sorry to spook you, ma'am. We're ranch folks from Preskit. We're looking for two outlaws that shot a deputy at Crown King two days ago and robbed the store. Did they stop here?"

She shook her head, but he could see she was about to cry.

"I reckon your man is gone. We don't aim you no harm. Could we water our horses?"

"I'd—rather—you rode on."

"Did those men stop here two days ago—"

Her knees collapsed and she fainted. He held his hand out for them to stay, dismounted, and went to her, removing the gun and setting it aside.

When he got on his knees and lifted her into a sitting position, she tried to twist away, unable to look at him, and began crying. "Don't touch me. Oh, dear God don't let them rape me—again."

His partners were there to help him. Hampt opened the door and Chet carefully carried her inside and put her on the couch.

"Ma'am, we want those men that hurt you," Chet assured her. "How long were they here?"

"The whole night." Seated on the couch, she turned her head away from him so he couldn't see her face.

"They leave at daylight?"

"Yes."

"Did they steal a horse?"

"Two of them, and left me some old plugs. My husband will be so mad."

"No, he won't, ma'am. He'll be glad you are still alive and those mad men didn't kill you. My name is Chet Byrnes, that's Leif Times, and the big man is one of my foremen, Hampt Tate. I ranch in the Verde Valley. My wife used to be Margaret Stephenson."

She gulped, then said, "I have met her. I am Gail Cloud. My husband's Clay. He's packing salt to his cows that are up in the mountains for the summer." She blew her nose in a handkerchief from her dress pocket. "I'm sorry to impose on you men. This has been the worst day in my entire life. Twice today I even considered suicide."

"Don't do that," Times told her. "Nothing is worth that."

"Lord, no Missus Cloud, those two worthless birds aren't worth the powder to blow them up, let alone them drive you do to that."

She nodded. "I know you men came a long ways today. See about your stock. I can make us breakfast—that's fast." She sniffed. "Will that be all right?"

"I can take care of the stock," Hampt said. "You show my boss man where things are and I know he can cook it and Leif can help him." The big cowboy went for the door.

"There's grain in the barn if you need some."

"No ma'am," he shouted back from outside. "We've got all that."

"I-I can make it."

Chet agreed and was glad she'd recovered a lot. "Just show us and we can do that and you be the boss."

Leif and she made the biscuits. Chet chopped up the potatoes and some onions for hash browns. He heated a skillet for them to fry in and worried about the flame under it heating it up. He put a couple tablespoons of lard in it to melt and went to cracking open brown shell eggs from a bowl she set out.

"You guys don't need a wife, I can see that. My, you have done this before."

"Mrs. Cloud," Leif said, "I need one. He has Marge."

"Well, a nice looking guy like you could find one in a minute up here."

"I have one in mind. But I fear someone has taken her."

Stopped for a minute, Chet turned his ear that way for a second to listen.

"Who is that?" she asked, putting a big steel sheet with floury sourdough biscuits on it in the oven to bake.

"Chet knows her. It's his sister, Susan Byrnes. Well, big brother, what do you say to that?"

"My sister Susie has been a big part of my managing our ranch operations in Texas. She is a very outspoken woman and you may be right, Leif, she is currently dating a man who ranches near Preskit."

"I know my competition, Tom Hanager—I know him real well, and if we ever can catch these two felons, I am going to pitch in and compete with him."

Chet shook his head. The boy was damn sure serious.

"Does he know your father, Chet?" she asked.

"Both my parents have died. I guess I am the patriarch for the Byrnes clan."

"See," she said. "You have an in right there, Leif."

Chet held his hands up. "I am not choosing husbands for my sister. No way."

"I am intrigued by all this. Why are you ranchers doing this?"

"Tell her, Leif," Chet said. The grease sizzled when he poured the potatoes in the skillet.

"How do I tell her nicely?"

"Tell her, she's a big girl."

"The sheriff is an office man. It all started when Chet was buying the Quarter Circle Z. The foreman who ran it, Ryan, had everyone who dealt with him afraid. Even the owner in the East wouldn't come back out here. Chet bought the ranch and ran him off, but Ryan shot a good horse out from under Chet. Then he ran and Chet went after him all the way to Hackberry. Then he hired a man and his boy to haul them back. He's in prison now at Yuma. Sheriff Sims took offense at that.

"Then someone stole horses from Mr. McClure's place. Shot his foreman and another cowboy in the chase. And Chet got them."

"Oh." She looked shocked at Chet. "You ended that at Rye, didn't you? I read that letter to the editor."

"Yes, ma'am." He used a turner to move the hashed potatoes and onion around in the skillet to brown them.

"The robbery-murder in last week's paper. You arrested those men?" she asked.

"And the ones that robbed the store in Camp Verde," Hampt said, coming in the room. He hung a large hand over his head on the kitchen door. "My boss is a busy man."

She frowned. "Why isn't the sheriff doing all this?"

Leif nodded. "Lots of us would like to know."

She shook her head in wonder. "I need to get the biscuits out of the oven,"

Chet opened the oven door and he stepped

aside for her. Next he stirred the scrambled eggs. "Besides, ma'am, I have a ranch to run. Now two of them. We're building one up on the rim east of Hackberry."

"I bet folks elect you when the time comes." She stood considering him as if in disbelief, and nodding firmly. "They will when the word gets out."

"We'll see when the time comes." Chet side-stepped for her to put the large tray of oven-hot browned biscuits on the table.

"You know those stage robbers that last year hung around up here?" Hampt said. "No one could stop them. He did that single-handed last fall."

"I do know his wife and that explains why she's his wife," she said, as if satisfied. "She knew a good man when he arrived here." Then she laughed and about blushed. "You three are a mess. I felt so terrible just thirty minutes ago and here I am laughing with men who were strangers. I am amazed."

"Good," Hampt put a chair under her and moved her closer to the table. "That is the last civil thing I'll do tonight, getting you at the table." He straddled a chair and sat down. "Here on it's everyone for themselves or they'll starve."

They were all laughing.

"Gail, we need a description of the horses they stole," Chet said.

"A bay and a sorrel. They have a T75 on their shoulders. The sorrel has one white hoof. My husband loves that horse, he calls him Sunny and the bay he uses to rope with. I know he's going to be screaming mad, but there was nothing I could do about it."

"No problem. We'll do our damnedest to get them back."

She quickly nodded.

"You better eat up, ma'am," Hampt said with a soft elbow in her arm.

"Clay will be back tonight. I'll be better then."

"Eat, you'll be fine," he assured her.

"You aren't married, Mr. Tate?"

"No, ma'am. It just never worked out. Mind you I'm not complaining, but with cowboy's wages there ain't hardly room for one. But I'm looking hard and I may have to get me a new occupation if'n I ever find one."

She shook her head as if she didn't believe him. "Where did these outlaws go?"

"We're leaving early to try to find them. We figured they might still be at Hassayampa City or they took a stage from there," Chet said between bites of his hot biscuit with grape jam. "If your horses are there we will board them and send you a note."

"Clay would appreciate that. The sorrel's his favorite horse." She got up to pour more coffee. "I am very grateful for the three of you to be here this evening."

"We appreciate you too, ma'am."

"How early will you all get up?"

"We better leave about four," Chet said.

"I'll have breakfast at three thirty."

"We ain't—"

She cut Hampt off. "You aren't imposing. There." She finished filling their cups.

They smiled and thanked her before they went outside to get some sleep. Chet looked at the million stars and wondered which one shone on those two bastards. He hated them before but worse than that now. A big job lay ahead for the three of them. Those two could slip away if they didn't push hard to capture them. He hoped daylight brought them more success.

Morning came too soon and in the cool predawn they dressed and headed for the house. Once in the lighted kitchen Chet could see she'd been crying some before.

"Morning, Gail. You all right?"

"I will be. Got to feeling sorry for myself." She swallowed hard.

"Things will ease up when he comes home. My, my, you're spoiling the posse with those cinnamon rolls. I could smell them clear down at the horse corral."

"I guess the others are coming?" She looked to try and see them.

"They're saddling the animals and packhorses." He poured himself some coffee in a tin cup.

"I have one question—kind of private and you don't have to answer it if you think it is."

"What?"

"Is your wife easy to live with?"

Chet laughed. "The easiest woman I can imagine.

We went on a camping trip to buy the other ranch for our honeymoon. Does that say anything?"

"She didn't mind?"

"No."

"Were you concerned about her?"

"Last year, yes. But I didn't know her then, until I guess she came to my aid when my nephew was murdered by those stage robbers."

She snickered and turned away. "Did she really pay all your bills?"

"Yes, and I made her take the money."

"I heard that too. I can see why—you are a leader of men."

"Thanks, but don't be too impressed. I'm just another Texas cowboy."

She gave him a small push aside to get to her biscuits and rolls in the oven. "No, I know better."

"Wow," Hampt said. "It is *larruping* smelling in here."

Everyone laughed.

They rode off before the predawn painted the eastern mountaintops pink. His gray was feeling his oats and they rode down alongside a dry branch until they topped another rise and could see the various houses of Hassayampa City in the first light. The structures were in the midst of some tall saguaro cactus. Fighting roosters crowed while milk cows bawled for their calves.

Chet found a man at the livery forking hay. He stopped him. The man, dressed in overalls, leaned on his pitchfork. "We're looking for two men that rode in here yesterday on horseback."

"Stolen ones?"

"Yes, they stole them from the Cloud ranch."

"I know Clay Cloud's horses when I see them. And them two galoots were riding them."

"Did they ride on?"

"I think they rode up Roble's Canyon to some buddy's place. Do you know him?"

"No, who is he?"

"Ross Harold. I never seen them come back from there."

"Another way out?"

The man nodded and spat tobacco aside. "It would be tough."

"How close can we get on horses?" Hampt asked, looking around.

"Oh, if I didn't want to be seen, I'd leave my horses at the spring."

"Is it obvious?" Chet asked.

"It runs water down that canyon."

"It's obvious." Chet looked at the mountain walls studded with the great cactus everywhere. Any way out of this place looked difficult, as steep as those mountainsides were around them.

"Let's water our horses, then ride up there."

Hampt joined him. Under his breath he asked, "You think they are still here?"

Leif came over to hear his answer.

Chet nodded. "Good chance they are."

"You men after them two?" the liveryman asked.

"Yes, we tracked them down from Crown King to where they stole the horses. They'd also mistreated Mrs. Cloud the night before. Two days before they robbed the store up there and shot Deputy Roamer."

"Can I go along to help?"

"Sure, if you won't shoot us," Chet said.

The man laughed, said his name was Stanley, and they introduced themselves and shook his hand.

"I'll get a horse to ride," Stanley said, and went to get him.

When he was gone, Chet told them, "He's a calm enough man to go along."

The other two agreed, busy watering the horses at his trough. Chet looked again where Stanley had pointed out Robles Canyon. It was a large gorge in the wall of mountain on the left, and beyond most of the scattered jacales. Were the shooters still up there? They'd be plain lucky if they did find them up there.

They rode around the small businesses, saloons, a store or two, and the stage depot where he had gotten off the hard seat in the coach for a short reprieve and stretched his legs. He recalled helping Marge off and back on the stage there under the stars that night on his first trip to Preskit. Lots of water had gone under his bridge since then. He felt good thinking about her. And a relief to know more about those two thugs who shot Roamer and raped Mrs. Cloud.

The trail up the canyon was under a few tall, gnarled cottonwoods. There was some thick brush and lots of small birds flitting about, choked in between the tall sheer cliffs. The ring of their shod horses was loud above the crush of the gravel beneath them. The trail wound upward and some buzzards drifted on the updraft overhead.

When he sighted the water spilling over a granite boulder, he stopped the others behind him.

"Is this the spring?" he asked softly over his shoulder.

"Stanley says yeah," Hampt gave a stage whisper.

"Hobble the horses, so no one can stampede them if they get by us."

They set into doing that, then, armed with their rifles, went around the small, clear spring pool and started up the steep grade. When he at last could see the shack against the bluff wall, there was no one in sight.

"It's pretty well open ground from here," Chet said. "We need to spread out and watch for any movement. Hit the ground at the first sight of any resistance."

The posse members nodded and they moved apart, rifles cocked and ready. The way was rocky and steep. Nothing moved. Then a sorrel horse raised his head up and looked at them from a rough pole corral.

"Stanley, is that Clay Cloud's red horse?"

"It is, sir."

The answer sobered him to the reality.

"Hold it right there!" someone ordered, and everyone dropped down to the ground.

"Listen to me," Chet shouted. "You send out those two men Ryder and Bender. Then no one will get shot I promise you—or else you will die with them. They're wanted dead or alive."

"We ain't giving up."

"Then put on your Sunday clothes, 'cause we'll bury you in them."

"Who the hell are you?"

"The men who trailed you from Crown King. Now get out here, 'cause we won't stop shooting till you all are dead."

Chet lowered his voice and told the others to fire two rounds in the windows of the cabin.

"Here's my reply."

The loud reports of their guns cracked the canyon silence in ear-shattering blasts.

"Hold your fire," someone inside shouted. "Hold your fire."

He nodded grimly. Two Hispanic women came out coughing on the dust.

"That may be a shield," Chet said sharply.

Hampt, on the right with his rifle at his shoulder, ran to the side to better see the outlaws coming out. He stopped and aimed clearly at the two men. "Where is the other guy?"

"I'm coming."

"Make it quick," Hampt said.

"You women step aside. Keep going. You men get belly down on the ground."

The posse members searched them for weapons and tied their hands in back. Stanley went and led the two Cloud horses out of the pen. Leif handed Chet the round-handle handgun that he'd taken off the taller outlaw.

He nodded as he examined it. "This is the pistol the store man mentioned he shot Roamer with."

"See if there's any money inside." When he said that the two women started to move to the shack. "Hold it there and sit on the ground right there."

They obeyed.

"I can guard them." Chet said to his men, "Look close for all of it."

"Hey I got rights. That's my money in there," the other tied-up man shouted.

"Hiding them makes you an accessory. You have no rights in this matter for my part. Do you know what they did to Mrs. Cloud?"

"I don't know."

"They raped her."

"I didn't do nothing."

"If I was the judge I'd hang you with your horse stealing partners."

"You can't do that."

He looked at the man. "I know where there's cottonwood trees at the base of this mountain that could stretch your neck, you better not keep challenging me."

Hampt came out with a bundle of money tied up in a shirt. "I think we got it all."

"Good." He made the three get on their feet and herded them to where Stanley had saddled the horses they stole.

"Put a lead rope on those horses. I don't want them getting away."

"What's your damn name?" the tall one, Ryder, asked.

Chet backhanded him and snapped his head around. "Shut up. I'm not listening to the worthless words you have to say."

"What about me?" Ross Harold asked.

"I ought to haul you to Preskit and let the judge fine you, but your women can let you loose when we get out of here. Not yet!" His shout made the two Mexican women quickly sit back on the ground.

The posse had their prisoners on the two saddled horses. They were started for the spring and off the mountain. Chet waited until the others were out of sight, then he started after them.

Leif led the procession off the mountain. When they were gone around the bend, Chet mounted the gray and followed them. He didn't entirely trust the man Stanley called Ross Harold, probably a bootlegger and someone who handled re-branded cattle. Some day he might have to ride back and catch him red-handed. Not his job this day—but he might need to consider it more seriously as the summer passed. Sims damn sure wouldn't do anything about the like. There were others in this country who needed rooting out and sending elsewhere.

When they rode out of the canyon, he caught up with Stanley and rode beside him. "What would you charge me for a buckboard to haul them to Preskit?"

"A dollar."

"No, I want to pay for it."

"To get rid of those two, I'd pay you."

"I want to keep going. I'm going to send Hampt to take the Clouds' horses back to them and then give the money back to the storekeeper up there. I'm going to have him give me a receipt. Then I'll have them locked up."

"I'll get a driver for you. He can bring the rig back."

"Thanks."

"I heard about you. I thought all this talk was bullshit and when I met you this morning, I saw you were none of that. You won't get paid a dime for this work. Why did a man with a big ranch have to go to find these criminals?"

"There was no pursuit by the law, and the bastards ruined a good woman's life."

"I'm sorry most about that." They dismounted at the livery. Word was out about the capture and several folks began flocking to the stables and asking questions.

"Who are they?"

"What did they do?"

"Why are they tied up?"

Stanley got their attention. "These men held up the store at Crown King. They shot a deputy sheriff who tried to stop them. They assaulted a rancher's wife and stole their horses. Mr. Byrnes, Mr. Times, and Mr. Tate are concerned citizens doing the job our lawmen should be doing. The horses and money will be going back to the rightful folks."

When he ended, the men and women applauded and came by to shake the three men's hands.

Chet listened closely to the crowd as they prepared to take the outlaws on to Preskit. Lynching them and getting it over was the word on many lips. He started for Stanley to tell him to hurry the buckboard deal as the crowd was turning angrier by the minute from what he heard. Not at them, but at the two in the back.

"Hold it." he raised his hands. "These men are my prisoners and I'll shoot anyone that tries to take them away from us. The law is working. Now you all can go on. Start moving."

"Your name Byrnes?" a man shouted at him.

"I'm Chet Byrnes. I am just a rancher. I am trying to stay out of this law business, but I am not doing a great job at it. That isn't here nor there. Yavapai County needs good law enforcement. I am just here to take these men in to the authorities. Thank you for dispersing."

Chet instructed Hampt on taking the Cloud horses back to them, then for him to take the storekeeper the money in the shirt. Then he needed to carefully count it with him, as well as bring a receipt from him for the prosecution attorney.

"I can handle it. Thanks, I'll see you at the ranch."

"Yes, come by Marge's. Leif and I will take them in to Preskit tonight and have them locked in the jail."

"You don't need any help here?" Hampt asked, looking as the crowd began to let up.

"Wait till we start out. Thanks. Is your man ready, Stanley?"

"Yes, his name is Lloyd Burks. Good man."

"Thanks again, Stanley, for all your help." He saluted him in the late afternoon sun's glare and the team struck a good clip on the Black Canyon Road, headed north for Preskit. By the time they reached the turnoff into town it was long past midnight. Chet had a time staying awake in the saddle.

"You want to go home from here?" he asked Leif.

"Naw, I'll make it and dislocate my jaw yawning. I'm sure pleased you let me join you. Now do you have an in with your sister?"

"No. She pretty well makes up her own mind. I certainly can't head her toward anyone, no matter how much I like you. You're on your own in that case."

"Thanks. You won't object to me trying?"

"No, it is a free world. I just don't want her hurt."

"Oh, I'd never hurt her. I'd just like to have her

look at me. I am not rich. I am not educated. Does she go to church?"

"Don't we all?"

"Yes. I mean is she into any brand?"

"Better ask her."

"I didn't join you to win your sister. I am one of your fans since you tracked down the Artman killers. I told my dad I wanted to help you again. I am not any great hero, but I am learning."

"I appreciate your help. I hope this is the last time I have to run down anyone. Only I don't believe it will be. Still the same, you need something or help on something besides winning my sister, come get me."

"Thanks. What don't she like?"

"Pushy people."

"Oh, I'll remember that."

"Good luck to you."

"I ain't leaving until they're in jail. Let me know how Hampt got along."

"Be glad to do that if he's not around."

"Where did he come from?"

"I'm not sure—" Gray spooked sideways at some grouse's booming flight in the night from the edge of the road. He got him calmed down and went back to riding with Leif.

"Hampt was a cowboy then that needed work last year, and he handles lots of things for me."

"Good guy to have on your side."

Chet agreed.

They came off the steep hill to the courthouse,

and Chet found the streets were deserted. He told the driver he'd pay for his room to sleep and to find Jenny's café and she'd feed him on his account. Frye's livery would stall his team too on his account as well.

"Thanks, I'm ready to sleep some. Sure glad we had no trouble back there. Folks were getting upset, but you see'd that and stopped them."

"It will be all right."

"Hell. We're here now for the most part."

Chet agreed as he reined up on the west side of the courthouse. Leif went in and got the night jailer.

"So you got them bastards shot Roamer?"

"Yes, how is he doing?"

"Fine, he's on crutches. Seen him yesterday in the Palace."

"Good. You need anything, I'll put this note with their names on your desk. Sims got any questions he can find me. We've returned the stolen horses and what money they had left to the storekeeper at Crown King."

"He probably will. Good night."

"How long you been up?" The guard made a face at him.

"Couple of days."

"My lord, you're a serious man."

"So is Times here. He's been up that long too."

"Get to bed."

The two men shook hands and he rode out to Marge's house to see the sun peeping up on the horizon. Jesus took his horse. Monica offered him breakfast and he thanked her, then went by her, kissed his excited wife and took his gun belt off, hung it and his hat on a peg. "I'm going to bed someplace. I really don't care." He looked at her out of bleary eyes.

"Can you climb upstairs?"

"I think so. I want to sleep for four days."

She laughed. "You will be up on a new project in lots less time than that."

In their bedroom, she pulled off his boots and helped undress him. Last thing he could recall was her kissing him—then he slept.

CHAPTER 18

By noontime, he'd taken a shower, shaved, and eaten some oatmeal. Seated at the dining table, he'd carefully explained his trip to the two women. They both, at points, asked him small questions, like Would Mrs. Cloud have shot him?

"No, even the men she should have shot got by her. No, that isn't fair, I think she's a very conscientious woman."

"I have met her," Marge said. "It takes a lot to ask a woman to shoot someone."

The second one they asked about was his mention of Leif and his sister.

"How old is he?" Marge asked.

"Early twenties. Quiet, but he's very alert. I told him I considered him an uncomplaining posse member, but I was not a go-between for him." Then he laughed.

"What will they do next?"

"Have a grand jury investigation. Then a trial."

"Will they be convicted?"

He nodded. "The court can't hang them. But they can sentence them to several years."

"Did you talk to them?"

"No. They are stupid criminals with no mercy for an innocent woman or a small storekeeper, or Roamer."

Marge returned with a piece of peach pie for him. She hugged his head standing beside him. "Monica made this for your return."

"Better keep her, she's great."

They laughed and he felt good to be home again.

"Your man Hampt just rode up," Marge said, looking out the bay window.

"Good, hide my pie." Then he held up his hands. "I am only teasing. You going to show him in, Marge?"

"Yes. He is such a nice big man."

"Well, boss man, they have the receipt of the money I paid back to Mr. Andy at Crown King."

"Did they say anything at the office?"

"They asked me what the receipt from Clay Cloud meant for his two stolen horses. I told them. The sheriff never came out and asked me a thing. All I talked to was a clerk."

"Sounds like what I expected."

"There's the same tickets I gave them and signed in case they get lost," Hampt said.

"Oh, Hampt they wouldn't do that," said Marge.

"Ma'am, I don't trust them."

"Put them in an envelope and in your safe," Chet said to her.

"Certainly. Thanks," she said, taking them from Hampt.

"Learn anything else?" Hampt took a seat and Monica brought him pie and coffee.

"Wow, thanks, ma'am."

"That is my welcome home pie."

"Glad I am included. I heard that the Hartley brothers are doing something."

"What is that?"

"The things I heard are, their plan is not working. The cattle they dumped on us up here are all over hell. They thought at community roundups folks would brand their calves for them and they could go in and collect them as two-year-olds. First, many were not branded. So they're being claimed as mavericks. Second, folks are eating them. Since they can't get them all up, I think from what I heard they are collecting them to drive on the upper end of our place."

Chet listened. "How many are on our land?"

"Tom and I figure fifty or more mother cows."

"Then we need to move them off and drive them down there before they drive more of them on us."

"What will they do with them then?"

"I don't care."

"We can take everyone and get them up in a week. We have a good tally on our own and they're all branded. We've worked hard to do that and we never touched a Hartley animal. Of course if they were mavericks, we branded them by the law."

"I know you and Tom have worked hard building a real tally. It is important we don't discuss this with anyone except you, me, and Tom. When we saddle up they won't have a warning and the cattle will be at their headquarters before they know what happened."

"Who needs to know?"

"Hoot for one, and get Victor to fix the outriders food, then take some of the men so we can get the ones on the far edge."

"Secret as I can be. I'll tell Tom this Thursday. I'll talk to Raphael and her father about their part. Will we start Monday morning?" Hampt asked. "And should we bring the loggers back?"

"No, we have enough down here. I may send word to Reg. But I can do that."

"What about JD?" Marge asked.

He shook his head. "I can talk to him but he has enough problems over there."

"Should I tell Tom about that situation?"

"Yes, but no small talk about our plan. I want them drove up here and they won't have a reason to ride on our deeded land."

"Was that why Loftin wanted to set up a camp at Perkins?"

"For a receiving place? Maybe. I figure they don't know how many they have and want to cut out a new range on federal land."

"Good thing they didn't know about your new place."

"Yes." He'd need to see Bo about his progress on closing the deal.

Hampt held the coffee cup in both hands. "Word is if you have three horses and can ride, they'll hire you."

"What do they pay?"

"Forty dollars a month. That ain't much for riding your own horses and having to find grub." Hampt shook his head. "They'll get some men hired but I doubt they get much work out of them."

"Good, we may be doing them a favor to ship them their own cattle."

Hampt laughed. "I don't know about that. I better go find Tom and make plans."

"Yes, do that. When will your father be back?" Chet asked Marge.

"Oh, when he gets through down there."

Chet frowned.

"My father has a lady friend down there."

"At Hayden's Mill?"

She smiled and nodded.

"Oh." Chet chuckled.

Hampt ate his pie, drank the coffee, and after thanking the ladies, he took off. Things were set now to get things done, and as quickly as they could do them.

Chet stood up, stretched, and decided he needed to talk to Bo about his progress. Marge agreed to go with him. After a short while he drove the team into Preskit. They stopped at Bo's office and he looked up from his desk when Chet stepped inside and nodded to his man seated and reading a *Police Gazette* magazine.

"You're going to be well informed."

Davis looked up. "He's still sober."

"Thanks. Well, Bo, where do we stand?"

"You own the Hackberry ranch, lock, stock, and barrel."

"Good. What else do you need?"

"Reg may want his own brand up there. I'll talk to him about it."

Bo nodded. "I have three sections of land available on the stage line route and the military road at the base of the mountains that hold the San Francisco Peaks."

"Are any west of that point?"

"All three are. The real estate company selling them for the Francisco Railroad wants twenty thousand a section."

"Wait until they shut down the track building again and offer them two thousand apiece."

Bo laughed. "The way these economic waves keep going through Wall Street, you may buy it cheaper than that."

"Good. It may be our best investment."

"Twenty miles east of there they are about worthless."

"I can see why."

Bo made a face like he had another idea. "I am

meeting with Jane. If I marry her can I be freed of these two *brothers*?"

"I will think about it. Has your fee for my work been paid?"

"No, but you will get a bill. Next week I am selling real estate. Several homes and small ranches."

"Being sober has helped your business."

"Yeah."

"Then realize that you are doing better because you're sober."

"Yes."

"Good. I may be out of pocket in the next few weeks. Marge can find me."

"Word's out you found the ones who shot Roamer?"

"Leif Times, Hampt Tate and I arrested them down at Hassayampa City a day ago."

"You think Sims has some pains in his ass over that?"

"I don't know."

Bo shook his head. "You better get ready for another job."

"We'll see."

"You know what I mean? Folks are really talking about electing you as sheriff."

"I have some ranches to run."

"That won't be all."

"Thanks." He left and drove Marge to the mercantile to get a few things while he went to see Jane while she shopped. He found her not busy.

"You know about the Hartleys' plan?"

"I've heard a little about it."

"They're going to round them up and push them on us."

She agreed and looked around. "Can they do that?"

"No, the Perkins is deeded land and there are no public roads. We will stop them but they know that."

"I think they're desperate enough to try."

He agreed. "Bo tells me you two are talking?"

She nodded. "We are. He's a great guy sober, but I don't know if he'll stay that way without his so-called brothers looking over his shoulder."

"That's your business. I won't interfere."

"Thanks. If I learn more about the others, I'll send word."

"Thanks." He tipped her five silver dollars.

She smiled and thanked him.

Then he went back to the buckboard to pick up his wife. She had some food items loaded in the back by a clerk and they went home.

"Things going good?"

"We have the ranch. I am going to have to ask Reg what he wants for a brand before we go forward."

"That's nice. Do you want to meet Raphael tonight and talk to him about moving their stock off our land?"

"Will your father agree to this?"

"Yes."

"Then I'll talk to him."

"Good."

"What will you do next?" she asked.

"I may need to stay down there while we gather those cattle and be sure it is going all right. Would you come along?"

"Of course."

He turned and kissed her on the cheek, then clucked to the team. "We'll slip down there Saturday. Tell Susie and May. We'll go to the dance and be there Monday when we spread out to retrieve their cattle."

"How do you think it will work out?"

"It may force them to sell some of their cattle."

She agreed. "They may shift their attitude toward the rest of us. I mean make a show of force against us."

"They can't fight every outfit."

"But you could be a good place to start." She smiled and shook her head. "I never expected to be in this much business as you stay involved in."

"Life ain't never simple."

Saturday they drove to the Quarter Circle Z. Marge made no plans to bring her tent and things down there. So once on the Verde, she and Susie, along with May, made some things for the regular potluck supper and laughed while he went to talk to Hoot.

"I'll be ready to pull out for Perkins and set up there. No problem. This came up fast?" Hoot asked.

"The Hartleys are hiring hands to gather their cattle. We needed to move fast in this case."

"Who's ramrodding it out there?"

"Hampt's handling that end. Tom is going after the closer cattle and using the lesser cowboys. They'll eat at the ranch and when we get this end cleaned up, then we'll go out and wind up at that end."

"You've got it planned well, then. Hell, Chet, we ain't greenhorns. We won't be long at this. I say in a week to ten days all their cattle will be at Mayer that are on this ranch and range."

"How many you figure are on us?"

"Tom say's there's over a hundred and fifty cows counting what's out west on our graze."

"That's a big herd. Didn't Ryan ever do anything about them being on his range?"

"Yeah, we ate them."

"That's a common style. A man was eating at his neighbor's and going home got sick. He swore to his wife it was because they'd eaten their own stock."

"Yeah, that's the way it goes." They both laughed.

"I can't see you having much trouble. It will all be over before they know it and they'll be loaded with them. They ain't got a bull of their own with any of them using all your bulls."

Later Chet wondered, riding up on top and surveying the rim north, what his nephew Reg had found up there that was occupying his time. It was tough to lose a woman like Juanita, and no telling what he was doing—but he'd show up in time.

Chet hoped he'd found some solace in a new country and a new project. He'd know in a few more weeks. Reg would be back, or else he might miss all the fun of chousing the Hartleys' cattle back home to them.

"Who else is in on it?"

"Marge's foreman Raphael and his three vaqueros are doing that up there."

"Good, her father is a leader on the high country ranch."

"Don't tell anyone, but he's down at Hayden Mills courting a lady."

Hoot chuckled. "That's interesting."

"I need to go talk to Susie. She knows she can help Victor if she wants to."

"Oh, yeah, thanks for getting me out here. It sure is a lot easier."

Two bold magpies flew in the tent to scout for some food. But they quickly left.

"They are nearly done on the cook shack roof. They're busy busting more shingles for it, but this will put us off a few weeks."

"They'll get it all done before fall."

Thunder roared in the distance. A summer shower could sweep up or down the valley. Anyone could use the moisture. He left the old man to his cooking and went to the house.

Susie was working in the kitchen.

"Marge around?"

"Upstairs cleaning up. What do you know?"

"She tell you about the latest deal?"

"Yes, she did. Said you, Hampt, and the Times boy went after them."

"He's not a boy, he's very serious. I bet he's older than you are."

"You must like him."

"He's a nice serious young man. Have you ever met him?"

"Oh, I danced a time or two with him."

"Did you get a bad impression?"

"Frankly, I thought he was an awful stiff shirt."

"Maybe you acted bored."

"I'd say he was kinda, you know, awed by me."

"Might have been. You and Tom still speaking?"

"Yes, thank you."

"Good."

"Any word from JD?"

"I think Reg told us all about his problems."

"I can't understand that. He saved her. I don't think she's entirely grateful for him."

"JD will have to figure it out."

"I think it's his pride keeping him there now."

"Oh." Chet blinked at her.

"What do you think then?"

"You may be right. I sure don't want him hurt, but it isn't a happy deal for him now."

She frowned and shook her head. "Some people never know when they're well off."

"I agree. But I am."

"Better go check on you own wife."

"Yes, mother."

She threatened to slap him but it was all in fun. He laughed halfway up the stairs.

They went early and the rest followed. Marge found some rancher wives and Chet talked to some of the men he knew. Tom was going to speak to the men individually that he met with at the meeting that Chet missed on his honeymoon concerning the Hartleys' threatened actions.

"How are those Kansas Herefords doing?" one man asked.

"Tom says good. We've had some good rain and the grass is doing all right."

"How many bulls you going to have to sell?" another man asked.

"We'll need some of them ourselves. Maybe two dozen of them."

"You got lucky."

"I didn't steal them. But he won't sell any more except as bulls."

"We've been hearing you're moving up on top." He tossed his head northward.

"My family bought a ranch site up there. There are no facilities yet and we are starting from scratch. My nephew Reg is up there lining things up. The deal has been closed. It belongs to us."

"How're you going to stock it?"

"Good question. I'm working on that."

"Were those two you brought in for Sims very tough?"

"No, they were dumb criminals. And cruel ones."

"How many does that make you delivered to Sims?"

"I haven't counted them." Chet wondered where they'd go with this.

"Too damn many."

"Boys, they're all in jail. That means they can't steal or murder us. Let's move on."

"Why's the Hartleys hiring all these cowboys?"

A man sitting on a box and whittling on a juniper stick spat and said, "They're going to gather up some of our stock and move them, with theirs, then bunch them on one range. That's their plan."

"Where?"

"I heard the head of the Verde and that country."

Chet shook his head. "They tried to set up at Perkins a month ago. That's deeded land. I ran them off. They will have to drive them up on the north rim and come back down west of there."

"They'd lose lots of cattle doing that."

"I don't care. They won't go in over us."

Heads nodded in agreement.

"You may have a war." One sharp-eyed man behind a snowy mustache looked hard at Chet for his answer.

"No, they won't have a chance."

The man bobbed his hat brim at him. "I'll bring my gun and help you."

"Thanks, I'd accept your help."

"I will too," came more voices.

Several more offered to back him and he raised his hands. "I am going to pray it doesn't come to this. But the Quarter Circle Z is not going to let them go in that way. Thanks."

They broke up and Leif came through them. "Is your sister here? I couldn't find your camp."

"She's here. We're eating at the main potluck."

He looked relieved. "Thanks." Then he half ran off. Chet recalled being that flustered by women in his time. Thank God, he had Marge. Whew.

The meal went well. He and Marge sat on a bench at the wall. He fielded many questions about his arrests. Several wanted him to commit if a draft was held for him to run for sheriff. He told them he was busy building his ranches and didn't know if he could give them the job they wanted.

"You know things won't get better in this country. New folks moving in and those on the run from the law figure that Arizona is a ripe place for them. This ain't going to get better, it will get worse, and we need effective law enforcement. Sims thinks you can put up wanted posters and collect them up. There's hundreds of them, but you and those others who helped you have run them down, before they committed another bloody crime."

"We got lucky."

"No, you're damn tough. That's what we need."

"I don't think he's convinced." Marge said to save him. "But I am sure he is considering it."

The older man centered his look on her. "You can help us."

She smiled. "I'll try."

The music started and he saw JD and Kay arrived in time to fill their plates. Of course, there was lots of food left. He and Marge slipped off on the floor into a waltz. He always felt good when dancing with her, and had escaped for a short while from the ones who wanted to draft him. The fiddle music filled his ears and the slight perfume she wore touched his nose. Time to count his blessings. Arizona Territory would someday be a great place, when the rough edges were planed off it.

"Are you concerned about not hearing from Reg?"

"He's a big boy and there aren't much ways to talk at a distance. I figure he's finding himself."

"Have you spoken to JD yet?"

"If he needs me he knows where I am. According to Reg, she rejected what I offered. Told him they'd make it. I was going to buy them some bulls and we sent them some saddle horses, since his are all older."

"Strange, isn't it? I have known her for years, and I can't explain all that must be going on."

"I'm more concerned about JD. But nothing I can do, obviously. I only stirred up a stink."

"What can you do?"

"We can talk about it later." People had come back to join them.

Tom and Millie were there and came by to visit. She wore a new blue dress the three women had sewn for her, and the outfit really flattered her.

Susie was over with Tom and his family group. He'd not seen Leif but figured he must be there. Poor boy had a bad case on her and he was losing ground fast in Chet's book.

"We're ready," Tom said when they were about alone.

"Good. I think we will shock them."

Tom nodded.

The evening went smooth. No fights among the drunks, and when it winded down, they loaded their wagons to go home or retired to their camps.

Marge reached over and squeezed his leg. "You have fun this evening?"

"I always do dancing with you. Guess I'm concerned how this cattle drive will turn out. But it's best that we end it now. It sure won't get any better in time, huh?"

"I realized you were occupied. The time has come."

He leaned over into her shoulder. "I thought so, too."

Sunday, Marge went with the women and two young boys to the church in town. Chet and Tom along with Hampt sat at the big dining table to make their plans.

"There are close to a hundred fifty T B branded cows plus calves scattered across our ranges. And several on this land."

"Fifty? Would that be close," Hampt asked, "in this end?"

Tom agreed. "I think so. But I've seen some new ones that have drifted upstream."

"We have an enclosure at Perkins where we can hold those cattle and it has enough feed for a week or so."

"Good, but I want them on the road to Mayer as quick as we can."

Tom nodded. "Yes, part of the shock will be for them to look up and see their cattle coming home."

"Does this move have any legal restrictions?" Tom asked.

Chet shook his head. "Their cattle are on our private land. We are returning them to their owners."

Hampt laughed. "I'd love to see the look on their faces when them cows come home."

"So would I," Chet said.

In the predawn light, Tom explained at the cook shack what happened next. Most of them smirking over the idea as their horses were saddled. The team was hooked to Hoot's chuck wagon, and in a short time things began to roll.

The hands around the ranch rode in three directions and the trap gates were open to bring them down.

Chet went over the books upstairs and Marge was busy with the girls baking or doing something. By noon Tom and his bunch brought in several T B branded cows with calves to the holding ground. He swung by the house. Chet came down to talk to him.

"There's more than I thought there were, but

we should have them in here by evening and can go help Hampt in the morning on the west side."

"Sounds smooth enough."

"Most have calves and the cows won't bust off if their calves can't follow. We've done well. Must be fifty cows in this bunch. We saw some of their yearlings but stayed with the cattle we had."

"I'll go help this evening. The girls have dinner fixed—go ring a bell."

"I will. Hope Hampt and them had as good a morning."

The girls had fixed chopped beef and gravy over rice and three kinds of pies. The crew, some whom were more like carpenters than cowboys, had got a big kick out of the drive. Lots of teasing about how one or the other about fell off their horses turning back an ornery cow.

Marge smiled at him. "Don't you fall off."

"I might. The yearlings might be harder. They are dumb anyway."

He saddled one of the roan horses. He tied two lariats on his saddle and rode out. The T B yearlings stayed a lot to themselves up in the junipers, so the first sweep brought most down in the open grasslands after playing merry-go-round with some of them. One threw its tail over its back and lit out.

Time to go to work. He took the lariat on the right side and fed out a good size loop because this was a pure longhorn. His pony narrowed the gap between them. He stood up in the stirrups and began to swing the loop over his head and the first toss landed on the steer's back. He remade the loop on the fly. Tossed it over half his head and the stub horns, then he spurred the roan past him and threw the rope over the steer's back. Then he turned left with a hard wrap on the horn and the steer collided on the end, and the force flipped him over on his back.

Chet rode up slow. The steer was fine and getting to his feet groggy like, and Chet rode in and flipped the rope off his head. "Now get back with the rest."

The shocked steer went off to join them but a lot slower than he left. Chet came past a carpenter on horseback who pushed him in with the others. "I'm all right herding but I'll leave that roping to you."

They both laughed.

As the bunch grew they made lots of dust and Tom came though it standing up at a trot. "I think we got most all of them. If you and two boys can take them to the pasture, three of us will make a big swing to check for any more."

Chet knew that left him four carpenters in the saddle, but the yearlings were mostly settled. "We can make it."

Tom and his bunch left and they drove the T B yearlings off the hills for the pasture gate.

With sixty or so young stuff soon locked inside, they closed the gate. The carpenters dismounted, holding their backs in both hands and threatening to walk back to the headquarters.

"Not me," Wayne said. "Them other hands ever

find out we did that they'd razz us till we're gray headed."

"You're right," another said, and got back on.

"You cowboys can call it a day," Chet said. "I'm off to find Tom and help them get the last ones."

"You ain't leaving without us. Those women folks of yours would tell the boys before their shirt tail hits their asses, how we chickened out."

So an amused Chet and his crew rode northwest to find them. The men with Tom had about twenty more, some cows that had hid out. Everyone fell in, pleased.

"Too smooth was all," Tom said. The real test probably would be in the rougher country in the west.

Chet nodded at Tom. "Tomorrow we'll see who can stay in the saddle."

"Victor's taking them up fresh horses this afternoon. I figure they've got a lot bigger workout than we did."

"This was slick," Chet told the crew. "Driving them up over Mingus Mountain might challenge us. I once owned a big roan steer who could have led them anywhere."

"What happened to him?"

"I sold him when I came back one year and had lost three good young men on the drive."

"That cattle driving made money, but it was tough, wasn't it?" Tom asked.

"Pure hell. I hated it so bad I made my brother take the last one, and they shot him."

They reined up in the yard and Marge came to

greet them. Susie was on the porch listening to the progress.

"We've got them in the big pasture. We'll go help Hampt tomorrow."

"Your nail drivers made cowboys."

Chet looked them over and then chuckled. "Damn good ones, too."

One of them crowded his horse in and said, "You bet Missus Byrnes, and not a one of us fell off his horse."

A hurrah went up.

CHAPTER 19

At predawn they saddled up. Tom cut out the two less likely ones to be real cowboys and told them to watch and guard the place while everyone was gone. They rode at a trot for the Perkins place.

When they reached the broad valley, Hampt met them.

"We've got most of the T B cows and calves gathered. There's two or three old Texas moss horns got away, but I rode back through the north country yesterday and only saw one run off. The boys should bring in the rest today. The Herefords up here and them won't hardly stay together with the longhorns, so they weren't as bad as we expected."

"How many big stuff have you gathered?" Chet asked.

"Two-fifty cows, not counting calves. There were plenty up here."

"They probably were pushed this direction by their men," Tom said. "We'd noticed an increase but couldn't catch them doing it."

"Tomorrow we can start driving them?"

"I'd say so," Hampt said.

"Good, we better tell Hoot."

The two men agreed.

"Put them in one herd then, tomorrow at the ranch?" Tom asked.

"That's a good plan if you feel we have the most of them gathered. I know we can't get every one. We move them there it will be a hard day the following one to get them on top. Raphael and his hands will have more T B cattle at her place, and they will help move them the next day to Mayer. If we can get them on the mountain that first day, we'll be in good shape to drive them to their place the next day. We may block lots of traffic on the main road, but we can get there."

His men agreed and he went to the house. Past midday he was back and dismounted. One of the carpenters armed with a rifle met him.

"Any trouble, Burt?" he asked the man.

"No sir, been pretty quiet."

"Good." He looked at the house and his wife came out the door.

"You're back. Is anything wrong?" she asked.

"No, but I have a mission for you."

"Good, what is that?"

He thanked Burt and went on to his wife. Arm across her shoulder, they went inside.

"Tomorrow the T B cattle will be here. Next day we will drive them up Mingus Mountain, which will block the road. Can't be helped. Then I want to rest them on the east end of your range, so if

Raphael gets your ranch cattle moved west we won't have any mix up and he can throw his T B cattle in with ours."

"By now he'll have most of their cattle gathered."

"We can add them to these."

"You will leave here day after tomorrow for the mountain?" He agreed, and she said, "So what if I ask Leif to block the road on top and tell folks there is a herd coming? I fear someone won't listen to my man because he is a Mexican and it might hurt his feelings."

"Yes, maybe have Leif get a few other ranchers to back him. If he's not too busy. If they can or know something they might try to stop us right there."

"I better get home then."

He kissed her. "I'll hook up the team. You be careful, too."

Susie, who'd been privy to their conversation, agreed.

Marge turned to her. "Why don't you go along? You've never seen my house or the ranch up there."

"Take me a few minutes to get packed. I'll do that." Susie looked pleased at the invite.

He felt better the two were going together, and ran to hitch the team. Burt helped him and soon the rig was out front waiting for them.

When they appeared, on the porch, the two men carried Susie's luggage to the rig. Loaded at last, he kissed Marge good-bye and told her he'd see her in a few days. He checked with May in the house before he rode back to join the crew in the west. On the ride back, he wondered if the Hartley brothers had any idea what they were up to. When they reached the top of the mountain, they would damn sure hear enough gossip about the movement thing to stir them up. In all his time in the territory, he'd not even met either of them, like they were avoiding him. He'd only met their foreman Loftin, in his outrageous try to intrude on the ranch.

The fat would be in the fire in forty-eight hours. Most all of their cows were straight longhorn and they'd been using others' bulls. Most of the calves trailing them were half British crosses—Shorthorn or Hereford. But none were from Hartley sires, and many of their stray cows had not been bred while wandering around and were open. Their plan to infest the range with these cattle was to let the others buy the bulls and they'd clip the coupons at roundup. They were about to get the whole coupon delivered for free.

He joined Tom and Hampt in camp who were certain they had the T B cattle for the most part off the Quarter Circle Z range.

"Marge is to have some ranchers up on Mingus Mountain to warn folks that the herd is coming up tomorrow. She was afraid the someone might give her foreman Raphael a hard time, so she's getting Leif and Gates to warn them at the head of that road that the herd's coming up."

"I can see that," Hampt said. "He's hardworking, but someone might cuss that Mexican out and go down anyway."

"I'm glad she saw that," Tom agreed.

"So am I. Susie went with her. So they can keep each other company."

"When we get on top, should Hoot come up there?"

"Good question. I didn't plan on that. He can fix supper at the ranch tomorrow night that we'll be over there. We better send someone to tell Victor—"

"He's here helping."

"Better go find him. We'll need to eat tomorrow night late at Marge's ranch and then have breakfast on the day we drive them to Mayer. Plus supper when we come back."

"I'll get him," Hampt said.

Shortly they had a conference and Victor said he could be up there and set up to do all that.

"You know that tank on the east end of Preskit Valley that belongs to Marge's family?"

Victor nodded. "I have seen it."

"Raphael will help you get water out there."

"No problem, I will be there, *señor.*"

"Good, see you there in two nights." He clapped the youth on his shoulder. "Marge and Susie are at Marge's ranch if you need them."

"I can do it, *señor.*"

"I know, but I bet they'll want to help you."

"I will check with them."

"Should we have everyone bring their bedrolls?" Hampt asked.

"Thanks, we better." Chet knew they were closing the problems that might occur. And everyone was working hard to make it smooth.

"The men have rested their best horses in their string for the drive," Tom said.

"We take on the mountain in the next morning. Tomorrow will be a short run."

They agreed.

Before dawn crept up, the crew had the cattle on the road to the main ranch headquarters. Hampt and another hand rode out front to clear the road for the herd. A big cow with a six-foot span of horns took the lead. She bossed things and proved herself the leader. The dust churned up by cloven hooves loomed on the kerchief-masked riders, keeping the slow ones up to follow the herd.

Lots of shouting, and individual riders bringing back the ones that tried to break aside.

Before noon, they were at the ranch and had driven in the herd, with lots of head-butting and social places decided, but it straightened out as the sun went down.

In the predawn morning amid the continuous cow bawling, Hampt and Chet took the lead and started up the road to take on the mountain ahead of the mossy-back lead cow and the two point riders.

Starting up the mountain, they met a man in a wagon coming down and he was almost there.

"Damn, I hoped I'd beat you," he swore.

"Did they warn you?"

"They did. But I planned to be past here." He cussed some more.

"If you stay hard on the wall side and park, they will probably pass you. If they damage anything look me up," Chet said.

The man agreed and put his team of mules as close to the bluff side as he could. Chet thanked him and they rode on. Halfway up, the cattle's bawling was hard in his ears, but Chet could look back in his field glasses and see Mossy coming in a swinging walk.

"They must have cut off the rest of the traffic," Hampt said after loping ahead to scout anyone else trying to come down. "I didn't see anyone else."

"Great, we're making good time."

Mid-afternoon, Mossy came up the last grade out of the canyon and on top. Chet and Hampt were with the three other ranchers. Leif, Gates, and a man named Helm were shaking hands with them. Several freight wagons, riders, and rigs were lined up waiting to go on.

Chet rode down the line and apologized to the folks waiting. Most said they'd make it. A few were indignant and he nodded to them. But the road committee had done their job right. They'd made the worst part of the drive and for all he could tell they were on top, or close to it.

When they got to the water, Raphael would have the T B cattle caught on his range waiting for them.

Leif rode in beside him when he returned. "Your wife invited us to supper. Gates and Helm said they needed to get back today. I'd like to stay for selfish reasons. Is that all right?"

Chet smiled. "They invited you. I'll see you at supper."

"Good. Did that guy get down there that won't listen to us?"

"Almost. I don't think he had a problem, but I'd wished he'd waited."

"He won't listen. Oh, I figure some guy by now has rode to tell the Hartley brothers."

"We knew someone would tell them."

"You concerned?" Leif looked at him hard.

"Always when you do things like this, you know the other side will try to stop you. I took that chance. You can't live all your life ducking confrontation. Their foreman challenged me in the road and told me they'd get what they wanted. Tomorrow they'll have these cattle back. I sure hope he'll be pleased."

Leif nodded like he understood. "Thanks. Dad said to tell you he'd support you any way you need us."

"You tell him thanks, when you get home. See you at supper. I'm going to check on Raphael."

"I'll ride with Hampt. See you later."

They parted and he set the roan horse in a short lope for the tank. Before he topped the rise he heard the cattle bawling from the other side. He reached the ridge and could see Raphael had gathered a couple hundred head of T B stock off his ranch. The foreman rode out to meet him.

"You must have made it, *señor*?"

"The lead cow came out of the canyon about a

half hour ago. They should be all on top soon. I see you have several head here."

"We got all we could. There may be one or two we missed, but come roundup we will get the rest."

"Thanks."

"What will those brothers do?"

"If you mess with a rattlesnake he will strike at you."

"Ah, *sí*, but how do you think they will do that?"

"I am not sure. I am ready for anything. Meanwhile those cows won't eat our grass."

"*Sí*, that is right."

"I may ride over to the ranch and check on the women."

"We are ready and your cook is set up. He has several barrels of fresh water and firewood."

"*Gracias, mi amigo.*" He swung by to talk for a minute to Victor and then rode on to the house.

Marge came out the back door with a nightshirt, towel, and soap to meet him. Susie backed her at the door.

"I use to get kisses. Now I get a bath," he teased, and the women laughed.

He kissed his wife and they headed for the sheepherders shower. "Everyone is fine. We are on top with the herd by now."

"Great, get clean." Susie waved him on.

"I really see why you never married, you had her," Marge said quietly.

"Some other women have said that before. She's a dynamic person."

He undid the gun belt, and began to undress after he toed off his boots. "It went well so far."

"Do you think they know about it by now?"

"Yes. It is up to them now, but there is near a thousand head going to their ranch tomorrow and it will sure force them to make a decision."

"Were there any problems?"

"I don't have all the facts, but things went well."

While he was under the shower, she shook her head. "Was it a bigger drive than you thought?"

"I knew there were several head on the ranch, but it exceeded my largest count almost double."

"Are any of the ranchers coming to supper tonight? I invited them."

"Leif is."

"Oh."

"The rest needed to go home."

"Does that put Susie on the spot?"

Soaping himself, he shook his head. "She's a big girl."

"She really is a nice person. She takes after you."

Under the flushing rinse water, he let go of the pull chain. "I don't know about that."

They both laughed.

The Hartley brothers would have a response. Toweling dry, he wondered what they'd try to do. Damn he'd like to simply ranch. There was no end to this kind of business to fight for what was his. Only time would tell.

CHAPTER 20

At the sound of horses at the front yard gate, Chet rose from the supper table and told her he could handle it. It was past sundown.

He could see Sarge was off his horse and had started for the gate.

"What's wrong?" Chet asked.

"They arrested Tom and Hampt both for rustling those cattle and took them to jail."

"Who arrested them?"

"Two of Sims's deputies." Sarge was out of breath. "We'd never let them take them, but Tom said for us to watch the cattle and notify you. And not to cause a fight."

"He was right."

"What happened?" Leif said from the porch with both women behind him.

"The Hartleys swore out a warrant for our arrest for cattle rustling. Sims's men arrested Tom and

Hampt. Took them to jail, Sarge said. Tom wanted no trouble and he did the right thing."

"What now?" Marge asked

"I'm going out to the herd. They're getting their cattle back in the morning. No matter what."

"I can go bail them out," Leif said.

"I can go with him and be sure they're out." Marge and Susie shared nods.

"Good. We're driving those cattle to their ranch at dawn."

"Has Sims lost his mind?" Marge asked.

"I'm not certain, but it was foolish, anyway." He'd damn sure never expected this to happen—arresting his own men to stop him.

"You take care of the herd and those men. We'll handle it on this end," Susie assured him.

Chet went for his horse on the run. Soon saddled, he joined Billie Cotton and Sarge going back to the herd.

"They said they had a warrant for you, too," Sarge said, riding close as they loped down the road under the stars.

"I'm not worried. A judge will back our move when he hears the whole story."

"Them deputies were pretty cocky. Weren't they, Billie?"

"Like two banty roosters."

They all laughed.

Chet found Raphael at his cook camp.

"I am so glad you came. Those deputies said first they wanted you, and asked where were you hiding. Tom made us all be peaceful. I think some of the men would have taken them. That deputy told the men that they all would be on trial for rustling if they didn't ride out and leave the country immediately."

"We ain't left yet," someone shouted. "I'd've damn sure cracked them over the head with my pistol."

"That was the plan—for you all to quit and to let these cattle scatter. In the morning I'll be riding up front with my rifle. They try something, you all stampede the damn cattle on top of them. They won't stop running until they're at least ten miles past Mayer. Then they can go find them."

"Yeah, we can do that."

"We will need a few guards tonight. Sarge will give you the orders. Break of dawn, we'll be on the road. Right now, Marge and Susie along with Leif Times are getting our men out of jail. They haven't won yet."

"They ain't going to either, boss."

"Thanks. I'll be here all night. You see anything wrong, wake me."

Victor woke him at four a.m.

With his concern for all their safety, his night proved to be a short one. At the cook camp, Tom and Hampt rode in while he was drinking his first cup of coffee.

"How was jail?"

Tom shook his head. "Nice to be out of there. When Marge and Susie got through with Sims's men, they both were less then two feet tall."

"Those deputies told your crew they'd be tried as rustlers, too, if they didn't immediately leave last night."

Tom looked around. "No one believed them, did they?"

"No. But they tried. I told them I'd ride up front with my rifle in the morning, and if they tried anything, to stampede the cattle through Mayer."

"I'm riding with you," Hampt said.

"I'll stay with our riders. But we can damn sure stampede those longhorns."

"Serve them right." Hampt went for coffee.

One of the night riders rode in and slid his pony to stop. "I seen six riders on the ridge southwest of here. Just made an outline."

"I'll go see if I can find them." Chet tossed his saddle on the hobbled roan. Hampt took off the hobbles. With Hampt in his own saddle, they short loped to the high point.

When Chet first saw the riders they were surrounded by more riders, and six men had their hands in the air.

"Who is that?" Hampt asked, unlimbering his own rifle and ready for action.

"Looks like some ranchers with Leif."

"Yeah, they're waving at us to come over."

"These men work for the T B ranch," Leif said, coming out to meet them. "My dad and some of the others came to be sure you delivered those cattle. We have them unarmed."

"Get them off their horses. Then make them take

off their boots and jam them in their saddle bags or tie them on their saddle. They can walk back home. We'll deliver their horses with the cattle."

One of the Hartley men shouted at his words, "Hell, man, there's thorns all over this mountain."

"Bet you didn't think about that when you rode out here this morning, did you? Now run for that far ridge and if I see you again, I'll shoot at you with my rifle."

"Go! Go!" The others threatened to shoot.

The shouting, foot-hurt cowboys hobbled out of sight, crying in pain.

"I'd've never thought of that," the senior Times said. "Are your men out of jail?"

"Yes, and ready to herd these to the T B ranch. Lots more were around than I had imagined; we have near a thousand head. Thanks to all of you for coming to help. Let's grab a cup of coffee and some grub. This may be a long day for all of us."

"Hey Chet, what was Sims thinking when he sent those deputies out there to arrest your men, and you, we heard?" a rancher asked him.

"That was the the Hartleys' first response when they learned we were coming. They thought my men would scatter under the rustling threat of arrest and they could gather these cattle and re-scatter them."

"Sims never rode out here and talked to you?"

"No, he doesn't talk to me."

Another rancher drove his horse in closer, leading their saddle horses. "He don't need to be talking to anyone for my part. We need a new sheriff. Byrnes would you run for office?"

"Boys, I'm way too busy."

"No, we want you. Things won't get straightened until we have a sensible man in there."

"My sister says I'm too tough to be elected. I call a spade a spade."

"She's way wrong. We need you."

"I'll consider it."

"Good," went up the cheer.

"Now let's move these cattle."

Five men with rifles led the procession, and it was mid-morning when they rode through Humbolt. A dozen more ranchers joined them there. Despite all of his miles, the roan horse was on his toes. He felt the excitement and danced through the small smelter town and on the road eastward.

They were about to the sign that marked Mayer's west side when a man on a fancy sorrel horse rode out to meet them.

"That's Carl Hartley," Hampt warned him.

Chet stood in his stirrups to direct him. "Carl, better turn your horse around and go east with us. No way to stop these cattle, except circle them. We aren't doing that."

"You sons a bitches ain't going to do this to me."

"These cattle will be on your ranch in three hours. You have no deeded land near where these cows were wandering into. They have been grazing on my private land, using my bulls to breed them, so they're going to your place today."

"You're new around here. This ain't Texas and you can't force me off the open range."

"Turn that horse around or get off the road. We're coming though."

Hartley stood in the stirrups to look for something. "Where are my men I sent to stop you?"

"They're walking home barefooted."

Hampt cocked his rifle and aimed it at him. "Turn that horse around, chuck that pistol in the road, or I'm going to blow daylight through you."

"You ain't—" He must have decided or knew Hampt well enough to know he meant it. He dropped the pistol in the road and turned his horse.

"When I get through with all of you, you'll all beg for mercy."

"Shut up or I'll shut you up." Chet said. "Your ranch is east of here, they say five miles. You can ride ahead and tell everyone there to get into cover. We will stampede these cattle downhill to your place. Some may even cross the river. From now on keep them on your own range."

"You must be Byrnes," Hartley said, like he had just recognized him. "You've got a helluva lot to learn about this territory and how it works, mister."

"Your rustling charges won't stick. I have too many witnesses and a good lawyer. And if they come back, I'll return them."

"This is free range out here."

"Not on my deeded land, it ain't. You feed them."

"You owe me for a new pistol too."

"Go warn them we're coming hard," Chet said, tired of listening to him.

"You ain't heard the last of this."

Hartley raced off on his horse and soon disappeared. The cattle were coming and when they reached the spot pointed out as the way to their ranch, the cattle were hurried off the road and pistol shots sent them racing home. Tails over their back, those longhorns could run, and they did in a cloud of dust as the crew gathered to watch and laugh.

They pushed the herd through Mayer with few problems and were soon moving again at a good pace on the open road. They had to jog their horses to keep in front of them.

Hard as they were running, they'd flatten any corral or yard fence they ran into. Chet would have liked to have been down there to see it. He nodded and said, "Let's go. I'm buying the beer in Mayer."

The crew shouted and fired their pistols in the air. It was wild. When they reached Mayer they went into Louie's Cactus Saloon.

"Start pouring beer," Chet told the main bartender. "These cattle drivers are dry."

"You the bunch brought those damn cattle through here in a wild charge?"

"You know whose cattle those are?"

"No."

"The Hartley brothers. They owned those cattle

and they were all on our range. Those boys think they own all the land in the county."

"Free range."

"No, we're changing that. Cattle belong around your property. And damn sure not on my deeded property."

"Those boys got some tough hands work for them."

"Tonight when they walk in here barefoot, I'll buy them each a beer and then they can tell you how tough they are."

"I never heard of that." The bartender shook his head.

"They're walking back from Preskit Valley—barefooted. How tough are they? I hope real tough. Set up another round, these boys been working hard."

"You sure?"

"I saw Hartley's men running like sheep over a mountain."

"I'll be damned. What's your name?"

"Chet Byrnes. I own the Quarter Circle Z at Camp Verde."

"Good to meet you. I've heard about you. You got them horse rustlers."

Chet nodded.

"Crew," he said to his men. "Down those beers, we need to get back. Victor and the girls got a big supper planned."

He paid the small bill and they waved good-bye to Mayer.

* * *

They reached Victor's camp and the big hunks of beef were browned on the spits and the iron lids clanged off the Dutch ovens for baked potatoes to lather with sweet butter, big biscuits, and lots of snapped beans cooked with smoky bacon. Hoot in a fresh white apron sliced off the beef in generous slices and the girls fixed their plates. Victor poured them coffee and kept things moving.

"Ladies, we ran those longhorns to the boys' front porch and on. And we made it back with all our toes."

Everyone clapped.

That night, in bed with his wife, she said, "I think you fixed them. Are you planning to go to Hackberry and check on Reg?"

"I better."

"Susie can tell you. Act surprised when she does. She spoke to JD last night when he came over from the Palace Saloon, pretty liquored up, to see what was wrong. He told her he'd made the wrong turn and would have to live with it."

"Nobody has to live with anybody if it don't work."

"Talk to her before you run off and do something."

"I will." He looked at the dark copper ceiling tiles and wondered what would happen next. No need in that boy falling in a bottle. He about had Bo weaned off it, and now JD fell into one.

If Susie didn't have an answer, he'd go get him himself. A family could be trying at times.

"Throw in that rancher, who wanted to know if I'd run for sheriff."

"Well?"

He smothered her with kisses. He didn't need any more of that business either.

CHAPTER 21

After breakfast, Chet told Tom to pay everyone ten dollars and tell them not to shoot out the lights in any town. They'd see them Sunday night and to be ready for work Monday morning. The whooping and hollering was loud coming from their camp when Tom got through telling them.

He felt almost sorry for the ladies of the night. Amused, he sipped on his coffee under the tent Victor had set up.

Hampt and Tom joined him over more coffee.

"Them boys are off to a wild time," Hampt said, straddling the bench to sit down.

"Aw, they deserved it," Tom said, nodding, satisfied that was the thing to do.

"If they run into any sore footed T B men they may have a fight."

His men laughed.

"That was damn best idea I ever saw pulled off on rascals."

"You see their foreman in that crowd?"

"I didn't. He may have quit and rode on," Chet offered.

"If he was smart, but I don't think he was that smart," Tom said. "What's next for you?"

"I need to go check on Reg. He'll hate that he missed all the excitement. Something up there has him involved, I guess. No doubt he's probably still upset about losing his wife."

"You and Victor going?' Hampt asked.

"I imagine my wife is as well. She likes camping and traipsing around."

"Millie would turn her nose up at that right now." Tom shook his head, like that would be impossible to get her to go. "She loves that new house so much, she about cries every time she gets up."

"Good. She deserved it."

"I sure appreciate it."

Hampt shook his head. "Tom and I were both out of work two years ago when you came out here. I thought he'll try ranching out here and go back—too dry. But I never knew the hell you had back there."

"You two never thought you'd be back on that ranch either?"

"Oh, hell no. Ryan had a tight fist on that baby."

Tom smiled. "When I quit him I knew we'd have it tough. But I never thought I'd go back there as mad as I was at the time."

"Well, we are loose from the extra cattle we've been carrying. We still need a hundred more cross cows for the ranch down there and to think about the upper place. We need it stocked next year."

"Can we buy yearling cattle down on the border and drive them up here?" Hampt asked.

"We might if we do it early enough and have some moisture," Tom said.

Chet nodded about that idea. "I bet Raphael has connections down there. I'll talk to him."

"That might work," Tom said, as if thinking the matter over. "They drive them clear to Montana from Texas."

"Whew, glad I don't have to do that," Hampt said, shaking his head.

"Well, some of us have to work." Chet rose, laughing, and stretched. "It went well. I better go in to town and settle these charges."

"I hope you get us off!" Tom teased.

"Oh, I will do that." He left them and rode back to the house.

Marge met him at the back door. "I have the two-seat buckboard ready to go."

"I saw it. We gave the men the rest of the week off and ten bucks to blow."

"Susie is going with us."

"Hey, fine." Monica gave him a fresh cup of coffee and Susie came in the kitchen.

"Marge said you were going with us."

She nodded. "I can't afford to have you in jail."

"You got some big plans coming up?"

"You can't ever tell."

"Marge and I are planning to go up and find your nephew."

"Lots of luck." Susie laughed. "I simply hope

that he's all right. Marge told you about JD the other night in town."

"What can I do about that?"

"She knows the lady; I don't. But he can come back to the ranch or go help Reg up on top."

"Maybe offer that to him."

"There is no need for him to stay there if they aren't getting along," Marge said.

"I am certain she's under lots of pressure. The ranch has lots of needs and she doesn't want my charity."

"It's JD's part of the ranch." Susie shook her head. "We won't interfere if we can help it."

"She might talk better to me than either of you," Marge said. "I can drive out there while we're in town and see what I can learn."

"We'd appreciate that," Chet said, with his sister's approval as well.

"Let's go to town then," Marge said.

He drove and Susie sat in the back row. Clouds were gathering and that pleased him. Any rain would be welcome, and they had the surrey top on this rig.

The two women talked over the seat and he kept the horse trotting all the way there. They went by the lawyer's office. Egan told him the whole matter was settled with the county prosecutor's office and the charges dropped. Sims had gone out of town to see about some wanted men.

Chet took that to mean the man didn't want to

answer any questions. Fine with him. He knew on which side of him he sat.

Marge had gone to Kay's place and he went to Bo's office. Susie was shopping at the mercantile and was going to be in Mrs. Churchill's to look for a dress if she wasn't at the store.

Bo, fresh faced, had his argument all prepared for him when he got there. "If I marry Jane and get a house to live in, can I shed these two?"

"Has she agreed to marry you?"

"All my indications from her are that she will."

"I'm not that certain she will. How is business?"

"I sold two houses and one small ranch in the past week. Is that enough?"

"No. You still act too damn anxious to go back to drinking and gambling."

"I swear I won't do that."

"She'd leave you quicker than a lamb can shake his tail if you did."

Bo pounded on the desk. "I need to be free."

"No, you're selling real estate and have an income. You could become an important part of this city—sober."

He collapsed in the chair.

"I'm going up north to see about that ranch. I'd look at that land up there you say is for sale."

Bo rifled through his files and handed him the sheets on it. "The west property may be the best. They have some stakes up there. I don't know if they'd help you find it or not."

"I'll find it."

"I heard they tried to arrest you night before last."

"We had a misunderstanding with the Hartley brothers. We settled it and sent their cattle home."

Bo shook his head. "The man with no fear. I still recall the first time I met you in the Palace Bar. I said then to myself, what a tough piece of Texas leather. Why, he might even buy that big ranch at Camp Verde."

"And I am glad that I did." Chet prepared to leave. "Keep selling land."

"What about what I asked?"

"I'll go see what she says and get back later. Stay sober."

"Gawdamnit! I am!"

He found Susie in a beautiful white gown having a fitting. *So much for Leif.* The bell rang over his head and he removed his hat for the two women fussing over the dress who, with their mouth full of straight pins, nodded hello.

"This is serious. Sorry I intruded."

"You'd found out sooner or later. Tom and I are thinking we will get married on September first."

He took a seat in a frilly covered chair and twirled his hat on his hand, thinking about all he and Susie had been through together. It was time she stepped into her own life, had some kids of her own—he guessed. It simply broke up the old ranch some more. He went back to the time they were winding up branding and the ranch horses were stolen. That was only yesterday—but it pushed on three or four years ago. Damn, time went fast.

"You haven't seen Marge yet?"

He shook his head. "No rush, we'll go to Jenny's café when you get through. She'll be along."

"We'll only be a few minutes more," the gray-haired Mrs. Churchill said, still on her knees making changes with her helper.

"No rush. You usually only get married once."

When the women finished the fitting, they left the shop and walked to Jenny's café. The usual crowd was there and Jenny did a double take at Susie when she went by. "We'll have seats in no time."

"Fine," he said after her.

She was back drying her hands. "And this is?"

"My sister Susie. This is Jenny who fed me and the boy the first time."

"I've heard so much about you from both of them. I feel I know you well. There are seats back there where those guys are getting up. You want the meat loaf on the daily special?"

"Two, and coffee," he said when she nodded.

Jenny was gone to serve the crowd.

"She's the one feeds the unemployed?" his sister asked.

"That's Jenny."

They were almost through with their lunch when Marge arrived and came in to join them.

"Learn much?" he asked her.

"Too much. Kay wants out of their arrangement. She has someone else in mind, I think."

"He won't leave?"

"She hasn't told him yet."

"Maybe she has and he isn't listening." He looked over at Susie.

"I can't talk for him. What do we do?"

"I'll ride over there and talk to him myself."

Marge looked disappointed. "I hate that. I introduced you all to her."

"Marge, it ain't your fault. People change their minds. I will go talk to him. He don't need to be getting drunk at night to forget his days. And sure not at his age. Reg knew something was bad wrong a few weeks ago. He rode out because he knew it and couldn't do a damn thing about it."

"That is settled in Byrnes ranch fashion. He will handle it," Susie said, and clapped on top of his hands. "That is why Marge and I both have you."

They laughed.

The next morning, he left the ranch before daybreak and rode for Preskit and Kay's place. It was a long enough ride to get himself squared away with things he aimed to say and do. Satisfied when he rode over the last hill that he had his story completed, he hoped the rest went smoothly.

He found JD refitting a plate on a bay horse. He dropped the hoof and wiped his face on his sleeve. "Everyone out of jail?"

"Yes and we sent a large herd of their cattle back to them."

"I never thought you could do that. There are several around here."

"On deeded land you can cut them out and drive them off."

"I guess I need to do that."

"Need help, holler."

"Need help for what?" Kay asked, joining them. "Marge was here yesterday. Today you're here?"

"Marge said, you two weren't getting along real well. I simply came by to tell him, and you too, I sure have a place for him if he wants to come back home."

"That might be a good idea. We haven't been getting along . . ."

"You want me to go?" JD demanded. "Just say so."

"I don't think we are right for each other."

"Well by gawd, I was fine when you wanted to split from him. Now you want me to leave well by gawd I'll do that and your damn ranch can finish falling down." He threw his short-handled hammer on the ground and stomped on it.

"Hey, take it easy. We all can change our minds. That ain't worth boiling over about. Go get your things. Kay, you need anything, either my men or hers will come help you."

She nodded, but never said a word. She turned on her heels looking close to crying and walked back to the house avoiding JD's angry exit with a bundle of his clothes and some more harsh words for her.

He saddled the horse he brought over and they rode back in near silence. At Marge's lane gate JD said he'd go on back down. Chet asked if he'd like to go find Reg and he said he'd see. And tell them later.

Susie had gone home earlier so she would be there when he got to the ranch. He dismounted heavily, and Marge joined him.

"How did it go?"

"He came back with me and rode on to the ranch. He's bitter. Feels like he was good enough to shelter her from her husband and now she's dumped him. Which she did. She went to the house in silence, I offered her help from either ranch if she wanted it. No answer."

"I'm so proud of you. You are a great guy and patriarch of both places. I know that was a damn sight tougher to do than drive those damn cattle over there to Mayer."

He laughed. He had her cussing again. He kissed and hugged her, then whispered in her ear. "Will Monica care if we go upstairs and take a nap?"

"I'm not sure about me letting you sleep, but hell no."

"Good." He swept her up in his arms and carried her to the porch. She damn sure was a bright spot in his world. A real bright star shining for him when he needed it the most. *Keep laughing girl. I love it.*

CHAPTER 22

Chet's plans were to leave on the next Sunday for the high country. That meant after the potluck and dance at the Camp Verde schoolhouse. Victor had the things ready—packhorses, food, Dutch ovens, utensils, tents, bedrolls, and a few folding canvas-wooden chairs as well. Plans were to catch him up at the sawmill on Monday and Marge had leased the honeymoon cabin for them that Saturday night. JD was going to catch them at the sawmill Monday night—if he decided to go along.

Tom had him shoeing horses, a good hard job to keep his mind busy.

There were lots of questions for Chet from area ranchers about moving the Hartley cattle at the Saturday night gathering.

"They arrested your men?" Jake Bowling asked him.

"Yes, the girls went and got them out."

"What in the hell does Sims have on his mind?"

"I'm not sure, he don't talk to me. But he took those Hartley boys swearing out a warrant for us stealing their cattle and served it. Tom kept them hands from killing the deputies. He and Hampt went peacefully, but them cowboys were mad as hell about it."

"What about you? I bet you were real mad about it too."

"Yes, that's why I sent the women to bail them out."

The small crowd laughed in agreement.

"They say that drive through Mayer was huge?"

"Cows and calves, I think close to a thousand."

"Hell, it was a big parade."

Marge drew him inside to eat, laughing about his being treed.

"I'm damn glad you got me out of there."

"Your sister went home. I'm sorry—" Marge bit on her lower lip. "Tom Hanager brought Kay with him, he said 'cause she had no way to get over here. I guess Susie couldn't stand it and left."

He closed his eyes. "Where was Leif?"

"I haven't seen him. How did she get home?"

"Knowing her she might have ridden home double behind him on his horse."

"Let's eat. You suppose Kay wanted Tom all this time?" Marge asked.

Warily, Chet shook his head. "I'm not sure about anything."

"They may have had an affair before she left her husband. I can't imagine her being such a bitch. I thought her to be my friend. Now I don't want to claim her."

There she went to cussing again. Oh well, he'd

taught people worse things than that. They had the cabin to themselves for the night. They could savor that time being all alone and carefree as they could get. He felt glad to admit they were still on their honeymoon.

Where was Reg? No telling. He was somewhere up there. He hoped they didn't pass him going west and him east and miss him. In that country they could do that. Had Leif taken Susie home? She might have asked him to. No telling how they'd work that out, or maybe not. But somehow, not seeing him there, he felt pretty certain he'd taken his chance at impressing her. Riding double back to the ranch with her was a good opportunity for him. He'd learn later all about it.

His good roan horses were at the cabin. Rio would come drive the team and the buckboard they came in back over to this ranch for their return. It was all set.

They left the honeymoon cabin for the rim at dawn. They joined Victor in the early afternoon in his piney camp, close enough to hear the steam driven blade whine through the logs. The mill man came down and joined them. They talked about his horses—they'd added more teams of mules in the past months. Chet had made a good buy on four teams of them from a freighter and sent them to Dave, who was in charge up there.

The operation was making the ranch money, so he decided to go on some more time hauling logs to the mill and hauling lumber out as well.

"It's going to be farther to haul up to our new

place, and the mules might do well hauling out there as well."

The mill man said, "I'm ready to start cutting lumber for it."

"We about have everything down there. We'll be wanting some framing lumber up there shortly. I may have an order when I come back."

"Good, we're getting some new business from out there now."

They left the mill the next morning and headed for the San Francisco Peaks, and turned west at the base. He talked to a few resident folks about where they thought they were on the survey, and worked west. Yes, he wanted the land in the west after he saw the craggy stuff closer to the road junction. He'd get Bo to find it and decide then what to buy. They rode on for the ranch site across the rolling grass country west of the peaks. Camped at night, they sat around the fire and listened to Victor's guitar, playing songs they knew and some ballads from his homeland. A coyote or two howled at the half moon, and they went to bed.

"I'm glad I have you out here all to myself."

"Oh, I enjoy every day we steal away from work."

"I thought we were making more work?"

"Oh well, it's fun."

She laughed and he hugged her.

They reached the ranch the next day. There was a wall tent set up and signs of ranch things Reg'd brought up there. A small corral had been built and used. There were some clothes on the line, and Marge smiled. "Now whose dress is that?"

He frowned. "I recognize that dress—Lacy wore it, when we were here."

"You think Reg moved her in?" Marge made a smirk of discovery and about to laugh covered it with her hands.

They both laughed at the notion and he hugged her off the ground. "I reckon things found a way."

Reg and Lacy rode in on jaded horses late in the day. Chet stood up when they dismounted, and thought they looked a little taken aback by their discovery of company.

"We've been working some mavericks. We've found about fifty head since we—well we got together. She's a real hand at roping cattle. We talked about getting married but it just hasn't been convenient."

"That's your business, not ours." Chet figured they were both grown-up people.

"How have you been?" Lacy asked Marge.

"Fine. We've came to see what Reg was up to. Let's you and I go somewhere and talk. I'm sure they have lots to go over."

"Certainly."

Chet showed Reg the chair.

"Lacy is quite a cowgirl," Reg began. "I bet she can outrope you. We were looking one day at some of this ranch and we saw this maverick sneaking down the canyon, and she said, "Let's get him," and by damn we did and branded him with your brand here using my cinch ring. I remembered grandpaw telling us how to do that once."

"You got irons now?"

"Sure, I went over to her family's ranch shop and made me two. One for the quarter circle and one for the z, and they work fine."

"Her father approve of her living here with you?"

"I guess. She told him she was leaving with me and he said 'you two be careful.'"

"So you two are thinking about getting married?"

"I think there's a justice of the peace over at Hackberry. We could go do it over there. She don't care about anything fancy. What do you think?"

Chet nodded. "That would be nice. But why not bring her over to the ranch and we can have a family celebration?"

"I'm sure she'd like to do that. I'll ask her."

"Fine. I need to tell you that I went and got JD before I came over here. He's at the Verde ranch shoeing horses, last I heard. Pretty shook up, but he'll recover in time."

"Good, I'm glad that's settled. Chet, Lacy's been damn good for me. Juanita ain't coming back. I hate that. She's not pretty like her and I think that is good, 'cause chances are I'd never find another like her. But she's a pretty person inside and the damnedest competition at roping I ever met. She don't miss nothing heading or healing. She's been a tomboy all her life. Her father don't have any boys. I see why she's like that, but I do love her. What do you say to that?"

"I wish you two the best. I don't believe you ever told me that much in one conversation in our lives. But I think you did a smart thing, found you a real woman."

"I have. Oh, my God I have. I guess I must have lost track of time, we've been so busy catching mavericks, we may have a large herd up here before long." He unbuttoned his shirt pocket and handed him the tally book.

#1 Yearling bull black cut and branded 7/22 by Lacy and me.

The list went on. Those two damn near had a herd already.

"That's neat. Hey, I didn't tell you, Susie was trying on a wedding gown in Preskit. But I think it may be over. Tom Hanager brought Kay to the dance. But there is another guy there I think took her home double on his horse."

"Oh no. That is funny. Who's he?"

"A young man your age who was trying to get her to look at him. He rode with me and Hampt and we got two sorry outfits that murdered an old couple for their money that they didn't find. The old man's brother stole it."

"What else have you been up to?"

"We took the T B cattle back to their ranch in Mayer, and Tom, along with Hampt, got arrested for stealing the cattle. I sent your aunt Susie and Marge to get them out."

"How many cows?"

"Cows and calves we drove near a thousand head to them and stampeded them off the mountain to their place."

"They offer any resistance?"

"Eight of their men they sent to stop us we made walk ten miles back, barefooted. We disarmed the one brother who rode out to stop us and sent him ahead of the cattle to the ranch."

"Hey, Victor has supper ready, guys, come on," Marge called.

"Coming."

They laughed about everything at the meal, and afterwards, the women did the dishes and Victor played the guitar for them.

Later that night in their own tent, Chet whispered in Marge's ear Reg's speech about his new woman.

"I'd say he's figured it out, and she is pretty, just being Lacy. And her roping ability really impressed him. She's as awestruck with him as he is with her. That's neat. Good, like I am about you."

"Don't lose it," he whispered. "I am too."

They laid out the ranch house on the site. Then the corrals and sheds. A sudden afternoon rain shower sent them to hide in one tent, and nickel-size hail peppered the canvas hard for a short while with lots of thunder and bolts of lightning rolling overhead.

He told about lightning running from horn to horn on those longhorns on the cattle drives and stampedes during storms. With his head in Marge's lap stretched out on the cot, the storm soon passed and the sun popped out.

The four rode out to catch some more mavericks the next day. Chet watched the two of them drive the first critter out of the junipers and into the vast open prairie. She rode in and headed this one, then she turned her horse aside and he went in and swept the hind legs with his loop. The critter was thrown on the ground and Reg dismounted and tied his three feet with a pigging string.

Chet had the second one making a wide circle on the end of his lariat. Lacy charged her horse to get behind him, tossed the loop around his leg, and then lifted the rope, and her horse flew backwards. They had two caught.

That day they worked twelve head. Lacy could brand with the best man and hold a yearling's leg while Reg cut out his manhood. They had mountain oysters for supper that night.

"See why we didn't come right home?" Reg asked.

"Are they like this all over up here?" Chet asked.

"They've worked the mavericks hard west of the Springs, but they didn't know that these were here. They got away from herds driven through. The old cows are slicker than these yearlings," Lacy said. "They're wilder too."

"We only have a dozen cows. The rest are yearlings, but we're getting them." Reg looked proud of their adventure, and of her as well.

What a mess, but they were having a second honeymoon and lots of fun, too.

"Mr. Byrnes?" Lacy asked him.

"Chet."

"Yeah you told me that before." She gave him a big slow grin. "If we go back with you to get married, can Fern go, too? She's like me, she's ain't never seen Preskit either."

"We don't care. We can't guarantee her a man, but she can have a good time."

"I appreciate that. Marge said you'd say yes."

"Lacy, when you get to know us, we are one big family."

"I can tell that. I'm proud to be becoming one of you all. I loved getting to guide you two around up here, and won't ever forget that man wanted a way to get water."

"We can buy her a wedding dress, can't we?" Marge asked.

"Hell yes, and a pretty one."

"Oh, my sister will die if you do that. Girls up here just get married in the same old dress they peeled 'matoes in a few hours earlier."

That set off a camp full of laughter.

"Hey, girl, this is the Byrnes outfit and we do things right."

Lacy nodded. "He's told me the story of how your father and his father-in-law came out of the hills of Arkansas to find a Texas ranch."

"Brave to come that far out, too." Chet said. "They were forward-looking folks in those days to make that move. Mexico still owned it and Santa

Anna wasn't having any white folks tell him how to do things. The Mexican army chased them all over Texas, and then one day they turned and whipped them."

"That was how they did it."

"Must have been tough."

Chet agreed. "Life's tough all over when you think about it."

"I'm sure it is." Then she snickered. "But I never figured on all this happening to me. Whew it's been fast."

He hugged her shoulder and kissed her cheek. "I'm just as grateful to you as you are to us." She may never know it, but she saved that boy's life.

"Suppertime." Victor called them in.

CHAPTER 23

Why was the ride home always longer than going out there? It always felt that way to him when he was traipsing back. He and Marge were still laughing, and the kids, as they called them, were too. They camped along the way, and Victor said he thought he could lead them down into Oak Creek off the top, and they could catch some trout to eat before they rode home.

Marge had been there before and when they got off the mountain, they fished in the canyon stream and caught several trout. Victor fried them in cornmeal and they peeled them off the skeleton and ate until they were stuffed. Then they rode home across the valley to the Verde ranch.

Things were really going on when they arrived. Tom Flowers had bought twenty new horses and they were all snorty broncs. The crew were all perched on the corral to watch the fun.

Susie met them and took the women to the

house, fussing over the bride to be and her sister Fern.

Marge filled her in on everything that happened or would soon happen.

JD looked half asleep when his older brother shook him.

"You all right?" Reg asked.

"I'm fine. When did you get back?"

"Right now. You going to be my best man in a couple of days?"

"Huh?"

"Be-my-best-man?"

"When?"

"I guess before the week is out." Reg shook his head at him. "Are you alive?"

"Hell, yes, I am."

"No, you aren't—you're deader than I was when I got here. Come on. I want you to meet my soon-to-be wife. She can outrope any man here."

"Huh?"

"Wake up damn it and live."

Chet smiled to himself. Reg would have little brother up and going in no time. Who could tell, he might meet Fern. She wasn't the cowgirl her older sister was, but he'd bet she could do her share of things on a ranch. And she could dance his boots off. *My lands*, he shook his head, this place was a mess.

About then Hampt arrived and stepped off his sweaty horse. "I know you rode off that night at the dance," Hampt said, laughing. "But our man Leif brought your sister home riding double on his horse that night."

"I figured he'd do that if he got a chance."

"His bank account with her went way up."

"Good. We like him."

"Damn right. He's a good fellow to know. How are things up above?"

"Reg and his wife-to-be have been gathering maverick cattle up there."

Hampt shook his head and frowned. "Very many?"

"Fifty head. He's got a tally book full of them."

"Maybe we should be up there catching them."

"That girl could rope a grasshopper. I roped with her. Those two make a great team."

"How did he find her?"

"She was the one guided Marge and me around when I bought the place. She showed him the ranch first off."

Hampt laughed. "You said he was a hand."

"Boss man, we've got few salty ones left to ride," Billy Cotton said from the top rail. "They ain't near as salty as Ono was when you first rode him."

"Not today, boys. I still ain't straight from that ride."

They all laughed and waved him on. He trekked to the house, went through the living room and to the kitchen. In the doorway he leaned on the frame.

Susie jumped up to tell him their plans. "We're going to town tomorrow and get her fitted in her new gown. They will get married at the schoolhouse at the potluck and dance. The pastor down here will marry them. Can they use that cabin you two used?" Susie asked.

"That's Marge's friend's."

"I can get it for them," Marge said, and smiled at Lacy.

"Fern wants to know if you know anyone who will dance with her?"

Chet winked at her. "You better wear soft shoes. If you don't dance over half the dances, I'll find you a partner."

"Don't trust him, girl," Reg's mother Louise put in, shaking her head. "He is too damn busy to help anyone."

They laughed.

"Millie showed Lacy her new house and she about cried," Susie said.

"That's the only plan they can build. Sorry."

"Oh, Chet, it is gorgeous." Lacy's lashes were wet.

"You're getting in the Byrnes family, darling."

Susie got her a towel to blot her face and eyes.

"Did you tell them how many mavericks you and Reg roped and branded?"

Heads swung to look at her and she nodded. "About fifty head."

"Really?" Susie asked.

She blushed. "I'm not a great cook or housekeeper, but I can rope stock."

Chet went over and kissed her on the forehead. "You don't need to take a backseat here, Lacy. We're proud you've joined us. And your sister, too."

Everyone agreed.

Since they were all going into town the next day, he and Marge stayed over.

Late at night, in bed, Marge whispered, "She is what he needed, isn't she?"

"I'd not have ordered her, but she is pretty inside and out. And she even challenges him and he loves it."

"What next?"

"I need to sell some steers. I need to check on my connections over there."

"What do you think about it?"

"I don't know, but someone knows how to sell cattle to those agencies. And I'll find them."

"Can I ask?"

"What's that?" He rolled over on his belly and propped himself up on his elbows.

"Are you financially sound?"

"Yes, we are. I salted money back from all those cattle drives that should last you and me, so what the future brings us I am not certain. It's in the lock boxes in San Antonio. Some is in the safe here and some is invested. But I dread runs on banks. Still, we need to make money each year to pay expenses and wages."

"My father has investments all over. I hope nothing happens to him."

"We'll sit down and go over it, one day. I have no reason to hide it from you. Susie has a good track of the plan."

She hugged him tight. "I trust you, but I know we talked earlier about it. Just making sure we are all right."

"No problem in that area—so far."

"I'm glad you're helping that girl."

"No. *We* are."

"Oh. I'm sorry."

"No problem. I know what you meant. You aren't crying?" he asked.

"Not much," she sniffed. "I'll be fine."

He cuddled her. Tired from all the traveling and being a woman was all. She'd be fine.

CHAPTER 24

No news from his requests of the Navajo agencies in Gallup, New Mexico Territory, when he checked the post office and the telegraph office. He found a letter or two for some of the cowboys that he would send on to the ranch. Most of that kind of mail went to the Camp Verde Post Office, but he also got most of his business mail at the Preskit post office. Maybe he needed to go meet with theses various agencies to make a deal, perhaps with one office. It was long ways to ride considering he might not sell one head of stock. It was still unclear what, if anything, the Hartley brothers were going to do against him for sending their cows home.

Word was out among the ranchers. "Send them home!"

He'd heard that over a hundred more head of cows plus their calves had been driven to their ranch by unknown donors. If they weren't going to show force, maybe they'd all be delivered back on their place. No, he expected them to strike back to reinforce their hogging up the range. But how?

He was at the Preskit Valley ranch and undecided about whether he dared to leave for three weeks, or should stay closer to his operation. They would finish the construction work on the Verde ranch soon, and plans were to take a crew to the Hackberry operational headquarters and start on it.

"You look upset today?" Marge asked him from across the living room.

"Just usual things pulling at me. What to do next."

She came over to him. He kissed and hugged her. "If I knew what to do next I'd be a lot more happy."

"You are concerned the Hartley boys are going to strike back at you over your efforts to right the graze business."

"Exactly."

"Until they try, how can you know?"

"Oh, my imagination may be running wild. I expect them to do something and it has me staked down here until they make a move."

"Why don't you go down to the ranch and check out your claybank stallion Barb, talk to the cowboys, and get back into being yourself?"

"If it's that damn easy, I'll do it."

"Good. I'll go along and visit with the women."

"At times, Marge, you can see through lots of the smoke that gets in my eyes."

"No, I'm just your wife."

He chuckled. "A whole lot more than that."

"I'll be ready to go in twenty minutes."

"That's quick enough."

She kissed him and hurried off. He started to go get the buckboard hitched and tie his horse on behind.

"Will we stay through the dance down there?" she called out from the stairs.

"Sure." He stalled in the doorway.

"Good. I'll pack another dress for that."

He waved and went to find Jesus. The youth was shoveling out the stables when he found him. With a bright smile he put down his pitchfork. "Ah, what can I do for you, *señor*?"

"Hook the buckboard up and saddle Ono and tie him on back."

"I can do that. My nephew Armador told me last night that he heard in Mayer that they would pay a thousand dollars for your head."

"I might sell it to them for that much. Who will pay that for it?"

Jesus turned up his hands. "Maybe those brothers. He didn't know."

"Thanks, I'll make sure they don't get it."

They both laughed.

Those damn outfits. He should have given that gun-packing Hartley a real lesson the day they returned his cattle. The big concern is they might get takers for that much money if they had it to pay the killer. He really thought they were stretched out bad for operating money. With no apparent sales of cattle, their income had no sources that he could see. They might need money. He might even offer to buy them out when he knew their debt. However, they might owe more than they could raise. No doubt there were many things going on unanswered—but who else in Mayer wanted him dead? Jesus's relative had heard something, and it no doubt was real.

On the spring seat with his wife, they trotted the team for the Verde Valley. In late afternoon they came up the lane to the headquarters. Susie came out on the porch, busy drying her hands.

"Well, at least you brought her with you this time," she chastised him.

He held his hands in the air. "Don't shoot."

Laughing, he helped Marge down. "Any problems?"

"No, but it is good you brought her, she can help us get ready for the wedding."

"There," Marge said. "I'm lucky I came."

Under his breath he said, "Ask her if she's riding double down there."

Marge looked at her hat brim for help. "You ask her yourself."

Susie frowned. "What is it?"

"Oh, I wondered if you were going to ride double on a horse going down there this weekend."

"It looked kinda bad. I don't need any reminders."

He tousled her hair. "I am picking on you."

"Hey, I know that."

"Truce?"

"Yes. Go look at cows."

"I'm going to go check on things. Don't mislead my wife while she's here."

He let Ono loose and checked the girth before he mounted him. By then Rio was there and took the buckboard to put it up.

How are things going?" he asked the youth.

"Oh, fine. We are very busy breeding mares to the stallion."

"That sounds good."

"I can't wait to see his new colts. Huh, *señor*?"

He nodded to the enthusiastic youth. "They should be great ones."

Then he rode up to the cook shack and spoke to Hoots who was taking a break standing outside.

"Where are the hands today?" he asked the aproned man.

"They went to Perkins. They're watching them Herefords close. Tom's pretty proud of them."

"Anything wrong up there?"

Hoot shook his head. "Not that he said."

"Good."

"I need to go to Gallup and find out about the different agencies of the Navajo and to sell them some of our beef."

"They're buying beef from somebody, ain't they?"

"Yes, all those agencies buy beef, but it must be some kind of a secret."

"Aw, hell boss man, you'll figure it out."

"Thanks for your support. Now if you worked there, I'd be in."

They both laughed. With a cup of his coffee in his hands, he asked Hoot, "You been by to see Jenny lately?"

"Yeah, when we were up at your wife's, I ran in there and had a nice visit. She's pretty proud of all of us out here. Though, she said she's saving lots of money not having to feed all of us. But she's pretty tenderhearted. And she's your biggest fan."

"She's a great person."

"I think you must have a helluva wife."

"Thanks, Marge is a great wife. I'm very pleased. We've both been with others, but we've real easy molded."

"Victor loves her. I never thought a woman of her means would ever simply go camping, but he says she loves it."

"I'm damn lucky. We're going to start on the upper place next."

"Hey, I'm happy here."

"I'm pleased you are. See you."

"Thanks for coming by."

"Sure."

His nephews rode in on their short horses. They weren't Shetland ponies, just small horses Tom had found for them. The right size and disposition, they could saddle and handle them.

"What are you boys up to?"

"Oh," Ray said, "we've been checking on cattle for Tom."

"Found anything wrong?"

"Not today. They all looked okay."

"Can we draw cowboy wages, doing all this?" Ty asked.

"I guess I owe you some wages. I'll tell Susie to pay you. What are you going to do next?"

"Fish."

"Catch some big ones," he said and headed west on Ono. His brother would have been proud of those two boys. Damn shame he wasn't there to do that too. He always had the machinery, buggies, and the rest in good repair, and he was fussy about them. Chet couldn't imagine himself involved in that kind of work day after day. Working cattle on horseback—he could do that every day.

His round of the east end was more an exercise. Calves were growing and soon their mothers would wean them. The number of roan and white face heifers trailing their longhorn cows would improve the herd when their own calves contributed to the ranch's output.

Reg and his wife-to-be Lacy rode in with the crew. Chet was there and hugged her shoulder and kissed her on the forehead. "Did you show them up today?"

A little embarrassed by his attention, she shook her head and smiled. "No, but those white-faced cattle are sure beautiful. They're doing great up there too."

"Good. You two ready to start building up there?"

"Sure. When do we start?"

"If we get a break, we can haul the lumber up

and set up tents. It might be a rough winter for both of you."

"Aw, we'll make it. I remember the day when we stopped at that big spring and we talked about building a ranch headquarters there. I never thought about it then even being a part of my life, never mind living there."

"We're getting company," Reg said, unsaddling their horses and indicating the riders coming toward the house.

Chet agreed, excused himself, and went off the hill to go see who it was and what they needed.

Leif was the lead rider, trailed by Gates and another rancher named Logan.

"We need to talk," Leif said.

Chet pointed toward the house. "We can talk up there. What's happened?"

Leif looked around, and in a low voice, said, "Carl Hartley got enraged and shot two cowboys who were driving some T B cattle back to their place."

"What happened next?" Inside the living room, he showed them to the furniture. They took various seats.

"One of them died and the other is in serious condition at Doc Melton's office." Leif sat on the edge of the couch, whirling his hat on his hand.

"Who were they?"

"Worked for Ira Tuttle. He was home with a broken leg from a horse wreck. The one died was

Dick Warner and Heath Rowland is the one in serious condition."

"I didn't know them, but I've met Tuttle somewhere. Was Hartley arrested?"

"No. He's vanished. Sims's deputies went up there and claimed they couldn't find him."

"I wouldn't think they could."

"There's lots of folks would like some of us to go look for him. We came to ask for your help."

Chet felt crestfallen. "I can't. My nephew Reg is getting married this Saturday."

Leif nodded. "We knew you were busy, but we figured you were our best bet to locate him."

Chet closed his eyes. Should he have turned them down? "I'm sure sorry but—"

"Is something wrong?" Marge asked, coming downstairs.

Chet stood up. "Some cowboys were shot yesterday. Carl Hartley shot two men in a rage, according to what I have learned so far, and he disappeared when Sims's deputies went to look for him."

Marge looked concerned at him, and chewed on her lower lip. "Have you decided what you should do?"

"They've asked me to help find him."

She nodded. "I imagine finding him as soon as you can is important?"

"Yes."

"I would think to finally be rid of him would be a relief." Everyone in the room agreed with her.

Chet shook his head over his own part. He was certainly torn apart by the whole thing.

"Marge," Leif said. "Those men were shot in the back. They never had a chance."

"I'm thinking about my husband. Carl is a worthless individual in my book. But he's not worth my husband's life."

"We agree," Gates said. "But Marge, he's stopped lots of this lawlessness and many of us look to him for his leadership."

She agreed with her lips tight together. "I don't tell him what to do. But that little horse biscuit is not worth wasting a moment on. I am sorry to intrude—I know you have come a long ways."

Chet nodded and sat down again. "Thanks, Marge."

She joined Susie at the kitchen door and they disappeared.

"Where did he go?" Chet asked. "Do any of you have an idea?"

"Maybe Tucson or Tombstone," Gates said. "The deputies never checked if he took a stage."

"You think he did?" Chet asked.

"It's about the only way, besides a fast horse, isn't it?" Gates asked.

Chet agreed. "I really have several things that need my attention here, besides the wedding. I'd love to help you, but my nephew is marrying a young lady we like and I am working on some other things I feel I can't leave. Sorry, but I really can't go."

"We understand," Gates said, and stood up. "We need you in the sheriff's office."

"Let's find a candidate. Isn't Roamer recovering?"

"Yes, but he says you're the man."

"Thank him. Be careful. I consider Hartley a coward who'd shoot anyone in the back."

"We will leave in the morning to try and find him," Leif said.

The men refused any food and stood up to leave. Leif excused himself and went into the kitchen, no doubt to speak to Susie. He came back shortly with no comment and Chet went with them to their horses.

He watched them ride out with his belly eating at him.

Marge hooked his arm and she broke his concentration on his guilty conscience.

"Thanks."

"I guess you have to say no sometimes."

"Sometimes."

"Two more days, you will have a daughter-in-law. Those two boys are really your sons."

"Yes, they are." He had to admit that.

"Good, come on, they can find that little weasel."

"I don't blame you for hating him, but I still have to laugh about that brazen bastard for propositioning you." He shook his head in disbelief over the matter.

"That was not funny."

"We may go to Gallup. I want to see those agencies firsthand."

"I'll be ready. You did the right thing, quit dreading."

"All right, but I won't." They both laughed.

He blinked when Susie came back inside and it struck him that she had gone out there to say something to Leif. He'd been so concerned over it all—he hadn't noticed. None of his business, but the turn of events sure meant she couldn't ride double to the Camp Verde dance and wedding.

The weekdays passed fast. He'd seen Lacy in her gorgeous wedding dress and her hair fixed. This attention and everyone fussing over her had consumed the cowgirl and he about laughed when she said, "I can't believe this is happening."

"Accept it. You will always have this day to remember."

"Since my father can't be here, will you give me away?"

"Why, sure."

"Marge said for me to ask you. Thanks."

"She's coaching you?"

"I guess."

"Where is Fern?"

"JD is duty-like showing her the ranch."

"Oh?"

She shook her head. "They've struck up a friendship. That's all."

"Good."

The wedding caused a crowd at the schoolhouse grounds. The women had baked six three-layer cakes for the occasion. The ranch crew barbequed a fat yearling on a spit for twenty-four hours at the schoolhouse site. There were Dutch ovens full of biscuits, German fried potatoes, green beans with bacon, plus brown beans and ham. Enough food there, he decided, to feed two armies.

And kids ran all over playing tag and rolling hoops, their voices shrill and excited, added to the atmosphere of a big event. There was music all afternoon. And some drinking like at most events, where the jug was passed and great things discussed like why it rained here and not there.

A report came from the three men who went looking for Carl Hartley, in a telegram from Gates: *Not known to be in Tucson.*

Chet looked at the far-off mountainside in deep thought. Not satisfied, he knew Hartley was under a rock somewhere. He hoped they found him. He'd best get on with his business. He'd give the bride away in a few hours. Neat job for him and he observed Aaron Waverly was escorting May Byrnes around the grounds. Susie had baby Donna and Louise's latest escort was sipping something with her under the tarp shade.

"What plans have we ahead of us?" Marge asked, nudging him out of his deep thoughts in the canvas chair.

"Don't spill me out." He laughed, recalling some wrecks they'd had with such things.

"With you all cleaned up I wouldn't think of dumping you."

"I guess Navajos come next."

"Buggy or horseback?"

"You want to go in a buckboard?"

"I haven't decided."

"Think on it."

"I will. We better mosey over there. The time's getting close."

"Who brought Kay today?"

"I haven't seen her."

"Oh, well, so much for that."

"Is JD occupied with Lacy's sister Fern?"

"I think they're simply friendly." He rode forward enough in the seat to get up. "I'm coming."

He marched Lacy up front, whispering to the bride. "Just enjoy today. Relax. It will be a big day but—"

"I don't want him to think I'm some country clod."

"You look lovely. To hell with the rest of them. This is your day girl."

"I can't hardly get my breath."

"Breathe deep, Mrs. Byrnes."

"Oh, I will. I just don't know if that will be enough."

"It will. You're fine and you look delicious."

She snickered and slightly shook her head at him. "Thanks, you'd boost anyone."

"Have fun."

"I will."

Her in place, he stepped back and took his seat with Marge.

"What's she laughing about?"

"Big secret." He hugged her shoulder.

The ceremony over, they crowded around the cake-cutting and after that the two newlyweds ran off in a white-and-red-streamer-decorated buckboard with tin cans tied to the tailgate. He went back inside for a plate of the barbeque and trimmings. He was enjoying the food with his wife, who was seated on the bench.

Ira Camp came by and took a seat close to them. A rancher in his fifties, days of hard sunlight had turned his face saddle leather brown. "I didn't want to interrupt you two eating. But I heard you were looking for markets for cattle. I ain't a big producer, but I could use a market too if you find one."

"I thought about the Navajos, Ira. All these tribes are getting beef and I could use the sale to them as well as you can."

"Anyway if I can help you, holler."

"Right now, I don't know, but in sixty days I may be the expert."

They shook hands on the matter and the evening moved from eating to dancing and more conversation. Afterward, Chet and Marge drove back to the lower ranch to find May and Susie sitting at the kitchen table, talking.

"May, is that cowboy a serious matter?"

She made a pained face. "He's nice. He's polite. He can dance. But I don't figure he'll get up enough nerve to ever ask me anything but *could we—ah, dance?*"

"I don't know him."

"Susie says he has a place of his own over near Strawberry Gap."

"He comes a long ways then?"

"Oh, yes, but I don't expect much more than a dance partner. He truly is bashful. But well mannered, and I get peppermint candy every week. Oh, I think he lives with his mother over there."

"I told May that we could go over there and meet his mother and see his place." Susie said. "But she's not ready for that."

May blushed.

"Peppermint candy ain't bad," Chet said. "I could send a scout or go look myself and tell you what I found."

May blushed some more. "Not yet."

After all the women's words on the wedding and how nice those two looked, he and Marge went upstairs to bed.

"I think you are right, Chet. She was beautiful tonight and he loves her."

"Pretty inside and out. He's got a hardworking woman."

"When do I need to be packed?"

"We can go this week. It will take us a week to get around or longer."

"I say we go horseback. That moves faster. And can we borrow Victor?"

"I am sure we can."

"Good. Let's go Tuesday morning."

He rolled over to cuddle her. "Good, that's over."

"Were you waiting for me to answer?"

"No, really I just needed a kick to get started." They both laughed.

Tuesday came faster than they planned, but by dawn they were headed off the mountain. Victor, with four packhorses and all the gear and food, was meeting them at the base. The sun was up when they met him and they left headed east by northeast for New Mexico. By evening they were camped at the small lake and turned in at sundown. Then up again in the cool predawn, and ready to travel. Saint Johns was their next stopover and they were tired enough after that day to turn in at sundown. Then two days later, they swung north and went by the agency at Shiprock.

A sub-agent, Daniel Carter, spoke to them at great length in his office. The beef contracts were sent out from the Gallup office and the requirements were listed on them. There were five agency sites that the livestock had to be delivered to. They usually received 150 head at Shiprock.

Chet narrowed his vision to consider the man's words. "You're talking about seven hundred and fifty head of cattle when you consider all the stations, then?"

"Yes, if the others need that many as well."

"I have driven two thousand head to Abilene, Kansas, from west of San Antonio. That takes near three months or longer. What do these cattle you receive look like when they get them here?"

"Much thinner than what they told us they would be when they arrived here."

"They must have gathered them in Texas and drove them here. I bet they were thin. That's lots of cattle every month—seven hundred fifty head, but I need to talk to the Arizona ranchers and see if we can line up that many cattle."

"Mr. Byrnes, we need those cattle here on the first day of the month, and be ready to give the rations to the Navajos," Carter said.

"No matter how skinny they are when they get them here?" Chet shook his head in disbelief.

"Yes, our agreement with the tribe is to have those cattle to butcher here on the first day of the month."

"How much are you paying now for beef?"

"I don't know. That is a bid process."

"Could I bid to deliver that beef too?"

"I am certain you can do that with the main agent, Fred Carlock, who resides in Gallup."

"Thank you, I will do that."

They shook hands, and he showed the two of them to the door.

"Thanks for stopping by. Come by anytime. I enjoy non-Indian company part of the time."

"Judy Bell, we gave her a ride to near her home, when her horse died in the shafts on the Marcy Road."

"She is a very intelligent lady. Maybe too intelligent for her own good at times. Indian men don't accept woman speaking out loud very well. But she has little fear."

"If you see her give, her my regards."

"I will do that. And so nice to have met you, Mrs. Byrnes."

"Thanks, I am his shadow." She smiled and nodded at the man.

"Hardly." Chet shook his head and they left the sub-agent's office.

"This could be big job," she remarked once they were outside in the sun. "To gather that many cattle each month. Have them in good condition during the winter when they arrive here. I don't see any great grass range up here to sustain them on, either."

"That has been going through my mind as well, Marge. Over west in Arizona there is some real grass country in this high country, but that's a good distance from here, and that region is not overrun with water. I plan for us next to ride on to Gallup and talk to this head man, Carlock."

"Fine." She hugged his arm and about swung on it. "I am finding this Indian beef supply business interesting, but it will be expensive as well."

"You're right." He kissed her cheek and looked around at the Indian women and children at the agency. Lots more to this beef business than he ever imagined. But if some other folks were doing it there was no reason if he could make money at it for him not to try.

"Where to next?" Victor asked, when they arrived at the camp setup.

"Gallup."

"That will take a few days."

Chet nodded in agreement.

Gallup was a sleepy town. There were several off-duty Army cavalrymen in town, he noted. The three took a twenty-five-cent bath in the Chinaman's place and a meal in a busy café.

Then Victor went back to camp to keep an eye on things and they went to find Carlock.

The tall thin man in a suit showed them into his office and offered them something to drink.

"Thanks, we just finished lunch. My wife and I are here to talk to you about the beef supply business and bidding on it. I spoke to your man at Shiprock a few days ago"

"Strange you brought that up. Two men were here from Texas this morning on the same matter. Where is your operation located?" After they sat down he did as well.

"Camp Verde, Arizona Territory. We have supplied some beef to the Yavapai Reservations."

"Then you know lots about the beef contract."

"No, sir. We have sold beef to them from time to time only."

"No doubt their supplier couldn't get there, then?"

"Actually my foreman, Tom Flowers, handled those sales. It must have been a reasonable price, he knows the business quite well."

Marge agreed.

Carlock smiled. "Our beef is supplied by some Texas businessmen. That is a long-range business to get beef delivered out here, and they end up late many times, especially in winter, due to snow."

"I can understand. I moved to Arizona last year from Texas. I can imagine the difficulties they must have."

Carlock leaned back in this swivel chair with a squeak of protest. "We take bids on these deliveries for a year. And before the last year is out, we had dealt with three different people. That is how hard it is to get cattle up here. I have been promised fat cattle and all we got were real thin ones."

"I can imagine. I drove several herds to Abilene, Kansas, from San Antonio."

"You know driving cattle can be troublesome. I have paid as high as fifteen cents a pound to the second party for them to deliver them, even then late, which is hard. Many of these Navajo people live in the far corners of these reservations and come to here and to the other agencies on day one of each month to get provisions, and they must wait and wait."

Chet agreed. "Could I ask your current bid price?"

"Eleven cents a pound. I am curious, is that what you expected?"

"I'd need fifteen cents to get them here in good flesh." Chet glanced over at Marge for her answer. She agreed.

"If—" Carlock tented his fingers. "If I got you word, how long would you require to get, say, six hundred and fifty cattle here?"

"Probably six weeks. I am building a new ranch near Hackberry and it is not stocked with cattle, but it might be where I'd begin the drive. And if

I had the notion you needed them I could have that many cattle on hand over there, say in a year. But we can supply you before then from our other large ranch."

"At what price?"

"Winter or summer?"

"Year round."

"Fifteen cents, and I would guarantee their condition"

"You're high priced, but I believe you'd deliver them."

"Except in high snow, in three weeks I could have them here. My problem is there are no telegraph facilities at Hackberry. Preskit has a dependable line. Take three days hard riding to get from Preskit to Hackberry. Then we'd have to gather the cattle."

"So you'd need a month's notice?"

"However, if I had a contract, I could graze those cattle over in northern Arizona where there's grass."

"What price?"

"Fifteen cents a pound."

"I'm only paying eleven now."

"But obviously they don't get here in time, and are very thin when they do." Chet could see this man wasn't getting what he needed and so it should be worth more.

He made a frown at Chet. "I could do this on a hardship clause."

"What is that?"

"A governmental agency, when all else fails, can

use their discretion in isolated places to keep the government's promise to complete a contract."

Chet laughed and shook his head.

"It isn't funny."

"Yes, it is. Do you realize the costs and work involved to get all this set up for us?"

"Many dollars I imagine."

"Several. But you're telling me that you need a dependable good supply of beef?"

"That's my main concern. And I believe that the current beef supplier won't deliver this next month's order on time."

"You mean September's cattle?"

"Yes, that's why they were here this morning."

Chet shook his head. "I could have those cattle here in October. September is almost here now. I can't make that delivery."

"I may have to accept that."

"I'm not here to tell you your business. If my outfit sets in, we will deliver." Chet sat back in his chair.

"What happens after October first?"

"This contract has eight more deliveries. Is that all right?"

"Yes. That's time enough to know if we can afford to do it."

"I can reach someone there by telegram. You said Preskit?"

Marge smiled amused. "It is Prescott, Arizona. Folks over there call it Preskit."

"I understand. But we can correspond?"

"Yes. We also have a dependable mail delivery from here to there."

"Oh. I am certain you do. Leave your mailing address and your name and how to wire you all with my assistant, Mr. Cooper, and I will send you an emergency contract. What else can I do for you this morning?"

"What will you do about September?"

"Try to buy them locally."

"Sorry I am not closer, or we'd get some up here."

"Thanks for the thought. If you have any doubts about October delivery, be certain to warn me."

"Yes sir." They shook hands.

"So nice to meet you as well, Mrs. Byrnes."

"Yes, and thank you."

"I don't imagine you will be coming back, ma'am."

"Oh, I might have to. But thanks again."

"Oh?"

"I can cowboy too," she said.

The man looked shocked.

Outside, after finishing their business with his assistant, she laughed privately. "Wait until he meets your niece-in-law Lacy. He thinks all women do is keep house or weave rugs like the Navajos do."

"Hey. He has lots to learn anyway." He hugged her shoulder. "This was our day. I'd still been writing letters if we hadn't come over here."

"Means you have lots more to do. Finding cattle every month will be a task."

"I thought about that. But we can do it. This

operation will not only really put us in the ranch business, but make us some good money."

"I think you're right. I'm glad we rode over here. You'd probably turn a buckboard over going home on the curves."

He kissed her. "And I guess we better go to church more often, the good Lord's taking care of us out here."

"I go quite often."

"Damned if you don't. Put in a good word for me then."

"You are high."

"Man couldn't get drunk and be as high as I am. Whew."

They rode back to the campgrounds on the near dry creek under some cottonwoods where several teamsters were parked. Victor came out to greet them.

"Did you have good day?" he asked.

"A wonderful day. You know all about how we got here?"

"Sure, why?"

"We have a contract to deliver beef to all five sub-agencies."

"No kidding?"

"No kidding. You may need to be the trail guide."

"Wow, you did have a day."

"We honestly did have a good day. We need to head home tomorrow. We have lots to do."

"How many head?"

"Six-fifty, October one, here."

Victor whistled.

"And every month thereafter," Marge said.

The trip home was uneventful. A few showers, but they didn't last long, and Chet had his eye out for a place to locate his cattle station. He stopped and talked to a man who had two windmills. Joseph McQuire was a tall man with a straight black beard and two wives. Chet decided he was a Mormon. The women visited while McQuire talked about his windmills. He made them himself and Chet decided the man might be a better mechanic on windmills than a cowman.

"You ever think about making them for a living?"

"What would I do with this ranch?"

"Why, sell it. Move to Preskit and have a shop set up to build the windmills. You could sell several I'd bet."

"You say that like it would be easy."

"How many cows do you have up here?"

"Eighty-seven plus calves, and four bulls. And sixty-five yearlings. The deed calls for a full section, six hundred forty acres."

"What would you take for it?"

"Ten buck an acre and throw in the cattle for a cash deal."

"Mister, you just sold a ranch."

"I'm talking six thousand dollars." His eyes narrowed to slits to gaze at Chet.

"I'll buy it."

"You'll what?"

"I'll have my man up here in four days to learn

all about the setup. You can collect the money from my land agent Bo in Preskit. He will have the papers to sign in his office when you get to Preskit and he can pay you."

"I better tell them sisters we've sold and we're moving to town. And shortly."

Back in camp, Marge ducked out of the tent with a sly look when she saw him come in. "What did you do here?"

"Bought this place, lock, stock, and barrel. We'll need it for a station to hold cattle on for the next drive."

"Who will you have run it?"

"Sarge, you've met him before."

"Yes, I like him."

"You bought this ranch?" Victor asked.

"Yes. It has grass and water."

"It sure does. I bet when I am an old man, I will tell my children's children that I was there when he bought two of those ranches."

Chet laughed and clapped him on the shoulder. "You better get busy then."

"Huh?"

"You don't have any children yet."

They both laughed. Marge shook her head in disapproval, but she laughed too before it was over.

"I think I have it worked out. We will send two wagons of things up here that Sarge will need, and they can haul McQuire's stuff back to Preskit for him. Victor is going to stay here and learn all about the ranch and cattle for Sarge. We're gong to push to the ranch and get busy on the cattle deal."

She held the back of her palm to her forehead. "Oh, my heavens, even my father could not have figured this out, and he's a real dealer at buying and selling."

So they left Victor and the packhorses there and made a long hard ride back to the ranch. Late in the night, both exhausted, they reached the ranch. Susie met them.

"Sorry to have to tell you, but Tom and Hampt had war today with Carl Hartley and his foreman. Tom was slightly wounded and Hampt thinks Hartley is wounded too. But those two got away and Hampt was concerned Tom's wound might have been worse and took him to the doctor in Preskit."

"Where's Hampt now?"

"Sleeping in the bunkhouse. He was caved in when he brought Tom back. Tom's fine, but he's sleeping, too."

"I need to sleep a few hours. Have someone get me up about five." Hartley had pulled his last stunt against him. He planned to settle this once and for all with that banty rooster.

"Where is Victor?" Susie asked, looking concerned in the flickering candlelight.

"He's at the new ranch."

"New ranch?"

"Oh, yes, and we have a large contract to deliver beef to the Navajos."

"Oh, my heavens, Chet Byrnes, how do you find into all these deals?"

"It ain't easy, either," Marge said, with a weary shake of her head, ready to go upstairs.

They all three laughed.

"Long story," he said. "But it could be good business." Then he and Marge went to bed upstairs. Under the covers, he hugged her tight and they fell asleep.

CHAPTER 25

Hampt, Tom, and Chet all sat at the end of the table in the chow hall under coal oil lamps that Hoot had to illuminate the room. Tom's right arm was bandaged, but he shook his head to dismiss any concerns Chet might have.

"So we have to deliver six hundred fifty head of cattle each month to the Navajos?" Hampt asked, looking doubtful after Chet had explained the contract.

"And you bought a place up on top in the east, for a place to bunch them at?" Tom asked.

"That's right. It has corrals, a house, sheds, and two windmills, plus some other water."

"Vic is up there learning all about it, huh?" Hampt asked.

"Yes, he's checking it all out for us. Plus eighty some cows, calves, and yearlings are in the deal. It's a nice place. A three-four day drive from the reservation and it has lots of grass. Maybe that far from here if you're driving cattle. The guy who owns it wants to build windmills rather than ranch."

"Hampt, when he heals, Tom is going to locate and buy cattle for this deal. You run this place when he's gone. I'll send Sarge up there to run that place."

"Fine, I wasn't worried that you hadn't done lots of thinking about it. But it's going to take a lot to find that many cattle."

"Oh, yes, but I have a plan, and most important," Chet nodded, "I count on you guys."

"It's worked out a damn sight better than I even dreamed," Hampt said, then he looked around. "Would you be upset if I courted your sister-in-law? That guy from Strawberry Gap ain't worth much and I'd really like to see if we could be happy together."

Chet swallowed hard. "May's been like a daughter to me. I can't say much else, Hampt. My brother Dale and her got along. Sure. Give it a whirl, she needs a life of her own."

Tom smiled at Hampt. "I wondered when you'd do that?"

"I didn't want to offend anyone. You two have sure been good to me. I just wanted to be sure it wouldn't make anyone mad."

"Tom, you aren't opposed to being a cattle buyer?" Chet asked.

"Not as long as I don't have to move my wife."

"No way. Anyone heard from the Hackberry newlyweds?"

Both of his men shook their heads.

Tom said, "I guess all is well on the mountain."

Chet agreed. They had about half of the first bunch of cattle to come from their own, but they'd needed maybe three hundred more head. They should be able to buy them for six or seven cents a pound and make from fifty to fifty-five per head. Buying cattle at seven cents and selling at fourteen should make about fifty-five bucks. That should make over three thousand dollars a drive, before expenses. That ought to work and make some real money over time.

"When do we need these cattle?" Tom asked. "I'll get some handmade signs up at the livery and mercantile about what we need. I suspect there will be plenty of cattle at our first cattle buying day."

"Then we can spread out. We need to buy at least three months' worth of cattle to start with," Chet told them. "So we have a backlog."

Tom agreed.

"Well, I need to take Marge home today. Where did you two run into that pair?"

"We went to see Gus Hamblin about buying his cows," Tom said. "He's got some good shorthorn cross cows. We were on the road to Mayer and they saw us and began shooting. We never said a word."

"I don't know what they were thinking," Hampt said. "I got my rifle out and they turned and ran, before I got a good shot at them. I saw Tom was hit or I'd've chased them down."

"Stray lead fragments hit my arm is what the doctor told me," Tom said. "He got them out. He thought the bullet might have struck a rock and the pieces of that hit me. I'll be fine."

Chet scowled over the matter. "I have had it with those Hartleys."

"We set a pattern. Others drove cattle back to them. Their range can't stand that many hungry cows."

Chet agreed. "Then they better sell them. Greed got them into that fix, not the rest of us."

"Be careful," Hampt said, with a serious look of concern. "This place needs you."

He thanked them, had a team hitched, and went back to the house. Marge was ready and they headed for the buckboard.

"What do they think?" she asked as he set the team in a jog for the road.

"They don't know why they drew fire. They ran away. Oh, yes, and I think May is going to get a new man of interest for her to check out."

"Who is that?"

"Hampt Tate. And he sounds damn serious."

"She's a very sweet person. And I like him as well, plus I know you do."

He nodded. "I am going into Preskit this afternoon and check on Bo and put him on clearing this new purchase with McQuire."

"You still have him under guard?"

"Of course. There is a woman in his life and I am hoping he marries her and acts like a sober person from there on."

"Will you release him then?"

"I will have to, but she could be a good steering person in his life."

"Is that why you married me?"

"Oh, yes."

She punched him lightly in the stomach. "Liar."

"What was I supposed to say?"

"Oh, boy, the guy who buys ranches with flair asks me that?"

"But he loves you."

She kissed him on the cheek. "That's why I stay with him." They both laughed.

"I don't know what I'd do without you." He clucked to the team to keep up their pace.

With a nod she squeezed his arm. "Me too. And I enjoy our honeymoons as well. But you have to be careful. That Hartley bunch is crazy."

"Obvious that he never left from what the men told me this morning. I will try to be back for supper."

"My poor cook must no doubt be upset by our wild lifestyle, but Monica will be all right."

"She's a good person." He reined up the team at the top of the grade over the Verde Valley. "We can take a few minutes to relax here and let these horses catch their breath."

"Good, excuse me. I'll be right back." She swung down and, her dress in hand, she went behind some junipers and soon returned.

They were at her house by noon and Monica came out, hands on her hips. "About time you two came back."

"Hey, we've been working," he said.

"I bet."

"No, Monica, don't pick on him," she said. "He really has been busy."

"All right, I'll let you off."

"Whew, I will catch something in town."

"I have lots to do yet today." He set Marge's two bags on the porch, kissed her, and hurried off, waving at them.

Later, in town, he found Bo working at his desk. He looked up as his guardian lowered the newspaper to nod to him.

"I bought a ranch. His name is McQuire and he'll be along to see you. He needs a place to build windmills and a big house. He has two wives. You can sell him something if you have a location like that."

"Two wives?"

"Yes, he has two. It would take that many to keep you straight," Chet said, and laughed.

"She said she'd marry me."

"Good, when?"

"When I am ready."

"You ready?"

"I think so."

"You get drunk she'll divorce you."

"This new ranch is?"

"He says a section of land and several cows, calves, and yearlings. It's on the cutoff from the Marcy Road going west."

"There's lots of territory."

"That is your business and why I keep you."

"If I marry her can I do it without these two?"

"We will have to see. I have more business to see about."

He spoke to Mr. Tanner at the bank about his cattle business. The man was interested in the project and felt a place for local folks to sell cattle might be just what the ranchers needed. They talked about his money needs that might arise in buying all those cattle. Tanner felt that the bank could help him. Chet left the bank feeling good about his conversation, and went to Jenny's for a meal.

"There's the man!" she said, and pointed him out when he came in the door. "My favorite rancher."

He waved down the faces who turned to see him as he entered the café. She came and hugged him. "You look wonderful. Where is your lovely wife?"

"Resting. We've been on a long journey."

"You here to eat?"

"Yes, ma'am."

She pointed out an empty table. "I'll get you a plate of food."

"Sounds good." He took the seat and she returned with his coffee. "All going well?"

"Yes. Lots going on."

"I heard Tom was shot?"

"He says he's fine. Tom, Hampt, and I had breakfast this morning on the ranch."

After his chicken-fried steak, mashed potatoes, green beans, and sourdough bread, he ate a piece of apple pie, and she joined him for some small talk. The ranchers had come back empty-handed, but he figured that when Hartley shot at his two men. Then he excused himself to head for Marge's house.

He left the town and was jogging the team eastward when three riders came charging out of junipers. With the lines he sent the team into a run for it. He jerked the rifle out of the scabbard on the dash. The shots from the three masked men were loud. With a glance back, he saw them gaining. As it was impossible for him to do more than guide the team, he looked for some cover, but aside from a few dusty junipers beside the road, he saw nothing that offered him any sanctuary.

Those riders kept closing in. He knew he needed to do something, and fast. He decided when he drew close to the next large clump of junipers that he'd need to try to make a break for it to the left. At the last minute he steered the team aside. The front wheels of the rig of the buckboard hit a bump and propelled him through the air. On the fly, holding the rifle, he hoped the land was sandy enough to cushion his fall.

Spitting grit, and still on the roll, he levered a shell in the chamber and came up on his knees to blast the rider on the right. The bullet caught the horse in the chest and he went nose down and did a cartwheel. The other riders veered off the far side of the road into some more junipers. Despite the pain from hitting the ground and the hard roll, Chet moved quickly, bent over into the junipers, knowing this was his break, too. Under the boughs he found his Colt was still in his holster, and that made him feel a lot more secure.

One masked man came running around a bush. Through the boughs he could see him and fired. He must have hit him with his shot. He went down and disappeared back out of sight. There were thirty minutes left before sundown, by his figuring. His count was three assassins trying to kill him. That evened things up better than three to one odds. His team and rig had circled back on the road and wouldn't stop until they reached Marge's place, and that should draw him more help.

Then someone was trying to mount a circling horse. He ended that so they didn't ride away—he shot the horse. When the horse crumbled, the shock-faced looking person dove for cover. The other ambusher fired four rounds in the juniper boughs around him, and Chet was three spaces over by then. He backed out and then chose another juniper to hide under to try to see where his enemies were hiding. Another shot and the gun smoke left him a target. He used the rifle and put two bullets close by and thought he heard someone call out in pain as he moved on to the right in the sticky needles under the tree.

He heard some profane language. Next their shots crashed over his head into the boughs. Two more riders arrived, and someone across the road shouted for them to get over there. Damn, his odds of survival went down. His not-so-easy light crash with the ground hurt his shoulder. But so far he was unscathed other than that, and it wasn't broken as far as he could tell.

Next thing he knew, he heard them ride off double, but they didn't come around where he could see or clearly shoot at them. He rose on his elbows, the thick smell of evergreen and rosin boughs in his face. He was covered in dirt and sticky patches of the juniper needles.

There were riders coming from the east. Those should be Marge's men—Raphael and his men. He rose and crawled out to see their sombreros. It was her man all right, and three other rifle-armed men with him. He rose, sore from his jump, and staggered out toward the road.

"Don't shoot, that is *Señor* Byrnes," Raphael shouted as they reined in their horses.

"You all right, *señor*?"

"They rode off double. Some of you carefully check over there, they may be wounded. I need a horse."

"Chocko, give him your horse," Raphael said. "The rest of you check carefully for them. I will go with the *señor*. If there is someone there, go get the sheriff to come and take him."

"*Sí*," Chocko said, handing the reins to Chet. "Boy, you really got dirty, *señor*." Then they laughed. Chet did too.

"But they didn't kill me," he said in Spanish, and they cheered.

In the saddle with his rifle in hand, he and Raphael tore out on their horses. He caught sight of their dust down the valley. Riding double, they wouldn't get far. Besides, the horses they rode were much fresher than the outlaws'.

"Who are they?" Raphael asked as they pounded down the wide swale.

"I think they may be Hartley and his foreman Loftin."

"Where will they go?"

Chet shook his head. "Maybe to a hideout those ranchers didn't find looking for them."

Raphael agreed.

"There are several abandoned mines and shacks down there."

"We'll find them." He hurried his horse.

"This time I will be with you to help."

"*Gracias, mi amigo.* We must put an end to this bunch."

"Oh, *sí.* The *señora* told me to bring you back in one piece."

"Thanks for her."

The smaller man agreed.

The two men took to a steep cow trail up the hillside that ran parallel to the valley. Chet's horse took the mountain in great lunges that jarred his sore shoulder. He glanced back and saw his partner was coming the same way. Sight of the others was gone, but he knew they went up this way.

Tracks showed they went down as hard as they came up. Then he saw them in the scattered pines on the floor of the next flat, still headed south.

"We need a long rifle," Raphael said.

Chet agreed and the powerful horse on his heels went back downward. Dangerous business, going off like this, but he wanted those two and had no time. Talus rocks slid under his horse's hooves, and he scrambled for his footing. To Chet's relief, they were off the worst of the steep slope and on another flat when he set out in a hard run.

He'd lost sight of them when his man came back to ride beside him.

"Any ideas?"

"There is an abandoned mine maybe a few miles farther."

Their horses were foamed in sweat on their chests and breathing harder with each thud of a hoof. They couldn't continue this pace much farther. Then he saw something and his partner pointed to a downed horse on the ground.

"That's their horse."

"*Sí.*" They slid their horses to a stop.

He flew off his mount. The sweaty horse lay on his side and breathed hard. The rifle in the scabbard was pinned underneath him. Good, they never got that one. His own Winchester in his hand, he studied the scattered pines and junipers for any sight of them. Then he heard a muffled, "Hurry."

He shared a nod with his man and they rushed toward the south. The grade was upward and he knew they were in the open too much of the time charging after the pair. His boots clambered over the black boulders spewed out from some volcanic source thousands of years before. The hard-breathing Mexican was keeping up.

Then he saw the weathered black boards of the mine tower and dropped to his knee. They could be up there. Too far a shot for a pistol, but if they had a rifle they were close to being in range.

"That's the Towson Mine."

"Will your men send us help?"

"It will be daylight tomorrow, I bet, before they can find us."

"Maybe your men can find us. His desk deputies couldn't find their own tracks let alone ours."

"That means we must take them, huh?"

"We can try. Keep an eye on that tower and the windows to see if they come to one and look for us."

"Get down!"

Chet hit the rocks and swung the rifle around. That puff of smoke came from the middle of the tower window. No need to shoot—they left that one. He'd thought they'd go higher to get a better shot at them.

"Listen to me," he shouted through his cupped hands. "If you don't give up and come out with your hands in the air, we're going to burn you out."

Raphael agreed. "That would make a big fire. How come I never think of that?"

Chet laughed. "You don't have an evil enough mind."

"I guess I don't. But I sure hate those men for what they did to you. How did you get so dirty? I never saw you like that."

"Wait. I think I heard him say they were coming."

"Good thing, or they could be roasted gooses, huh?"

The two watched for them. Someone was packing the second man, obviously wounded. They stopped in the open.

"Be careful, Raphael. They aren't defanged rattlers yet."

"*Sí*, I understand."

"Keep your rifle ready, they may try something yet. You go more to the left so we aren't easy to shoot at."

"I savvy. I don't see any weapons."

Step by step, they covered the ground. Any wrong movement and he intended to shoot them down.

"We ain't got no guns."

"Just be damn sure you don't," Chet warned them.

"Who is the wounded man?" his man asked.

"That's his foreman who's shot. Carl is the other man."

"You bastards killed my brother or I'd never gave up."

"What in the hell did you expect me to do? Let him kill me?"

"I'll get you, Chet Byrnes, if it takes all of my life."

"Better not waste it." He checked them for weapons. When he finished, he told them to sit down on the ground.

"Raphael, go get some more horses. This job is over."

"No, it ain't," Carl said.

Filled with rage, Chet set down his rifle and jerked the shorter man up to his feet by a fistful of his shirt. "Listen, weasel, in Texas I'd already have hung you. I can still do it here and probably get a hero's welcome in town, but I'm not going to. I want you and your worthless foreman here to rot in Yuma prison. Or maybe bake. Now count your blessings 'cause I can still hang you if you're going to run off with your filthy mouth at me."

Hartley never said another word. Raphael went for help. Chet set in to guard the two men after he tied Hartley up. Loftin was in pain from his gunshot wounds and moaned a lot. He might not make it, but Chet did not consider himself enough of a doctor to help him. It was a live or die situation, and he had no hand in it either way.

Coyotes yelping broke the night and the cooler air set in on the wings of a soft wind. His belly complained of hunger and he wondered how upset his wife must be. First the buckboard arrived home with a driver and the sun had gone down. All she knew is that he'd gone after them.

He could still recall the sight of her in the buckboard seat when she came to help him after the road agents had killed his nephew Heck. She looked like an angel to him that day with wings and all. Up to that moment, she'd been a woman of interest, no more. But he saw her sincerity then, and the following days she helped arrange for Heck's burial and the rest. The whole effort on her part left him with a deep place in his heart for her. He couldn't wait to hug and kiss her.

These two meant nothing to him. They could face the judge and be banished to prison—good enough for the likes of them. But his family and the ranch operation were beginning to work. His cattle deal with the Navajos would move them forward. They'd soon be in the position they held in Texas—one of security.

After midnight, they carried a torch, the one leading the posse held high. Chet rose stiff and sore with his rifle in his hand. He heard her cry out his name and she came holding her dress high on the run.

She flew into his arms—crying. "He said you were all right. But I had to know that. Are you—all right?"

He clutched her form tight to his chest and smelled her sweet-smelling hair. "God, yes, I'm all right. Now you're here. It's been a long night, but it's over."

"You know his brother is dead?"

"I heard that. No loss. Did the sheriff come this time?"

"Of course not. We didn't bother. These are my cowboys and a few neighbors. They want you to take them in. You ran them down, you and Raphael need to show them what you've done."

"I'd only stir up more trouble with Sims."

"No, it's time you made an appearance and people can see how much you do for them."

"All right. All right. I'll do that for you."

He took the reins to the horse he'd ridden there from Raphael and thanked him.

"No, I want to thank you for what you have done for me. I want you to be my best man, too."

"When is this?"

"In a few weeks."

"Who are you marrying?"

"Why, Monica, of course."

Chet nodded. "Of course. Monica will be a good bride for you."

"*Sí*, I love her, *amigo*. We have that wounded man loaded, but he is not so good, no?"

"He's in bad shape. Is there a wagon at the road?"

"*Sí*. They brought her out here in that. Then she took a horse."

"We can take him in that rig to Preskit."

Raphael nodded, looking very serious under the stars. "If he lives that long."

With grim agreement, he clapped the man on the shoulder. "He came to kill me. But that is all we can do from here."

Then he boosted his wife back on her horse and mounted his own. The men were headed back for the road. He pushed his mount in close to her and they held hands for a short moment.

It would be way past dawn when they reached Preskit. The solemn posse, in a parade of wagon and horseback riders, came off the steep hill to descend to the courthouse, turning heads and gathering a large crowd when they reached Whiskey Row and turned south. At the west door of the courthouse a deputy came outside and frowned at them.

Chet pushed his horse in closer. "These two men are wanted. The one in the wagon is badly wounded and needs medical attention. Carl Hartley needs to be locked up."

"You don't run the sheriff's office. I will need to contact him and see what this is about."

"What is your name?"

"Guy Masters. Why?"

"I will see the new sheriff fires you. There are warrants for both these men on his desk. Either you accept them as prisoners or we will lynch them."

"Are you threatening me?"

"I am not threatening you. I am telling you what this posse can do."

"I have no orders—"

"Get me a rope, Raphael." Chet held out his hand.

Her foreman pushed his horse in close and handed him a lariat.

"All right, but I am only holding him for twenty-four hours."

"Masters, if you cut him loose, you will serve a term in Yuma for breaking the law. Take him in the jail. Raphael, take that buckboard down to Doc's place and get Loftin some medical attention. He won't run off. Take the dead man's body to the funeral parlor."

He reined his horse back as two of the men

herded Hartley. "I'm buying drinks at the Palace. One round. Thanks."

He rode his horse across the road and handed the reins to Marge. "I need to pay for these drinks. I won't be long."

"Will we eat breakfast at Jenny's?"

"Sure. I can hitch him. Go over there and order us some food."

She smiled. "Go pay your bar bill. I'll have it waiting for you."

"Thanks." He went inside and waved the bartender over. "Two beers each for my men."

The bartender climbed on the bar and counted fourteen men. "Dollar and a half."

He put the money on the counter. Jane came by and nodded. "You must've arrested them?"

"Willis is dead. Carl and his foreman were arrested."

"I like Bo sober. I am going to marry him."

"Keep him that way. I'll buy the dress."

Her brown eyes flew open. "You'll what?"

"My wife will help you choose a wedding dress. I'll tell her all about it and she will send you a note to meet her. Good luck."

"Thanks." She looked about to cry and left him.

He waved good-bye to the men at the bar and went for his horse. He had a breakfast to eat and his belly said he was ready.

On the big bay horse, he rode the three blocks to Jenny's and dismounted. It looked like there was a crowd. He shrugged and went in to find his wife.

"Over there," Jenny directed him.

"What in the hell is going on in here?"

"This is a meeting of the Byrnes for Sheriff Committee. We are holding this to convince you to run for the office."

A cheer went up.

He frowned at his wife. Their breakfasts were set before her.

"I knew nothing about this."

"I am starved. I'll eat. You have the meeting." He took up the napkin and sat down.

"We didn't expect you to be here, Mr. Byrnes," a small gray-haired man said, standing up. "But since you are here, all of us want to encourage you to run for sheriff."

He held the cup of coffee in his hands. The warmth felt good. Its aroma filled his nose and he nodded at him. "My ranch operation grows more extensive. I really don't have the time. Your members can find a good man who will do the job."

"You seem to end up doing all the sheriff's jobs for him. We heard you brought the Hartley brothers in this morning."

"They started shooting at me. I returned fire."

There was a snicker. Then another older man stood up. "Mr. Byrnes, we hope you will reconsider and become our sheriff."

"Maybe at a later date. Not now."

Jenny came by. "You need to see Mr. Tanner at the bank today, as well."

He frowned at her.

"He knows we are friends, and he said he had an important matter to discuss, and that it was private."

"I'll go by and see him. Sorry we can't go home yet," he said to Marge. "I told Bo's bride-to-be that you would help her pick out a wedding dress and I'd go the cost. You will need to send her a note when to meet you."

"Do I know her?"

"No, but she's tough enough to keep his wheels on tracks."

"Fine, you going to see Tanner now?"

"Why don't you shop and I'll do that?"

"Fine. I'll be at Grace's shop. You reckon May will need one too?"

"Considering Hampt and how he moves, yes."

"I'll get ideas for both. How big is this other girl?"

"Four foot two, maybe."

"Oh, she's short."

"Yes. I'll go see Tanner. Want a boost on your horse?"

"No, take him with yours. When you get done I'll ride home on him."

"Good. Thanks, everyone. Sorry I can't help you." He insisted he pay for the two breakfasts and Jenny at last took his money.

The bank was two blocks down and one north. He tied the two horses to the hitch rack and entered the lobby. Tanner's secretary, a young man, immediately stood up at his desk and came to greet him.

"Thanks for stopping by, sir. You knew Mr. Tanner wanted to speak to you?"

"I got the word at Jenny's café. Is he in?"

"I will tell him you are here."

"Fine."

The young man returned and took him to Tanner's walnut-lined office.

"Good to see you. I hope I did not interrupt your life."

"No, I was in town. We brought in Carl Hartley, and his brother is dead."

"That is my problem. We were going to foreclose on the T B ranch shortly. But I have neither the knowledge nor the help to do that. But you do. Have a seat, Mr. Byrnes."

"What do you intend to do?"

"Try to rescue the bank's money. They have borrowed several dollars to make up this ranch and while they might once have had some capital of their own, I fear they have spent it. Repossessing any property is never good business for a bank. Could you make a profit out of running their operation?"

"I doubt it; they have more cattle than this country can hold. They have no pool of bulls, hence many cows don't get bred. Second, the offspring many times become mavericks and, once weaned, that is what they are. Anyone can legally brand them."

"What can we do?"

"Sell the open cows and reduce the herd to a workable size. There are many ranch buyers that want a place that will work. I think the T B could be straightened and gotten into shape in a year. Now unless you have lots more in it than I think, it could then be sold."

"What would you charge to do it?"

He closed his eyes. "Expenses and a commission. How does that sound?"

"Sounds manageable to me. How will you do it?"

"Find a foreman and three damn tough cowboys to start."

"Who would they be?"

"I am not certain. But I'd have to pay off his crew and hire them and do it quick."

Tanner agreed, then he leaned back in his chair.

"I can fit some of these cattle in my Navajo deal. We have to get rid of lots of those cows or none of us will have any feed."

"People have complained to me about that."

"And they did like I did, drove them to their place."

Tanner agreed. "I'll need to have our lawyer file papers on that then."

"When will you do that?"

"I imagine tomorrow. Why?"

"I want to take my boys over there at dawn and take possession of the place then. Otherwise those men will take anything loose for what they consider their pay."

"I guess no one will be able to complain. You say the Hartleys are either dead or in jail?"

"Yes. I don't care but I want what is theirs to be there when I take over."

"Go ahead and do that. And give me a report as soon as you can."

"I am going to use six hundred fifty head of cull cows for the October delivery. They should have some flesh on them and fit my needs. That will help reduce the numbers. How many cows do they claim?"

"My last list was two thousand."

"Then I can take that many to the ranch I have on top and let them fatten until November. That will be a good number left—say four to five hundred super cows. Of course we don't know really how many they have and how many are of any account."

"Right. I trust you implicitly to do the right thing."

"If I don't, it will be an honest mistake." They shook hands and Tanner was left to go see his lawyers.

Chet left the bank and headed for the dress shop with both horses. The bell rang when he entered and the women working looked up and smiled.

"I'm coming," Marge said. "Look at this the dress for you-know-who."

"Looks lovely."

"I need the other girl's size."

"We can get it. We need to get home."

"Oh, in a hurry?"

"Something has come up."

"Oh, yes, you spoke to the man?"

"Yes. I can tell you on the way."

Outside he boosted her on her horse and they

set out. When they were over the hill with fewer people around, she turned. "What now?"

"We are dispersing the T B ranch for the bank."

"Hartley's place?"

"Yes, they are foreclosing and I am dispersing it for them."

"What comes first?"

"Fire the help and start over. I plan to sell the cows down about fifteen hundred head on my Navajo project. I have no idea what they have, but Tanner said two thousand head. We will see."

"My lands, you will sure be spread thin doing all this."

"We can handle it."

"All right, but no more riding after these outlaws."

"Darling, I'll try not to do that again."

Then he laughed and she shook her head. "It isn't funny now. It's damn serious."

He'd damn sure know more about that before the sun came up in the morning.

CHAPTER 26

His crew was gathered in the predawn on the last rise above the T B ranch. Some banty rooster was crowing about something and there was a light on in what he considered the cook shack and stove smoke in the air.

On his hoof-stamping horse, JD rubbed his shirtsleeves in the morning chill. "I hope they've got breakfast made when we get down there."

"If not, we'll make some," Chet said. "Spread out. We're taking the place. I don't expect any trouble, but I'll not put up with any, either."

"Billy, you be sure there isn't a horse wrangler out by the corrals. If there is you can herd him up to the cook shack."

"Gotcha." He turned his horse and went more north than the others to get beyond the dark corrals filled with sleeping horses and a few shuffling around in them.

When Chet rode, up a man in an apron was about to ring the triangle.

"Go ahead, we need to talk to everyone."

"Huh? Who in the hell are you?"

"Your new boss. Ring it."

"Yes, sir." He rang it.

Sleepy cowboys came out of the bunkhouse and stared at the horseback riders sitting on their mounts outside in the dim light.

"Who in the gawddamn hell are you guys?"

"Keep walking, the answer is up at the cook's place."

"I asked—"

"I don't give a dime what you asked. Shut your mouth and keep walking."

"That's all that's in there," one of the Quarter Circle Z riders said, and remounted after checking.

Everyone inside the cook shack, Chet addressed them. "I am the new boss of this ranch. It has been taken over by the bank in Preskit. I am looking for cowboys that can ride and rope. We're going to disperse the livestock and you will be in the saddle a lot. I can pay anyone wants out. I can also pay the back pay but I am only paying it at cowhand wages."

"What's that?"

"Twenty-five a month."

"Hell them Hartley brothers was paying more than that."

"How many months they owe you for?" Chet demanded.

"Three months."

"That's seventy-five dollars."

One man spoke up, "They was paying me sixty a month."

"One's dead, the other in jail, I won't pay you and you can go up to the jail and see what he'll give you."

The man ducked his head and shook it in disgust.

"Any more questions?"

They shook their heads.

"After breakfast, I'll set up to interview each of you and pay you. I don't want one damn thing taken from the ranch that ain't yours. If you do I'll see you spend three years in Yuma. Am I understood?"

"Yes."

"Good. Eat. Is there food enough for all?" he asked the cook.

"I can fry some more eggs and pancakes, sir."

"Do that. My boys have been up all night."

"Yes, sir."

Counting the horse wrangler, who came in last, there were seven hands. JD met each one and shook his hand, then did the book work while Chet paid each one.

He interviewed each man at a desk he made from some boards and a barrel. He sat behind it on a ladder-back chair. JD was beside him, writing it all down for the record.

"How much did they owe you?"

"Three months, sir."

"Name?"

"Wiley Jinks."

"Age?"

"About eighteen, I guess. I ain't got no record of my birth."

"Where you from?"

"Where was I born, sir?"

"Yes."

"Arkansas. A tornado wiped out my family when I was twelve. I survived. I went with a family to Texas. But all they needed was a slave so I joined a cattle drive and helped the cook. In time I got to be a drover. But they had real bad storms back there every time I went to Kansas, so next time I drove some cattle out here. And I stayed. They don't got any tornados out here."

"You want to cowboy for me?"

"Yes sir, I'd be proud to."

"I'll hire you. Have you been here three months?"

"I been here six."

"I heard they had not paid you men for the last three months."

"That's right. That would be fine with me. I thank you, sir." He took his money and smiled.

Chet asked him if he brought a horse and he shook his head.

He didn't offer the grumbler a job. Figured he was a gunman, not a cowboy. Besides, he didn't like Jay Ponders's ways.

"I've got a horse coming to me," the man in his thirties said, then he looked around like he was bored with the whole deal.

"You ride him in here?" Chet asked.

"No, but they promised me one when I left."

"I told you they were in jail or dead. All I owe you is seventy-five dollars. Get on shank's mare and ride away."

"Hey, I made a deal."

"The bank won't pay for it."

"Listen, a deal is a deal."

"Those people aren't here. I'm the boss. You aren't getting a horse out of me or the bank. Move on."

"Partner, your hearing is bad. He said move on," Hampt came over and took the man by the shoulder.

For a minute, things looked like they'd break loose. But considering Hampt's size and deep voice, enough had been said, and Ponders went for his things. The other obvious gunman, Curly Brown, had a bill of sale for a brown horse with the Bar K brand on his right shoulder.

Chet called on the horse wrangler, Mike Martin. "You know this man's horse?"

"Yeah, he's a bay horse. He's up with some others on the mountain."

"Is he sound?"

"Yes, sir. Pick him a like horse out of the ones here. I'll make him a bill of sale and he can sell me his. That all right, Brown?"

"I guess so."

"Save you waiting around all day. Go choose a horse with him, Mike, then you come back," Chet said.

Henry Judson came next.

"Where do you hail from, Henry?" Chet asked the gangly youth.

"Bossier City, Louisiana, sir. I don't want to go back there and I like working cattle around here."

"Good, we need real cowboys to work this ranch. No horse?"

"No, sir."

The next one came up.

"What's your name and where do you come from?"

"Buck Temple, Texarkana, sir. I ended up here like Wiley. We drove cattle out here from Texas and stayed."

"Bring a horse?"

"No sir, and I'd be proud to work for you."

"Next?"

"That's Mike Martin, the short bronc twister and wrangler," JD said. "I sure like him. He's coming back. He got Brown a horse. What about the cook?"

"Do you men staying here like the cook?" He looked over the men standing there.

"I ate better. But I damn sure ate worse," Wiley said.

Buck smiled. "Shirley ain't half bad for a ranch crew cook."

"We could hire a worse one. JD's the ranch boss from here on. He'll hire and fire all the help. We need to round up a mess of these cows and ship about fifteen hundred head. There's way too many on our ranges. I have a place up on top for them and then we'll ship them. You work for me and you may have to go elsewhere to do what needs to be done. We start in the morning sorting out the cows to sell and then push them to the north ranch. How many British cross cows are there?"

"Not a whole lot." Buck said. "Most are long-horns."

"If they have a good cross calf on them keep them. Especially heifer calves."

Everyone nodded. "Any longhorn bulls on the range, I want rounded up."

"JD wants to get an idea about the cattle here. So saddle up, day one is about to begin."

"You ride in on a horse?" he asked Mike. When he shook his head, Chet paid him.

"JD has to run this ranch. How is the remuda?"

"For this many cowboys, all right. What are there, four and me?"

"Yes."

"We'll need more horses."

"You have a team for the chuck wagon?"

"We do. Four mules."

"Can Shirley handle them?"

"I'd need to drive them around a few days."

"Do that. JD, we need to go talk to your cook."

"Yes, sir. And thanks for all you two done. I know them other guys appreciate it. Them gun hands you let go kinda ran things at the bunkhouse and elsewhere. All the crappy jobs them guys got, and the Mister Bigs kept their own boots propped up."

"JD and I figured that out before the sun came up."

"Where did the cocky foreman go that I met in the road?"

"Took a powder about two weeks ago. Took

AUTHOR'S NOTE

I want to assure the fans of the Byrnes Family Ranch series that according to my publisher, we have two more books to go, at least, after this one. Book Two, *Between Hell and Texas*, sold well and several fans wrote me asking about the future of the books. The Spur Awards judges made Book Two a finalist in the 2012 contest; that meant one of the top three books in the category. The Fictioneer Award's judges also chose it as a finalist in their contest. By the time this one is published we will know of any other awards.

I write books for readers, not for judges or awards. And I am as proud of my fans as I am of any awards, but it is nice to get recognition from my peers. As a young man growing up, I read every western book I could get anywhere. I could consume a paperback western in one night in high school and college. I've walked and ridden over lots of the land in these novels. My wife and I dragged an RV around the West to lots of these places for almost twenty years.

I walked the streets of Tombstone in the pre-dawn and thought I heard Doc and Wyatt talking to me. Been to the Chiricahuas and know why the Apaches loved those mountains. Swam, fished, and floated the Verde River in a truck-tire inner tube near Fort McDowell. Looked all over the Superstition Mountains for the Lost Dutch Mine as a young man. I am not the guy that did everything, but I've seen and researched lots of old newspapers and try to keep things in place.

Gary Goldstein, my editor, and I go way back. Years ago I introduced him at a writer's conference and then had to leave the room. My friends told me when I left the room, Gary said, "There goes the next Zane Grey. I mean it. He will be that and more."

Thanks, Gary. Thanks, too, to my lovely agent, Cherry Weiner, who never takes no for an answer. And all the folks that voted for me in True West's poll, when they announced in 2011 that I was the greatest living western fiction writer. *I liked the "living" part.*

To my wife, Pat, and my grown daughters Anna and Rhonda, who pushed me in this western writing business, thanks too. I really enjoy it.

I don't have a secretary, but I do answer e-mails. My webmaster, Duke Pennel, keeps a schedule up on dustyrichards.com. You can e-mail me at dustyrichards@cox.net or write me at P.O. Box 6460, Springdale, AR 72766.

Thanks, folks. May God bless you, and all of America.

—Dusty Richards

three ranch horses and I wasn't sure Carl give him them."

JD nodded that he heard him. "Not big losses, are they?"

"They were mortgaged property, we might look in on that case."

Shirley Taylor was the eighth boy in his east Texas family. His mother always wanted a girl and when he came along, she called him Shirley.

"Well, we're going to cut cattle back to five hundred mother cows here and try to make a ranch out of it," Chet explained. "We plan to take them to a ranch I bought up on top. So you may have to move with those cattle. I will sell them by the first of November and you can come back here unless we need you up there. Either way I can pay you a hundred dollars for back pay and pay you forty dollars a month for three months. Your job grows, I'll pay you more than that."

"I guess I'm lucky then," the large-bodied man said. "I figured they'd lose this place and I'd set out all winter with no job. Proud to be a part of your outfit."

JD shook his hand and so did Chet.

"We spoke to Mike about driving the mules some," JD said. "You be certain that wagon is sound and make a list of things you need now, and then later a three-month list for the trip up there. I'm going to be here so we can work together on it."

"Good," Shirley said and laughed. "That's a big weight off my shoulders. And them gun hands gone suits me fine."

JD walked outside with him. Hampt and the others were mounted up and had Chet's horse ready.

"You need something, don't forget to ask. Oh, I need that piece of payroll for Tanner and I'll make a record of it."

"I'll start a ledger on the keeper cows and try to find out all I can in the next week."

"Be set to move those cattle up there in two weeks."

"Whew, that's a tough schedule."

"We need a tough one. This needs to be done. Most of those calves at McQuire's have enough size and we can cull them and then bring the good ones down to the Verde ranch. Tom wanted more cows there anyway. Then they won't mix in with the sale cattle."

Hearing it all, Hampt shook his head, sitting on his horse. "Boys, daylight's burning. This place is in good hands. Let's get back." He rode over and gave Chet his horse. "We're headed back to Verde."

"I need to stop at Marge's. I'll be there at sunup. We go get the McQuire herd tomorrow. Tell Hoot him or someone needs to go up there and cook for that deal. He'll probably send Victor. Make arrangements, get the horses you'll need. Rio can wrangle them. Sarge should be up there by now and know more."

Hampt nodded his head. "You got anything else we need to do?"

Chet broke down and smiled at him. "Maybe sweep my office."

His men rode on. He'd catch them.

Dismounted, he checked the girth. He'd better go see his wife. He hadn't had much time with her lately and while she knew he was busy, he still needed to pay her some mind. Besides, he missed her—everything from her free laughter to her wonderful body. For a minute he closed his eyes. This damn territory was busy and as much work as Texas ever was.

He rode in and learned that Marge and Monica were in town getting Monica's dress fitted for her wedding. She and Raphael planned to tie the knot—shortly. The date escaped him. He took off his clothes in the back room, tied a towel around his waist, and picked up a bar of soap to walk on his tender soles to the sheepherder's shower. The water was warm and he soaped himself down, then rinsed. He heard a team coming and hurried to dry off.

His horse was still hitched up there so she'd know he was home.

He came around the corner and she met him, running into his arms. He lost the towel and she peered down before kissing him again. "You're naked."

"I only have a towel." He swiped it up and put it around him. When he looked up he saw something was wrong.

"Anything bad happen?" The damn towel would stay if he held it with one hand.

She chewed on her lower lip. "No."

"What's wrong?"

"I-I may be going to have a baby. Now don't shout. Twice before I've lost them. My record is not good in this matter. But I had to tell you."

"Of course. I'd hug the fire out of you, but for holding my towel. That is wonderful news and we won't pin our hopes till we see if it will stay in there, right?"

"Yes. My—"

"I don't care about before. If we can have a child, I'll be pleased. But Marge I am always proud of having you and we have each other. Thank God."

She laughed through some tears. "Let's go find you some clothing."

"I agree." Hugging her arm, and the other one holding his towel, they went for the house.

He breathed in the turpentine smell on the wind. A lucky man with a new future and maybe a son or daughter. Either would suit him.

Thunder boomed and they hurried the last fifty feet. Another shower was going to baptize the land and them if they didn't hurry. Whew, those big raindrops were like ice on his bare skin.